HONOUR ~THY MOTHER

HONOUR ~THY MOTHER

T. C. BADCOCK

BREAKWATER BOOKS LTD.

Honour Thy Mother is one family's story of passion, possessiveness and punishment, as a brother and sister come full circle in tracing their roots.
Set in Quebec and rural Newfoundland, the author captures both language and landscape. His true-to-life characters will remain with the reader long after the last page is turned.

—Danette Dooley, independent reviewer

They say revenge is best served cold. Well, get a knife and fork because T.C. Badcock has created a real page turner where the icy setting of Newfoundland's South coast is as cold as the revenge in Honour Thy Mother.

—Jeff Gilhooly, host of CBC Newfoundland's radio show *On The Go*

Badcock creates a brilliant mosaic of love, joy, sadness, suspense and dram through the characters and landscapes in his latest novel. A young girl's marriage to a dysfunctional husband and her odyssey from Roberval, Quebec, to Dark Harbour, Newfoundland, will have universal appeal to all readers.

—Frank Galgay, author

A great piece of work by an author that appreciates the hardships of living in earlier outport Newfoundland and the warm feeling of love and attachment.

—Beaton Tulk, former premier of Newfoundland and Labrador

BREAKWATER BOOKS LTD.
100 Water Street
P.O. Box 2188
St. John's, NL
A1C 6E6
Canada

Library and Archives Canada Cataloguing in Publication

Badcock, T. C. (Thomas C.)
Honour thy mother / T.C. Badcock.

ISBN 1-55081-204-1

I. Title.
PS8553.A285H66 2004   C813'.54   C2004-904321-8

Interior Design: Carola Kern
Cover Design: Rhonda Molloy

The Canada Council | Le Conseil des Arts
for the Arts | du Canada

We acknowledge the financial support of The Canada Council
for the Arts for our publishing activities.

We acknowledge the financial support of
The Government of Canada through the Book
Publishing Industry Development Program
(BPIDP) for our publishing activities.

Printed in Canada

EDICATION

For TJ
There's never a moment when you don't fill my thoughts.

And for the mother of my children whose father, George King,
was the victim of a fishing industry accident.

One

FRANCINE STEPPED OFF the boat onto the community wharf at exactly 10:00 a.m. on November 12th, 1951. She would have felt better had she known that her pursuers were convinced that she was somewhere else. Nevertheless, she felt that she had made a successful escape.

She had arrived. She had read about Dark Harbour when she was still in the convent and dreamt about going there. In her wildest dreams, however, she had never imagined what it was really like. It seemed as if everybody in the community had come down to greet the boat and she discovered later that, in fact, they had. The visit of the coastal steamer was their only contact with the outside world and its arrival was the most excitement that the residents had. Francine held tightly onto Michel's hand as they watched the cargo being off-loaded and placed on the wharf. Winter had arrived and, depending upon the harshness of the weather, this could very possibly be the last delivery of necessities to the community until spring. One man checked invoices against deliveries while the passengers waited for their trunks to be lifted off the boat. The wind was cold, but it didn't seem to bother Michel, who watched with amazement as the large pallets were lifted by crane from the boat to the wharf. Sally Patten, who had befriended them on the steamer, spotted them and, with her suitcase in hand, walked toward them.

"Well, Francine," she said, laughing. "This is Dark Harbour. What do you think of it, maid?"

"It's, ahh," she paused, looking around, "not exactly what I had expected."

"Well me dear, you better get used to it because we expects that this boat here is going to be the last one you'll see until the spring. So you better not want to leave."

"No, no, it's nothing like that. It's just that I never thought it would be so isolated, but it's a perfect setting for my book, so we'll be staying," she avowed.

Sally turned her attention to the crowd on the wharf, scanning the excited faces for that of Millicent Fudge. Francine had been able to arrange everything except a place to stay in Dark Harbour. Sally had told her that Millicent had a large house and boarded the doctor whenever he came, so she might consider giving them room and board. "She has to be here," Sally said. "Everybody in Dark Harbour is on the wharf." Then she spotted Millicent.

"Millie," she called out. Francine looked in the direction of Sally's call and saw a middle-aged woman wearing rubber boots and dressed in a man's jacket return the wave. As soon as she did, Sally beckoned her to join them. Pushing through the crowd, Millicent headed in their direction.

"I see that you made it back, Sally. Couldn't stay away, could you?" she spoke as she drew close to them.

"No, maid, I couldn't," Sally said as she turned toward Francine. "Francine, this is Millicent Fudge, and she's the one I told you about on the boat. Millie, this here is Francine and she's come to Dark Harbour to write a book about us and bide here a spell. Her and her boy there, Michel, needs a place to stay and I told her on the boat that you boards the doctor when he comes around, so you might want to give them room and board."

"Welcome to Dark Harbour," Millicent said as she stretched out a hand covered by a heavy woolen mitten. Francine stretched out her leather-covered hand and it disappeared inside the large mitten as they shook hands. "Thank you," Francine said.

"How long are you planning to stay in Dark Harbour?" Millicent asked.

"It will probably take me at least two years to do all the research I need," Francine lied convincingly.

"My God," both women said in unison, and then looked at Michel who was still amazed as he continued to watch the cargo being off-loaded. "What about your husband?" Millicent asked.

Francine paused for a moment and lowered her eyes a little. "My husband was in the Air Force and he was killed in a terrible accident last year," Francine lied for the second time.

"Oh, I'm sorry to hear that," Millicent said sympathetically.

"Yes, me dear, I'm sorry to hear that, too. So it's just you and Michel?" Sally asked.

"Yes, it's just the two of us, and we really could use a place to stay. I'm willing to pay fifty dollars a month for a home for the two of us."

Millicent gasped and looked at Sally. Fifty dollars was as much as her husband earned in two months of fishing. She couldn't believe what she had heard. "Good God, we don't have a hotel and our bit of grub is rough, and I certainly don't expect you to pay that kind of money."

"You mean that you'll give us room and board?" Francine said expectantly.

"Don't you want to see it first?" Millicent asked, still in a mild state of shock about how much money Francine was willing to pay.

"I'm sure it will be fine, as long as it's warm and large enough for Michel and me."

"My goodness, yes, it's warm and you don't have to sleep in the same room as your boy. The doctor used to sleep over when he came, but now he stays up there," she pointed to what could have been any one of the houses up the slope from the wharf. "So we gave the bed to me brother. I'll have to find another bed for him, that's all. It's just Joe and me and we only sleeps in one room," she explained.

"Good then," Francine said, smiling. She reached into her purse and fumbled with her money until she found a fifty-dollar bill. She passed it to Millicent. "Here you are, Mrs. Fudge, our first month's payment in advance."

"Call me Millie," Millie corrected her, "and there's no need for that. Fifty dollars is far too much for a roof over your head and a bit of grub."

"No, no, I insist," Francine said. She extended her hand toward Millie and pushed the bill toward her. Millie's hand closed around it. She started to laugh. The longer she looked at the fifty-dollar bill, the harder she laughed. Francine and Sally looked at each other and began to laugh too. Finally, Sally spoke.

"What's so funny?" she asked as Millie continued to look at the bill.

"This is the first time I ever saw a fifty-dollar bill." She stopped laughing for a few seconds to answer.

"That's more money than I ever had in my life before and you know something?"

"No," the other two women said.

"I can't even spend it. Who has enough money in this place to give me change?"

Sally left them still laughing, satisfied that Francine would be very comfortable living with the Fudges. Michel continued to stand beside his mother throughout the off-loading of the boat and occasionally would look up at his mother and then point to something particularly interesting to him. Finally, they watched as Francine's two trunks were delivered to the wharf.

"Those are my two trunks coming off now," Francine said to Millie as both mother and son pointed at them simultaneously.

"Good," Millie said. She left them for a few seconds, walked over to the man who was checking the deliveries, said a few words and then returned to Francine and Michel. "Everything's fine," she called out as she neared them. "Me husband, Joe, will have them delivered to the house as soon as they finish unloading the boat. Come on, let's go up to the house before we freeze fast to the wharf."

Millie and Francine held Michel's hands and together they walked the short distance from the wharf to the Fudge's home. Michel didn't want to leave, but Millie promised him that they could come back down again a little later, after they had warmed themselves. Reluctantly, he agreed. During the walk, Francine took the time to look at her new home.

This could very well be the end of the world, she thought to herself. There was a foggy haze over the entire community, which was set into the side of a hill at the end of a harbour. All of the houses were the same shape and painted the same dingy white. Each house was just a few hundred feet from the shore and there were dozens of small fishing boats either moored in the harbour or tied up to the sides of wharf. There were no trees, no grass, nor any signs of other vegetation. The walk took only a couple of minutes, but it was slippery and uphill from the wharf. There were less than two dozen houses in the entire village, and Millie proudly informed Francine that the population was ninety-three. They had a little church with a school in its basement, and despite the fact that they had no electricity or running water, she wouldn't think of living anywhere else.

The Fudge house was the same as all the others. Built into the side of the cliff on a foundation of flat stones, it was heated by a wood stove and lit with kerosene lamps. It had an outhouse and chamber pots under the beds were used in the night-time or during inclement weather. Barrels in the porch, filled with water drawn from a well, served as the water supply. The whitewash on the clapboard had faded, but as soon as the door was opened and they stepped through the porch into the kitchen, Francine felt the warmth of both fire and family. Millie moved the kettle to the middle of the stove as she continued to talk non-stop while showing them where they could put their belongings.

Millie and Joe Fudge were both raised in Dark Harbour and had married seventeen years earlier. Joe was born into a fishing family and he continued the tradition. Millie was also born into a fishing family and it was natural that she should marry a fisherman. She was alone most of the day while her husband fished, as did all of the men in the community, and she had desperately wanted to have children. Though they had tried, Millie had been unable to get pregnant and she and Joe had both resigned themselves to the fact that they would never have their own children. With the arrival of Francine and Michel, she knew that for at least the next two years, she wouldn't be alone when Joe was out on the water.

Joe arrived nearly an hour later. He was a big man with a heart to match. He was well over six feet tall and had a mop of red curly hair. His face was wind burned and looked as if it had been frostbitten on several occasions. He carried the trunks as if they were extensions of his arms. His big smile was infectious. Whenever he spoke, Francine couldn't help but smile as she answered his questions. He tried talking with Michel, but each time he did, Michel hid behind his mother's skirt. But the tiny smile that appeared on Michel's face as he peered out from behind Francine was an indication that it wouldn't be long before the two became friends.

The family ate at 3:30 p.m. because it would be well after 9:00 before Joe got in off the water and had the fish salted. Michel went to bed at 7:00 and Francine followed soon after. The bedroom was cold and Millie had shown her where the lamp was and how to light it. Michel would have to sleep with her tonight until they could get another bed for him in the morning. Francine felt better with Michel in the bed with her anyway, at least for the first night in their new home. An hour later, the house was in darkness, as the Fudges retired for the evening. They were both happy that Francine and Michel had come to stay with them.

It was still dark the next morning when Francine woke with a start. She sat straight up in the bed and stared into the darkness for a few seconds before she realized where she was. It was cold. She shivered and then quickly lay back down and covered herself. She felt nauseous again this morning and hoped she wasn't coming down with something. The next few days would be very busy ones and she needed to be healthy. Suddenly, her stomach heaved. Instinct told her to head for the bathroom, but there was no bathroom. She remembered the chamber pot beneath the bed, and just as she found it and pulled it out, a stream of vomit covered the bottom. Twice more she heaved into the large china bowl. Francine bent over it and heaved once more, but there wasn't anything left to come out. Relieved, she lay back down again. It had to be the worry and the travel that was making her sick.

As she lay wondering what the problem was, Michel stirred beside her. Today she would make arrangements to get him a bed of his own. He turned over and grunted. Francine smiled as she brushed the hair out of his eyes and drew the heavy blankets up to his neck, tucking his arm underneath. She pushed the chamber pot under the bed and lay on her side. She stared at the closed bedroom door and could see light through the cracks around it. She felt for her watch on the tiny table beside her bed and strained to see what time it was, but it was too dark. Voices from beyond the door told her that the Fudges were up, so reluctantly she crawled out from under the warm blankets and cracked the door a little to give herself enough light to dress.

Noiselessly, Francine left the room and stepped into the hall. At the end of it she could see light coming from the downstairs and she made her way toward it. The stairs creaked as she walked down them, holding the banister. It was cold and smooth and a little loose, she discovered, as she leaned on it to feel her way down the dark stairs. The voices grew louder as she got closer to the kitchen and so did the aroma of breakfast. The floor felt cold through the knitted slippers that Millie had given her the previous evening. She paused for a few seconds before stepping into the warmth and light of the kitchen. As she did, she glanced at her wristwatch; it was only 6:15 a.m.

"Good morning," Millie beamed at her as soon as Francine appeared in the doorway. She was standing over the stove with one hand holding the stove damper and the other forcing a huge piece of wood through the opening as the flames licked around its sides.

"You looks like you've been rode hard and put away wet," Joe laughed as he sipped tea from a saucer.

Francine smiled weakly at him in response. "I'm feeling a little peaked this morning," she explained.

"Don't mind him," Millie said, as she finished filling the stove with wood. "There's no need for you to get up this early," she continued, as she cleared a place at the table for her. "Come on and sit down, and have some breakfast. You'll feel a lot better after you've had a nice cup of tea, and we gets something inside of you that'll stick to your ribs."

Francine smiled her agreement and took a place on the bench across from Joe. Compared to Millie, Francine felt she must have looked like something half-starved. Millie was at least two hundred pounds, if she was an ounce. "How'd you sleep last night?" Joe asked as she took her place at the table, "and where is that boy of yours?"

"Very well, thank you," Francine answered, "and Michel is still asleep."

"Well, if we're going to make a fisherman out of him, he can't stay in bed until dinner time," Joe said, laughing.

"He's just a baby, you bloody fool," Millie responded good-naturedly as she placed a large mug of steaming tea in front of Francine. "Get off your lazy arse and go down to the stage somewhere," she continued, as she nudged him with one of her very large arms. Joe was a big man, but Millie's nudge still pushed him along the bench and the tobacco and paper he had started rolling into a cigarette fell to the table in front of him. He just laughed as he scooped it up and tried again.

Francine put a heaping teaspoon of dark sugar into her cup and then cooled the tea with fresh cream from a chipped jug. The cream was very thick and flecks of cream floated to the top as she stirred. She took her first sip as Millie placed a huge slice of toasted bread on a plate beside her. Seconds later, it was smothered in butter and blue-berry jam from a preserve jar. Her unsettled stomach forgotten, she drank the hot tea, ate the warm toast and chatted with Millie.

The house was less than five years old and was modern by Dark Harbour standards. It had three bedrooms, a kitchen, living room and a big porch where a large wooden barrel sat filled with drinking water. The large kitchen window looked out over the bay and Francine could see that the cold Atlantic wind had whipped the water into whitecaps. Plain, home-made, blue and white checkered curtains hung at the window, matching the oilcloth covering on the table underneath it. Beside the table were two benches. Hanging from the beamed ceiling was a kerosene lamp that provided the only light and the cherry yellow wallpaper assisted the lamp in brightening the room. The floor was covered with well-worn canvas, but the most prominent feature of the room was a large couch that Millie referred to as a daybed. It was pushed into a corner by the stove and beside it was a knitting bas-ket and a half-finished man's sweater. It was comfort, Newfoundland style, and it had a warmth to it beyond that provided by the stove. On the wall over the stove hung a tiny little plaque with the words "God Bless Our Home."

Joe left the table with his second cup of tea in hand and as he walked across the floor to the daybed, a sleepy-eyed Michel appeared at the kitchen door.

"Well, me son, we're not going to make a fisherman out of you if you spends all day in the bunk," Joe teased with a smile. Michel ran to his mother and buried his head in her lap.

"Did you sleep well?" Francine asked as she picked him up and sat him on her knee. He didn't answer his mother, but eyed Joe very nervously with one eye, as he pressed the side of his head into his mother's breasts.

"Don't let that old fool bother you, me son." Millie said in a surprisingly soft voice. She reached forward to smooth his ruffled hair and he dug deeper into his mother's chest.

"Now, Michel," Francine chided him, "you don't have to be afraid of Millie or Joe. They won't hurt you."

"That's right, sweetheart," Millie responded. "I'll get you some nice hot tea with milk and a big slice of toast with jam. How would you like that?"

Michel nodded without lifting his head.

"After you've had your breakfast maybe you'd like to come down to the stage head and see me boat," Joe offered expectantly.

"You have a boat?" Michel perked up, looking in Joe's direction. No one was more surprised than Francine to hear her son's question.

"Yes, I have a boat," Joe answered.

"Can we go for a ride?" Michel asked a little more boldly.

Joe laughed. "No, not in this wind. I'm building a new boat for next year and you can come down and help me if you likes. That is, if it's okay with your mom," Joe suddenly remembered to add. Michel turned and looked up into his mother's face.

"Please, mom," he begged.

"It's really cold outside, sweetheart, and I don't want you catching a cold," Francine answered.

"Oh, there's no need to worry about that. Joe keeps the stage warmer than the house. You haven't got to worry about the cold and it's only a hundred feet or so and they're there," Millie said as she reached to smooth Michel's hair for the second time. This time he didn't resist.

Francine paused for a few seconds and then looked at her son. "Okay then, but you have to be a good boy and do everything that Joe tells you."

Joe quickly jumped up from the daybed and practically ran across the kitchen to where his coat was hanging on a hook beside the door. His smile could only have been bigger if he had been laughing.

"I'll run down and get the fire going so it'll be warm when you gets there," he said as he finished dressing. "Now, you eat your breakfast and put on your warm clothes, and by that time I'll be back to get you. Okay?"

"Okay, Joe," Michel said, with a smile to match Joe's.

Millie filled a cup with equal amounts of milk and tea, carefully buttered a thin slice of toast, and smothered it with blueberry jam.

She cut it into tiny squares and slid it toward Michel, who had left his mother's lap and was sitting on the bench beside her. As he took his first bite, Millie looked at her young house guest with a love that she knew would grow much deeper the longer he spent in her home.

Michel ate quickly and, as he did, Francine returned to their bedroom to get his clothes. Millie took them and laid them on the open oven door to warm. Then, as Francine watched, she dressed him. Francine repeated her previous instructions while sipping her second cup of tea and Michel nodded his impatient agreement. A few minutes later, Joe entered the kitchen and hand in hand the two new friends left for the stage. When they were alone, Francine asked Millie about their new hometown.

Dark Harbour was located at the western entrance to Great Bay Below and was sheltered from the winds by several small islands and high cliffs. Francine found out later that the proper name of the bay was Great Bay de l'eau, which, when translated from French, meant Great Bay of Water. The community had been settled for nearly fifty years, and it got its name from the dark, deep water in the harbour. There were only about twenty or so houses in the entire community and each was built on the rocks, close to the water, with the cliffs serving as a backdrop. The houses didn't have basements; it would have been impossible to dig into the bedrock. Instead, the houses were built right on top of the rock with flat pieces of shale used to form a footing. They were all the same shape and usually about the same size. They were built close to the water and in full view of the harbour. There were no roads connecting them, but footpaths wove between the buildings. The only access to the community was by boat.

Every resident was a fisherman or the dependant of a fisherman. Every fisherman had built a wharf to moor his boat and to offload his catches of fish. The wharf was built by driving long logs into the harbour floor to form a fence and the inside was filled with rocks. Then a floor of planks and logs covered the rocks. Finally, a shack called a stage was built.

It was a hard life where the sea took the men, childbirth took the women and countless other diseases took the children. Their only link to the outside world was their boats and the coastal steamer. A doctor came to the community by boat every couple of weeks during the summer months only. For the remainder of the year, they had to do without professional medical care. Fortune was the closest large community and it was an hour away by motor boat in good weather.

After their first few weeks in Dark Harbour, Michel had developed a relationship with Joe that Francine had prayed he would have with his father. Michel had not even mentioned his father after their second week away from him. He loved their new home and, despite the biting wind that blew across the barren coast, he spent a great part of his days outside. Joe Fudge couldn't have been happier. Francine paid them for room and board, but he enjoyed Michel's company so much that, after the first month, he didn't want to take the money. Both Fudges fussed over Michel as if he were their own son. And Joe showed him off to his friends as proudly as any father showed off his son.

December was biting cold and the fishermen spent their days doing repairs to their fishing gear, getting it ready for the next spring's fishing season. The ground was already covered with six inches of snow and the last of the boats were being dragged out of the water onto the beaches. The winter storms would soon lash the coast and, if the boats were not beached, they could be blown out to sea in a winter's storm rage, or crushed by ice in the spring.

Joe needed a larger boat and he had begun to build it a week before Francine and Michel came to live with them. This was to be his winter project. Two other men fished out of his boat and the old boat had become too small for the three of them. Besides, it had become so waterlogged and heavy that it pushed a lot more water than it should have. Last spring, Joe had cut a new keel from the root of a spruce tree, and it had been drying in the stage ever since. Last week he had begun to shape it. The previous winter, he had cut the logs he needed and after having dried out, they had been carried over to Reg Tibbo's mill to be sawed into planks. Now, in addition to all of the other things he would have to do to be ready for the start of the spring fishery, Joe would be building his new trap boat.

Michel spent every waking hour with Joe and together they worked on the new boat. Joe had sawed a two-foot length of plank and Francine had painted Michel's name in bright red letters on it. Joe, despite being a very skilled fisherman, had never gone to school and therefore could not read or write. A fisherman didn't need to be able to read or write to catch fish, but it was a tradition to name a new boat and the nameplate was displayed proudly on a shelf in the stage. When the boat was finished, it would be nailed onto the front. Then everybody would know that Joe Fudge's new boat was named Michel.

Michel soon learned the names of all the tools and what each was used for and took great pleasure in passing tools to Joe whenever he asked for one. Otherwise, he played with the wood shavings. The floor was made of round poles covered with rough planks, and there were several cracks through which Michel dropped little objects and watched them fall into the water below. A little pot-bellied stove made the shack quite warm. They went to the stage at 8:30 a.m. every morning, except Sundays, and left only for meals. They worked until 3:30 p.m. and every evening at supper Michel took great pains to explain what they had done today and how he had helped Joe.

Francine visited the stage every day and brought them either their morning or afternoon snacks. Michel was always happy to see her and showed her what they had done since the last time she had visited. He knew the names of the various parts of the boat and would point out where the cuddy was going or where the wheelhouse would be. Francine was very proud of her son and when she looked at Joe's face she saw in his eyes a pride that she wished she could have seen in Denis's eyes.

Francine told the Fudges that she had come to Dark Harbour to write a novel. It was a believable story and she spent a portion of every day using the typewriter she had purchased in Halifax. Of course, she wasn't writing a book and didn't have the first idea of how to begin, but she had to give the impression that she was writing so that Millie would be convinced. She carried a notebook with her everywhere she went and began recording her experiences in the community. She wrote about the people she met and what they did. She drew portraits of the residents and landscape sketches and people quickly began to associate Francine and her notebook. Many of them asked what she was doing and, after telling them, they were only too willing to share their own stories. She was very convincing and soon everybody knew who she was and what she was doing in Dark Harbour. What they didn't know, however, was that in addition to recording her present day situation, Francine was recording the events that had made the move to Dark Harbour necessary.

She had also convinced them that her husband had been killed earlier in an airplane accident. She had chosen Dark Harbour very carefully because of its isolation. There were only two radios in the entire community and no newspapers. But she would have to change her story now that she was pregnant. That was the only explanation for the fact that she had missed at least two periods and for the morning sickness she was experiencing. With all of the disruption, she had failed to be as attentive as she usually was. She would soon be forced to provide an explanation. It would just take a little while to think of a believable one.

Two

FRANCINE AND MICHEL's first Christmas in Newfoundland was their most enjoyable ever. In the time that had passed since they arrived, Francine had met everybody in the community. Many of them she now knew by name and she felt as much a part of Dark Harbour as anybody else there. Despite the cold and the isolation and the lack of basic amenities, Francine couldn't think of anywhere she would rather be. Her only regret was that she had arrived too late to order presents to have them delivered to the community before Christmas. But that regret was short-lived because very few people in the community actually gave store-bought presents. There was little money for such a luxury and much of the fun of Christmas in Dark Harbour was making Christmas presents.

Millie showed Francine how to knit and even though she spent every spare moment at it, there was still a sleeve missing on the sweater she was knitting for Michel for Christmas. On Christmas morning, though, when he opened his presents and found the sweater that was identical in colour and style to Joe's, he insisted on wearing it for the remainder of the day.

A few days after Christmas, Francine got her first exposure to mummers. It was just after supper and a loud knock was heard on the kitchen door. Michel ran to open it and then ran for his mother. Standing in the doorway were six people dressed in combinations of men's and women's clothing, shouting, "Any mummers 'lowed in?"

No one could remember where the mummering tradition came from, but it was like an adult version of Halloween. Adults would dress up in the most outlandish clothes they could find, cover their faces and go from house to house. The residents of the house being visited had to try to guess who they were as they danced around and disguised their voices when they were asked questions. They remained covered until they were correctly identified. At first, Michel was frightened of them, but as their identities were eventually revealed and he began to recognize them, he became comfortable with the entire charade. Before the Christmas season was over, Joe and Millie took them mummering and Michel had the time of his life. Francine did, too.

By the time Christmas had passed, Francine was even more convinced than before that she had made the right decision to come here. She and Michel had readily adapted to their new lifestyle. Francine continued to write in her diary and it contained a record of everything that had transpired since they had left Toronto, as well as what had impelled her to leave. She made very comprehensive notes about their day to day routine. Nobody suspected that she was anybody other than a writer and her daily typing convinced Millie, who, in turn, convinced everyone in the tiny community.

Francine learned how to bake bread and to prepare various traditional fish dishes. She introduced the Fudges to several Quebec dishes and she and Millie became as close as sisters. They confided everything in each other, or nearly everything, and Francine quickly became a respected member of the community. The residents were members of the Church of England faith and despite her strict Catholic upbringing, Francine readily adopted her new religion. She taught a Sunday School class, sang in the choir, and had filled in for the school teacher when he was absent for three days with the flu.

The harbour filled with ice in mid-January and the *Bar Haven* had made her last call in late December. Until the spring came and the ice was blown offshore, the community was totally isolated from the outside world. Their only contact was a short wave radio at George Buffett's place, but it was only used in medical emergencies. Mary Poole was the nurse and since there was very little she could not handle, it was rarely necessary to use the radio for medical purposes.

By the beginning of February, Francine knew that she was five months pregnant and was having difficulty hiding her weight gain. After breakfast one morning, and when Michel and Joe had left to work on the new boat, Francine decided it was time to confide in Millie.

"Millie," she began as they sipped their tea and looked out the kitchen window at the ice clogged bay, "I have something to tell you."

"What is it?" Millie asked.

Francine paused for a few seconds, having practised what she was about to say countless times in the past few months. "I'm pregnant."

"I know," Millie said quite calmly.

"You know?" Francine said, quite surprised.

"I may not be able to have children of me own, Francine dear, but I knows the symptoms of a pregnant woman. I heard you vomiting in the mornings, and despite your best efforts, you couldn't hide the life that is growing inside you. I figured it was your business and when you were ready to tell me, you would."

"Millicent Fudge," Francine said, smiling, "every day I spend with you, the more you amaze me. Why didn't you say something?"

"It's like I said, when you were ready to tell me, I knew you would. You had to tell me before you went into labour," she replied.

Millie laughed and they embraced on the bench as they sat at the table. Francine withdrew and looked straight into Millie's eyes. "You're a good friend, Millie. I don't think I've ever had a better friend, nor will I ever," she admitted as tears welled up in her eyes.

"Now, now, don't go getting all mushy on me," Millie said as she lifted up her apron and dried Francine's eyes.

"I know I told you that my husband died before he could have fathered this baby, and that was a lie. I didn't know you very well when I told you that, and I don't want to tell you anymore lies. So please, don't ask whose baby it is and maybe some day I'll be able to tell you everything." Francine lowered her head a little.

"Listen here now," Millie said. "Everybody has a secret or two and you're no exception. You know that whatever you tells me, I'll keep secret and when you're ready, just let me know and I'll be all ears. Until you are, though, you remember that you told everybody that your husband died in an accident over a year ago, so we'll have to come up with a story to satisfy the busy bodies. Leave that to me. Okay?"

Francine nodded her head in agreement.

March was colder than anybody could remember. It snowed every day and the ice remained in the harbour through April. Francine and Michel watched from the kitchen window as Joe and several other men killed the first seals. Francine was a little reluctant to taste the meat, but Michel couldn't get enough. Eventually, Francine tried it too, and after several more meals, she grew to enjoy it.

In May, the weather changed and one morning they woke to find that the wind had blown the ice out of the bay. By the end of the month, all of the snow was gone and the fishermen were getting ready for the spring fishery.

Francine felt as big as a whale and had to be careful when she made the walk from the stage to the house. Millie held her arm and they walked together slowly but surely. During the last week of May, with the assistance of most of the able-bodied men in Dark Harbour, Joe and Michel launched their new boat. Michel sat proudly in the front as the men pushed the new boat over the logs along the beach and into the water. Just as they reached the water's edge, Joe jumped into the boat. Everybody commented on how well the new boat sat in the water. The *Michel* floated proudly.

Joe had fashioned a makeshift life jacket for Michel out of trap floats and Francine had to laugh at him sitting on the boat seat with Joe, looking happier than he had ever looked in his short life. Joe held onto him with a grip that ten of the strongest men in Dark Harbour would not be able to release. Francine recognized what was happening. Joe was replacing Denis as Michel's father and on several occasions she had heard him referring to Joe as "Dad". At first she wanted to correct him, but now she wasn't sure. It couldn't do any harm and, besides, every boy needed a dad.

It was on the sixth of June when Francine felt her first labour pains and knew her baby had decided it was time to greet the world. The wind had whipped up the water and Joe had to wait for it to die down before they could go out to tend his traps. It was shortly after lunch when they were sitting at the kitchen table playing "forty-fives" when the first pain struck.

"Owww," she exclaimed, just as Joe was beating her Jack of Hearts with his Five.

"Don't take it so serious," Joe laughed as he drew in his trick and then came back with the Ace of Hearts.

Francine dropped the remainder of her cards and put her hands to her swollen belly. "It's not the cards," she smiled weakly. "I think Michel is about to become a big brother."

"Oh, me God," Joe said, dropping his cards as well.

"You go get Mary and tell her what's happening, then get back here right away and look after Michel. This might be a long day," Millie said calmly as she stood up and moved the kettle to the centre of the stove.

Michel had been playing on the floor with a few odd shapes of wood when suddenly he stood up and walked over to his mother.

"You okay, Mommy?" he asked as he stood up on the bench and put his tiny hand on her cheek.

"Yes, son, I'm okay." She kissed him on the cheek and he returned to his blocks.

Millie helped Francine up the stairs to her bed to await Mary Poole. Before Francine got into bed, Millie stripped off the sheet and put a large piece of plastic over the mattress and then replaced the sheet.

"No need to ruin the mattress," she said as she finished.

Millie had just finished helping Francine with her nightdress when she heard the door open downstairs and listened as Mary walked directly up the stairs.

"Well, at least it wasn't the middle of the night," the old woman joked as she came into the bedroom and threw her coat and headscarf on the floor in the corner. Mary Poole had been delivering babies longer than both of the two other women had been alive. She had come to Dark Harbour from Fortune nearly twenty years earlier and she was the community doctor, nurse and veterinarian. She had not received a single day of formal medical training, but she mended broken bones and administered drugs as well as any doctor could, every person in Dark Harbour agreed.

"You get some hot water and some towels and I'll see when this baby is going to be the newest resident of Dark Harbour," she said to Millie, turning her attention to Francine.

"This is your second baby, right?" she spoke to Francine as she pulled back the blankets and examined her. The room was cool and Francine was glad because she was perspiring profusely.

"Yes, it is," Francine said, and then closed her eyes as the contraction forced her to tighten. "My water just broke," she said, smiling.

"Good. Any problems with your last birthing?" Mary asked as she continued to examine Francine, hoping that the conversation would help ease her discomfort.

"Noooo," Francine replied.

Mary Poole, however, was not comforted. The repeated pressure of her thick hands along the underside of Francine's belly first alerted her to the woman's unease.

"Is everything okay?" she asked. She took a closer look at Mrs. Poole, noticing that her forehead had wrinkled with concern and her pleasant smile had now been replaced by a concentrated, measured look in her eye; as if she had found something, but wasn't quite sure what.

"Is everything okay, Mrs. Poole?" she asked again impatiently when the woman did not respond. Mary breathed deeply,

"This baby is breech."

"What does that mean?" Francine asked, confused. She didn't recognize the word. Her native tongue, even after living in Toronto for over four years, still precluded her from knowing all the nuances of the English language.

"Your baby, deary, wants to come out feet first."

"But…But is that normal? Can you do that?" Her voice rose in excitement.

"Well, it's not entirely normal, but it does happen. I've delivered breech babies before, we've just gotta be extra careful, that's all." Mary gently patted Francine's stomach as she pulled the bedclothes up over her. The terror on her face scared even the guarded nurse. Her heart went out to the young mother as she watched Francine's lip quiver, clearly on the verge of tears. But she caught herself, realizing Francine's need for reassurance. She smoothed her hair, "Now you listen here, deary, you can do this, It's just going to be a little bit harder than last time, that's all. Ain't nothing that ain't been done before." Under normal circumstances, if they had been in a hospital, a breech birth would have not been a cause for alarm. More than likely, the doctors would have performed a Caesarean Section to avoid trauma to the mother and the baby. But the nearest hospital was over one hundred miles away. It could have been a million miles for all the good that would do now. If Mary had somehow known about the breech position before labour had started, she might have been able to turn the baby. Often, massaging, bathing and similar relaxation techniques could induce turning, but by now labour was too far along. The baby would have to be delivered naturally. Mary had not lied to Francine; she had performed breech deliveries, but only a handful. And only half of those had survived.

Francine had had only one contraction since Mary had arrived, so it would be a little while yet before active labour began. It was safe to leave her for a short time. She also wanted Millie to be aware of the circumstances before hand. She spoke to Francine in a soothing voice, "Now I'm going to go downstairs and help Millie with the water and towels. You time the contractions and when I get back you let me know how far apart they are. Okay?"

Francine nodded and then was left alone. A single tear slid down her cheek from the tears that had been welling up in her eyes since Mrs. Poole had explained the situation. "Please God let my baby be okay," she whispered to an empty room, closing her eyes. The weight of the heavy blankets became unbearable as the next contraction waved over her. She struggled to throw them off, and was left with a single sheet. On the third contraction, Mary returned.

"How are you feeling deary?" she asked as she entered the room.

"Okay, I guess," Francine said weakly.

"How far apart are the contractions?"

"Two minutes."

"It'll be soon now then."

Another contraction came and passed. Francine clenched her teeth trying not to scream, but a sound came out anyway. Mary took a cold wet cloth and laid it across Francine's perspiring forehead. Thirty seconds later, Francine called out in pain again. As she did, Millie returned to the bedroom with a steaming kettle and a second pan filled with cold water. She poured their contents into two large ceramic bowls.

Mary removed the cool cloth from Francine's forehead, folded it and dried the perspiration off the rest of her face. Once finished, she rinsed the cloth in the cool water, wrung it out and then replaced it. As she did, Francine struggled through another contraction.

"There only about forty-five seconds apart now," was Mary's response. She threw back the sheet covering Francine and bent her legs into the birthing position to examine her. Sure enough, the baby had moved down into the birth canal and Francine was fully dilated.

"It'll be soon now," Mary stated. "Francine, this is going to be a little bit different than when you had Michel. I want you to prop yourself up on your hands and knees. The baby will have a much easier time coming then. We're gonna take it nice and slow." Francine did as she was told. Millie had let go of her hand, but as soon as Francine assumed the position, she came to her side again and took her hand. It was already white from the pressure Francine had been exerting on it as she held on. Prompted by Mary, Francine began to push, but the pain was nearly unbearable. She couldn't remember it hurting so much the previous time.

"That's it," Mary said.

Millie continued to wipe the perspiration from Francine's face. She tried to soothe her by gently rubbing her shoulders with her free hand. The feet were showing through the vaginal opening. The skin was now torn and bleeding profusely. There was a lot of blood and Mary reached for more cloths to soak it up. She was now pale, almost green, as Millie continued to hold her hand and offer words of encouragement. Millie felt Francine grow weak as her knees began to buckle, but she implored her, "C'mon now, Francine, be strong, be strong for your baby." Francine straightened.

Millie grasped Francine's shoulders while she strained, but the loss of blood had made her very weak. She pushed as both women offered support.

"Okay, okay, it's coming. Keep pushing," Mary said as they watched the baby's legs gradually become visible, then the torso, shoulders and, finally, the head. Mary quickly picked up the baby, making sure the umbilical cord was not wound around its neck. She cleared the breathing passages and then expertly cut the umbilical cord. Then the baby made its first sounds. Francine groaned as she felt contractions begin again. Seconds later she delivered the placenta. Hearing the baby's first sounds she formed a weak smile, rolled onto her side as if in slow motion and fainted. Mary looked at Millie and exhaled a big breath of air. "Good,"

Millie left Francine's side and found a blanket to wrap the newborn. Because it was premature, it was not a big baby, perhaps six pounds, but blood continued to flow freely from Francine. Millie tried to staunch it, pressing a clean cloth to the area, which slowed the flow just a little. But the damage was done. The bed was soaked in Francine's blood.

Millie took the new little girl to the warmth of the kitchen. Joe and Michel were waiting for them. "This is your new little sister," Millie said to Michel as she walked into the kitchen. Michel ran to greet her and Millie bent down for him to see.

"She looks all yucky," Michel said as he looked at his sister for the first time. Millie and Joe laughed.

Both of them looked on as Millie washed and wrapped the baby. She was covered with tiny bruises caused by the difficult birthing process. They would disappear in a couple of weeks. But there was a more pressing problem. She would soon want to be fed and Francine's present condition made that impossible. They didn't even have any bottles. Millie wrapped the child and placed her on the day bed. Joe and Michel stood over her and watched.

While Millie cleaned the baby, Mary remained in the bedroom and attempted to stop the bleeding and help Francine. Finally, she managed to stop the flow of blood, but she knew that it was probably too late. She left Francine sleeping and went to the kitchen.

Joe filled a pan with hot water for Mary and she washed off the blood without speaking. Once finished, she looked at Millie and then at Joe.

"Why don't you take Michel for a walk," she said to him. Joe knew what that meant.

"Come on, buddy," he smiled to Michel. "Let's go down to the stage and see what's going on."

Michel didn't need to be coaxed. He raced to the porch and quickly put on his boots and jacket. A few minutes later they were walking hand in hand down the hill. Mary waited until they were gone before she turned to Millie.

"It don't look good," she said as Millie dipped her finger into the warm milk and tried to teach Michel's sister how to suckle.

Millie looked up without speaking.

"The poor girl has lost a lot of blood. She should have lost the baby, but she's not going to make it herself. She's just lost too much."

Millie had already guessed that herself.

"She's sleeping now, but I don't think that she's going to last much longer." Getting up from the chair she said, "I'll go back up with her," and she left the kitchen and returned to Francine's room.

Tears formed in the corners of Millie's eyes, and she wiped them away with the back of her hand.

Francine was awake when Mary returned. She turned her head as Mary entered the room.

"You have a beautiful baby daughter," Mary smiled at her as she picked up her nearly lifeless hand. Francine tried to return the smile, but her lips were dry and she was very weak.

"Water," she managed.

Mary ran back to the kitchen and returned with a glass of water. She put her hand behind Francine's head and helped her while she took a few sips. Mary let her head fall back to the pillow and for the next several minutes neither of them spoke.

"Can I see my baby?" she asked, after she had finished drinking.

Mary called out from upstairs and a few seconds later, Millie appeared with Francine's baby. Mary propped her up a little in her bed while they waited for Millie.

"She's beautiful," Francine said as she looked at her daughter for the first time. "I've always wanted to have a little sister for Michel." Her eyes were heavy and she closed them after she finished speaking. Mary waved the two of them away. After they were gone, Francine spoke again.

"I'm going to die, aren't I?" Francine asked, suddenly.

"No, deary, don't go talking' like that. Of course you're not going to die," Mary lied.

"You must tell me the truth." Francine spoke quietly. "You must. If I'm going to die, then I have to talk to Millie. Please!" she pleaded. She tried to raise her hand, but did not have the strength.

Mary looked down at her charge. She couldn't lie. "You've lost a lot of blood, deary. I just couldn't stop it."

"Thank you for my little girl," Francine said. "At least she's okay."

"Yes, she's a beautiful healthy baby."

"I have to speak with Millie," Francine whispered as she turned and looked into Mary's face. "Before it's too late…" she trailed off.

Mary left the room and went down to the kitchen. "She hasn't got much time and she wants to talk to you," she explained as she took the baby from Millie's arms. Millie raced up the stairs to Francine. She took her hand in hers as she sat on the edge of the bed.

"Millie," Francine said as soon as she felt her friend's hands on hers.

"Yes," Millie answered, with eyes full of tears.

"There's something I have to tell you." Francine laboured hard to get the words out. "My real name is Francine Forest, and Michel and I ran away from my husband in Toronto. He must not find out where we are. I have a lot of money in my bag." She tried to point to it. Her eyes remained closed. "You take it and you raise Michel. When he's eighteen, I want you to give him all my things. And there's a lot more money that he will get when he's twenty-one. Do you understand?"

Millie nodded and managed a low, "Yes."

"You must raise my little girl, too."

"Yes."

"Michel must go to school and get an education."

"Okay," Millie managed, and her tears dripped down on their hands.

"You're a good…" were the last words that Francine Forest spoke.

Three ~

NEARLY EVERYBODY IN the tiny fishing village came to the funeral, which meant cod traps that would normally be hauled in the early afternoon were put off until later. It was a cold, windy day. The weather on this bleak, weather-beaten coast of Newfoundland was unpredictable at best. It was the second week of June, but it was bitterly cold and everyone in the small church had dressed for it.

The church was small and perched on a hill at the back of the town. A narrow path led up to the church and from the wooden platform in front of the door worshippers could view the entire village. There wasn't much to see though; a ring of houses around a cove filled with fishing boats.

The church seemed to have a Norman influence to its architecture. A crude sort of four-sided steeple had been built atop the structure and it was covered with graying clapboards that had soaked up whitewash many years earlier. On all sides of the steeple, rough, louvred windows allowed the heavy, monotonous claps of the bell to escape. Today it clapped at intervals of fifteen seconds. A funeral toll.

Both sides of the tiny church were lined with windows filled with panes of clear glass clouded by the salt air spray. One single stained glass window portrayed an angel holding a harp, contrasting sharply with the rest of the drab building. It looked out of place and was obviously a gift from some generous parishioner.

Surrounding the structure was a pointed picket fence and its lean was a testament to the futility of trying to drive the posts into the rock. It had been futile. It too had been whitewashed, but it had been so long ago that it made little difference. The large door at the entrance to the church was twice the height of a normal person and the metal

hinges, rusted by the sea air, extended half way across it. It was painted white and the rust from the hinges had washed down its front.

Despite its many openings and closings, the huge door squeaked
as Joe pulled it open for his family. Most of the seats were taken as
he closed the door behind them and walked toward their pew. The
pews were made of rough hewn lumber, a couple of inches thick, but
many years of use had rubbed them smooth. A large pot-bellied stove
was fixed to the floor at the back of the church and the wood that
Joe had brought earlier was crackling noisily and generating too
much heat for those at the back and too little for those at the front.
The floor was also covered with rough hewn lumber, fit together
with meticulous care, and a Manila hemp rug covered the aisle up
through the pews to the altar that had obviously been constructed
with more care than the pews had been. Covering it was a small
draped cloth with a religious insignia on its front. Behind the pew
stood Reverend Foote who had arrived earlier that morning. To his
right, Francine lay in an unfinished wooden box that was her coffin.
It had come from the Forsey's store and would be replaced when the
next supply ship called.

Millie walked to her pew carrying Francine's baby in her arms
while Michel walked up the aisle holding onto Joe's hand. They nodded their greetings to the families who shared the pew and then
 waited silently for the service to begin. Michel sat between the two of
them and tried to look around to see the others. He looked up at Joe
as if to say something, but Joe put his index finger across his lips and
mouthed a silent "Shhh."

These were a poor people, ravaged by the weather and exploited
by the greed of those who owned the fish plants where they sold their
catches. They fished on an open sea and exchanged their wares for
credit at the store of the owner of the fish plants. Always, without
exception, at the end of the fishing season they remained indebted to
the store, regardless of how much fish they sold. Their clothes were
simple and reflected their lifestyles. A good deal of the clothing was
purchased on credit in anticipation of a future sale of fish, clothes that
were cheap leftovers from the Montreal garment industry, where so
many of the fish plant owners had ties. But churchgoing presented the
opportunity to put on one's "Sunday best." Most of the women were

accomplished at sewing and made their own clothing, purchasing the material from stores in St. John's, or having it sent by relatives who had moved to the city. The material was then delivered on the coastal boats. It was obvious that most of the younger children's clothing had been handmade and passed down from sibling to sibling. The women's dresses were also handmade and, because of their meagre resources, dresses were of a material and colour to make them wearable at many occasions: the serious and the joyous. The men wore dark trousers, dark jackets and white shirts and their neckties depicted an array of different colours. Their faces had been burned by the summer sun and frozen by the winter wind. Their hair was trimmed close and high above their shirt collars.

The church was full even though the people of Dark Harbour had only known Francine for a very short time. Seated in the pews in the small church they looked like people who were practised in this type of ceremony. Few of them had ever ventured farther away from their homes than their fishing boats could take them out in the morning and back in the afternoon. They were fishermen and the families of fishermen and they were God-fearing people. Death and funerals were regular occurrences in Dark Harbour and the church services were always well attended regardless of the weather.

As Reverend Foote lifted his eyes up from the Bible, the congregation sensed he was about to speak and suddenly the shuffling of feet and the whispering subsided.

"We are gathered here today to pay our last respects to Francine Forest," he began. "Francine was in our community for only a short period, but during that time she became a respected and loved member of our community. Her class in Sunday school had many good things to say about her and her lovely voice added much to our choir. She came to Dark Harbour to write about us, but God has called her for another purpose." He suddenly lowered his voice and continued. "But Francine has left behind two lovely children." He paused to point at the two children between Joe and Millie.

The service was short, but as usual, Reverend Foote conducted a nice memorial service. The Twenty-third Psalm was recited in unison and Rock of Ages was the only hymn sung. The hymn books were shared between couples, but there wasn't a dozen amongst them who could read the printed words. It was a practised ritual, committed to memory and recited.

Millie, Joe and the children were the first in line behind Reverend Foote as the coffin was carried from the church and down the hill to the cemetery. Joe had selected the pall- bearers and a shoulder injury he had incurred a few days earlier prevented him from being one of them. The wind had subsided a little as they left the church and over-sized snowflakes were drifting lifelessly to earth. Each melted the instant it struck the wet ground.

The funeral line was solemn as it winded its way down the hill to the cemetery a few hundred yards from the church. Another picket fence surrounded it, but it was obvious from its appearance that the ground was much softer here than where the church was located. There were no headstones; only wooden crosses set into the ground bearing names and dates. The schoolteacher was always asked to write the appropriate words and numbers on a piece of paper, which the fisherman would then carve on the cross.

They waited until everyone was in the cemetery. Those who had been first to arrive stood impatiently staring into a hole that was des-tined for all of them one day. The Minister went first, followed by the Fudges, and took his position at an end of the grave, opened a worn Bible and began reading.

Millie never heard what he had to say. Her thoughts were on the first day that Francine had arrived in Dark Harbour and the friend-ship that had developed since then. She held the little baby closer to her breast and reached to touch Michel. Michel responded by looking up at her. It was a sad day for everybody and Millie wanted it to end, but she realized that the next few days would be just as difficult.

Millie still thought of the room as Francine's room and she felt a little strange as she began the work of opening the dresser drawers and sorting through Francine's clothes. Francine's clothes felt expen-sive and had fancy stitching. They were soft and smooth as she touched them to her face. The smell was also definitely Francine's. She tried not to, but she couldn't stop the tears that ran down her cheeks. Francine had been a good friend to her and her death would be very difficult to overcome.

Millie had never been to school. There were fourteen children in her family and she was the oldest. Her job had always been to help her mother. School couldn't teach her anything that would help her with that responsibility, so she stayed at home. She could tell the denominations of money, knew her ABCs, and could write her name and her husband's, but that was the limit of her literacy. Until now she had never had a need to read or write anything other than those few simple requirements. As she carefully sifted through Francine's belongings, making a pile of the papers and a pile of the clothing, she wished she could read what was on those papers.

What clothes fit her she would wear and what didn't she would distribute to the other women in the community. This was expected. There were lots of papers and books and other printed things which, when everything was sorted, Millie gingerly deposited in one of the large steamer trunks. In it she also placed the typewriter and several pieces of jewellery. They would be kept for the children. There were also several pictures she could only guess were members of Francine's family. She turned one over and on its back was written "Linda". Millie recognized the name because that was also the name of one of her sisters. Millie looked at the picture and wondered if it could be Francine's mother. There was no resemblance, however, so she concluded that it was not. Anyway, she now had a name for the baby. She would christen her Linda.

The pictures, papers and everything else that she would give the children when they were old enough were placed in Francine's trunk. Finally, all that was remaining were the two purses. Millie recognized the smaller one as the one Francine carried with her from day to day. She couldn't remember having ever seen the other one.

Reluctantly, she picked up the first purse and then drew it to her breast. She closed her eyes for a second and then slowly lowered it to her lap. Michel, who had been playing in the other room, came in the bedroom and climbed up on the bed. He snuggled up beside her, with his thumb in his mouth. She bent over and kissed him on the forehead. She stared into his face for a few seconds and realized that she loved this little boy as much as any mother could love her child. He was tired and wanted to go to bed. She turned back the sheets, lifted him up and placed him under them. He would sleep for an hour before supper. Millie then picked up the purse again and pinched the two little clips that held it shut. It came open and, embarrassed, Millie reached inside and withdrew its contents.

There were the usual things that a woman such as Francine would carry in her purse in addition to several pieces of paper. Millie gathered them together and placed them in the trunk along with all the other papers. One envelope remained and Millie could see that it was full of money.

There was a lot of it, more than she had ever seen at one time. She tried to count the change first, but gave up when she couldn't add beyond a few dollars. She then turned to the paper money. It was in no particular order, but there were assorted denominations. Millie could not determine the total worth of the numerous bills, so she just piled them together and laid them on the bed beside the now sleeping Michel. Then she turned to the large purse.

Millie removed several small envelopes from it and carefully laid each on the bed with the others. Inside each was a small book with only a few pages and, after examining them, she returned them to the envelopes. One was a little larger than the others and was sealed with a large elastic band. Millie removed the band and as she did, the envelope and its contents fell to the floor.

It was like slow motion as the envelope slipped from her hands and bills scattered over the hooked rug. Millie raised both hands to her mouth and sat hypnotized by the mess of bills on the floor. For nearly a minute Millie stared down at the scattered pile of one hundred-dollar-bills. She had never seen so much money in her life. She didn't know whether to laugh or cry. She suddenly shivered.

"What have you done, Francine?" she whispered, staring at the spilled money on the floor. Michel stirred beside her and Francine's words came back to her. "You take it and raise Michel."

It was nearly 6:00 p.m. when Joe returned from delivering Reverend Foote to Cow's Head. He smiled weakly as he closed the door behind him. He removed his jacket, hung it on a nail beside the kitchen stove and then sat at the table as Millie passed him a plate of oven baked beans piled high on a chipped china plate. Silently, she sliced several thick slices from a loaf of fresh bread and put them on a plate in front of Joe. As Joe was buttering his bread, she filled his cup with steaming tea. Finished, she poured herself a cup of tea and sat on the bench across from him.

"How was the water?" she finally asked as she sipped her tea.

Joe shovelled the beans and bread into his mouth and then tried to speak. "It was a bit loppy when we got underway, but it calmed down by the time I got ready to come back."

Millie continued to make idle conversation as Joe ate his supper. Finally, she couldn't hold it in anymore. "It's an awful lot of money, Joe," she blurted out.

Joe didn't look up from his meal; Millie paused for a second.

"Did you hear what I said?" she asked.

"I'll pay Ralph Forsey for the coffin. Don't worry about it," he said, trying to console her.

"No, it's not that, you bloody fool," Millie scolded. "I went through the things in Francine's room and there's an awful lot of money. There must be thousands and thousands of dollars."

"What?" Joe started, staring straight at her.

"Yes, there's more money than I've ever seen in me life before. I couldn't even count it," she answered with a joyless smile on her face.

"Where is it now?" Joe asked, stupefied. He was barely able to formulate the question and, though famished, had stopped eating altogether.

"It's in the room. I didn't know what to do with it so I just stuffed it back into her bag. Before she passed away, poor child, she told me that I should take it and raise Michel and the baby. I didn't dream that there was so much money. And you know something else?"

Joe shook his head, holding a forkful of beans suspended half way between his mouth and the plate.

"She told me that there was a lot more money and Michel would get it all someday."

Joe finally shovelled the beans into his mouth and swallowed hard. "Let me see it," he managed.

Millie pushed herself back from the table and went to the bedroom. She returned a few minutes later with Francine's two bags. She pushed the dishes away from the center of the table and carefully set the two bags down. They both stared at them and then, after a few seconds hesitation, Millie reached for the smaller of the two. She squeezed the clasp, removed the bundle of bills, and placed them in front of Joe, who pushed back his dinner plate. He wiped his hands on the front of his sweater and picked up the money. With his thick hands, scarred from hard work and salt water, he picked up a bundle with his left hand and, with his right hand, carefully laid each bill onto the table. Both were silent. Millie just stared at him. It was as if he had suddenly learned how to count.

Joe examined the bills in the pile and once finished, he stared at it for a few seconds and then at Millie. She pulled away from his stare and reached for the larger purse. She squeezed the clasp and reached inside. Joe gasped as her hand reappeared with another bundle of bills, considerably larger than the first. Millie placed it on the table beside the smaller pile. Neither of them spoke.

"It's all ours, you know," Millie said, breaking the silence.

"What do you mean, it's all ours?" Joe asked with a tone of disbelief in his voice.

"Francine said it's ours. Before she passed away, she told me that it's ours, to be used to raise her children. We're supposed to make sure that Michel gets himself some education."

Joe's eyes flickered between the piles of money and Millie.

"Reverend Foote said that the children are ours now, so then the money is ours, too," Millie said, trying to rationalize her decision.

"Does he know about this money?" Joe asked suddenly.

"No, of course not. There's not another living soul that knows about this. Do you think that I'm foolish or something?"

Joe didn't answer. He was thinking. He saw the piles of money as a new boat, a couple of new traps and some new gear that would allow him to fish longer and farther out from the shore. He wouldn't have to come home every night, or every time the wind blew. He could steam into a cove and wait out any wind. He looked up from the piles of money and saw that Millie was staring at him. He suddenly felt guilty for what he had been thinking. Millie could see the change in his eyes.

"What's the matter?" she asked.

Joe paused before he spoke. "I was just thinking that this money could get me a new boat. A long liner."

"You just built a new boat," Millie commented.

"Yes, but that was just another trap skiff. With this money I could get a real boat."

Millie didn't respond. She just stared at her husband. Her gaze hardened. The money wasn't for them. It was for the children. Her husband's comments saddened her. He was thinking of himself. She lifted her gaze to chastize her husband and the instant she looked into his eyes she knew that Joe Fudge had never had a selfish thought in his entire life. The boat would give them a better life.

"Yes," she said, smiling at him. "I think that Francine would have wanted that. She told me that they would someday get more money. We just have to make sure that we don't spend everything and that we do as Francine wanted. Michel has to get an education."

"Yes," Joe nodded. "I only wish, though, that we knew how much money we got here," he said, frustrated at not knowing just how wealthy they were.

"Maybe we can call the schoolteacher and get her to count it for us," Millie offered.

"No," Joe snapped. "We don't know her. We can't trust her not to tell other people about this."

Millie nodded her understanding and agreement. They continued to stare at the money. Millie was first to break the silence.

"How about if we write down all the numbers and then ask the teacher to add them up for us. We could tell her that it was the weight of the fish you sold last summer or something like that. Then I could ask her a few questions so we could understand how much we would have left after you got your boat. Would that be okay?" she asked.

"Yes, maid, I think that would work. Get a pencil and some paper and start writing down the numbers."

Joe moved the kerosene lamp to the table. They sorted the bills by denomination, and then, once the numbers were recorded, Joe rolled each bundle of bills and secured them with string. Together, they examined the sheets of paper and the bundles stacked at the center of the table. Then they methodically took all of the bundles and carefully placed them in the larger of the two bags. Millie folded the sheet of paper. After tea, they checked on the sleeping children and retired for the evening.

By 4:30 a.m. the next morning, Joe had eaten his breakfast and was on the water. Millie kept busy, but the hours dragged by until finally it was 8:30 a.m. She dressed Michel and Linda and pulled a shawl over her head and shoulders. With the folded sheet of paper in her apron pocket, she walked the couple of hundred feet to the church, which housed the basement schoolroom.

Sarah King had just started the fire and was rubbing her hands in front of the stove as Millie pushed open the door to the tiny schoolroom and closed it behind her. She turned to greet her visitor.

"Why, good morning, Mrs. Fudge." The schoolteacher smiled at her. She didn't acknowledge the children.

"Good morning to you too, Miss King," Millie answered.

"What brings you to school this morning?" she asked.

Millie walked toward her, still holding Michel by the hand. She let his hand drop and placed the baby on a desk before removing her shawl from her head and letting it drop to her shoulders. As she did, she reached into her apron pocket for the paper. Finding it, she passed it to the schoolteacher.

"Miss King," she said, "this here is all the lobster pots that Joe and his brothers have scattered all around here. Joe said to me a couple of nights ago that every year there seems to be less and less of them. So I told him to count them all at every place where he got them stored. Then I'd get that nice Miss King to add them all up for us. Then every spring he can count them again and if there's any missing he would know. Would you mind, Miss, adding this up for me?" she finished as she handed the paper to her.

Miss King took the paper. "Yes, of course. No, I mean, no." She laughed. "I wouldn't mind adding this up for you. Why don't you just have a seat beside the stove and I'll do this for you."

Millie smiled her appreciation and sat at one of the student's desks closest to the stove. Michel stood beside her. Miss King stepped up on the platform to her desk and quickly began to scribble on the paper. A few minutes later, she returned.

"Your husband and his brothers have three thousand and eleven pots," she smiled proudly.

"I didn't think anybody had that many," she commented.

The amount was a shock to Millie. The number kept repeating itself. She just stared without blinking.

"Mrs. Fudge, are you okay?" Miss King asked, noticing the change that had come over Millie.

"Yes, yes, fine thank you. I think my husband may have counted the stored pots in some of the coves more than once," she laughed, trying to make light of the amount.

"Well, I suggest you have him count them again. I wouldn't mind adding them for you when he is done, but he should do it before the end of this week because this is the last week of school and I am going home for the summer," she said.

"Yes, thank you. Thank you very much, Miss King," Millie said. Then she remembered that Joe had said he could buy a new boat for about two thousand dollars. "If they had two thousand less than that number, how many would there be?" she asked sheepishly.

It seemed like a strange question, but Sarah King had heard more than her share of strange questions since she had come to Dark Harbour a year earlier. "They would have one thousand and eleven," she quickly calculated.

"That would be more than enough," Millie said as she turned to pick up the baby and hurry Michel out the door.

Millie raced home, barely able to contain herself. She made herself a cup of tea and as she sat at the table drinking it, she saw Joe tying his boat up at the wharf. She got up from the table, moved the kettle to the center of the stove, and broke several eggs into a pan. By the time they were ready, Joe was at the door.

Michel ran to him as he entered and jumped up into his arms. "Can I come down and watch you clean the fish?" he asked as Joe hugged the little boy and then sat him on a chair beside him at the table.

Joe nodded his head and Michel smiled his widest smile.

"Did you see the schoolteacher?" he asked, turning to Millie as she placed a plate of eggs in front of him.

"Yes, I did," Millie answered.

"Well?" Joe asked impatiently.

"We have three thousand and eleven dollars," Millie stated.

"Oh, my God," Joe said. "I never dreamed it would be that much.

He turned his attention to Michel. "We're going to have a new boat, Michel," he said, grinning from ear to ear. "And do you know what we are going to call her?"

Michel shook his head.

"We're going to call her *The Francine*. Yes, we're going to call her *The Francine*," he said as he stirred his tea and poured a little into his saucer to cool.

Four ∼

MICHEL WAS SIX and a half when he started school. It was September 6, 1954, and a year earlier he had started calling Millie and Joe "Mom" and "Dad". Maybe it was because Linda had always called them Mom and Dad. He talked about Francine often for the first year after her death and he cried a lot when Millie tried to explain to him that his mother was now in heaven with the angels and wouldn't be coming back. On a couple of occasions he even mentioned his father, but his memories of him were very vague. As time passed, he mentioned his real parents less and less and Millie knew that was probably for the best. The first time he called her Mom it sort of slipped out, but then one day he just gave up calling her Millie altogether. Millie and Joe knew that one day they would tell him everything they could about his mother and give him all of her things. Hopefully, everything he needed to know would be found in the steamer trunk.

Michel had grown into a very handsome little boy and Millie guessed that he must look like his father because he did not look much like Francine. He was pleasant and he followed behind his adoptive father like a shadow. There wasn't a person in Dark Harbour who was prouder of his child than Joe was of Michel. Except perhaps Millie, who was equally close to Linda. Like Michel, she was very bright and had been blessed with good health. She uttered her first word at seven months and she was walking at ten months. Now, at age two, she had an excellent vocabulary and spoke with the accent of a born and bred Newfoundlander, for indeed she was.

Michel liked school, or at least pretended to, but he enjoyed going fishing with his father more than anything else. On many occasions he mentioned to Joe that he wanted to be a fisherman like him, but Joe reminded him each time that if he didn't go to school, he wouldn't be permitted to go out on the boat with him on Saturdays. And Michel would have done anything for the opportunity to go fishing with his father. Millie made it very clear to him that not only was he required to go to school, but he was expected to do well there. He did, but it was very obvious to his teacher that Michel had only one love, and that was fishing.

He was eleven when Joe first let him take *The Francine* out from her mooring in the harbour to the fishing grounds. *The Francine* was the best boat in Dark Harbour and Joe treated her with no less care than he did his children. He caught more fish than anybody in Dark Harbour and it meant a lot to him that he owned his boat and all the gear outright. He paid cash for his engine and all of the lumber was cut and then sawn in Reg Tibbo's mill. He had bought her keel and gunwales because he was unable to get what he wanted in Dark Harbour and he had paid cash for those as well. She was five years old and thirty-five feet long. She was powered with a nineteen and one-half horsepower Lister diesel engine and a crew of three fished off her deck. This morning though, she had a crew of four as Michel stood on an apple box beneath her wheel and steered her out of the cove toward the first of two cod traps that they would haul before lunch.

Joe stood beside his son, giving him both encouragement and directions. The heat from the engine and the stench of diesel fuel filled the little cabin as the other two men sat on the bunks sipping their tea and smiling their encouragement to the young man. Michel smiled proudly as he stared out through the salt-stained window and gripped the wheel so tightly that his knuckles were white. He wasn't strong enough, though, to work the throttle lever, so Joe moved it to the orders of the new young captain.

"Open her out, Dad," he ordered as they cleared the entrance to the harbour. Joe pulled back on the lever.

"Aye, aye, Captain," Joe responded, and at the same time winked at his two brothers.

The engine sound increased in pitch and the stern of the boat dug a little deeper in the water in response to the increased power. The boat surged ahead and left a trail of white foaming water astern. The little punt that *The Francine* pulled behind danced on her wake.

Gradually, *The Francine* levelled and as she did, the smile broadened on Michel's face. He glanced across at his father and caught the wink Joe had flashed at his brothers.

It was a beautiful morning and there was hardly a ripple on the water as they steamed out of the harbour and into the bay. Once outside the protection of the harbour, however, the calmness was replaced by the constant North Atlantic swells. The gulls squawked their resentment at being forced to fly out of the path of the oncoming boat as Michel guided them to the first trap. He steered the boat like a seasoned fisherman and reached their first cod trap a couple of miles from the harbour just as the sun was rising.

The cod trap was a marvellous invention and Michel knew exactly how it functioned. It was used by most fishermen and had evolved over the years into a very effective tool. Michel knew the names of every part of the trap and as they neared it he passed control of the boat over to his father and then walked out onto the deck with his uncles. They were younger than Joe and had been fishing with him ever since they had become old enough to fish, which in Al's case had been twelve, and Mel thirteen. And like their older brother, neither had gone to school.

The cod fish was the most predictable of marine specimens and every year during the months of June to August, it left the deep ocean waters and followed its main food source, the caplin, in to the shallow water. There the cod gorged themselves on the tiny silver fish. During this period, inshore fishermen, like Joe, made their living.

Joe carefully guided the boat to the buoy, which marked the point where the leader rope extended across the top of the open box. Twenty feet from it, he threw the engine into neutral and coasted into the centre of the box. Mel hooked it with the gaff and pulled the rope over the stem of the boat. As he did, Joe shut the engine off and the swell of the Atlantic Ocean tossed the boat up and down. Al jumped into the little rowboat being towed behind *The Francine* and took up a position directly opposite them. He pulled on the mesh and draped it over the side of his boat. Below them, swimming aimlessly in circles, were, they hoped, enough fish to fill their boat.

For the next hour they began the process of "hauling the trap". This was the most enjoyable aspect of fishing, yet the most physically

strenuous. It took an hour to bring the bottom of the trap to the surface and there was no way of telling if there were any fish in the trap
until the bottom was in sight. It could be very disappointing, but they
wouldn't be disappointed today. Al was only twenty feet broadside of
them now and with each pull of the mesh, the boat drew closer.
Michel peered over the side of the boat into the darkness between the
two boats. He could see shapes below him and he knew they were fish.
He spotted a couple of flashes of light and everybody knew, without
speaking, that they had trapped a few salmon as well. They would be
smoked and kept for winter. Michel pulled now with more enthusiasm than when they started. Mel nudged Joe and they both smiled as
they watched Michel. Joe was very proud of his young son.

The water suddenly began to churn as the fish were drawn to the
surface. "How many do you think we got this morning, Michel?" Joe
called to him.

"I bet there's ten thousand pounds there, Dad," he answered.

"Yes, by, I'd say you're not far wrong," Joe said as they secured
the wall of trap to keep it from falling back into the ocean. The other
two men laughed as they watched the huge bag of fish between
the two boats.

Michel left his position and made his way to the stern where he
found a dip net and passed it to his father. He found a second and
passed it to his Uncle Mel. In unison, they dipped the nets into the
bag of fish and began scooping them into the belly of the boat. As the
fish were removed, more net was pulled and the remaining fish were
forced to the surface. Finally, after an hour and a half of dipping, they
sat exhausted, looking at the nearly ten thousand pounds of fish dying
in the bottom of the boat.

There wasn't much time to examine their handiwork because there
was another trap to be hauled before they could return to Dark
Harbour. Once all the fish were aboard, the net was thrown back out
of the boat and it slowly sank to the bottom. The doorway ropes were
released and as the boat steamed to the next trap, the big square of
corks settled back into place, opening the doors once again for the fish
already queued at the leader.

There was nearly ten thousand pounds of fish in the second
trap and by 11:00 a.m. they were back at the wharf. These were the

big spring fish and would be split and dried. If they sold the fish "green", not cleaned, they would get two cents a pound. They would sell the fish green in July when the fish were smaller, but these large fish, after they had been salted and dried, would fetch twenty cents a pound. The fish would lose a full two thirds of their weight during the curing process, but even after the salt was paid for, they had made nearly five hundred dollars this morning. Joe would take two shares, one for himself and one for his boat, and his brothers would get a share each. Unfortunately, it was a very short season and bad weather prevented them from doing this every day.

Millie and Linda were standing on the wharf as Joe guided the boat toward it. Michel was standing at the bow holding the big mooring rope and Mel was at the stern. Joe masterfully guided the boat beside the wharf and as he did, Mel jumped onto it and threw the stern rope over the gump. At the same instant, Michel jumped over the bow and threw his rope over another gump. The stern rope stopped the boat and, using both ropes, they slowly drew the boat tight to the wharf and it bobbed gently up and down as it rubbed against the old car tires hanging from its sides. Most of the people in the community had only seen pictures of a car and even though it would be a long time before the first automobile arrived in Dark Harbour, the tires had been there for many years.

Millie looked down into the boat. "Look at all the fish, Linda," she said as she held onto her daughter's hand. As they both peered over the side of the wharf, one of the fish, with a few desperate flicks of its tail, skidded across the top of the others.

"They're still alive!" Linda shouted excitedly as she pointed at the fish and then turned to her mother. They had repeated this process a hundred times before, but Linda still found it fascinating.

"Yes, they are," Millie laughed. Linda looked at her father and, without speaking, he picked up a single fish from the thousands in the boat and climbed up the ladder onto the wharf. It was one of the dozen or so salmon that they had caught.

"You fellers take one of them for your dinner, too," he called to Al and Mel as he stepped up to the wharf. Playfully, he swung the fish at Linda and she dug her head into her mother's skirt.

Joe crossed the length of the wharf. He picked up a knife and, holding the salmon's tail, raked the knife back and forth across its length, making the silver scales fly into the air like snow. When he was satisfied that it was sufficiently scaled, he dipped it in a large wooden vat of water beneath the table. With the sea water dripping from it, Joe laid it on the table and expertly slit the fish's throat and ran the knife the length of its body. He laid the knife on the table and then, in a single motion, he removed the guts and twisted off the salmon's head on the edge of the table. Seconds later, there were a half dozen slices of fresh salmon ready for frying. Twenty minutes later, Joe and Michel were seated at the table eating the fish.

After lunch, the work of cleaning the morning's fish began. It was noon and by four o'clock they would have to be finished so that they could repeat the process again. Mel was already back on the wharf when Joe and Michel left their house. Al was just arriving.

As they walked down the hill, the scene in front of them was something they had witnessed more times than either of them could remember. One side of the wharf was filled with rough tables spaced about ten feet apart. On the opposite side of the wharf, men were busy pronging the fish from the holds of their boats onto the wharf. Sea gulls were everywhere and at each table several men and women were busy cleaning fish. A couple of other boats from Dark Harbour had also returned with their catches and they also had to get their fish cleaned so they could return to hauling their traps later that afternoon. Joe had the largest boat in Dark Harbour and he also had a hoist to help them with the work of getting the fish from the boat to the wharf.

When Joe and Michel reached the wharf, they found their rubber clothes where they had left them before lunch and pulled them on quickly. Al took control of the hoist while Mel filled the large bucket attached to it. The surface of the wharf was quickly covered with fish. Michel picked up a prong and began the work of filling up the wooden box at the end of the table. Joe sharpened the knives and watched as Millie and Freda, Mel's wife, walked down the hill to the wharf. Al's wife would babysit the children today. Tomorrow it would be Millie's or Freda's turn. They were also dressed in rubber clothes and took their positions at the table like they had thousands of times before.

Freda took a knife from Joe and a fish from the box. With a practised skill, she slit the throat and opened its belly. She slid it along the table to Millie, who removed the liver and threw it into a large empty vat at her feet. The liver would be stored in large drums and sold later for cod liver oil. She then reached into the belly of the fish, removed its guts and threw them over the side of the wharf. Gulls fought to devour them before they sank to the gut-covered bottom. Before the guts hit the water, Millie, holding the body of the fish with her left hand, pressed down on its head and twisted it off across the edge of the table. Finished, she slid the headless fish across the table to Joe.

A "V" had been cut into the side of the table where Joe stood and a thin piece of wood had been nailed beside it. Joe slid the fish so that the tail was facing away from him and, with his left hand, he held the fin of the fish against the piece of wood. With a wide-blade knife that was turned up at the end, he cut into the fish near its tail. With the tip of the sharpened edge bent inward, he then slid the knife the length of the fish, cutting into its backbone. Turning the fish around so that the tail was toward him, he did the same thing on the other side. Then, holding the fish firmly, he cut underneath the backbone and it flew over the side of the wharf while the fish fell into a large vat of water. He was starting the procedure over again almost before the first fish had hit the water.

Al finished offloading the fish and then took a position beside Millie. He also began splitting the fish. In the meantime as the vats became full with the split fish, Michel used a dip net to scoop the fish into a large wheelbarrow. As soon as it was full, Joe took the wheelbarrow and strained to push it the length of the wharf to the stage at its end.

The stage was a weather beaten house of wood and no effort had been made to plug any of the holes where the planks that covered the walls didn't quite meet. A wooden ramp led up to it and the same kind of boards that covered the walls covered the floor. Fishing equipment was hung in no apparent order on the walls and on one wall directly across from the entrance was a large bin filled with several thousand pounds of coarse salt. Beside it was a large square pile of fish. Joe pushed the wheelbarrow to the pile while Michel found a second empty wheelbarrow and returned to the wharf.

Joe took the shovel that was leaning against the salt bin, filled it and threw its contents on the wooden floor. He repeated this process several times until an area about six feet square was covered. He then carefully removed each fish from the wheelbarrow, one at a time, and laid them flat, belly up, on the salted floor until the salted area was covered. Next, he shovelled salt over the white bellies of the fish; he repeated this process until all the fish were covered with the salt. He then brought the empty wheelbarrow back to the wharf where Michel had another one filled and waiting for him.

Everybody knew his job and it was not unusual to see children as young as Michel working alongside the adults. Boys or girls, it made no difference. So far, Michel was the only one of the Fudge children who was old enough to help; it would be a couple more years before Mel's or Al's children could join in.

Once the fish were offloaded, Mel readied the boat for its return to the traps again that afternoon. He made sure that there was lots of fuel and then, with a mop and bucket of seawater, he scrubbed the hold and the deck of *The Francine*. All the gear was stowed away and when everything was in shipshape, he joined the others and helped with the cleaning of the fish.

At 2:30 the women were finished. Mel and Al finished splitting the last of the fish and then helped Joe with the salting. By 3:30, two new piles of fish were salted in their stage and they took a cigarette break and proudly admired their handiwork. In twenty-one days the fish would be taken from the salt, washed and spread out on the large fish flakes behind the stage for drying. That was what Millie and the other women would do while the men were out fishing. In a couple of days, the first fish they had salted this year would be ready for washing. But for the men, their work had been done.

It was 10:00 p.m. before the second catch of fish had been salted. They had nearly fifteen thousand pounds when they hauled the traps in the afternoon. It had been their best day in a long time. Two weeks of catches like today and they would have their money made, but days like today were rare. For the next two days, heavy seas kept them ashore and kept the fish in deep water.

By the end of August, the trap fishery was finished. It had been a good season for Joe and his crew and they had nearly four hundred thousand pounds of fish cured or nearly cured. When the fish went out to the deep water and they had removed their traps, they could begin with the gill nets and the trawls. Then, if they could get another couple of good months, they would have an excellent year.

During the first week of September, *The Crosbie* tied up in Dark Harbour and for the following two days it took the fishermen's catches. None of them knew exactly how many pounds they had. They depended on the skipper of *The Crosbie* to tell them that. No money changed hands, there was only a credit voucher to be used for purchasing whatever they needed at the owner's store. Joe asked for three vouchers. He got a voucher worth thirty-eight thousand dollars for himself, and Mel and Al each got one worth nineteen thousand dollars. The extra share Joe took was to take care of the expenses of running the boat, such as fuel and equipment purchases and repairs.

The feudal system enslaved the fishermen in no less a fashion than the Irish potato farmers were enslaved by their landlords. The fishermen had only one market for their fish. There was no bidding and no going to another person to see what he was offering. There was only the person buying their catches and the fishermen either took what he was offering or they starved. Everything they needed was supplied by the merchants, who charged what they wanted for the fish they wanted. They paid only enough for minimum subsistence and the payments were not made in cash, but in kind, with the fishermen given credit in the merchants' store. Regardless of the price the fishermen were paid for their fish or how much they caught, at the end of the fishing season they were always indebted to the merchants.

In a society when people were thrown in prison for their debts, this system ensured that the merchants would keep the fishermen fishing. The fishermen were a proud people who paid their debts and had little to show for work that kept them dependent. They were a people taken advantage of by a merchant-controlled society in which they were mere pawns. The only actual cash the fishermen ever saw would come from a fortunate meeting with a factory ship owned by the Russians or the Norwegians. Otherwise, everything was bought and sold on credit. A few years earlier, though, faced with mounting provincial criticism, George Crosbie had agreed to give the fishermen five percent of their sales in cash.

By mid-September the trawl and gill net fisheries were fully operational. Both of these types of fishing were considerably more dangerous than the trap fishery and accidents were prevalent. Joe had watched his father become entangled in a trawl as it was being set and before the boat could be stopped and reversed it was too late. He had been dragged to the bottom and drowned. His body lay at rest just a few feet from Francine's.

Gill nets were constructed very similarly to the leader on cod traps except that there was no box for the fish to swim into. They were usually strung together in quantities as many as fifty and sunk into five or six hundred feet of water. It was a simple principle. Fish swimming in those murky depths could not see the mesh, ran into it and became entangled.

Trawls, on the other hand, consisted of ropes as long as half a mile with string attached to them at three feet intervals to which were attached hooks and bait, usually squid. Both types of fishing were very effective and fishermen could be expected to catch half as much as they did with the trap fishery.

The danger with trawl fishing was obviously the hooks, with the gill nets it was not so obvious. Both of these fish catching devices were recovered from the ocean bottom with winching devices and, oftentimes, hands and arms got in the way. The real danger came from when they were being set; they were coiled at the stern of the boat and as the boat went forward the net or trawl was thrown off. Many fishermen had lost their lives after being pulled overboard by a gill net or a trawl.

By mid-November, the 1959 fishing season had ended. The weather had been so bad that they had only been able to get out a couple of times in the entire month. On November 17th they had removed all of their gear from the water and the next day a storm front blew in that lasted the remainder of the week. But Joe and his crew had nothing to complain about. They had a good fishery and had a lot to be thankful for. However, as the 1959 fishing season came to an end, Joe and Millie had more on their minds.

Michel began school again in September. He was in grade five this year and every morning Millie had to fight with him to get him there. Then, when she managed to get him to school, he fought with the teacher and ran away more often than she could remember. He spent every waking hour he could down on the wharf and wanted nothing more than to be able to go fishing with his father. Both Joe and Millie threatened that he wouldn't be permitted to go out with Joe on Saturdays unless he went to school throughout the week, but it did little good. He had developed into a strong-willed boy who was a big help to his father and Joe enjoyed it when he was out in the boat with him. They were at their wits' end as to what to do and Millie was especially disturbed because of her promise to Francine.

Fortunately, Linda was exactly the opposite of Michel. She was in grade three this year and loved school. On the teacher's recommendation she had skipped grade two and went directly to grade three from grade one. By November she was far ahead of the others in her class. But Millie was disappointed. She wished that Michel was like Linda. After all, Linda was a girl and, in her opinion, beyond the need to be able to read and write, any additional schooling was a waste of time. Linda could be expected to marry someone from Dark Harbour and to raise her family there. Michel was the one who needed to get an education and maybe do something else besides fishing. Millie had promised Francine on her deathbed that she would do everything she could to see that Michel got an education, but it didn't look like it would be a formal education.

Five ⮴

MILLIE AND JOE could not provide much help to Linda and Michel with their schoolwork. The best they could do was to ask if they had done their homework and hope that they were telling the truth when they said they had. Michael and Linda were not only brother and sister; they were best friends. They rarely fought because Michel was as passive as Linda was aggressive, and she usually got her way anyway. Michel was fiercely protective of his sister and everyone knew a disagreement with Linda meant a disagreement with Michel. as well.

They also loved to play practical jokes on each other. Many mornings Michel would get up to go fishing and, upon pushing his feet into his rubber boots, his movement would be suddenly stopped by a rubber ball or a wad of rolled up paper. Linda would put little pans of water on the half-open door to his bedroom and when Michel would push it open the water would splash down over him, followed by the pan. She would try to stifle her giggling, but she always gave her location away. After the first few times, Michel grew wise to her joke, but pretended he didn't know her hiding place. He would quickly track her down and chase after her. Still, she kept engaging in the joke, knowing she'd be caught but revelling in the sound of Michel's shouts and playful chasing.

Linda was usually asleep when Michel left in the mornings, and he would sometimes place a pan of water at her bedside. When she awoke and sleepily touched her feet to the floor, she stepped into a pan full of cold water. Some mornings he would make a black mark on her nose with soot from the chimney lamp. One morning he put a pair of her underwear in her school bag and it was not until she arrived at school and started unpacking her bag that she discovered them, sitting a top her books. That only worked once because Linda never again left the house without checking her bag, but it was a long time before her schoolmates let her forget that morning.

As they matured, their relationship also matured. Each recognized the other's strengths and came to appreciate them. Michael had a heart as big as the whole of Dark Harbour and he always had a kind word and an encouraging comment no matter what the circumstances. Linda was more serious and although she, too, could find humour in most situations, she was more solemn. Michael's gentleness grounded her. Despite their different personalities, no two people loved each other or respected each other more than Linda and Michel.

Linda grew into a beautiful young girl and Millie and Joe commented often on how pretty she was. There was only a slight resemblance to Francine though, and, as of yet, Linda still hadn't been told that Millie and Joe were not her real parents. There would be lots of time for that. She made friends easily and consistently excelled at school, despite having a different teacher each year. The isolation was very hard for some to bear and teachers usually only stayed in Dark Harbour for one year. But they all had high praise for Linda. Their only regret was that they didn't have the resources to give her more. Each one of the teachers practically begged Millie and Joe to send her to Fortune where she could get a better quality education. When their requests were denied it was always assumed that they couldn't afford to send her away. Of course the real reason was that they couldn't bear to be parted from her for two or three months at a time. And Millie remembered her promise to Francine.

It was Michel for whom they wanted to secure a better education, but as much as they hated to admit it, when he reached the age of fourteen, they had to accept the fact that Michel had learned every-thing he wanted to from school. The teachers had been telling them this for some time now. Michel became a full-time fisherman without graduating from grade eight.

Michel was not stupid, though. In fact, his father considered him brilliant when it came to fishing. He had only to be told or shown something once and he instantly mastered it. He worked harder than anybody else and Mel and Al completely agreed with Joe's decision to give Michel a full share when he joined the crew of *The Francine* full-time. Initially they thought it might mean a little less money for them, but with the speed and untiring effort that Michel put into his work, they didn't lose money, but, in fact, made more.

Michel had learned enough in school to be able to count, read and write, but it had been obvious from the beginning that he had very little interest in school. He was only six when Joe had built *The Francine*, but he still remembered how it was done and a couple of years later when they built the little punt, he could show Joe exactly how to do it. He could build a lobster pot, sew mesh in a trap and, if the engine failed to start, he knew the steps to follow to find the problem. When he started fishing full-time, he knew as much about fishing as men who had fished most of their lives.

It was the summer of 1962. Joe and his crew had been selling most of their fish to the fish plant in Harbour Breton. The price of salt fish had dropped so low that it was better for the fishermen to sell their fish green. When they considered the price of salt and the time they had to spend cleaning and salting the fish, it just wasn't worth it and because there was no cleaning involved, they had more time to catch fish, so Joe purchased a third trap that they hauled twice a day. They were getting three cents a pound in credit in the fish plant store, instead of cash.

The demand for dried fish hadn't dropped off, though; if anything, it had increased. Most of the fish plants in this part of Newfoundland were owned by a company called Fish Products of Canada. This company was, in turn, owned by a much larger company with head offices in Toronto. No one was sure who the parent company was, but they were sure of one thing: they had a monopoly on fish purchasing in their area. Shortly after they gained control of the fish plant in Harbour Breton, the price of cod suddenly dropped. From a business perspective it had been a stroke of genius. Traditionally, the fish merchants purchased the salted and dried cod from the fishermen for six or seven times the price of green cod. But if they bought it green and salted and dried it themselves, they would make even more of a profit. Therefore, they dropped the price and manipulated the fishermen into selling them the cod green.

If the fishermen had another market for their dried cod, they would have found that the price was nearly thirty cents a pound.

Additionally, the merchants had very creative people working for them when it came to weighing the fishermen's catch.

It was Linda who first brought this to Michel's attention. She was ten, but much wiser than her ten years. It had been a long day and Michel, as the youngest member of the crew, had to fuel the boat and make sure everything was ready for the next morning. The others, including Joe, had gone home. Michel was alone when Linda walked down the wharf toward the single light on the boat.

"How much fish did you get today?" she asked him as she stood on the wharf and looked down into the boat. A bulb had been rigged up to a tractor battery and the light for the boat spilled over onto the wharf. With the only other light in the community provided by kerosene lamps, it was easily seen from all around. Everything and everybody cast long ghostly shadows and it looked as if some giant hand was holding a flashlight from high above.

"Oh, hi," Michel said as he looked up to the wharf. "Does Mom know you're down here?"

"Yes," she replied sarcastically.

"Well, I figure we got between twenty and twenty-five thousand," he called up to her.

"You sold it all green, I suppose?" she asked. Despite her young age and openly announced dislike for fish, she knew all the expressions associated with the catching of them.

"Yes, of course," Michel responded.

"Well, how much was it exactly?" Linda pressured him.

"I don't know. The slip is in the wheelhouse."

Linda stepped aboard the boat and up the two steps to the wheelhouse. A nail had been driven into one of the walls of the cabin and pushed over it were several pieces of paper. She pulled off the top one and strained to see it in the light. It was a wrinkled second copy and the writing was barely legible. After much effort she was able to make it out.

Joseph Fudge, Dark Harbour. Green Cod, 17,200 pounds.

Linda turned and replaced the paper over the nail through the same hole. Michel was just finishing up. He unscrewed the light bulb over his head and suddenly the only source of light was the moon and the kerosene lanterns from the houses around the shore. She stepped up to the wharf where Michel was waiting with his hand held down to help her up. She took it and together they walked to their house. She put her arm through his as she had seen her mother do to her father so many times in the past.

"You said you had between twenty and twenty-five thousand pounds today, didn't you?" she asked as they walked together.

"Yes," Michel answered.

"The slip says you had seventeen thousand two hundred pounds," Linda said proudly.

Michel stopped and held her arm between his and his body.

"No way," he said, coming to a sudden stop. Linda just stared through the moonlit night into his face. Michel returned her stare for a few seconds and then, taking her hand, they walked the remaining distance silently.

Joe and Millie were sitting at the kitchen table when their two children walked through the door.

"Are you tired, sweetheart?" Millie asked Michel.

"Sweetheart?" Joe laughed in his direction. Michel didn't react. Instead, he kissed his mother distractedly and walked to the stove and hung his heavy woolen sweater on a nail behind it before returning to the table and sitting next to his father.

"How much fish do you figure we had today, Dad?" he asked as his mother put a cup of tea beside him. It was nearly 9:30 p.m. and they always had tea and biscuits before going to bed.

"A little more than seventeen thousand pounds."

"But, Dad, I was sure we had between twenty and twenty-five thousand pounds. The front hold was full and we've had twenty thousand in that one lots of times."

"Yes, I know, son, but that's what Willie said we had. We had big fish today and they take up more space than the small stuff, so that was probably why."

Michel still wasn't convinced, but before he could protest further, his father changed the subject.

"And what did you do today, little Missy?" Joe said, turning to Linda and letting Michel know that the conversation had ended.

"Oh, not much, Daddy," Linda answered, but her mind was still on what Michel had said. She had a particular interest in books about

Newfoundland and the fishery. When Michel voiced his concern over the discrepancy in the weight of the fish, she thought of something she had read a few weeks earlier. She walked over to her father and slid up under his arm to sit on his lap.

"Daddy?" she asked.

"What, honey?" Joe replied as he tried to drink his tea without spilling it on her.

"Could I go out on the boat with you and Michel tomorrow?"

Millie had been at the stove shoving in another junk of wood. She almost dropped the damper when she heard Linda's request to Joe. She stared at Joe with complete disbelief. Joe stared back at her.

Joe laid down his cup and twisted Linda on his lap so he could see her face.

"What did you say?" he asked.

"I would like to go out on the boat tomorrow?"

"I've asked you dozens of times if you would like to come with us, and you always said no. Why the sudden change?"

"Now that school is finished for the summer, there's not much to do around here. So can I?"

Joe looked at Millie and she shrugged her shoulders. "Well, okay, but if you get seasick you'll spend a pretty miserable morning because we can't come in until all the traps are hauled. That is, if your mom says it's okay," Joe added.

"I won't get seasick," Linda said confidently.

"You're joking, aren't you?" Millie said to Linda as she returned to sit at the table beside Joe.

Linda was still sitting on her father's lap. She shook her head.

"No, I'd like to go out in the boat and see Dad and Michel catching fish."

Millie couldn't believe her ears. "It's against my better judgement, but I suppose it's okay. But only if the weather is fine."

Joe was pleased with Millie's decision. "What about some rubber clothes for you?" Joe asked.

"There's a set that Michel used to wear when he first started going out on the water and I think that with a few adjustments we can get it to fit her," Millie offered proudly. She left the table and returned a few minutes later with an old rubber jacket and trousers. She tried to shake the wrinkles out of them as she entered the kitchen.

"Oooooh, they look and smell terrible," Linda said as Millie helped her on with the trousers and then the jacket. The pants were much too long and the sleeves of the jacket hung nearly to the floor, but after a few folds, Linda would at least be able to walk and use her hands. Millie promised to alter them to fit her properly if she decided she wanted to go again. She was secretly convinced that she would never have to make the promised alterations. She was sure that this would be Linda's first and last fishing trip.

Michel roused his sister the following morning at 4:30 a.m. "I've never been up this early in my life," she complained, rubbing her eyes as she joined the others for breakfast. "I don't think the porridge is even awake yet," she laughed as she poured the milk over the steaming mixture.

"There'll be no complaining about the grub on my boat," Joe said sternly, winking at Millie.

Linda almost dropped the milk jug at the sudden harshness of her father's voice, but when she looked at him his wide smile belied his mood and she laughed along with the rest of them.

Before breakfast was over, Millie gave Linda a set of orders that would probably have taken three or four kids to remember. She then issued orders to Joe and Michel, the gist of which was that Linda was to stay in the cabin and if she made any effort to move out of it, Joe and Michel were empowered to lash her to one of the bunks. As they were leaving, Millie whispered in Joe's ear as she kissed his cheek. "Look after our little girl."

Joe just nodded.

It was a pleasant surprise for Mel and Al when they saw Linda walking down the wharf with her brother and father. She looked awkward in her brother's rubber clothes and she squeaked and squealed with every step she took.

"You'll never be able to sneak up on a moose in that outfit," Al called out as she approached.

Linda walked in front of Joe and just as Mel was about to laugh, Joe held his finger across his lips. Mel changed his greeting and treated her as a fellow fisherman.

"Good morning, matey," he spoke. "You won't get seasick on us now, will you?"

"I don't think so," she answered, although the look on her face was a little less confident than the previous evening when she had answered the same question. Mel held out his hand and helped her aboard the boat.

"Okay, young lady, now you go into the cabin like your mother ordered," Joe said as he stepped onto the deck. Linda did as she was told and stepped through the cabin door. Michel stepped up to the wheelhouse. The smell of diesel fuel almost made Linda gag, but she swallowed hard. The engine had been started and the heat from it was already radiating into the tiny cabin. As she tried to get her bearings, Michel called down from the wheelhouse.

"Have a seat on one of the bunks until we get underway," he said, "and then I'll let you steer, okay?"

Linda nodded and listened as the crew called out instructions to each other until the boat left the wharf. Shortly after, the other three men joined her in the cabin.

Michel kept his promise and once they had cleared the harbour entrance, he let her steer the boat. The sun was not up yet and she had no idea where they were going, but she was pleased to see that there was a light on the front of the boat in case they encountered any other boats.

A half hour after they had left the harbour, Michel asked her to return to the cabin because they were approaching the first trap. Almost as if on cue, the sun suddenly appeared on the horizon and before the doorways to the trap had been hauled up and closed it was light enough to see everything that was going on.

Linda spent all of her time in the cabin unless her father gave her permission to leave. When they hauled the second trap, her father let her out on deck while they scooped the fish into the boat. Fortunately, the seas were relatively calm and she was able to walk about without fear of falling. She watched intently as they scooped in the fish and everyone made sure that she stayed back from the net and the fish. She didn't need to be reminded of that. She was not out there to see how they caught fish. She had another purpose.

It had been a particularly good morning catch and, after all three of the traps had been hauled, they had what they estimated to be thirty thousand pounds. The front hold was full and it held twenty thousand pounds when full. The stern hold was half full and both holds were the same size. As the last trap was settling back to the ocean floor, Michel pointed the boat in the direction of Harbour Breton. It was about a twenty-minute trip to the fish plant and before they had finished their tea, they were there.

Michel guided the boat expertly beside the large wharf and underneath one of the several cranes. As they were tying up, Willie Wareham appeared. Willie was a fish plant employee and was about Joe's age. "Good morning boys. How'd you do this morning?"

"Not bad, by," Joe answered. Willie stared down from the wharf into the open holds.

"Yes by, not bad at all," he said and then he spotted Linda peering out through the open cabin door. "Looks like you got a new captain this time out," he said.

Linda disappeared back into the cabin.

Another man soon appeared and he unlocked the crane and lifted a large wooden fish box from the wharf onto the deck of *The Francine.* Al and Michel climbed down into the forward hold and began filling the box. In the meantime, Linda found the stubby pencil and a piece of paper she had managed to sneak into the pocket of her jacket before leaving the house. As the first box was being lifted onto the deck, she tugged on her father's sleeve.

"Daddy," she asked, "how many pounds are in one of those boxes?"

"Five hundred," he responded without turning around.

Linda wrote the amount on her piece of paper and then watched as the rest of the fish was off loaded. Finally, forty-five minutes after they had docked, the last box of fish was being lifted onto the wharf. It wasn't quite full, so it was lifted up and onto the scales. Linda watched what was happening and then quickly left the cabin and climbed up to the wharf. She stood beside the scales as Willie moved the weights until they balanced on the bar.

"How much does it weigh?" Linda asked shyly.

"Two hundred and eight pounds," he answered.

Linda turned away from him and scribbled the "208" with the other list of numbers. Quickly she added them and put the paper and pencil in her pocket. "28,208" was written neatly below all the others. She then walked over to where her father was standing.

Willie took a few minutes to add up the numbers and when he was satisfied that they were correct, he passed the clipboard to Joe. He took it and, with a practised hand, scribbled his "X" below the total at the bottom. Linda strained to see and tugged on her father's arm until she could. "25,208" was marked in big numbers just above where her father had marked his signature. Before he could pass it back to Willie, Linda took it and walked over to him. Joe stood with his mouth open, looking on in surprise. The remainder of the crew and the crane operator who had watched her take the clipboard focussed on her.

"Mr. Wareham," she said as she approached him.

"Yes, Missy," Willie said, with a smile on his face.

Linda reached into her pocket and retrieved her paper. She unfolded it and held it up for him to see. When she began to speak all eyes were on her. "As each box was lifted off the boat I marked it on my piece of paper," she began. "After they were all off, I totalled them and the amount I came to was twenty eight thousand, two hundred and eight pounds. You've made a mistake of three thousand pounds."

There was silence for a few seconds and then Willie's sardonic laugh could be heard by everybody on the wharf, including those other fishermen waiting to have their fish weighed. He turned and, still laughing, began to return to the fish plant. Joe looked at his daughter and spoke softly.

"Are you sure, sweetheart?" he asked.

Linda nodded.

"Willie," Joe called out. Willie kept walking. "Willie," Joe called again. This time he stopped and turned. "My daughter says that you've made a mistake of three thousand pounds when you gave me credit for my fish."

Willie walked back to where Joe was standing with Linda. "Listen, Joe Fudge," he began as he bounced his index finger off Joe's chest. "I've being weighing fish here for as long as you've been fishing. I bought fish from your poor father before he drowned. I don't make mistakes."

"Well then, the only thing I can say about that is that you're a thief, Willie Clarke, because if my daughter says that we've got twenty eight thousand, two hundred and eight pounds of fish, then that's what we have," Joe said, bouncing his finger off Willie's chest.

Willie paused for a few seconds. The smile left his face and he turned very cold. "First you accused me of making a mistake, then you accused me of being a liar, and now you're calling me a thief. I don't know what's got into you, but you're putting an awful lot of faith into that brat of yours," he finished, pointing at Linda.

The word "brat" was barely out of his mouth before it was replaced by Joe's fist. Joe's hands were hard. Half a lifetime of having them submerged in seawater had made them that way. When that hand was fashioned into a fist, it was as hard as rock and it felt like rock as it contacted Willie's face, sending him flying across the wharf. Joe started for him again, but Mel and Al grabbed him.

Michel looked at his father. He had never seen him like this or heard his father raise his voice before. Now, in front of them, lying unconscious on the wharf, was the first victim of his father's anger. A hatred burned in Joe's eyes and were it not for his brothers, Michel feared what Joe might do.

The crane operator rushed to the aid of his boss, and patted his flushed face. Suddenly, a crowd had gathered and they looked first at Willie and then at Joe. Everybody knew everybody else and, like Michel, most of them were shocked by Joe's behaviour. He brushed away his two brothers as the crane operator managed to revive Willie. Another man helped him to his feet and he stood wobbly, staring at Joe. Joe spoke first.

"Listen, Willie Wareham, and listen well. Our disagreement was between us and if you ever call my daughter a name like that again, there's not enough men in Harbour Breton to stop me from drowning you off the head of this wharf."

Willie just rubbed his jaw.

"Now, my daughter said that you made a mistake of three thousand pounds when you gave me credit for my fish. I said that you've tried to steal three thousand pounds of fish from me. Now," he continued, "we're going to count those vats of fish and then add them up again. If there's what you say is there, then I'll tear up this credit slip." He waved the slip in the air for the twenty or thirty men who had gathered. "But," he continued, "if my daughter's right, you had better make out a new slip before the last vat is counted. And you'll apologize to my daughter." Joe turned his attention to the crowd. "Is there somebody among you who can do figuring?" he asked.

A young man stepped forward. "Yes, Joe by," he said, "I can count them for you."

"Just a minute, just a minute," Willie spoke for the first time since he had regained consciousness. "There's no need for all of this. We just have a misunderstanding here. Maybe, just maybe, I made a mistake like the little Missy said. There's no need for any of this, Joe. I've been busy this morning and I had a late night. Let's just say that you have what your little girl says you have and leave it at that."

Joe looked at his daughter. She nodded her head and Joe turned to Willie. "There's just one other thing, Willie Wareham, and that's the apology."

"Yes, sure, Joe." He walked over to where Linda was standing. "I'm sorry, Missy. I apologize for what I called you."

Linda stared straight into his eyes. She curled her index finger and signalled for him to bend down to her. He looked puzzled as he did what she had instructed. When his face was a few inches from hers, she reached with her hand and turned his head so she could speak into his ear without the others hearing.

"Mr. Wareham," she whispered, "you've been stealing from my father ever since he's been selling his fish here." Willie made a motion to straighten up, but Linda put her other hand behind his neck. "From now on, I'm going to be checking and if there's another mistake like this morning, I'll tell my father. Understand?" she finished.

Willie stood up and nodded his understanding and agreement. Linda pointed at the clipboard on the wharf and held out her hand. The new credit note was the fastest and most accurate one that Willie had ever written. Once finished, he passed it to Linda. She signed her name on the bottom with perfect penmanship.

The men on the wharf clapped enthusiastically as they watched the new credit note being passed to Linda. Joe Fudge looked proudly at his daughter and had it been dark, his glow would have lit the entire wharf. He walked over to her and, instead of the expected hug, she was very surprised as he reached for her hand and shook it warmly.

The trip back to Dark Harbour was a happy one for the crew of *The Francine*. Mel and Al, who had been shocked at the position taken by their brother, expressed their relief that Linda had been right. But it was Michel who saw the value in what his sister had done.

"I knew we had close to twenty-five thousand pounds yesterday," he said, shortly after they got underway. "Willie Wareham has been stealing from us and we didn't even know it." The others nodded their agreement, but Linda remained silent. She sat on the bunk looking at the piece of paper she had scribbled her numbers on. As they neared Dark Harbour, she spoke for the first time since they had left Harbour Breton.

"Dad," she said. Her father looked in her direction. "I have some bad news."

"What is it?" Joe asked with obvious concern in his voice.

"Dad, I've added up these numbers at least half a dozen times since we left Harbour Breton and you know what?"

"What?"

"I made a mistake."

Suddenly the only sound in the boat was the roar of the engine. No one spoke. Everybody looked at her.

"There was only twenty-seven thousand, seven hundred and eight pounds. I made a mistake of five hundred pounds. We've been paid for five hundred pounds too much."

Millie was standing on the wharf waiting for them. A few hundred feet from the wharf the engine stopped. She suspected engine trouble. Then she watched as three grown men and a half-grown man appeared on the deck in a fit of laughter. She also watched as Linda stood in the doorway of the cabin with a puzzled look on her face.

Millie breathed a sigh of relief. At least they had taken care of her little girl.

she had already told Linda in the last few days. It was an emotional goodbye and Linda promised her mother that she would write every day. Tears ran down their faces as they embraced and said goodbye until the Christmas break.

Linda had never been on a train before. A porter helped her to her seat and her father made sure that her trunk was stored in the baggage car. The window was open beside her seat and she stuck her head through it and called to her family. They came running and followed the train up the ramp. Millie continued to shout instructions until the train was out of earshot.

Linda remained standing with her head out the window until her family was out of sight. She reluctantly pulled her head back into the car and was startled to find a young man seated beside her.

"Hello," he said with a heavy accent.

"Hello," Linda answered shyly. Then she recognized him. It was Bob Humby. They had met a few years earlier at a Reach for the Top contest in Fortune. The organizers had sponsored a get-together after the competition and he had asked her to dance. She had refused and had regretted her decision for the remainder of the evening.

He was glad to have company for the trip to St. John's, as was she, and they chatted like two old friends. Upon finding out that he was a second year Education student at Memorial University, she quickly overcame her shyness. Her greatest fear had been the trip to St. John's and then the trip from the station to the university. She had never been farther away from home than Fortune and, for her, St. John's was the other end of the world. As soon as Bob told her he was a student, she felt a wave of relief sweep over her. She had a million questions and Bob patiently answered all of them, even though by the time they reached their destination she was beginning to repeat herself.

Bob lived at the university residence. Linda would also be staying at the university and when they arrived in St. John's, Bob suggested that he pay for the taxi, but Linda would hear nothing of it. She didn't mind getting free advice, but she insisted on paying her fair share. If he really wanted to do something for her, she offered as consolation, he could show her where and how she could register. Then he could help her find her classes. He enthusiastically agreed and all the while Linda couldn't help but notice how much she enjoyed his company.

Bob helped her get familiarized and gave her the "one movie tour", as he called it; she had to agree to see at least one movie with him and he was going to pay this time. She agreed. They shared an English class together, but because he was an Education student and she was a pre-Law student, Linda had chosen different classes. She enjoyed her studies and excelled in all her subjects. She studied every night until 9:00 p.m., whether she needed to or not. Saturdays were left free to see the sights and stores in St. John's and to go to the movies with Bob. Before the end of September, they were already going steady, but they would not allow their friendship to interfere with their studies. She was as ambitious as he was and their families had made many sacrifices to send them to university. The very least they could do was to study hard and to pass their courses.

During the first month Linda wrote to her mother nearly every day. There were so many new things happening and she wanted to tell her mother all about them. More importantly, the letter writing was a time in which she could forget about where she was and think of home. By October she was writing less often as she gradually began to make friends and did not have such an emotional need to connect to home. She had been homesick, but was adjusting to her second home. As well, her studies demanded her attention. She wrote to Michel once a week, and Lori read all the letters, including the ones to Millie. Lori also wrote their responses. Because Dark Harbour only got mail once every two weeks, when it did arrive, there were at least a dozen letters for the Fudge family and that evening was spent reading them. They alternated between Joe's house and Michel's, and it was always an excuse to celebrate.

In mid-November, with the arrival of *The Crosbie*, there were seven more letters, two for Michel and five for Millie. Michel and Lori came over a little after 6:00 p.m. and Lori began reading Michel's mail first. Linda told Michel about a few of the things she had seen in St. John's during the past few weeks and how much she was enjoying her studies. Michel missed Linda, even though he never openly admitted it, and he enjoyed hearing from her as much as the others did. She asked questions about how the fishing was and when the baby was due and Lori underlined each question to be sure she answered them when she wrote the reply for Michel.

As soon as the first letter was finished, questions followed and Lori would read the relevant passages again to provide the necessary clarification. When there were no more questions, she turned to the next letter.

The second letter was in a different envelope. It was brown and the name and address were typed; it looked very official. Lori looked at the name and the address and read it aloud.

"Michel Matte, care of Francine Matte, Dark Harbour, Fortune Bay, Newfoundland."

The colour suddenly drained from Millie's face as she turned and looked at Joe. His pipe hung from the corner of his mouth in disbelief at what he had just heard.

"This isn't for you, Michel," Lori said, not having noticed the change that had come over Joe and Millie. "I'll drop it off tomorrow and tell Jean to send it back..." Her voice trailed off as she looked at the back of the envelope and read the address. "Royal Bank of Canada, Robie Street, Halifax, Nova Scotia."

Joe and Millie still had a dazed look about them as Lori laid it beside the first letter and reached for the next one. Millie finally managed to speak.

"I'll drop it off to Jean," she said hoarsely as she picked up the envelope and stuffed it in her apron pocket. "I have to speak to her about Sunday's choir practice. I'll give it to her then," she lied.

Lori read the rest of the letters and, for the first time since Linda had been writing, Millie wasn't paying attention. She didn't hear what Lori was saying. For the remainder of the evening, Joe and Millie looked at each other nervously. Every few minutes she patted the letter in her pocket, wishing it would disappear.

Lori and Michel finally recognized that something was wrong, but neither of them indicated that they were aware of the change that had come over Joe and Millie. After Lori and Michel had left, Millie took the letter from her pocket and turned it over and over in her hands. "You know what it is, don't you Joe?" she asked.

"I think so," Joe answered.

"It's what Francine talked about before she died. She told me that when Michel was twenty-one he would get a lot more money. This is it. I know it is. What are we going to do, Joe?"

Joe rubbed his face with his rough hands. "I suppose we're going to have to tell him. He has a right to know."

"I knew this day would come," Millie managed. "I've been putting it off because I didn't know how to do it. I think we've waited too long. Oh, Joe, what are we going to do?"

Millie buried her face in her hands in desperation. Joe felt equally helpless, but both of them knew that the time had come when they had to tell Michel who his real mother was. However, that was part of the dilemma; they really didn't know who his real mother was. They had only known her for less than a year and she was as big a mystery now as when she had first arrived. Perhaps more. They had learned a lot about her in the short time they had lived together, but there was so much more they didn't know. Finally, Joe got up from the table and walked to the stove. He moved the kettle to the centre. "Millie," he spoke, "it will only be a few more weeks before Linda is home and when she is, we'll show her the letter and then tell them what we know. You get Francine's old trunk down and we'll let them go through it after we've told them. That's the only thing I think we can do."

Millie nodded her head in agreement. Joe was right. That would be the best thing to do, and she only hoped it wouldn't ruin their Christmas. Before this evening, she was really looking forward to Linda's visit. Now, she was confused and the uncertainty of everything unsettled her.

Michel and Joe picked up Linda in Fortune on December 14th. Fortunately, seas were calm and there was no ice, but it would have made little difference; they would have gone for her anyway. Her train was due in at 2:05 p.m. and it arrived at 3:10. She got off the train with a very handsome young man and they kissed before he wished her a Merry Christmas. He then ran into the waiting arms of an older woman who they guessed would be his mother.

"What's this all about, young lady?" Joe chastised her mockingly as she turned and spotted them for the first time in months.

Linda gasped and ran the few steps to her father and embraced him. "I've missed you Daddy," she cried, tears in her eyes. "I missed you, too," she said to Michel as she let go of Joe with one arm and drew Michel close to them. "But where's Mom?" she asked, looking around for her.

"Your mother is not feeling very well, sweetheart. She kicked up quite a fuss to come, but I made her stay home. You should have been there."

Linda laughed. "Yes, I can just imagine. But it's nothing serious, is it?" she asked with obvious concern in her voice.

"No, no, she's just getting old," he laughed. "She woke up this morning with a splitting headache, that's all."

Linda looked at her brother for confirmation. He nodded his head.

"Come on, let's get home before the wind starts to blow," Joe said as he took the two of them by the arms and made his way to the wharf. "Your mother is waiting for us and you know your mother. If we're not home soon, she'll have half the people in Dark Harbour out looking for us."

The wind had come up a little and it had whipped the water into whitecaps. Michel had to throttle back on the engine, but still waves washed over the bow of the boat. The trip normally took an hour and a half, but it was well past 6:00 p.m. before they rounded the point and entered the calm of the harbour.

"There's our house," Linda said excitedly as it came into view. It had been snowing for the past few days and the usual blue-grey tint to everything had been painted white. Footpaths to the houses had been shovelled and the walls of snow were several feet high on either side of the paths. Electricity was still not available tothe community and the dull shine of the kerosene lamps filled the windows.

"What's Mom up to, trying to save kerosene?" Linda asked as they neared the wharf. She could see that there wasn't a light in the window of their house.

Michel looked. "Maybe she's up with Lori," he said as he pointed to his house and the light in his kitchen window.

The boat had barely touched the wharf as Linda jumped up from the deck onto it. It was covered with several inches of snow and she slipped and fell. Both Joe and Michel howled with laughter once they saw that she was unhurt.

"I see you still got your sea legs on," Michel joked as he left the boat and helped her up. Linda smiled weakly and brushed the snow off her clothes. More carefully this time, she made her way up the wharf to their house. Joe and Michel finished tying up the boat and, taking a suitcase each, followed in her tracks.

Linda was out of breath by the time she reached her door. There was a light inside, but it was not very bright. She stamped her feet to knock off the snow and then burst through the door. The smile on her face in anticipation of her mother's greeting went from ear to ear. She swung the door closed behind her and peered through the dimly lit kitchen. She spotted her mother sitting in her rocking chair near the stove. The lamp wick had burned down and the fire was low in the stove. Linda removed her coat and hung it behind the stove. She removed her boots and found a pair of her old slippers. She continued to smile in anticipation of shaking her mother awake as Joe came into the kitchen. Linda smiled and held her finger to her lips.

"She's asleep," she whispered. "I'll go into the bedroom," she said slyly. "You wake her up and tell her that I wasn't on the train. Then, when she's having one of her fits, I'll run out into the kitchen."

Joe laughed silently and smiled his agreement. He finished taking off his coat and boots and then he waved Linda to the bedroom. When he was sure that she was there, he pushed on Millie's shoulder. "Get up and get my supper, old woman," he called out.

The rocking chair moved back and forth and Joe could hear Linda's giggle from the bedroom. Joe pushed her again, this time a little harder. The chair moved back and as it did, Millie moved forward, only she didn't stop. Joe had turned his back and then he heard the thump. He turned to find, lying on the floor beside the stove, the lifeless body of his wife of thirty-five years.

Five days later, the weather cleared and Millie was taken to Fortune where an autopsy revealed that she had died from a stroke. The headache had been the clue, but, as the doctor had said, even if Millie had been in Fortune when the stroke occurred, there would have been little hope. She was brought back a couple of days later. Several attempts were made to dig a grave, but the ground was already frozen solid and it would have to wait until spring. Her coffin had been sealed in Fortune, and she would remain at the little house at the cemetery until the frost left the ground in the spring.

Joe was the strongest of the three. Linda cried until there just weren't any more tears left. Michel didn't cry in front of the others, but at night he sobbed himself to sleep. Family and friends were a great comfort. Reverend Welsh tried to tell them that it was all part of God's big plan. Joe cursed him.

Christmas was nearly unbearable. Lori cooked dinner for them, but they didn't have a tree or any decorations in either of the houses out of respect for Millie. Linda reluctantly agreed to go back to school on January 7th, and Joe spent his first night alone in their house.

By the middle of January, Lori finally convinced Joe that the time had come to dispose of Millie's clothes. He reluctantly agreed, saying that he didn't want to forget Millie. Lori was very understanding and explained to him that Millie would want her clothes given to people who could wear them. Joe knew she was right and he also knew that the time had come when he had to tell Michel who he really was before something happened to him. He asked Lori to bring Michel with her when she came over to pack up Millie's things.

Lori's baby girl arrived the next day. That delayed the disposal of Millie's things, which suited Joe just fine. According to Lori's estimate, she was almost a month overdue by the time the baby arrived, but she was otherwise healthy and her delivery was fairly easy. "It was her time," old Mrs. Poole said, after she had delivered her. They decided to name the baby Millicent, and Joe was very pleased, but he said he would not attend the christening. He was still not on speaking terms with God.

It was the first happiness the Fudge family had experienced in a long time. The baby seemed to draw the family together. As he had done with Linda many years before, Joe talked to the baby like she was already grown and she fell asleep many nights in her grandfather's arms. When they were alone he told her how much her grandmother had been looking forward to seeing her, and he always dried his eyes in her blanket before Lori and Michel could see that he had been crying. A couple of weeks after Millicent's birth and having regained her strength, Lori reminded Joe that they should dispose of Millie's things. He agreed again and made up his mind that when they came over, he would tell Michel everything.

It was a cold, snowy, Tuesday afternoon when Lori and Michel came over to his house. Lori cooked dinner and before she could start gathering Millie's belongings together, Joe said that he had something to talk to them about. They sat at the kitchen table like they had so many times before. Only this time Millie was absent.

"What is it, Dad?" Michel asked as they sat down together.

Joe took a couple of puffs on his pipe before he began.

"Michel, what I have to tell you is the most difficult thing that I have ever had to do in my whole life. We were going to tell you and Linda when she was home at Christmas." His voice cracked and he drew on his pipe again and coughed. "Of course, all that changed when your mother," he paused, "when Millie died."

Michel looked at Lori for some clue as to what his father was about to tell them. She just shrugged her shoulders. Millicent made a cry on the day bed that momentarily got their attention. She had a couple of sucks on her pacifier and then went back to sleep.

"Michel," Joe continued. "I am not your real father."

"What?" Michel cried. He looked at Lori again. "Dad, you've gone through a lot in the last couple of months."

"No," Joe interrupted him. "Let me say what I have to say." He reached out and touched his son's hand. "I know this is an awful shock to you, but you've got to listen to me. Don't make this any harder than it already is."

"Okay, Dad." Michel laughed uneasily.

"This is hard, son," Joe began again. "Millie was not your real mother. Your real mother was Francine. At least that is what she said her name was. When she was dying she said to Millie that her real name was Forest. She came to Dark Harbour when you were a little boy, not quite four. She told us she was a writer and her husband had died. She boarded with us, and Millie and your mother got to be real close. You see, we couldn't have any children of our own, and when you came to live with us, we both learned to love you as if you was our own. Then we learned that your mother was pregnant when she arrived in Dark Harbour. Anyway, she had a hard labour with Linda and she died giving birth to her. We didn't know what to do with you and your sister so Reverend Foote suggested that we keep the two of you and rear you up like you was our own."

Michel hung on every word, glancing back and forth between Joe and Lori.

Joe tapped his pipe on the ashtray. "Your mother only lived with us for less than a year and we really never got to learn very much about her at all. She also had a lot of money with her and she wanted us to have it. We used some of the money to build *The Francine*. That's where the name came from. We named her after your mother. Also, she had a picture of a lady named Linda. That's where we got Linda's name from."

Lori had been holding Michel's arm. She looked like she had seen a ghost. Michel broke free from her grip, got up from the table and paced the centre of the kitchen. He wrung his hands and shrugged his shoulders and appeared to be carrying on a silent conversation with himself. Joe relit his pipe and drew slowly, waiting for a reaction from Michel. He stopped pacing a couple of times and stared at his father as if in a trance. Then he resumed his pacing. Finally, Lori decided to break the silence.

"Joe," she began, "did this woman leave anything that would give us a clue as to who she was?"

"Oh, yes," Joe responded, happy that someone was finally speaking. "Do you remember that letter we got before Christmas that Millie said she'd bring back to the post office because it wasn't for Michel?"

Lori nodded as Joe got up from the table and went to a drawer in the dish cabinet. He rummaged through it and drew out the letter. He returned to the table and passed it to her. Lori took the letter and looked again at the name. "Yes, I remember. It's for a Michel Matte. I thought you said her name was Francine Forest?" she asked.

"That's what I thought," Joe answered.

"Maybe we should open it and see what's inside," Lori offered. She passed the letter to Michel who looked at it for several moments before speaking again.

"Yes, that's probably what we should do," he said, passing the letter back to Lori.

Lori took it and held it up to the light. She then gave it a shake to move the contents to one end before ripping off the other end. She reached inside, pulled out a single piece of paper and carefully unfolded it. As Michel and Joe watched, she began to read.

"It's from the Royal Bank of Canada in Halifax," she began.

P. M. Reagan, Manager
Royal Bank of Canada
Robie Street
Halifax, NS B3K 4R4

Dear Mr. Matte:

As per the instructions left by your mother, Francine Matte, we are hereby informing you that we are holding on deposit for you the sum of one hundred and eleven thousand, two hundred and six dollars and seven cents ($111,206.07). Additionally, as per your mother's instructions, we have a safety deposit box of which the contents are also to be forwarded to you.

This is a considerable amount of money and to ensure that everything is in order, we ask that you confirm the instructions left by your mother and provide confirmation that, in fact, you are the Michel Matte referred to by Mrs. Francine Matte.

We trust that this does not inconvenience you. Once we receive your instructions, we would be very pleased to further assist you in any manner we can.

Sincerely yours,
P.M. Reagan, Manager

PMR/mb

Both men waited until Lori had finished reading. Then, in unison, they spoke.

"How much?"

Lori looked at the letter again. "One hundred eleven thousand, two hundred and six dollars and seven cents," she repeated.

"My God," Michel said, "what the hell is this all about?"

Joe just shook his head. "I didn't know anything about this, son. I swear. I do know that she did have a lot of money with her when she came to live with us. I think it was three or four thousand dollars. After paying for *The Francine*, we still had nearly a thousand dollars left. Your mother deposited it at a bank in Fortune, and we were going to use it to send you to university. That was what your mother wanted. But when all you wanted to do was to fish, we decided to use it for Linda. But this money is news to me."

Michel got up from the table and began to pace again. The others remained silent. Suddenly he stopped and stared at his father. "Did she leave anything else here so we could figure out who she was?" he asked.

"Yes, yes," Joe said excitedly. "Millie filled a big trunk with all of her things. We put it up in the attic a little while after her funeral. She brought two trunks with her. The other one Linda took with her to university."

"Where's she buried, Dad?" Michel suddenly thought to ask.

"Up in the graveyard," Joe answered.

Michel paused for a second. "This is just too much," he said.

"I know this must be an awful shock to you, son, but we always said that we would tell you and Linda about this when you turned twenty-one. As I said, we were going to tell you this Christmas past. Then after what happened, I got afraid that if something happened to me and you found out some other way, what would you and your sister think of the two of us?"

Michel stopped his pacing for a second. He looked at his father and tears welled up in his eyes. "Dad, you'll always be my father and Mom will always be my mother, no matter what." He walked toward Joe with his arms outstretched.

"I'm sorry, son," Joe said as they embraced.

It was an emotional scene and even Lori had to wipe her eyes with her apron. She gave them a few moments and then spoke. "You said there was a trunk, Joe?"

"Yes, there is," Joe answered as he pushed himself away from his son and dried his eyes with the back of his hand. "Come on, son, help me bring it downstairs."

The old steamer trunk was in one corner of the attic and with the aid of a flashlight they found it and carried it downstairs. It barely fit through the opening and they were perspiring profusely as they placed it in the centre of the kitchen floor. Both men sat at the table as Lori walked to the trunk and lifted the heavy cover.

For the next hour, Lori moved the contents of the trunk to the top of the kitchen table and the floor beside the table. As each item was removed, Joe tried to provide an explanation as to what it was.

"She said she was a writer," he offered when Lori lifted out the typewriter. "Those were her purses and her jewellery," he said as they were also taken out. In one of the purses they found several bankbooks; one was from the bank that had sent Michel the letter. There were dozens of pictures that Joe confessed he had never seen before. "Millie packed away her things," he repeated several times. There were also several dresses and scarves that obviously Millie had decided were too nice for herself or to give to others. And there were several bundles of papers, each sheet filled with typewritten words. Finally, the trunk was emptied and Michel stared at the pile of things that he hoped would tell him who he was or who his mother was.

They stared at the pile for a few minutes and neither of them knew where to start. "We'll have to read all of those papers," Lori said. "Then, we might be able to tell who she was. But we have to do something else before then."

Michel and his father each looked at Lori with a blank stare. She held up the letter to remind them.

"This letter is already three months old," she explained, looking at the date. "The bank is waiting to hear from you, Michel, about all this money. I think we have to write them and tell them what you want them to do."

Once again the two men looked at her for advice.

Lori knew that they expected her to come up with the answers, but she wasn't sure she had them. "Maybe we should write Linda and ask her what we should do," Lori suggested.

"No," Michel snapped. "Until we know what this is all about, I don't want Linda involved. You know how close she was to Mom." He paused for a second and looked at Joe. "She's still Mom. The other woman, Francine, may have been my real mother, but she's not my mom." Joe was happy he had said that. Michel turned his attention back to Lori. "We don't want Linda worrying about this right now. We'll tell her when she comes home this summer, if we've got it all figured out by then. Now, what are we going to do about the letter?"

"I suppose we're going to have to write them," Lori answered. "But there's a problem."

"What's that?" Joe asked.

"Michel's name is Fudge, not Matte. We don't even have a birth certificate for him. How can he convince the bank who he is?"

Michel and Joe knew that what she was saying was true. There was no way Michel could prove who he was without a birth certificate. Reverend Foote was the person who had told them that Millie and Joe should look after him, but he had retired many years earlier and they had lost track of him. Maybe though, with the birth certificate and the bankbook, the bank would be convinced. "Your birth certificate could be among all of these papers," Lori commented as she reached for a pile.

Millie had tied strings around each of them and Lori carefully untied each string and sifted through the papers. Finally, she held up a piece of paper from the third pile and smiled.

"I've got it," she said. "I've got it."

Michel and Joe got up from the table and looked over her shoulder as Lori read it aloud.

"Michel Claude Romeo Leblanc. Born to Denis and Francine Leblanc (nee Matte) at the Toronto General Hospital on March 16th, 1948. This is all we need," Lori said, proudly.

Michel took the paper and walked to the centre of the kitchen. "What did you say my name is?" he asked.

"Michel Claude Romeo Leblanc," Lori recited.

Michel continued to stare at the piece of paper. "Until now," he said, "I always thought I was Michel Fudge from Dark Harbour. When I got married, I gave my wife my name and our baby has my name. I don't even know who I am anymore." Michel paused and shook his head. It was obvious that the new information was weighing on him. "Who the hell am I?" he asked, tossing the piece of paper in his father's direction.

Joe could feel his son's pain, but he couldn't answer his son's questions. "Maybe I shouldn't have told you any of this," he whispered.

Michel looked at his wife and then at his father. "I'm sorry, Dad. I know this is not your fault. Do you see why I don't think we should tell Linda about this yet?"

"We still have the problem of the money and stuff in Halifax, though," he said, looking at Lori for advice.

Lori paused before answering. "Okay, then here's what I think we should do. We'll write to the bank and tell them to keep the money there in a savings account for now. We have your birth certificate and there's got to be a record of your mother's death up at the church somewhere. We'll send everything off to Halifax. So for now, we'll just tell them to send us what's in the safety deposit box and see if that will tell us more about who you are. Does that make sense to you?" she asked them both.

They nodded their heads in agreement.

"Great. Okay then, let's put all this back in the trunk and tomorrow, first thing, we'll get a record of Francine's death and I'll write a letter to the bank. Then we'll start going through all of those papers. We'll find out who you are, Michel." Michel looked at his wife solemnly, nodding his head before he lowered his eyes to the floor and took a deep breath. He wanted to believe her.

Seven ∽

FRANCINE FOREST SAT uncomfortably in her seat enroute to Toronto from Montreal on July 14th, 1946. It was 2:20 p.m. and she had left the train station in Montreal twenty minutes earlier. The heat was nearly unbearable and although she couldn't see it, she knew her face was flushed. Her clothes stuck to her damp body like static cling and despite her best efforts she could not get them to hang loose. She wiped her damp forehead with her gloved hand and then looked to see that it was not only damp, but slightly discoloured. For a moment she wished she were back home where, at about this time, she could be swimming. But Roberval was over one hundred miles behind her now and it was too late to change her mind. She had never been more than ten miles from home in all of her nineteen years, but before this day was over, she knew she would be much farther away than that.

Francine tried to put thoughts of home out of her mind. She recalled having heard on the radio how Queen Juliana of the Netherlands had sent tulip bulbs to Ottawa the previous month and hoped that someday she might visit the city to see them. She loved flowers, but her mother had never seemed to have the time to plant flowers around their home in Roberval. She shook her head to try and stop from thinking of home and then looked around to see a distraction. All the other passengers were engaged in conversation and glanced over their faces and caught bits of conversation. A man in the seat in front of her was addressed as Mr. Hamilton and it caused her to remember reading about Canada's first drive-in movie theatre opening in Hamilton. She imagined what it might look like, chuckling to herself as she pictured sitting in the back of her father's old pickup truck watching a movie. She could only imagine what a movie was, having never seen one. She hoped she would get to see one during her time in Toronto.

During the trip from Roberval to Montreal there had been so many things to see and experience that she hadn't had the chance to think much of home. She had never been on a train before and was naturally very nervous, but now, on the second leg of her journey, thoughts of home flitted through her mind. Her father had taken her to the station in his truck accompanied by her mother who cried a lot and kept telling her to be a good girl and to do what she was told. She had never seen her mother so emotional. Her father however, seemed to take it all in stride and acted as if this was something he did every-day. He surprised her however, when he finished speaking with the porter, by reaching for her and hugging her so tight she could barely breathe. He turned after releasing her and walked back to the truck without looking in her direction. Her father had not embraced her since she had been a very little girl and her mother looked more shocked than she did. The hug only caused her mother to cry harder as she also hugged Francine and said goodbye.

Francine's father was an old friend of the porter, who had assured them that they had nothing to worry about. Once they got underway, he chatted with Francine a few minutes and told her again not to worry. She appreciated what he was doing for her and felt confident that she would at least get off at the correct stop and find the right train to Toronto. In Montreal he made sure that she located the right train and, before leaving, pulled a pocket watch from the inside of his coveralls, flipped it open and notified her that her train would be leaving in less than an hour.

That was half an hour earlier. Her train was already there in front of her and through the windows she could see the porters making everything orderly before the passengers boarded. It was very warm and the stench of diesel fuel hung in the air, irrating her throat. She looked around and located a drinking fountain a little distance from her and decided to get a drink. She had some lemonade that her mother had made for her, but she would save that for when she was on the train.

She lugged a canvas bag with her and it was so heavy that she could only walk a dozen or so steps before she had to stop and rest, but her efforts were rewarded when she reached the fountain. To her surprise, the water was cool and she was careful not to drink too much because her mother had cautioned her about using public toilets. As she headed back towards the train, she considered her strategy, which was to find a comfortable seat on the train and to spend the entire trip looking out the window. She had promised her mother that she would write and tell her about everything she saw and the more she saw during the trip the longer her letter would be.

As she neared the platform, she looked at the signs on the side of each passenger car: Montreal-Toronto. She looked up at the imperious mass of glass and steel. This train was bigger than the one that had brought her to Montreal and there was a plaque welded on the side of the engine: Montreal Locomotive Works. She moved a little closer to examine it and, as she did, a loud noise punctured the air. Her hand flew to her chest as she jumped back in terror, nearly falling as she tripped over her bag. Her other hand, used to muffle her scream, was abruptly pulled away as she used it to balance herself. She heard some-one snicker and looked to see a young boy holding his mother's hand and pointing in her direction. Then she realized that it had been the train whistle. She managed a feeble smile as she picked up her bag and walked back to the bench, vowing not to leave it again until the train was ready to board.

When Francine boarded the Canadian National Railroad train it was stifling inside and the red leather window seat was hot. Her clothes quickly attached themselves to her skin as the perspiration dampened her thin cotton dress. Her mother had insisted she wear a singlet beneath her blouse and she now wished she hadn't because it made her very warm. She could feel the water dripping down the small of her back as she tried to sit up straight. The window was partially open, but she couldn't feel a breeze. She reached to try and force it all the way open, but all she succeeded in doing was soiling her new white gloves.

As the other passengers boarded she noticed that most of the seats in the car were occupied and she was in one of the few bench seats that only had one passenger. She shifted a little to the outside as she watched a large man enter from the front of the car and stagger down the aisle. He was dishevelled and wore grey trousers that looked like they had been slept in. His jacket was thrown over his left arm and he held a carpet bag in his hand. He used his right hand to steady himself by grabbing the top of each seat as he staggered up the aisle. His shirt was open at the neck and both ends of his tie hung over his very substantial belly. It had been several days since he had shaved and the closer he came to Francine's seat the harder she prayed that he would sit somewhere else.

"Is this seat taken, Missy?" he asked as he smiled through teeth that were irregular and very badly stained.

Francine hesitated for a second trying to find the courage to lie about a friend who would soon be joining her. "No, sir," she finally blurted out as she moved as close to the window as she could without looking up.

Out of the corner of her eyes she watched as he raised his carpet bag over his head and strained to put it into the overhead luggage rack. She could see the hairs on his huge belly bursting out through the recesses between the buttons on his shirt. He seemed relieved that he could manage such a feat and, once finished, he sat down, removed a filthy handkerchief from his pants pocket and wiped the sweat from his forehead and face. He breathed very heavily and the more he moved, the stronger his stench became. Francine was sure that he had not had a bath in weeks and hoped he wouldn't speak to her. She held her perfumed gloved hand over her nose to mask the terrible odour and moved even closer to the window. A few minutes later, his snoring served notice that he was asleep.

The heat and the smell were overpowering. She couldn't keep her hand to her face for the entire trip, but as soon as she removed it, the stench returned. Francine looked around for another seat, but couldn't see one. She wished she had lied about waiting for a friend.

The train finally got underway and the little breeze she felt from the open window was a welcome relief. She rested her feet on the bag that held all of her worldly possessions; she couldn't possibly have lifted it to the luggage rack. In it were two new dresses, a second pair of shoes, a few toiletries, several undergarments and numerous other casual articles of clothing. She had carefully selected a few of her favourite books and other special things that she simply couldn't leave behind. The bag was filled to capacity, but her most guarded possession, her money, was stuffed into her undershirt and occasionally she would press her hand against it to ensure it was still there. Her father had warned her not to let her belongings out of her sight because, as he put it, "There are lots of people travelling the trains just waiting to prey on young, innocent girls such as yourself." She wondered if the person beside her was the kind of person her father had told her about.

Francine was indeed a picture of innocence. Her polished black hair was tightly tied in a bun at the back and held with a bone clip that her grandmother had given her. She wore no makeup and her face was tanned a deep brown. Everything about her contributed to her beauty. Her lips were full and slightly parted, her nose small and slightly turned up. Her eyes were green and matched the broach pinned at her throat that accented her long neck.

She was attractive and tidily dressed in a manner that revealed her upbringing. Her mother had made her dress from very colourful, yellow cotton purchased a few weeks earlier. It was homemade but stylish. Her petticoat had been made from an empty one hundred-pound sack of Robin Hood flour that had been bleached and washed several times to make it soft, then dyed the colour of her dress. A ribbon of frilly material had been sewn on it to make a hem. A knitted white sweater with cotton gloves that she wished she could take off contributed to a mature look far beyond her nineteen years.

The Forests were a working class family. Francine figured she would end up like all her friends; married with a half a dozen children, living out her life in Roberval with a dairy farmer. It had never occurred to her that she would be moving to Toronto. When she allowed herself to dream, it was about becoming a nurse, although she knew her mother would never let her pursue such a career. She had read a lot about the English colony off Canada's east coast and thought that after her training she might like to go to Newfoundland and become a circuit nurse to the numerous isolated communities. The Sisters encouraged her and even found her some reading material. She had read that some of the communities were French speaking and with her abilities in both languages, she felt that she would be especially qualified. However, with the offer from Monsieur Leblanc, her entire career goals changed.

Five weeks earlier, Mother Superior had asked her if she would like to go to Toronto and become a live-in French teacher for the children of the Leblanc family. Once she over the initial surprise, she could barely contain her exuberance, but she knew that she first had to talk it over with her parents. Mother Superior had also informed her that she was her first choice, and Monsieur Leblanc would like to have an answer as soon as possible.

Her mother, not surprisingly, opposed the idea. She was a French Canadian, Catholic mother, who expected the half a dozen grand-children and the dairy farmer son-in-law. It was the traditional role of a wife and mother and she expected that her daughter would adhere to tradition. She did not want her daughter going out into the world alone pursuing a lifestyle that was not only foreign to her, but foreign to Francine as well. She wanted her daughter and her grandchildren nearby. The fact that her daughter had continued in school for as long as she had went against the tradition of the Forest family. When Francine informed her at dinner that evening that she would like to move to Toronto, her mother became very excited and immediately informed her that it was out of the question. Her father, however, was much more liberal in his thinking and was proud that his daughter wanted to leave home and become independent. He wanted to know all of the details and Francine had them for him.

She had been asked to go to work for a man originally from Roberval who had moved to Montreal. In 1933, Romeo Leblanc, then a very successful businessman, had moved to Toronto and had become one of the wealthiest men in the city. There wasn't anywhere suitable in Toronto where Mr. Leblanc could send his children to learn French, so he decided the best thing to do was to bring somebody from Quebec to teach them. So, he decided to call back to his home town and see if he could find a teacher. He had visited the convent and asked Mother Superior to find him a teacher. Francine was her choice and, in exchange for room and board and eight dollars a month, she would become the French tutor of the Leblanc children. She had an excellent command of both languages and Mother Superior recommended her highly for the position. She dearly wanted to go and eventually, after a great deal of coaxing and pleading, both parents agreed.

That had been a month and a half earlier. She smiled a little as she thought about what might be in store for her. She couldn't wait to get to Toronto and to see the city. She was very excited about tutoring the Leblanc children and hoped she would be a good teacher. That was more important to her than anything else. She closed her eyes and folded her hands and whispered a prayer. "Holy Mother, protect me and show me how to be a good teacher." As she finished her prayer she felt a hand on her shoulder. She opened her eyes.

"May I please see your ticket, Miss?" a porter asked her.

"Yes, sir," she answered as she pulled the string on her little cloth handbag and rummaged through it for her ticket. Her left elbow struck the sleeping drunk and he grunted. He had fallen asleep with his hands folded across his chest and his ticket held to his body. The porter pulled it out, punched a hole in it and replaced it. Francine found her ticket and passed it to him. He punched it, passed it back to her and, as he did, he looked toward the rear of the coach.

"Would you like to sit in another seat, Miss?" he asked with a big smile.

"Why, yes!" Francine replied. "Yes, I would. Thank you very much."

"Well, then, let's get you one," the pleasant porter answered as he shoved the fat drunk's shoulder.

"Sit up and let the little lady out," he growled at the drunk. Instantly he came to life, sat up straight and swung his legs out into the aisle.

Francine reached for her canvas bag and squeezed out between him and the seat in front of her. The porter took her bag and led her to the rear of the coach. He pointed to an empty seat. "I think you'll be a lot more comfortable here, Miss," he said as he placed her bag in the rack over her head. "Don't worry," he comforted her. "Nobody will steal your bag as long as you're on my train." He seemed to be able to read her thoughts.

"But don't forget to take it with you when we get to Toronto, will your Miss—" he left the inquiry hanging.

"Francine," she said to him with just as big a smile as his. "My name is Francine."

"Well, Francine, you have a pleasant trip and if there is anything you need, you just stop me. I'll be walking through the cars every twenty minutes or so. And my name is Harry," he whispered.

"Thank you, Harry," Francine said smiling as the porter turned and worked his way up the aisle.

Francine settled back in her new seat. She looked out the window and then quickly remembered her money. She patted her chest. It was still there. Mr. Leblanc had sent her fifty dollars to pay for her trip and any other expenses she might incur. She had used some of the money to purchase material to make new clothes and some more to pay for her ticket. The balance was still safely tucked in her shirt.

After what she guessed must be at least two hours since she had left Montreal, she felt a little hungry. Her mother had packed her a few sandwiches and she left her seat, reached up, undid the flap to her canvas bag, retrieved her lunch and returned to her seat. She ate while continuing to take in all the sights as they sped through the country- side. She finished her first sandwich, then carefully opened the mason jar and drank half of its contents. Her mother made great lemonade and it quenched her thirst despite the fact that it was no longer cold. She carefully replaced the cover, set it on the seat beside her and bit into her second sandwich. The thick bread was still fresh and she folded the paper across her lap to keep the crumbs from falling on her dress. The rattle of the rails and the gentle movement of the train were very soothing. Francine felt content.

After she finished eating, she carefully folded the paper, crumbs and all, and put it and the empty mason jar back into her canvas bag. It felt good to stand up again and she pulled her sticky clothes from her body. She tried to brush some of the wrinkles out of her dress despite the rocking motion of the train but eventually gave up and took her seat.

The scenes that flew by as they sped toward Toronto kept her attention and the time passed quickly. She could hardly believe it when she heard Harry announce that they would be arriving in Toronto in thirty minutes. He stopped and asked Francine if some- body would be meeting her. She informed him that there would be. He appeared pleased, reached up, removed her bag from the rack and placed it on the seat beside her. He winked at her and then continued through the car. She watched him leave and then reached for her handbag and found the telegram.

To Miss Francine Forest
Fm Mr R Leblanc
Message
Upon arrival in Toronto go to Post 16 Stop Driver will be there
holding sign with your name Stop Introduce yourself and he will
drive you home Stop

Francine looked at the word "home". This was indeed going to be her new home. She folded the telegram and put it back in her bag. She wondered what time it was. The train was scheduled to arrive at 8:01 p.m. and she was anxious to see how close to that time it would be when they actually arrived.

Shortly after Harry made his announcement, Francine got her first look at Toronto. It looked very much like the first scenes she had seen of Montreal earlier in the day. The buildings were huge and the closer she got to them, the larger they appeared. The ride became noisier as the tracks crossed streets and she watched as the cars stopped and waited for the train to pass. The scene that unfolded in front of her seemed one of total chaos.

There were so many people, cars, and large trucks all moving with such purpose that it was a mystery to her how they didn't all crash into one another, let alone where they all came from. The closer the train got to the city the more congested it became and the mystery and the intrigue of Toronto grew. She wondered how anyone could ever find anything. To her relief, she was able to catch a glimpse of a clock at the top of a large church steeple. It was 7:45.

The train slowed considerably as it approached the city. Many of the passengers were already standing up and had removed their baggage from the racks. Some were even walking toward the doors. She guessed they must be quite close to the station so she got up from her seat and stood in the aisle and once again tried to sweep the wrinkles from her clothes, but couldn't. Satisfied that she was as presentable as she could be considering the circumstances, she picked up her bag, made her way with the others toward the door and waited for the train to stop. Everybody was talking and straining to see outside. Finally, the train stopped and a breeze blew into the car when the doors opened. It was the same smell as Montreal.

Francine stepped down from the train onto the concrete platform and surveyed her surroundings. She had arrived in Toronto. There were thousands of people and every one of them seemed to be going in a different direction. She looked around for Post 16, but couldn't see any posts at all. Then she heard somebody beside her asking for directions to Post 22. She waited until he had his answer and she then asked directions to Post 16. The young man in uniform just pointed behind him. It seemed as if he anticipated the questions and pointed instead of answering.

He had pointed in the direction of a big building with a glass roof. She could see people going in and out and she walked toward it. The weight of her bag was hurting her arm, so she stopped for a few seconds and changed hands. A few feet from the entrance she stopped again. She had never seen revolving doors before. She stood examining the situation for a few minutes and then made her move. Cautiously, she approached them and then quickly jumped in as they came around. She hoped she wouldn't stumble and feared the worst, but before she knew it she was stepping out of them and into the lobby of the Toronto Union Station.

Francine had never seen such a place before. There were thousands and thousands of people among the benches, shops, signs and posts.

She uttered a sigh of relief as she saw a post with a number on it. The posts extended from the floor to the glass ceiling. She spotted number 12 and carefully pushed her way through the crowd to 16. As she approached it, she saw a young man in uniform with a cardboard sign. "Forest" was printed on it in big bold letters and she approached him with a big smile on her face.

"*Je m'appelle Francine Forest,*" she called out to the startled young man as she laid down her bag and grabbed his arm, not realizing that she had spoken to him in French.

He turned and looked at her with a blank stare.

"My name is Francine Forest," she quickly countered in English having realized what she had said. "That's my name on your sign."

Apparently he seemed unconvinced that Francine was the young lady he had been sent to pick up. Francine wondered if it was because of her accent.

The young man lowered his sign and took the ticket from her hand. He looked at it for confirmation and his face blushed slightly. He looked up from the ticket to her face and smiled apologetically to the attractive woman in front of him. "Is that all the baggage you have?" he asked as he reached for her bag.

"I can carry my own bag, thank you very much," she said as she grabbed the bag from him.

He wasn't expecting her reaction and it took him by surprise. He stopped for a moment and suddenly smiled and took off his hat.

"I'm sorry, Miss Forest, " he apologized. "I'm Roger and I'm here to pick you up. I must take your bag. It's my job."

Francine considered this information for a moment then smiled and passed her bag to him. "Lead the way."

It was quite warm as they exited the station into the Toronto evening. There were cars and people everywhere as she followed Roger up the street. He changed hands on the bag several times before they eventually stopped beside a big, black, shiny car. "Is this our car?" she asked when they stopped.

Roger laughed. "No, it belongs to Mr. Leblanc," he said as he held open the back door for her. He slammed it shut behind her and put her luggage in the trunk.

Francine had never been in a car before. There were lots of them in Roberval but she had never actually been inside one. She had been in her father's truck lots of times. It was hot inside and the seat was made of leather. She hoped it wouldn't be a long trip because she was already perspiring.

"You can crank down the window if it's too warm for you back there," Roger called out as he got into the driver's seat. Unlike the train, the windows rolled all the way down and by the time she had finished, the car was moving and the breeze felt good.

Francine asked him a million questions as they made their way through traffic to the Leblanc home. She couldn't see the tops of the buildings from inside the car so every time they stopped she leaned out through the window and looked up. Roger laughed at her as she "wowed" at things he had seen all his life. Gradually, they left the downtown area and moved out to the suburbs. The Leblanc home was on the outskirts of the city in Meadow Pine and, despite being tired,

Francine would have enjoyed nothing more than to have stopped and walked around the city. She longingly looked out the back window and saw the city disappear behind her. An hour after they had left the train station, they arrived at the Leblanc home.

She couldn't believe her eyes as Roger stopped the car in front of two huge metal gates. Roger left the car and picked up a telephone from a small box built into the high stone wall that ran along either side of the gates. He said something and seconds later the huge gates swung open. Roger drove through them and Francine watched through the back window as the gates swung closed behind them.

The road beyond the gates was paved, winding and narrow. Roger skillfully steered the car and Francine held on to a handle above her window to hold herself steady. There were trees on both sides of the road and despite her best efforts, she couldn't see anything through them. A couple of minutes later they reached their destination and the scene in front of Francine almost took her breath away.

It was as if they had left the darkness and entered into the light. Branches from the large trees hung over the road up to the mansion and blocked out the sunlight. Suddenly they came out of the trees into a big open area filled with sunshine. In front of them was the Leblanc home. It wasn't a house: it was a mansion. Roger steered the car around the circular driveway and stopped in front of the mansion. Francine just sat in the car and stared out through the window. Roger got out and went to the trunk and lifted out her bag. Francine was still sitting in the car when Roger walked to her door and held it open for her.

"Are you going to stay in there all night?" he laughed. She didn't hear him. She couldn't have heard a cannon firing beside the car. Roger reached in and grasped her by the arm. "We're here," he said as he tried to encourage her to get out. Roger's touch startled her. She reached his proffered hand and stepped outside.

She had to look up to see the mansion. About ten steps led up to it and a large spacious veranda ran the entire length of the front of the house. On it were several white chairs and tables with umbrellas. On each table were flowers that looked like they could have been cut from the beds they had passed coming up the driveway. The entire house was white and two big round pillars in the front supported a large overhanging roof. On each side of the pillars were two huge bronze lions. The front of the mansion was filled with windows and on each side of them were white shutters. Between the two pillars and nearly twenty feet back from them were two large doors.

The lawn in front of the mansions was as green as the house was white. It was perfectly manicured and there were numerous beds of flowers scattered throughout it. Beside each bed of flowers was a tree and as the evening sun set, the trees cast long shadows across the lawn. Francine had never seen such a beautiful scene before. As she took it in she heard voices coming from somewhere and she walked around the car and looked in the direction from which they had come.

The voices were coming from her left and she could see an area enclosed by a high, wire mesh fence. She looked toward it and could see some people dressed in white, playing tennis. She had seen a picture of a tennis court in Life Magazine, but it was nothing like this. Beside the court was a large water fountain and a sculpture of a young boy was standing in its centre. Water was coming out of his penis and pouring into the pool. Embarrassed by the sight, she turned back to the scene in front of her.

Hedge, about eight feet high and three feet thick, lined both sides of the driveway leading up to the house. It was a slightly different colour green than the lawn and Francine could see a man trimming it a few hundred feet away from her. To her right was another large area surrounded by a low fence. She could hear children's voices coming from its direction and she suddenly heard a splash. It was a swimming pool. She thought of Roberval and the stream she liked to swim in. She wished she could be swimming there now.

Francine continued to survey her new home until she heard a door opening, followed by a voice.

"Did you have any trouble finding her?" she heard as she turned.

"No sir, I didn't. We just had a little mix up with her name, that's all," Roger said as he turned and winked at Francine.

The person in the doorway was an older man. He looked to be about sixty. His hair was white and what little he had ringed the sides of his head. He was dressed in a black suit with long tails and beneath it he was wearing a white shirt and a funny looking tie.

"Hello Miss Forest," he spoke, making the same pronunciation error as Roger. "I'm Joseph, the butler."

"Hello, sir," she answered.

"Please call me Joseph," he responded. "Everybody else does."

"Then you must call me Francine," she quickly added.

The two men just looked at each other and smiled. Their look said that she had a lot to learn.

Joseph turned slightly and signed with his open hand toward the door. "If you'll just come in, Mr. Leblanc is in his study waiting to greet you. He expected you fifteen minutes ago. He doesn't like to be kept waiting."

Francine quickly ran up the steps through the door. She stepped inside. The cool air felt good on her warm face as she walked into the mansion. The inside was as magnificent as the outside. The ceiling was almost as high as the ceiling in the train station. Hanging from its centre was the largest chandelier she had ever seen in her life. The walls were covered with paintings and some were so large that they wouldn't fit on the outside wall of her house back in Roberval. In front of her was a beautiful marble staircase. She didn't know how she would ever find the words to describe it all to her mother. At the top of the stairs was a big picture of a woman dressed in a long white gown. She was beautiful. Francine suddenly felt a hand on her arm and Joseph began leading her to her left.

"Pretty impressive, isn't it?" Joseph asked as he led her to the study. All she could do was nod her head. Joseph chuckled lightly. "It had the same effect on me when I came to work here for the previous owners thirty years ago." he laughed.

Francine would have liked to just sit in the cool room and look at everything, but before she realized it they had reached the door to Mr. Leblanc's study. Joseph knocked gently on it, paused for a second and then slid the doors into their recesses in the wall indicating to Francine that she should enter.

The room was both a study and a library and there were more books there than she thought existed in the entire world. There was a library at the convent, but it was insignificant compared to the books in this room. She walked into the room and slowly turned in a circle. She heard the doors slide together behind her.

"*Bienvenue chez nous, Mademoiselle Forest,*" she heard, and turned to greet Monsieur Romeo Leblanc.

Eight ∽

THE TRANSITION FROM Roberval was a little difficult, but Francine soon settled into the routine of the Leblanc household and as it got closer to her first Christmas away from Roberval she thought longingly of home. She was still happy she had made the decision to move to Toronto and had grown to love the Leblanc family. Monsieur Leblanc was often absent from home on business and he had left his children's French education completely to Francine's discretion. During their initial meeting in his study, he had informed her that he wanted his children to be able to communicate with him in his native tongue. How she achieved this was her decision. If she had any disciplinary problems with them she was to bring it to the attention of Joseph. Francine assured him that she didn't anticipate having any problems with his children. She loved children and was confident that she would get along very well with them. And they would learn to speak and understand French.

The Leblanc children, Alain and Marie, were very well-behaved intelligent children. Alain was ten and his sister was twelve. Despite the fact that they belonged to a very wealthy family, they didn't fit Francine's impression of what wealthy children were like. They were friendly and pleasant and very nice. Despite the fact that they were chauffeur driven to a private school and had almost everything they wanted, they were friendly and pleasant and treated Francine courteously. They were eager to learn and eager for companionship. Because of where they lived however, very few children ever came to visit them on a regular basis, so they regarded Francine not only as a teacher, but as a friend. They weren't used to receiving instruction from someone as young as Francine and this, coupled with the fact that they lived in the same house, led to a relationship of mutual respect and friendship.

Joseph ran the household. Both Monsieur and Madame Leblanc were absent quite often and Joseph had been charged with the responsibility of ensuring everything ran smoothly. And it did. He treated Francine like a member of the Leblanc family and always referred to her as Mademoiselle Forest. There was also an older brother, Denis, but he was rarely at home. He lived and worked at Camp Borden, north of Toronto. He had been in the war and had decided to remain in the Air Force after it was over. He rarely came home and when he did it was for very short stays. He usually came home for Christmas though, the children informed Francine, and he would be coming for a few days this year. She looked forward to meeting him.

Francine didn't have long to wait. Shortly before Christmas and nearly six months after she had arrived at the Leblanc household, she met Denis. He was Alain and Marie's step brother, she learned from Alain when she questioned him as to why Denis didn't resemble either Alain or Marie. Denis's mother and Monsieur Leblanc's first wife had died of pneumonia when Denis was twelve and, according to Alain, Denis looked like his mother. Like every other girl who had met Denis, Francine was awed by his good looks and would soon be captured by his very charming personality.

It was nearly 11:00 a.m. and she was in the library when she heard the very distinctive ring of the front gate telephone. After it had rung a second time and she didn't hear Joseph attempting to answer it, she laid down her book and ran to answer it.

"Hello," she answered.

There was a pause for a few seconds. "Hiya, sweet thing. Push the button will ya?"

"Who is this?" she asked. She could barely restrain herself from responding with the same arrogance and insist that she wasn't anybody's "sweet thing."

"Who is this?" the voice answered.

"I am Mademoiselle Francine Forest. I am Alain and Marie's French tutor."

"Yes, of course. Marie wrote and told me about you. Are you as pretty as she said you are?"

Francine felt her face flush a little. "Oh, I don't know," she said, flustered. "Unless you identify yourself," she quickly countered, "I'm hanging up this telephone and calling Roger."

She could hear the voice laughing before she finished talking. Roger was certainly not the most threatening person she knew, but in the heat of the moment he was all she could come up with. She waited for him to finish laughing.

"I'm Denis and I've come home for Christmas," he said, still laughing.

"Well, my better judgement tells me that I should let you wait out there until I can find Joseph, but you sound just silly enough to be Denis, so I'm going to let you in. But if you're not—" She didn't get a chance to finish as she heard a click. She paused for a few seconds just to spite him and then pushed the button to open the gates. A few minutes later she heard the front doorbell and, after the second ring, she realized that Joseph was not there to answer it.

Francine walked to the door, pulled back the curtain and took a peek at Denis. Standing outside the door was the most handsome man she had ever seen. He was tall and dressed in a blue military uniform that seemed to accent his well-proportioned body. Perched on the side of his head was a canoe-shaped hat and above his left pocket were two silver wings joined by a maple leaf. Beneath it were several coloured pieces of cloth. Above his right pocket was a black piece of cloth and on it were the letters *Leblanc*. The sight of Denis caused her to straighten her dress and smooth her hair before she pulled open the door.

"I thought you were actually going to keep me standing here until you found Joseph," he said as he brushed by her and into the house. Just as she was closing the door, Joseph appeared.

"Monsieur Denis, we weren't expecting you," Joseph greeted him. "Madame Leblanc will be so surprised and pleased." At that moment they heard a squeal from upstairs and they all looked in its direction.

Madame Leblanc was standing at the top of the stairs in front of her picture. "Denis!" she called out. "What are you doing here? When did you arrive? How—?"

"Whoa, Linda, slow down," Denis interrupted her. "Let me get my gear stowed and I'll answer all your questions. I drove down from Borden and I was on standby all night so I could use a shower."

"Yes, of course. I understand," she said as they met at the bottom of the stairs and hugged. A few minutes after that, Denis was in the shower and Francine sat alone in the library thinking about him.

Denis was able to spend four days with his family and during that time, Francine got to know a little about him. He was twenty-two years old and had joined the Royal Air Force in 1942. He had flown twenty-three missions in Europe and had been shot down over Germany. Luckily, he had not been captured and returned to fly another seven missions before the war ended. After the war, he returned to Canada and joined the Royal Canadian Air Force.

He gave the appearance of an unusually gentle man for somebody who had undoubtedly dropped bombs and killed hundreds of people. He didn't like to talk about the war, but he loved to talk about flying and spent hours with Alain and Marie talking about planes and the feeling of soaring through the air. They would all buzz about the house like they were on bombing and strafing runs. The two children idolized their brother and during his short stays, Francine learned, they would spend nearly every waking minute with him.

Francine was fascinated by him. He was like no person she had ever met. There was something about him she couldn't figure out and it intrigued her. He had a sort of aura. It was not surprising that shortly after word got out that he was home, every available young lady in the area called on him, but he only paid them cursory attention. Francine was attracted to him, like all the other girls, and her feelings for him increased on the second day of his visit when the four of them went for a walk in the snow. He held her hand while they walked through the woods, citing some obscure military practice about walking with a lady. Even through her thick woolen glove and his leather flying glove, she felt something more than his hand. He seemed to always be smiling and whenever she was with him his smile seemed to be contagious.

Like all his previous visits, Denis could only stay a short time and the night before he was due to return to Camp Borden, his parents held a party for him. Monsieur Leblanc had been very disappointed when Denis joined the Air Force and even more disappointed when he decided to remain in the services after the war. He wanted Denis to work with him and though he had offered him more money for a month's work than he would earn in an entire year as a flight lieutenant, Denis refused. Romeo Leblanc had learned to accept his son's decision, but at every opportune moment he would let him know how much he would like it if Denis resigned his commission and came to work with him. But Denis loved to fly and he loved the Air Force, so nothing could make him change his mind.

Francine thought the party was fantastic. Nearly one hundred people were invited and she commented to everybody she was introduced to that it was the most wonderful party she had ever attended. For most of the guests it was just another party, but for a young girl from Roberval who had never attended such an event, it was considerably more. Roger had driven her downtown and she had spent an entire month's salary on a dress. It had been worth it because she was as beautiful as Denis was handsome. She tried to catch a glimpse of him all evening and each time she did he was dancing with a different attractive girl. She spent most of the evening sitting between Alain and Marie dreaming of Denis asking her to waltz. But he never even acknowledged her presence. He looked incredible dressed in his uniform and every time he held a girl in his arms, Francine wished it were her.

A couple of young men asked her to dance, but she politely refused saying that she had to stay with the children. After a few had asked and had been turned down, nobody else bothered. She was not a very good dancer, despite her practice with Alain a few days earlier, and she didn't want Denis to see how awkward she was. Then he would never ask her. She did dance once with Alain, grateful that her awkwardness could be explained by saying that she was dancing with a much shorter partner. On one occasion she noticed Denis looking in her direction, but as soon as their eyes met he turned away. Toward the end of the evening and during one of the few times when she wasn't subtly looking at him, he suddenly appeared in front of her.

"Would you do me the honour of dancing the next dance with me?" he asked while standing in front of her and gallantly holding out his white gloved hand.

His sudden appearance took her by surprise and she swallowed hard. Her heart raced with anticipation as she looked into his smiling, handsome face. He waited confidently for her to take his hand.

"No, thank you," she lied, not knowing why or how she managed such a statement. But it had the effect she wanted.

The smile suddenly disappeared from his face and he straightened up. He had never been refused a dance for as long as he could remember. He was not used to rejection and it was obvious.

"I...I...I beg your pardon," he stammered.

"No, thank you," Francine repeated. "I have to stay with the children," she said as she reached for both of their hands.

The children were as shocked as Denis. They had seen her looking at him all evening and couldn't believe what they had heard.

"You don't have to stay with us," both children said in unison. But their words didn't affect Francine's resolve. Denis just looked at the three of them, backed away a few steps and then returned to the dance floor. Francine watched discreetly as he reached for a beautiful young lady sitting on a chair beside a wall. She never hesitated and was in his arms instantly, her prayers obviously answered. Denis looked in Francine's direction smugly as if to let her know she wasn't the only fish in the sea. But Francine was not looking any more. She had achieved her goal.

At 11:00 p.m. Francine left the party and went upstairs to help the children get ready for bed. In just a short time, she had become much more than a tutor and seemed closer to them than even their mother. Madame Leblanc was born into an affluent Toronto family and her picture graced the society pages almost daily. She was kept busy with her involvement in a number of the city's charities, holding the chair on many of them, and had an office in the mansion similar to Romeo's where she could manage all her social engagements. She was quite pleasant and nice, but preferred to leave the rearing of her children to the help. Nevertheless, she did take an interest in the children's education and always treated Francine with respect.

Francine waited outside each of her young charge's rooms until they called to say that they were in bed. She then went first into Alain's room. Alain was a typical young boy and his clothes were strewn all over the room. If she ever had a child of her own, she hoped he would be as easy-going and free-spirited as Alain. Francine picked up his clothes as they talked about the party. He was planning to go skiing tomorrow and he reminded Francine to lay out his ski clothes. She did and when she finished hanging up his clothes, she touched her fingertips to her lips and touched his forehead.

"*Bonne nuit*," he managed quite proudly.

"*Bonne nuit a toi, aussi, mon cher*," Francine responded. She flicked off the light as she was leaving and then went to Marie's room.

Marie was much neater than her brother. Her clothes had all been put on hangers and hung in the closet. She was in her bed, lying on her back as Francine entered.

"Mademoiselle Forest," she said somewhat hesitatingly.

"Yes, Marie."

"Would you mind answering a personal question for me?"

"No, I don't think so."

"At the party this evening," she began, "all you did was stare at Denis. Even I could tell that there was nothing more in the world you wanted than for him to ask you to dance. When he finally did, you said no. I don't understand."

Francine laughed. "You're a pretty observant young lady," she chided as she sat on the edge of her bed and lightly pinched her cheek. "You see, Marie, Denis was aware that I was looking at him and he concluded I wanted to dance with him. He knew that as soon as the party began. But he waited for a long time before he asked me. If I had agreed to dance the first time he asked, he would treat me the way he treats the other girls. So, I said 'no.' We're women, sweetheart, and we should never let men forget how special we are. As soon as they do, they get tired of us and, perhaps, go looking for somebody else. Do you understand now why I couldn't dance with him the first time he asked?"

"I think so," Marie smiled at her, "but you do like him, right?"

"Yes, I like him a lot, but don't you go telling him that in one of your letters, will you?"

"I won't, I promise, but if he asks you to dance again, you will agree to dance with him, won't you?"

"Maybe. Now you get some sleep. Before you realize it you'll be going to dances by yourself and finding yourself in the same situation. Go to sleep now, and we'll talk about it some more in the morning." Francine stood up from the bed, leaned over and kissed her on the cheek.

Francine left the room and returned to the party. A waiter approached her and offered her a glass from his tray. She reached for it instinctively and walked to a chair alongside the wall, sitting down. Only after taking her seat did she guess from the bubbles that it was champagne. She had tasted the fruit punch several times throughout the evening, but had dared not try the champagne. She watched the bubbles exploding in each glass as the waiter served his laughing customers. Finally, she decided to taste hers and lifted her glass and took a sip. It was terrible. It was bitter and the bubbles got in her nose. She was rubbing it profusely when she looked up and Denis was sitting beside her. She tried not to show her excitement.

"Tastes terrible, doesn't it?" he asked, laughing.

"Yes, it does. So why does everybody drink it?" she asked.

"Because it's champagne and everybody drinks champagne," he said, purposefully emphasizing the folly of his statement. "Otherwise, though, are you enjoying yourself?" he asked changing the subject.

"Yes, very much so," she responded, resting the glass on top of the napkin on her knee.

She looked at him. "Are you?"

"Yes, I am thanks. Where are Alain and Marie?"

"It was past their bedtime. They've gone to bed."

"Well, if that's the case, then you can't have any excuse for not dancing with me."

"It was not an excuse when I refused the last time," she said correcting him. "I have responsibilities."

"Yes, yes, but you also have a responsibility to me."

"What do you mean?" she asked, surprised.

Francine looked at him and laughed. His playful smirk betrayed his attempt at solemnity but, nonetheless, she could not resist him. She smiled in acquiescence, stood up and placed her glass on the table beside her. Her heart pounded as Denis took her hand and led her to the dance floor. Little did she know that his heart was beating just as fast.

She was a clumsy dancer and she knew it. She had never even been to a real dance and she had only had the opportunity to practise with Alain for two days before the party. Fortunately they were dancing a waltz and it was the easiest to master. Denis held her hand in his and she prayed she wouldn't perspire. He was very light on his feet and moved her effortlessly across the floor. He was as graceful as he was handsome and she felt safer in his arms than she had at any time before in her life.

Francine had never felt like this before. She was aware of nothing other than the touch and the smell of Denis. His open hand placed securely on the small of her back guided her through the maze of dancers and she felt as if she were floating. She was oblivious to the music and when it stopped she continued to move as if it were still playing. Denis's hand pressed against her back and the increase in pressure brought her back to reality. She let him go and joined the others in applauding the band.

They had a single dance and then he returned her to her chair, where they immediately engaged in conversation. They forgot that there was anybody else in the room and talked as freely as two people who had known each other all their lives. They reflected on their dramatically different pasts and their plans for the future. Denis wanted to fly until he was too old to get into an airplane and Francine wanted to find another family whose children she could teach once Marie and Alain were able to speak French. They laughed and frowned and acted hurt and happy as they chatted about anything and everything that came into their minds. They quickly became very comfortable with each other.

The other young ladies in the room grew envious of Francine. It was obvious that she had the undivided attention of her partner. There was no doubt that Denis was one of the most eligible bachelors in Toronto and anyone of the girls would have given anything to change places with Francine. The two of them talked and laughed, oblivious to everything around them. They were still talking when everybody else had left.

But their encounter was far too brief. Denis had to leave early the next morning to return to his duties at the Camp. He knocked gently on her door as he was leaving. "Good morning, are you awake?" he called out from the hall outside her room. His voice and his knock got louder until she finally heard him. She looked over at the clock on her night table after she had switched the lamp on. It was 5:10 a.m.

"What is it?" she asked in a hushed voice, instinctively pulling the bedclothes up around her.

"It's Denis. Would it be all right if I wrote you or called you on the telephone sometime?"

Francine smiled sleepily. "I'd like that," she answered. "I'd like that very much."

Francine changed after that evening. She had known Denis Leblanc for just a few short days yet he had made a deep impression on her. She had feelings for him that she had never experienced before. The children saw the change in her as did the other members of the household. She seemed to be always smiling, lost in a fantasy world filled with schoolgirl daydreams. Only the mention of Denis's name seemed to get her attention. Nothing could upset her, not even when Alain called her Madame Forest instead of Mademoiselle Forest.

On January 4th she received her first letter from Denis and though she considered letting him wait she could not resist answering him the same day. He telephoned when he received her letter and then, to everybody's surprise, he came for a visit the last weekend of the month.

They spent every waking moment of the weekend together. They began their day with breakfast very early in the morning even before the cook and the other kitchen staff were in the kitchen. Denis made her his "famous" omelette and they sat at the breakfast table and she complemented him and said how wonderful it was even though she hated mushrooms. By the time they had finished breakfast, the rest of the household were up. They left the kitchen a mess and didn't hear the gasps from the cook as they raced out of the mansion.

It was Saturday and after breakfast Denis said he wanted her to go with him to Toronto where he had a surprise for her. Roger was outside getting the limo ready for Mr. Leblanc and when he saw the two of them come out he immediately opened the rear door. Denis ran around to the driver's side, hopped in, leaned across the seat and opened the front passenger door. "Get in," he called out to Francine.

Roger slammed the rear door and moved to hold the door for Francine.

"Tell Dad that I've taken the car. Get another one from the garage for him," Denis called out to Roger as Francine stepped into the car and sat down. The limo sped out of the driveway with Roger standing with his forage cap in his hand.

Denis made Francine move over on the seat so that she was closer to him and they chatted as he drove into the city. She wanted to know where they were going, but all he would do was smile. She didn't have long to wait, though, because twenty minutes later they had arrived at their destination.

She waited in the limo and ten minutes later Denis returned, opened the door for her, and held her hand as she got out. "What are we doing here?" she asked as she looked at the huge building beside them.

"This is my surprise," he said smiling. "I'm taking you flying." He led her toward the hangar.

She paused and his hand slipped from his. "I've never been in an airplane," she whispered. "I think I'm afraid."

Denis laughed. He walked beside her, put his arm around her shoulder and nudged her forward. "Don't be silly," he admonished her. "This is what I do for a living. In case you don't remember, I'm a pilot."

Francine didn't want to be afraid but she couldn't help it as Denis strapped her into the back seat and then got into the front. He slid back the canopy, started the engine and went through the pre-flight checklist. He told her everything that he was doing and what she could expect. He told her not be afraid and that she would love flying just as much as he did.

The small airplane taxied down the runway and Denis waited for a few minutes to get clearance and then powered up the engine. They began to creep forward and then quickly picked up speed. Francine was forced back in her seat and she whimpered as the airplane sped down the runway.

To console her, Denis kept talking and as the airplane slowly lifted off the runway and she experienced flight for the first time, his voice seemed to be the only sound she could hear. She reached ahead to feel his shoulder and it helped. Slowly the airplane levelled and reluctantly, Francine opened her eyes and looked down. They were at four thousand feet and as she looked out through the window she gasped. Denis laughed.

They stayed up in the air for an hour and when it was time to return to the airfield, Francine's fears had disappeared. She loved the experience and made Denis promise that they would go flying again.

Denis even suggested that she learn to fly herself which caused her to laugh uncontrollably. Here she was a little girl from Roberval who just a short few months earlier had never even been in a car and now someone was suggesting she learn how to fly. He life was changing in ways she had never imagined.

Their time together passed too quickly and before they realized it, it was time for Denis to return to Camp Borden. The afternoon that he was supposed to leave they kissed for the first time. For Francine, it was the most beautiful thing she had ever experienced. Denis could feel the strength leaving her body as he held her and at that moment he knew that this was the woman he would someday marry. Of all the girls he had been with, not one of them had affected him like Francine. He hadn't even looked at another girl since he started seeing her and he realized to his surprise that he would never want to look at another girl again.

By March they were together at least twice a month. Denis showed up at the mansion whenever he had a couple of days off and the more time they spent together, the deeper they fell in love. Denis took her shopping, they went for long drives and went to only the very best restaurants for lunches and dinners. They met many of his former girl-friends at several of their stops and they looked enviously at Francine. Denis introduced her proudly to the who's who of Toronto. Several times their pictures appeared in the society pages of the newspapers and one reporter even wrote an editorial on how the most eligible bachelor in Ontario had finally found the woman who was going to tame him.

In June, Denis proposed and Francine accepted. They wasted no time in setting a date and shocked the Leblancs by announcing that they would be married on July 8th. Francine called Roberval after they made their announcement to the Leblancs and left a message that she would be calling back in one hour. It was a very emotional telephone call an hour later as daughter told mother she was getting married.

Francine's letters to her mother after the engagement became more frequent as she poured out her heart to her. She called occasionally, but her family didn't have a telephone of their own and she had to leave a message that she would call at a certain time to ensure that her mother was at the store where the telephone was located.

Her mother did not accept the engagement gracefully. She had objected to Francine going to Toronto in the first place and when she received Francine's letter announcing their engagement, she became quite distressed. She had known Romeo Leblanc as a young girl and she was aware of his rise to fame. She knew of his son because he had visited Roberval on a couple of occasions and she had watched the girls swoon over him. All she could think of was her young naive daughter being taken advantage of by a big city playboy.

She expressed her feelings to Francine in her response and it troubled Francine that her mother felt the way she did. However, she said that she, too, was aware of Denis's past, but she loved him and he loved her and she wanted her mother to trust her judgement. She poured her heart out to her mother. She wrote about how she felt and asked her mother if she had felt the same way about her father when they fell in love. She telephoned her and Denis spoke with her and he told her that he loved Francine more than he could put into words. He was very convincing and, reluctantly, she gave her blessing.

Her mother could tell that her daughter was very happy and they looked forward to going to Toronto, paid for by Monsieur Leblanc, to attend the wedding. That was all her father talked about to friends and, indeed, to anybody who would listen. Then the unexpected happened.

It had been a routine training mission. Denis had flown it a hundred times in the past. But this time something went wrong. An investigation conducted by the flight safety people determined that the cause of the accident had been equipment failure. Denis had been forced to bail out at an altitude much too low to safely eject from the airplane. His parachute had opened without a problem, but the heavily forested area into which he crashed had been unforgiving. Unable to avoid the trees, he sustained extensive injuries upon impact and the Flight Rescue Team had to be very careful not to further injure him as they lowered him from the trees.

After the engagement, Denis had changed his next of kin notification so that Francine was called first. The calmness of the spring afternoon teaching Alain and Marie was shattered when she heard the deep voice of Denis's Commanding Officer, Wing Commander Rick Melenchuk, on the other end of the phone. He tried to downplay the seriousness of the accident, but Francine could detect the concern in his voice. The accident had happened nearly eighteen hours earlier and, though he apologized for the delay in advising her, he would not provide her with any of the details over the telephone except to say that Denis was fine and in the hospital. His injuries were serious, but not life-threatening. That, in Francine's mind, could mean any number of different things. However, Wing Commander Melenchuk was resolute in his position. She would have to wait until she got to Borden to discuss the details of the accident with the Camp Surgeon. As it stood, she was still just his fiancé, not a member of the immediate family and he had already provided her with more information than he was permitted to under regulations.

Roger was immediately instructed to get the car ready for the trip to Camp Borden, while Francine frantically tried to find Linda. They finally located her two hours later in Downsview where she was doing volunteer work with a women's group and they picked her up on the way. Denis, of course was not her natural son, but a mother could not love a son more than she loved Denis. She fainted when first told the news and had to be helped to the limousine. She regained her composure a few minutes later, but, like Francine, sobbed all the way to the camp.

Travelling the final couple of miles to the camp, Francine couldn't help but notice the sudden stark contrast between the previous disorder and expansiveness of rural Ontario and the rows of trees that lined both sides of the road signalling their entry into the outskirts of the camp. It seemed to imply a world of order and regularity. The appearance of aircraft and tank displays led them to conclude that they must be very close to the entrance and suddenly in front of them a Military Police shack appeared, straddling the centre of the road. Roger identified them. They were expected and after a moment's pause were directed to follow a Military Police vehicle. They stopped only for a few moments after departing to permit a group of marching soldiers to cross the road and, ten minutes after arriving at the front gate, the limousine pulled up in front of the hospital.

Francine and Linda were escorted into the hospital by a miliary policeman. He must have radioed ahead because a man dressed in white with a stethoscope around his neck was waiting from them at the entrance. He greeted them, introduced himself as Doctor Grant and explained that Denis had been in surgery for five hours and the surgeons had been lucky to save his arm. He quickly added that, "He would never pilot an aircraft again." He had broken both his legs and had been hung up in the trees for nearly two hours waiting for the Flight Rescue Team. He went on to explain the details of the accident and the surgery as they walked toward Denis's room. Eventually, he continued, they did manage to get him back to the camp, but his right arm had been badly mangled and the delay had only made the situation worse. With physiotherapy, Denis could only hope to regain fifty percent range of motion. His days as a pilot were effectively over.

The surgeon took great care to explain Denis's condition and once he had answered their questions, he led them into Denis's room. Doctor Grant pushed open the door and held it on the inside for them to enter. Linda and Francine gasped and covered their mouths with their hands when they saw him.

Denis was the only patient in the room and he lay in the bed, flat on his back, with several tubes draining fluid out of his arm. There were two bags of clear liquid hanging on a metal rack over his head and tubes leading from them into the back of his left hand. At the point where the tubes entered his hand were patches of white tape and they were stained lightly with blood. His face was covered with scratches and his lips were cut and swollen. His eyes were like little slits cut into his severely swollen face. Both of his legs were in casts and they were held up off the bed with ropes hooked into pulleys affixed to a post at the foot of the bed. A nurse was sitting on the side of the bed holding a glass from which he sipped water through a straw. She put it on the side table and left with Doctor Grant as Francine and Linda entered.

"You didn't have to go to all this trouble just to get me up here to visit you," Francine smiled at him as she leaned over and kissed his bruised and cut forehead.

Denis attempted to smile back at her, but she could tell it hurt because of his grimace and his swollen lips. "Am I still handsome?" he whispered.

"You're the handsomest man in the entire world, sweetheart, and I'll love you even if you look this ugly for the rest of your life."

Denis tried to laugh, but it hurt too much. Linda moved to the other side of the bed, leaned over and kissed her stepson on the forehead. "You've got us all worried you know," she said. Her eyes were red and her once flawless mascara had run down her cheeks.

"You look worse than I do," he whispered to her. She immediately left the side of his bed and looked at herself in the mirror over the sink. She gasped at the sight of her face and then proceeded to rub frantically with her hand to erase the mascara streaks.

"Do you hurt?" Francine asked, turning her attention back to Denis.

"Only when I laugh," he whispered again his voice scratchy and then tried to draw a smile with his finger on his face.

"Doctor Grant told us that you're going to be okay. I told him that you just did this because you have cold feet and don't want to marry me. But you're not going to get out of being my husband that easy," she said as she leaned forward and kissed him again.

"I love you," he managed.

"I love you, too, and I want you to get better as soon as you can."

Denis was still very weak and the doctor, realizing this, came back to the room and informed the ladies that they should end their visit and let his patient get some rest. They reluctantly agreed to leave, but not before promising Denis that they would be just outside his room.

Francine and Linda left Denis's room and were shown back to Grant's office. An officer from Denis's squadron was already there and he volunteered to provide whatever assistance they needed. Francine made it very clear that she had no intention of returning to Toronto until Denis had improved significantly. Linda opened her purse, found her wallet and passed a handful of bills to Francine. Flight Lieutenant Walker indicated very quickly that he had arranged a room for her in the Officer's Mess and she could stay there as long as she wished. There would be no charge for whatever she wished to have. Linda indicated that she would be returning to Toronto to let the family know first hand about Denis's condition and she insisted that Francine take the money in case Denis might need something. Francine reluctantly agreed. They then said a tearful goodbye, with Linda promising to send Roger back with clothes and other personal items for her.

An hour later Francine had been shown her accommodations and given the opportunity to freshen up. Fortunately, the hospital was just a short walk from the Officer's Mess and with the Doctor's concurrence, she returned to Denis's room where she remained nearly night and day for the seven weeks of his recuperation. On the day of his release, Doctor Grant finally explained to him that because of the irreparable damage done to his arm he would never be capable of piloting an aircraft again. It was a scene that Francine would never forget.

The news devastated Denis. The Air Force and flying meant everything to him. The doctor attempted to explain that there were many other jobs he could perform and still remain in the services, but Denis would have no part of it. He was a pilot.

He never said a word on the trip down to Toronto despite everything Francine did to get him to talk. When he arrived at the mansion he immediately went to his room and locked the door. In the following weeks he refused to see anybody and barely touched the trays of food that were left outside his door. Finally, he stopped picking up the trays all together and only after his father threatened to call a locksmith did he promise to unlock the door.

Denis's behaviour troubled Francine. She loved him with all her heart. The accident may have scarred his perfect body, but in no way did it diminish her love for her husband. In many ways she loved him more. She longed to tell him that, to help him, to love him, but he shut her out.

Francine was anxious to see Denis after Romeo had informed her that the door was unlocked. She gently knocked on the door and when he didn't answer she knocked again. When there was still no response she slowly pushed it open and walked in. Denis was awake and sitting up in bed. She hardly recognized him. He had lost at least twenty pounds and his face was covered with a two-week-old scraggly beard. He stared straight ahead and seemed oblivious to her presence.

"How are you feeling today?" she asked in a gentle voice, walking to his bedside. Denis never responded. "Honey, please talk to me," she pleaded sitting on his bed. Denis continued to stare straight ahead. Francine could hold it in no longer. She buried her face in her hands and began to cry. She loved him with all her heart and he had returned her love. But now it was one-sided and Denis wouldn't respond. Her crying didn't change his resolve. She got up from the side of the bed and walked around to the foot board until she was looking him straight in the face.

"Denis," she spoke, "I love you and I will always love you. Why are you doing this? Why are you shutting me out? You are the man I want to marry and the man I love. I didn't agree to marry you because of what's on the outside. I love you because of what's on the inside."

She waited for a reaction. She got none.

"I'm pregnant. I'm pregnant with our baby."

Denis's eyes twitched. Francine had not received that much acknowledgement before.

"We're going to have a baby, sweetheart. It's your baby and she'll need a daddy. I'll need a husband too. Please, please talk to me. I know what you're going through. My God, please talk to me."

Francine fell face forward onto the bed. Her face was between his feet. She sobbed. As she lay there sobbing she felt a hand on the back of her head and she lifted it and looked at Denis. He looked at her for the first time since leaving the hospital. She smiled at him as she wiped the tears from her cheeks.

"What do you mean 'she'?" he said as he returned her smile.

Those were the first words he had spoken in weeks. "Welcome back, sweetheart, welcome back," Francine said as she climbed up the bed to kiss him.

Nine ～

FRANCINE WOKE. THE cramp was so severe that it had awakened her. She looked at the alarm clock on the table beside her bed. It was 3:17 a.m. She hoped her labour pains weren't starting. She stared sleepily at the clock and watched the hands move from minute to minute, black mark to black mark. Each minute seemed like an hour. Shortly after 3:23 a.m. she felt another pain and by now she was fully awake. "Owwwww," she yelled, holding her stomach with one hand and clutching the bedclothes with the other. She looked at Denis and admired his ability to sleep despite the noise she was making. She guessed it was because of his military training and having to sleep wherever and whenever he got the opportunity. He was curled in a fetal position and sleeping like a baby. She reached across the bed and shook him. He only grunted. He had worked late at the car dealership last evening and had not arrived home until nearly 11:00 p.m. He had been working long hours ever since he started there two months earlier. Francine shook him again. "Honey," she whispered, in a raspy voice.

"Yes, what is it?" Denis answered, in a sleep-filled voice. He pulled the sheets up and nearly covered his head despite the fact that the room was quite warm. At least Francine felt warm.

"I think our baby wants to get out."

"That's nice, dear," he said as his voice trailed off.

In any other situation, she might have found his inattentiveness amusing. She reached for the lamp, turned it on, threw back the bed covers and carefully rolled herself out of bed. She felt as if she was big enough to give birth to a whale. She paused for a moment, looked down at her sleeping husband and smiled. The light and her movement about the room finally roused him and he turned to look at her empty side of the bed. From the bathroom she heard him call out.

"Do you need any help in there?" he asked. Francine had to go to the bathroom at least a half a dozen times a night and most times he offered assistance. This time, however, it didn't sound like his heart was in it.

"No, but maybe you should call Roger," she answered.

Denis paused for a moment before reacting. "I'm not sure that helping my wife to the bathroom is in his job description."

"Do you think he would mind driving me to the hospital then?" Francine said as she came out of the bathroom dressed in her robe and holding her bag.

Denis paused for a second like he had been instantly frozen. Suddenly he came to life, threw back the covers and jumped out of bed, all in one fluid motion. "Do you mean that our baby is coming?" he shouted as he ran to her.

"No, I just decided to wake you up because I thought you were getting too much sleep," she said, sarcastically.

"Oh my God, oh my God," he said. He stared at her for a second, opened the bedroom door and yelled to Roger. "Roger, get the car. It's time!" Roger lived in rooms over the garage, so no matter how loudly Denis yelled, he would not have heard him. Satisfied with the attempt nonetheless, he raced to the closet to find his clothes. As he was dressing, Marie appeared at the door, rubbing her eyes.

"What's the matter?" she asked.

"I have to go to the hospital," Francine explained. "Would you call Roger and tell him to bring the car around, please?"

Marie instantly turned and ran to the intercom to call Roger. Seconds later, the rest of the family appeared at the bedroom doors, one at a time. Each asked what the problem was, except for Linda who knew immediately what was going on. She ran to Francine's side, took her overnight bag, threw it toward Denis, put her arm around Francine and led her downstairs.

The rest of the family followed and by the time they got to the front door, across the veranda and down the steps, Roger was just pulling up. He jumped out and ran around to open the door for

Francine, but Linda was already holding it open. She helped her in and then stepped in beside her. Denis, with Francine's bag in his hand, got in on the other side. All three doors slammed simultaneously and Roger threw the car into gear and raced down the driveway toward the hospital.

Under normal conditions, the drive would have taken twenty minutes, but they arrived twelve minutes after they left the mansion. Fortunately, traffic was very light and at 3:41 a.m. Roger stopped in front of the emergency entrance. Francine's contractions were now two minutes apart.

Denis raced from the car and returned barely fifteen seconds later pushing a wheelchair. Linda helped Francine into it and then pushed it through the entrance. Denis ran in front of them as Roger returned to the limousine and found a legal parking space.

A few feet from the nurse's station, a nurse took over from Linda and instructed her to remain and fill out the admission forms while she pushed Francine to her room. She did as she was told and ten minutes later Denis, Linda and Roger were pacing the floor of the waiting room.

At 6:21 a.m., March 16, 1948, Michel Romeo Claude Leblanc drew his first breath of life. Had he been a girl, it would have been Rolande Linda Esther. The birth had not been a particularly difficult one, and when Francine heard her son's first cry she knew that the miraculous event was something she would want to experience again. It was worth every moment of discomfort. She could hear him crying as the nurses cleaned him and she tried to raise herself in the bed to get the first glimpse of her son. She didn't have very long to wait, however, because a few minutes later the seven pound, twelve ounce baby was placed across her chest.

Francine had dreamt about giving birth and even as a little girl she had longed for this moment. She turned back the blanket and looked at her son for the first time. His skin was pink and his eyes were closed. Surprisingly, he had a lot of hair. "He looks like a little kitten," Francine said as she lovingly looked at her baby and then kissed him on the forehead. The others in the delivery room laughed.

"Your husband and your mother-in-law are outside, and if I don't let them in soon they're going to break the door down, especially your mother-in-law," Doctor Harris informed her. "Are you ready to see them?"

"Yes, I am, but could someone just wipe my face with a damp cloth before you let them in? I don't think that I have ever sweated so much in my life," she laughed.

A nurse wiped and dried her face and then with the help of a couple of nursing assistants, slid her onto a bed with wheels. She was then wheeled to a private room. A few minutes later Denis and Linda were shown in.

"I'll give you five minutes and that's all," Doctor Harris said to Linda and Denis outside Francine's room. "The new mother has worked very hard to give you a son, Mr. Leblanc, and she needs her rest." Doctor Harris lectured them knowing full well it would do little good. Linda pushed by him and rushed to her daughter-in-law's side. She peeled back the blanket a little and looked at her first grandson.

"Oh," she gasped, "he's the most beautiful baby I've ever seen."

Denis leaned forward, kissed his wife and then looked at his son for the first time. He stared for a few seconds and then touched his face. "You know something, Linda," he said, without expecting a response, "you're right. He's the most beautiful baby I've ever seen, too." He turned his stare from his son to Francine. "How are you feeling, sweetheart?"

"I'm fine," she answered, looking at her husband as he kissed her. "And if they're all as easy to have as Michel, then I'd like to have at least half a dozen more."

Francine suddenly remembered Roger. "Where's Roger?" she asked.

"The doctor wouldn't let him come in," Linda said.

"Well, can you please thank him for getting us here so fast?" Francine asked.

Denis and Linda assured her they would and the trio chatted for a few more minutes. The nurse soon appeared as promised and informed them that the baby needed to be fed and Francine needed rest, so they would have to go. They could return in a few hours and by that time Francine would be fully rested. Reluctantly, they left.

Three days later, Michel and Francine were allowed to go home. Denis took a half day's vacation leave and arrived at the hospital at 2:45 p.m. He had driven home to have lunch and then Roger drove him to the hospital. Francine had just finished dressing as he entered her room and a nurse was dressing Michel. Though concealed by an armload of balloons and a huge bouquet of flowers, Francine still recognized her husband. The enormity of the event overwhelmed Denis. It eclipsed the feelings of hopelessness created by the accident. Becoming a father made him feel like a man again. They hugged each other and then the nurse, despite Francine's objections, wheeled her and Michel to the hospital exit. Several of the hospital staff stopped them to say goodbye and congratulated them. They were both relieved to be outside, where Roger proudly held the door as Denis helped his wife and son into the limousine.

Denis held his son during the drive home and acted like the prototypical new father. He talked to Michel in baby talk, promising him that in a few weeks they would go fishing with his grandfather. Both Roger and Francine laughed at the silly things Denis promised his son. When Denis told him that they were going to play "catch" later that afternoon, Francine reached across the seat and took Michel, playfully telling Denis to "Give me my son before you turn him into as big a fool as you are." He reluctantly passed his son to Francine as they neared home.

The staff at the mansion had prepared a large "Welcome home" sign for Francine and Michel and it hung on the stone wall beside the gate. As they drove up the driveway, Maxwell, the Leblanc's gardener, stood beside a beautiful flower arrangement that spelled out "Michel" in various coloured flowers. There were still a few patches of snow, but somehow Maxwell had managed to have flowers planted for their homecoming. All of the staff were outside as they pulled up in front of the mansion and several of them rushed to hold the door open for Denis and Michel. Choruses of "Welcome home" echoed through the foyer and were quickly followed by "Thank yous" from Denis and Francine.

Michel had arrived a few weeks earlier than expected and there were still a few things that Francine wanted to get for the nursery, but Linda had taken care of everything. She was waiting at the door of the nursery anxious to unveil the room to its new owners. Entering slowly, both parents looked at each other in disbelief at the opulence of their son's bedroom. There were stuffed animals everywhere and a collection of toys that he wouldn't be able to use until he was at least six-years-old. Francine looked at Denis, realizing from whom he had inherited his silliness. Obviously, Linda had the same lofty plans for Michel as her son. He was her first grandchild and Denis's first child and there was a natural tendency to want to give him everything. But Michel was sleeping and even if he weren't, it would be several years before he could appreciate what Linda had done for him.

Each member of the staff stopped by the nursery in the course of the next half-hour to congratulate Francine and to see Michel. All of them brought little gifts and both parents thanked them sincerely for their thoughtfulness. The Leblanc family treated their domestic help like members of the family, involving them in most aspects of the Leblanc family life. There had not been a baby born to the Leblanc family since Alain, eleven years earlier, and this was an occasion to celebrate.

Monsieur Leblanc came home early to see Michel. None of the staff could ever remember him leaving work early unless someone was sick. He, too, had a gift with him, but instead of a teddy bear or some other token gift, he carried a single envelope. He walked into the nursery and everybody went quiet. When he had left home on a business trip a few days earlier he had not been a grandfather. Now, admiring his grandson from the doorway, he finally felt his life was complete. He approached Francine, who held Michel in her arms.

"*Bonjour, mon petit bébé,*" he spoke. "I see that you have the prominent Leblanc chin," he said as he gently pinched the baby's chin. The others laughed. "Unlike your grandmother, I have something that is a little more useful to you than all of this stuff," he said as he waved his arm to indicate all of the toys. "I have, for you, five thousand shares in our new company." Linda gasped. Even she was not aware that her husband was forming a new company. "The new company was listed on the Toronto Stock Exchange this morning and I am proud to say that by noon the shares had increased in price from a listing of two dollars, to two dollars and twelve cents. But," he said very seriously, "your father will have the voting rights of these shares until you are eighteen years old. You don't understand what that means, but that makes no difference." Romeo took the stock certificates and tried to fit them in the infant's hand. Realizing that he could not succeed, he pushed them up the front of his nightshirt. Everybody laughed. "And," he finished, "here's another five thousand shares for my beautiful daughter-in-law for giving me such a handsome grandson to take over Leblanc Industries from his father."

To Francine, it all sounded rather aristocratic. She was not used to such extravagant gifts and did not fully comprehend the implications of Romeo's generosity. She had never even seen a stock certificate. Examining her own and then removing the others from under Michel's shirt, she saw that they looked like money, but were much larger and much more colourful. Everybody gathered around to look at them as Romeo used the opportunity to slip away and return to his office. This was his first grandchild and he was immensely proud, but, as was his nature, he wanted to reflect on his good fortune. His wife had winced a little when he had referred to her as "grandmother", but he was long overdue in becoming a grandfather, and didn't at all mind being called "Grandpa."

Forty-five minutes later, Linda hustled everybody out of the room and told them that the new mother and baby needed their rest. Nobody argued and soon only Denis remained with mother and son. Francine's arms were tired and she stood up from the rocking chair and passed Michel to Denis. He took him after getting instructions similar to those Francine had given him in the limo. Cautiously, he sat on a padded banquette that took up one entire wall as she readied their son's bassinet. After she had finished, she glanced at the clock on her night table and saw that it was time to give Michel his first feeding. Denis returned his son to his mother as she walked to the rocking chair and then watched her breast feed. He knew then that he loved her more than he could ever love her again.

Michel was a good baby and he only woke twice the first night. By the end of the second week he was only waking up once a night. Francine fed him just before midnight and then it was usually three or four o'clock before he woke again. Denis said he would get up with his son but, unfortunately, he could not take care of the feeding.

Francine chided him that he was only using that as an excuse. However, when Denis was at home, he spent as much time as he could with his son, even though Michel spent most of the first two months of his life sleeping.

Francine and Denis made love in the third week after Michel's birth, and Francine wished that she would get pregnant again. Even though he had initiated their lovemaking, she got the impression that Denis's heart was not in it. It had been nearly three months since they had made love, and she expected their reunion would be even better than before. Before Michel was born, Denis wanted to make love every night, and they usually did. He had always made Francine feel desirable, as if she was the only woman capable of pleasing him. He was normally sweet and gentle, but tonight he had been very rough. Her breasts hurt and he had scratched her back. He was different and she wondered if her husband no longer found her attractive.

It was nearly a week before they made love again and then it was because Francine initiated it. In fact, as they had finished, she could tell that she was the only one who had climaxed. Denis seemed to have changed. It seemed like lovemaking was more of an effort to him than it was worth. Francine wondered if it was because of his work. He left the house very early in the mornings, returned very late at night and rarely saw either Francine or Michel awake. Francine was devoted to Michel, yet his father was a stranger in his life. Though she couldn't understand why, it seemed as if Denis was ignoring his son. Four months after Michel's birth, they had their first fight.

It was nearly 11:00 p.m. when Denis got home. Francine had been asleep when he had left in the morning and she had barely seen him all week. It was Friday night and he had promised her the previous week that they could go into Toronto and see a movie. She was in bed reading when he came into the bedroom. He didn't even acknowledge her, but instead went straight to the bathroom, where she heard him turn on the shower. A few minutes later the door opened and he came back into the bedroom in his pyjamas. He walked around the bed and got in without speaking. He pulled the sheets over himself and turned away from her.

Francine was amazed by his behaviour. She had been sitting up in bed reading and was surprised that he didn't at least say good night to her. She closed the book and placed it on the night table. "Honey, is there something wrong?" she asked.

"I'm just tired," he answered, "and I want to go to sleep. Would you turn off the light, please?"

Francine turned off the light and snuggled down in the bed. She curled up behind her husband and put her arm around him. "Is something the matter, dear?" she whispered. She moved her hand up to his chest. Denis reacted and turned toward her. He put his arms around her and kissed her passionately. It had been nearly two weeks since they made love and Francine could tell that Denis was ready as he pressed hard against her. She pressed back.

The foreplay was practically non-existent as they fumbled with each other's clothes in the dark room. As Denis was pulling off Francine's nightgown, they heard a cry. "It's Michel," she whispered, pulling her nightgown back on and jumping out of bed.

"God damn him," Denis said as Francine hurried out of the room. She stopped for a second at the doorway after Denis's comment, but continued on to Michel's room.

Francine could tell what the problem was as she pushed open the door that had been installed between their room and the nursery. Her son needed to be changed. The smell was terrible. She changed him quickly, put a pacifier in his mouth and then returned to bed. She got in and Denis's back was to her.

"What was it you said when I was leaving?" she asked.

"I said God damn him," Denis answered, quickly and loudly.

Francine could not believe her ears. "What?" she shouted as she sat up in bed and turned on the lamp.

Denis remained turned away from her. "Ever since that kid came into the house, it's been a madhouse. He's crying all the time and every time we try to make love, he wakes up."

"What do you mean, every time we try to make love?" Francine asked in an equally loud voice. "We haven't made love for such a long time, I'm surprised you even know how." She waited for an answer but didn't get one. "What are you trying to say?" Francine asked, shocked. "He's a baby and he wakes up to be changed and to be fed. I can't understand this. He's our son and you're sounding like, like...I don't know what you're sounding like," she said, frustrated. "You can't mean what you're saying. You're just working too hard. I'm sure your father never intended for you to work the hours that you're working."

Denis turned over and sat up in bed. He looked straight at Francine. "How the hell would you know? All you have to do is to stay home and look after the brat. You don't understand what I do and, for Christ sake, don't you ever patronize me. You have no idea of the pressure I'm under. The pressure I'm under to perform. We've tried to keep it a secret that I'm the boss's son, but it's impossible. So now everyone's taking out their miserable frustrations on me. Then I come home and the two of you pick right up where the others leave off."

Francine realized that Denis was just looking for a fight and the more she talked the more upset he became. She reached over, turned off the lamp and turned away from him. She knew that Denis had not been as romantic as he usually was for the past few weeks, but it wasn't until now that she realized the full extent of his resentment. This was her first indication that something was really wrong. She wodered if it was because he was jealous of Michel. But he had nothing to be jealous off. It was too silly even to consider. She had to convince him to take a few days off so they could go away for a little vacation and be alone. They could easily afford it. Linda would love to have Michel to herself for a few days. She would talk to Denis about it in the morning, she concluded, and wisely decided not to pursue it tonight.

Denis got up the next morning, showered, had breakfast in the library and left without even talking to her. Francine had breakfast set up on the balcony in the hopes that he would join her, but when he left without even acknowledging her she knew that their problems were serious. Michel was in her arms and Denis had not even kissed him goodbye. That was a first. Francine went back upstairs after he had left and laid Michel on the bed as she drew a bath for him. She decided to get in the tub with him. She dropped her robe and then pulled her nightgown over her head. As it dropped to the floor, she looked at herself in the full length mirror. She had been very fortunate. She didn't have any stretch marks and the bulge in her stomach had completely disappeared. Her breasts were still much larger than normal, but she knew that within a few months they would also return to normal size. She turned a little and tried to examine herself in profile. She was still a very attractive woman. Surely Denis's lack of sex drive could not be attributed to her. She walked naked to the bedroom, picked up Michel and together they got into the tub.

After lunch, Francine took Michel for a walk. She pushed the carriage quickly and used the daily walks with her son as a means of getting some exercise. There was a beautiful path that went all the way around the grounds and it took her nearly a half hour to traverse it completely. In addition to using the walks to get fresh air and exercise for both herself and Michel, it was a chance for her to think. And she had a lot to think about. The dream of the perfect marriage and the perfect life was deteriorating. She would confront Denis this evening when he came home and try and resolve their differences. It was a beautiful afternoon so she decided to walk the path a second time and formulate her plan to talk with Denis.

It was nearly 10:00 p.m. when Denis finally arrived home that evening. Francine was lying on their bed when he came into the room. "Hello, honey," she spoke as he pushed open the door. He did not respond, but instead walked into the bathroom and closed the door. Francine picked up her bookmark from the bed, placed it in the open book, closed the book and put it on the night table. She folded her arms across her chest and waited. Five minutes later Denis came out of the bathroom, dressed in his pyjamas, carrying his suit, shirt and tie over his arm. He hung his clothes in the closet and then got into bed. He lay down and turned away from Francine.

"I don't know what the problem is, Denis," Francine spoke, quietly, "but if there is something I did, then I wish you would tell me what it is." Denis did not acknowledge her. She waited for a few seconds and then spoke again. "Denis?"

"What?" Denis snapped.

"Is something wrong?" she demanded to know.

"What makes you think that there's something wrong?" he answered sarcastically. He continued to lie on his side facing away from his wife.

"Well, for starters, there was the conversation we had last evening, if you could call it a conversation. Then, you left this morning without saying goodbye to Michel, and tonight when you came into the bedroom and I spoke to you, you didn't even answer me."

"Are you keeping a record or something?"

"No, I'm not. I just would like to know what is wrong with you. Have I done something to you?"

"No, you haven't done anything. That's it. You never do anything. You're so predictable, Francine. I bet I can tell you everything you did today."

"What does that mean, I'm predictable? I live here in this house, I teach French to two children and I am the mother of a small baby. Of course I'm predictable. What do you want me to do, go in to Toronto and sell myself on the street corner or something?" Denis did not answer. She decided to take a different approach and be reasonable even if he wasn't.

"Sweetheart, I know you've been working hard and you're trying your best to earn the trust that your father has given you. But there comes a time when you've got to take a break. Nobody, especially not your father, expects you to work as hard as you're working. I was thinking this morning how nice it would be if we could get away somewhere for a few days. A long weekend, perhaps. We could leave Friday morning and come back Sunday night. Maybe we could take the train to Montreal or even go all the way to Roberval and visit with Mama and Papa. I think you'd enjoy that and I'm sure that all of our relatives in Roberval would love to see us, and especially Michel. It would be a nice restful few days. Or we could go somewhere else if you like. We could leave Michel at home and just the two of us could go away for a few days. It doesn't have to be this weekend. It could be whenever you want. How does that sound to you?"

Francine waited for a response but none came. She touched him on the shoulder and he grunted. He was asleep.

Ten ~

FRANCINE WOKE EARLY and got up to finish the details for Michel's first birthday party. Denis had not come home again last night, the second night in a row. And he hadn't bothered to call to say he wouldn't be coming home. She had asked his father if he knew where Denis was and was told that he had probably worked late and decided to stay in the city. Denis had a room at the Leblanc Hotel just for that purpose, Romeo reminded her. But Francine wondered just what "that purpose" was. Was it only a room to sleep in? Denis had lost all interest in her sexually and she began to suspect the worst. She tried not to think about it and was glad when the telephone rang. "Hello," she said as she picked up the receiver. She waited for a response and when there was none, she spoke again. "Hello, who's calling, please?"

"It's Denis. I won't be able to get home for Michel's party."

This was the first time Francine had spoken to her husband in days. "Where are you and why haven't you called?" Francine snapped at him.

"I don't want to talk about it now. Tell Michel I'm sorry I can't be there. I have a lot of work to do."

"No, I won't tell him you're sorry," Francine shouted back at him. "That would be a lie and I won't lie to my son the way you have been lying to me. I don't know why you're treating me this way, why you won't even talk to me." She paused for a second to wait for his response. "Denis, are you—" She didn't get a chance to finish. The silence indicated that Denis had hung up the telephone. Francine held the receiver to her ear a few seconds longer to make sure Denis was really gone. She couldn't understand what was happening. She slammed the receiver down and then stared at it wondering what had come over him. She turned to leave and saw Georgette, one of the downstairs maids, looking at her. Georgette quickly looked away and continued her polishing.

Michel's birthday party was almost as grandiose an affair as his parents' wedding. As before, Linda took charge of the event and nearly fifty children, varying in age, attended the celebration. Including parents and attendants, over one hundred and fifty people filled the grounds of the Leblanc mansion. It was March 16th, 1949, and in addition to her many other abilities, Linda had been able to influence the weatherman. It was a beautiful spring day. The grounds had been transformed and it looked as if a circus had come to visit. Several tents had been erected and inside each tent performances would be held throughout the day, the show times were posted outside the tents and a masterful job of scheduling had been accomplished so that a maximum of twenty-five people viewed each show. Linda had hired seven clowns and three magicians and they entertained the children and parents as they wandered the grounds and queued to see each show. The magicians pulled coins out of their ears and gave them previews of what to expect when they got inside. Each tent held something for everybody. There was something special for children and parents alike and nobody went away disappointed.

By 4:00 p.m. the shows had come to an end and all the guests gathered in the large central tent to watch Michel blow out the one big candle on his massive birthday cake. Gifts were stacked behind the table holding the cake, which Linda would let him open in due course, and then give the majority of them to one of the orphanages in the city.

At 10:20 p.m. Denis pulled into the driveway. Francine was still in the library when she heard the front door open. She listened as it closed and then heard the footsteps on the stairs. She thought that it must be Romeo. She found a book and then went upstairs to the bedroom. As she opened the door she heard the shower. She took her book and went to her side of the bed. A few minutes later the bathroom door opened and Denis entered the room. He looked at her. "Don't start anything," he said, glaring at her.

Francine looked at her husband as he spoke. She didn't know who this person was. It certainly wasn't the man she had married. The man who had been devoted to her and his son. "I'm not going to start anything, Denis. Whenever I ask you what's wrong, you start to rant and rave. You haven't seen your son for three days, and today you couldn't even manage to get home for his birthday party."

"I told you not to start anything," Denis shouted at her. "For just once, just shut up and leave me alone."

"Like you've been leaving me alone?"

Denis walked over and stood in front of her. Francine was taken aback by the hatred in his face, hatred she couldn't understand. She looked down at her book. Without warning the book went flying across the room and hit the wall. The force of Denis's slap turned her sideways and the involuntary movement of her arms had flung the book across the room. Her face burned and tears welled up in her eyes. She had never been slapped before. The left side of her face felt like it was on fire. She reached to feel it and as she did, Denis grabbed her by the upper arms and lifted her off the bed. "I told you not to start," he yelled at her with his mouth just a couple of inches from hers. Spray from his mouth hit her face. It was hot. He stared at her for a second and then threw her to the bed. Her back hit the brass headboard and it rattled. She forgot the pain in her face as the pain in her back heightened.

Suddenly, the look on Denis's face changed. He hovered over her and looked at her in a way he had never looked at her before. "You bitch," he said as he slapped her again, but this time it wasn't so hard. Francine wasn't sure, but he seemed to be getting pleasure out of what he was doing. She remained sitting up in the bed and both of her hands covered her face. Denis reached again and this time ripped the front of her nightdress, revealing her breasts. He stared at her and then bent over and forced his face into her chest. He grunted like a pig as he sucked her nipples. He was like an animal and when he lifted his head, Francine pushed him away and he fell backwards to the floor. His look changed again and he paused for a split second, then recovered, grabbed some clothes from the closet and went into the bathroom. A few minutes later he reappeared, fully dressed, and left the bedroom.

Holding her back and her face, Francine hobbled to the bathroom and looked in the mirror. Already her eye was bloodshot and the entire side of her face was red. She turned, pulled up the back of her nightdress and examined her back. There were two red streaks where she had hit the headboard's brass railing. Tears streamed down her cheeks and dropped onto the front of her torn nightdress. Her face and her back hurt, but she pride hurt so much more. This had to be a dream. A horrible nightmare. Who was the person who had just slapped her? It wasn't Denis. It wasn't her husband. But it was. She sat on the toilet seat and covered her face with her hands. "What's wrong with him?" she asked aloud.

On those few occasions when Denis came home, he fought with Francine. Every time she tried to talk with him he found some excuse to turn things around and blame her for the deterioration of their marriage. She wanted to take the honeymoon they never had, but Denis laughed at her whenever she suggested it. Francine finally resigned herself to the fact that hers would be a loveless marriage and began spending more time performing charitable work. She had become well known in the Toronto community and her marriage into the Leblanc family and association with Linda reserved her a place in elite social circles where she was recognized wherever she went. But even charitable work was tiring, and when Denis refused to consider a vacation, Francine decided that she would take a vacation by herself. After the summer was over, Francine and Michel went to Roberval for a visit.

The visit with her family and friends in Roberval was very restful and Francine enjoyed her stay tremendously. Unfortunately, Francine had neglected Michel's French language training, and he could only smile a lot when his grandparents talked to him. Even before her mother had expressed her disappointment that she couldn't talk with her grandson, Francine knew what her priority would be as soon as they returned to Toronto. Despite that inconvenience, mother and son had a wonderful visit and Francine promised that she would visit more often in future. It had been over two years since she had seen her parents, and that was unacceptable. She made a vow when she left that the next time she returned, her son would be able to understand and speak a little French. Before she left Roberval, she paid a quick visit to the convent and Mother Superior.

They were only gone for a week, but when Francine returned, she was met at the house by Denis who, surprisingly, was home at 2:15 p.m. He was standing on the veranda outside the main doors and

Francine could tell by the sullen look on his face that he wasn't in a very good mood. Michel was sleeping, so Marie took him upstairs to finish his nap. Denis never spoke, but stood outside the door with his arms folded. He stared at her as Roger unloaded the trunk and carried her bags up to her room. Francine waited until he had finished and then took a little package that her mother had given her for Linda from the limousine. As she neared the top of the steps, Denis took her arm and escorted her to the library.

"Just where the hell were you?" he yelled at her as soon as the door was closed.

Francine looked at her husband. She hadn't seen him in over a week. His face was drawn and he looked much older than she remembered. "I tried to reach you before I left, and I left a message at your office," Francine managed. "Besides, everyone else knew exactly where I had gone. I took Michel to Roberval for a week. Michel has not seen his other grandparents in over two years, you know."

"I don't care how long it's been since they've seen him. You will not take my son out of Toronto again without my permission," he shouted at her as he walked toward her menacingly. "Understand?"

"No, I don't understand. You're seldom home, and when you are Michel is asleep. He doesn't even know who you are and now you're telling me that I can't take him to see my parents without your permission?"

As Francine looked to Denis for a response, she saw a noticeable change come over him. He was not used to being talked back to. Without warning he swung his right hand up and the back of it struck Francine full in the face. She saw stars and the force of the blow drove her back against the wall. She raised her hand to protect herself as Denis approached her again.

"Don't you ever lecture me, you little bitch," Denis screamed, and spit from his mouth sprayed on her face. There was a hatred there that she recognized from before. He turned as if to leave and, instead, stopped at the door and locked it. He paused for a second and then returned to where Francine was standing against the wall, holding her right cheek.

"I have given you everything you own and I can take it away from you," he yelled as he started at her again. "My father may have thought you were an innocent young virgin, but I know the difference." Then, without warning, Denis struck her again with the back of his hand. She had tried to protect her face by covering it with her hand, but it did little good. The back of her hand stung, and, frustrated, Denis grabbed her hand, pulled it from her face and then slapped her with the palm of his other hand. The noise was like a gun shot and it echoed around the room. Francine began to sob uncontrollably as she slid down the wall to the floor. Denis reached down for her, grabbed her two forearms and lifted her to her feet. He stood looking at her as she cringed in preparation for another slap.

"I have tried to teach you how to behave, but you just won't listen," Denis spoke in a much lower voice, his speech measured. His right hand slowly left her forearm and he moved it to her breast. Francine was surprised by this sudden change. "You know what you have to do to please me, and you just won't make the effort," he spoke again in the same soft voice. Francine opened her eyes and looked at her husband and as she did, Denis reached down the front of her blouse and ripped it violently. Her body was jerked violently toward him. She was able to stop her face only an inch in front of his. Before she had a change to recover, he yanked at the blouse a second time, and this time her bra broke.

"Why are you doing this to me, Denis?" Francine sobbed. Denis never answered her. He squeezed her breast hard as he bent over and buried his face in her chest. "You're hurting me," she said, but he ignored her. He was becoming aroused and Francine could feel his erection pressing against her.

"Shut up," Denis ordered. He squeezed her breast hard and it hurt her. She tried to squirm away, but he forced her against the wall. The more she squirmed, the more he seemed to enjoy it and as she moved, he lifted his head from her chest and kissed her. His breath was hot and his stubby beard irritated her burning and bruised face. She tried to turn away, but with his left hand he held her face. Her lips hurt as he pressed hard against her. His hot breath came in short pants. Slowly, Denis moved his hand from her breast, down to her crotch. Moving his hand under her skirt, he drove his hand in hard and Francine screamed with the pain. She tried to protest and as she did, he removed his hand and slapped her again. Francine hung her head and closed her eyes.

Francine knew that the sounds from the library could be heard by somebody. She wondered if she should scream. Why hadn't somebody come to see what was the matter? There were people in the house. Denis grunted like an animal as he forced Francine down to the carpeted floor. She lay on her back with her hands to her sides, afraid to move, afraid to scream. Her blouse was ripped open and her face was bruised and bleeding. Denis stood over her, undid his belt and let his pants and underwear drop down to his ankles. He looked down at her for a few seconds and then dropped to the floor. He lifted her skirt and ripped off her flimsy panties. Francine chose not to resist. She could sense that the more she resisted, the more he enjoyed it. She made up her mind at that moment that their marriage was over. Denis Leblanc didn't exist anymore. An animal had taken his place. He leaned forward over her and forced himself inside her. She bit her lip to keep from calling out. She would not resist and she wouldn't give him the pleasure of seeing her hurt.

The rape lasted only a few minutes. She felt his liquid inside of her and she knew he was finished. Francine kept her eyes closed. She heard Denis doing up his pants. "If you ever disobey me again, I will see that you never see Michel again. Do you understand me?"

Francine did not acknowledge him. He kicked her foot with his.

"Do you understand me?" he yelled again.

Francine nodded.

"Good, now get up and get dressed, you ungrateful bitch, or the next time I'll kill you," he finished as he turned and left the library, pulling the door closed behind him.

Francine lay on the floor for a few minutes. She couldn't believe what had just happened to her. She had been raped. Her husband had raped her and he had enjoyed it. She put her hands to her bruised face, patted it gently, and decided quickly that she should get up before somebody came in and found her in this condition. She pulled her torn blouse together to cover her naked breasts and stepped out of the remaining untorn leg in her panties. She then picked up her bra and panties and pulled her skirt back down around herself. Every part of her body hurt. But the hurt she felt inside was much greater than the physical hurt. Maybe it would be an easier pain to bear if she could understand why she was being treated this way. Or, if she could understand what was wrong with Denis. What had changed him? Maybe it was something she had done. But she quickly discounted that thought. She had been a loyal and loving wife. Every time they met, he beat her, but this would be the last time. She gathered herself together and quietly walked toward the door.

Francine opened the door slowly and looked out through the crack. The only way to her room was out the library door and up the stairs. Fortunately, there wasn't anybody in the foyer. She opened the door a little wider and then pulled it all the way open and raced up the stairs. She prayed that she wouldn't meet anybody on the way to her room. She took the steps two at a time, and once she reached the top, she raced down the hall to her room. She hoped that Michel was still sleeping. She reached her bedroom door, pulled it open and stepped inside. She was alone. Nobody had seen her.

In the bathroom, Francine looked in the mirror. Her blouse was in tatters and her face was red and bruised. How would she explain this to Linda and the children? Had they heard Denis raping her? She filled the tub with water and then got in. She would never let him beat her again. She didn't care what it took. Denis Leblanc would never beat her again.

Francine lay in the tub of hot soapy water and tried to wash away the pain and the hurt. Holding a mirror in her hand, she examined her bruised face. She had done nothing to cause Denis to do this to her. He had changed and their marriage was over. She just had to figure out how to get away and take Michel with her. Denis might let her go, but he would never let Michel leave. That would be her challenge. And it was a challenge she would accept and win. Michel could not be influenced by the monster his father had become. She would not allow this to happen.

Eleven

IT HAD BEEN nearly a week since the rape incident, and Francine had not seen nor talked to Denis in that time. He had come to the mansion on a couple of occasions when she was away and taken Michel out for a few hours, but he always had him back before she returned. She didn't know why he now wanted to spend time with his son. She thought of getting a divorce the day after the rape and actually looked in the telephone book for the name of a lawyer, but then quickly rejected the idea. She convinced herself that Denis's behaviour had to be related to his father's death, or pressure from work, so she decided that she would give him another chance. She knew she shouldn't, but she had little other choice. He was a very powerful man and he knew a lot of powerful people. If she were to pursue a divorce, Denis's lawyers could undoubtedly misconstrue her intentions and she could end up losing Michel. There was no way she would ever let that happen.

Francine and Linda had become very close after Romeo's death, and they did a lot of things together. Romeo had been twenty-five years older than Linda and she was closer to Francine's age than most mothers-in-law. The two women normally tried to have lunch in the city and take in an afternoon movie at least once a week. Today's plan was to meet at *La Maison Rouge* for lunch and Roger delivered her there at exactly 12:30 p.m. The doorman opened the door to the limousine and held her hand as she stepped out.

"Good afternoon, Mrs. Leblanc," the young doorman said as she stepped onto the sidewalk.

"Good afternoon to you, too, George, and thank you very much," Francine replied. The doorman hurried to hold open the restaurant door for her and as he did she heard her name being called. She turned to greet her caller.

"Hello, Mrs. Leblanc," a very handsome and well-dressed man said as he approached her with a large bouquet of roses.

"Hello," Francine said timidly.

"I have a little gift for you," he said as he passed her the bouquet of flowers and then kissed her on the cheek.

Francine, more than a little bewildered, took the flowers. "Who are you, and why are you giving me these?" she suddenly remembered to ask.

"Let's just say that I'm a secret admirer," the man said, and he turned and walked up the street, leaving Francine standing there holding the flowers. She followed him with her eyes until he turned a corner, and then she turned to the doorman with a dazed look on her face.

"Pretty flowers for a pretty lady," the doorman blurted out as he held open the door for her. Francine went into the restaurant without speaking. She was still wondering who the man could be when the maitre d' asked if he could take the flowers for her. Before handing them to him, she pulled out the card and read it as she walked to her table, where Linda was already seated.

"You're late," Linda greeted her as she sipped her martini. The waiter held the chair for Francine and she sat down, still a little dazed.

"The funniest thing just happened to me as I was coming in here," Francine said.

"Well, hello to you, too," Linda said, sarcastically.

"I'm sorry," Francine apologized. "Hello."

Linda laughed. "Why the puzzled look?"

"Well, as I was getting out of the limo, a very handsome young man came up to me, kissed me on the cheek and gave me a dozen roses. I have no idea who he was."

"Was there a card?"

"Yes," Francine replied, "but it doesn't tell me who he is or who the flowers are from." She passed the card to Linda.

"From a secret admirer," Linda read aloud. "So, what is this, you're having an affair so soon?" Linda said impishly.

"Don't even joke about that," Francine snapped back.

"Okay, okay. Maybe it was Denis and he's trying to make up. I know he gave you a real going over in the library when you came back from Roberval."

Francine's eyes widened. She leaned in closer to Linda, looked to either side of the table to make sure no one could hear her and whispered, "You could hear him raping me?"

Linda paused for a few seconds and looked at Francine. "Rape?" she asked.

"Yes, rape. Why didn't you come in and help me?"

Linda sipped her martini. "A husband can't rape his wife," she said after she laid down her glass.

"Well, he raped me, and he'll never rape me again. I think he actually enjoyed it."

"He's been under a lot of pressure since his father died. I'm sure that in a few months he'll return to his old self," Linda explained in his defence.

The waiter placed Francine's wine in front of her. She picked up the glass and drank nearly half its contents before she spoke again. "Yes, maybe," she said.

The two women had a wonderful lunch and went to see *All About Eve* at the theatre near the restaurant. The theatre was a wonderful place to forget you troubles and Francine revelled in the ability to lay her worries aside for an hour and a half. Unfortunately, however, it ended much too soon. They continued to talk about it as they came outside and found Roger waiting for them. They had enjoyed the performance so much that they promised each other they would go see it again next week.

Francine went to bed alone again that night and she fell asleep thinking about her secret admirer. Michel had been a little restless the previous few nights and each time she was just about to fall asleep he cried out. He had stomach cramps and if they weren't better by morning, she would call Doctor Best and ask him to drop by. The combination of Michel's cries and her thoughts about the man at the entrance to La Maison Rouge disturbed her. Denis had not given her flowers since Michel was born and even though she didn't know who her secret admirer was, she appreciated getting the roses. Maybe they were from Denis, though, as Linda had suggested.

Maybe it was his way of apologizing. She closed her eyes and prayed that it was.

Michel was still complaining of stomach cramps in the morning so Francine called to find out if Doctor Best could drop by. His nurse said that he was very busy all day in his clinic, but if it was an emergency, he would certainly come. Otherwise, if she could bring Michel around at any time, he would be very happy to examine him. Francine confirmed that she would be by around 10:00 a.m. and an appointment was scheduled for that time.

They left the mansion at 9:30 and Roger dropped them off in front of the medical centre with ten minutes to spare. Francine took Michel's hand and together they walked up the stairs to Doctor Best's office. As soon as they entered the waiting room, they were shown into his office.

"Hello, Mrs. Leblanc, and hello to you too, Michel," Doctor Best greeted them as the nurse followed them into the room and closed the door behind her. She picked up Michel and lifted him up to the examination table.

"Hello, Doctor," Francine said. "I'm sorry to have to bring Michel in on such short notice, but he's been having stomach cramps for the past couple of days and he's also having trouble sleeping."

"That's quite okay. I must apologize for not being able to come out to your home, but you can see how busy I am just by looking at all the people out there in the waiting room."

"Yes, I understand, and there is no need to apologize," Francine replied as she watched the doctor take off Michel's shirt.

The nurse assisted Michel, who was a willing patient. Once his shirt was off, Dr. Best warmed his stethoscope on the palm of his hand and then placed it on Michel's back. It was still a little cold and Michel withdrew a little. The doctor moved it around from his back to his stomach.

"Has he been having regular bowel movements?" the doctor asked.

Francine paused for a second and then answered, "I'm not sure."

"How about it young man," Best asked, "have you been doing your poop?"

Michel looked at his mother and then shook his head.

After a relatively short examination, Doctor Best indicated to Francine that she could dress Michel. As she did, the doctor reached for a prescription pad and began to write. When he finished he turned to the two of them.

"I don't detect anything wrong with Michel that couldn't be cured by a good bowel movement. There's a lot of rumbling going on in that belly of yours," he laughed while moving toward Michel and gently pushing in on his stomach with his index finger. "Give this to him and then call me in a couple of days. I'm sure this will do the trick," he finished as he folded the paper and passed it to Francine.

It was nearly 10:30 a.m. when Francine and Michel finished seeing the doctor and exited the building. Roger was leaning against the limousine as they came out. He dropped his cigarette as soon as he saw them and held open the door. Just as he did, Francine heard a familiar voice. She turned, and following her out of the building was the same man she had encountered yesterday. This time he was holding a bunch of daffodils. Francine turned and stared at him as he walked toward her, passed her the flowers and kissed her on the cheek.

"For you, sweetheart," he said as he turned and walked up the street.

"A secret admirer, Mrs. Leblanc?" Roger asked in a voice loaded with innuendo.

Francine didn't answer him. She just got into the car and Roger drove them back to the mansion. She looked at the flowers on the seat beside her and remembered the scent of the man who had given them to her. He was quite handsome and she liked the way he dressed. If she saw him again she would insist on his telling her who he was before she let him get away.

By the following day, Michel's cramps had disappeared and he had returned to his usual happy self. He was into everything and had to be watched all the time. He tended to spend most of his days outside, with his nanny and various members of the mansion staff taking turns going outside with him. Today was Saturday and to everyone's surprise, especially Francine's, Denis had come home last evening. She had been in bed when he came in and took a few things from their bathroom. But he never spoke, and she guessed that he must have slept in one of the guest bedrooms. She was eating breakfast when he came into the dining room.

"Good morning, Denis," she spoke.

"I'm taking Michel for the day," Denis replied.

"You actually remember his name?" Francine asked sarcastically.

"Don't start with me this morning, Francine. I'm taking my son to the circus for the day, and I'll bring him back later." He turned and left without waiting for a response. Francine finished eating. Actually, she was glad that Denis had decided to take Michel for the day. She had planned to go downtown shopping, and she hated leaving Michel with the nanny staff all the time. And she certainly couldn't take him with her.

At 10:15 a.m. Roger drove her downtown and agreed to pick her up at 4:00 p.m. at the same place. She had a couple of charity balls to attend in the next couple of weeks and she needed some new clothes, so she had decided to use today as an opportunity to get them. Francine wandered from store to store looking at clothes and examining gowns that a few years ago she would not have even dreamed of owning. Now she didn't even look at the price. Her father-in-law's bequest had made her a very wealthy woman. Her name alone demanded respect. She was very well known in the stores she frequented, and all her bills were sent directly from the stores to Denis's accountant and paid in turn. She had a little more than twenty-five hundred dollars deposited monthly into her account and she currently had a balance of nearly twenty-five thousand dollars. She had very little need for money, and when she did she could write a cheque, of which an ample supply lay in her purse.

Roger picked her up at 4:00 p.m. as arranged and drove her to the stores to pick up her purchases. She had found everything she needed and remained in the limousine while Roger went into the stores and came out with her packages. He was his usual talkative self and they chatted during the drive back to the mansion.

Upon arriving home, Roger carried the packages to her room and Francine unpacked them. She drew a bath and then had a quiet dinner alone. She was in the library at 9:15 p.m. when she heard a car drive up. Running outside she found Michel just getting out of his father's car and he ran toward her as Denis got back into the car and drove away.

"Did you have fun today, honey?" Francis asked as she kneeled down and Michel ran into her arms, wrapping his arms around her neck. Francine could feel him nodding his head in response as he pressed his cheek against hers. She stood up and took him with her. Together, they went into the mansion and up the stairs to his bedroom. Francine could barely keep him awake as she quickly bathed and dressed him and put him into bed. He was asleep as she pulled the sheets up to his chin and kissed him on the cheek.

Francine sat on the edge of her son's bed for a few minutes and just stared at him. Everything in her life seemed so perfect. She had the most wonderful son in the world, and she couldn't have lived in a more beautiful home. She dressed in the best clothes money could buy and ate the finest foods. Her friends and acquaintances were from some of the wealthiest families in Toronto and her charity work was very rewarding. But one thing was missing. A husband. A husband who loved her. A husband who came home every evening after work. A husband who she had dinner with, talked with, laughed with and then took her to bed and made love. She couldn't remember the last time she made love. She didn't want to cry, but tears came anyway. She forced herself to stop thinking about Denis and dried her eyes with the silk belt of her robe. Sufficiently recovered, she bent over and kissed Michel again before leaving his room.

The next day was Sunday, and Francine was scheduled to spend the afternoon at the Children's Hospital. Linda had asked her to accompany her while they distributed gifts to the less fortunate children. Francine enjoyed this part of her charity work the most, and as she distributed the pyjamas, toys and other gifts, she got a great deal of pleasure out of the children's smiles. This time, though, as she got off the elevator on the children's ward, she suddenly saw something that she had not expected.

"Francine?" A tall, very good looking young man spoke to her as she got out of the elevator and started up the hall. She turned to greet the voice. She looked at him for a few seconds and then spoke.

"Richard?"

"Yes, it is. My God, you're the last person in the world I expected to see here."

"Well, I certainly didn't expect to see you," Francine said, smiling as she walked toward him and threw her arms around his neck. He reciprocated, and as she kissed his cheek, he kissed hers. Francine withdrew first and then, still holding Richard's arms, she looked up into his face.

"What are you doing here?" she asked.

"Francine?" Linda broke in before Richard could answer.

"Oh, Linda, I'm sorry," Francine said as she turned and walked toward her, holding Richard's arm.

"Richard Berthiaume, this is my mother-in-law, Linda Leblanc. Linda, Richard. Richard, Linda." Each held out their hands. "Richard and I were friends back in Roberval. I haven't seen him for, oh, I'd say, nearly five years."

"Yes, it has been that long at least," Richard offered.

"I'm very pleased to meet you," Linda said, "but if you'll excuse me, I have a lot of kids waiting for these things," she said, pointing to the clothes on the stretcher beside her.

She turned to leave and Francine spoke. "Linda, I'm sure you can deliver these things without me. I'd like to get reacquainted with Richard. I'm going downstairs to the cafeteria. Could you come down after you're finished?"

"Yes, of course. You two go ahead," Linda said.

"You've got time, I hope?" Francine quickly remembered to ask Richard.

Richard looked at his watch. "Yes, I've got a few minutes, but only a few, so let's hurry," he said as he took her arm, turned toward the elevator and pushed the button.

Richard had been Francine's first love. In fact, he had been her first kiss. She could still remember that kiss. She was fifteen and it was the first time she had ever been kissed by a boy. It was the most horrible thing that she had ever experienced up to that point in her life. They had been going steady for nearly a month before Richard had tried to kiss her. Her girlfriends had offered her suggestions and advice about kissing, and she had practised on the back of her hand, but she was not prepared for Richard's kiss. It probably was his first kiss, too, and it just didn't work out well. But after that first one was out of the way, each and every kiss after that was a kiss to remember.

Richard and Francine drank their coffee and reminisced. Richard only had twenty minutes before he had to leave for a meeting. He had come to Toronto a couple of years earlier and gotten a job working for a hospital supply company. He had an appointment with the administrator of the hospital at 2:30 and couldn't miss it. But in the few precious minutes they had, he wanted to know everything she had done since leaving Roberval. She tried to tell him as much as she could and was disappointed when Richard looked at his watch and said that he really had to leave. He stood up, bent over the table and kissed her full on the lips. Francine had almost forgotten what a kiss felt like, and was grateful she was still sitting because she felt herself go weak.

"Richard," she said, as she stood up to say goodbye, "let's not be strangers. I'd love to see you again. Can we have lunch or something sometime? I really would like to catch up on everything that's been happening in your life."

"I'd like that very much, France," Richard agreed. She had not been referred to as "France", a nickname that her friends in Roberval had given her, in a very long time. Richard pulled a little appointment book out of his pocket. He thumbed through the pages. "I could meet you on Tuesday, if that's okay with you?" he asked.

"Yes, that would be fine, but could we make it somewhere a little more comfortable than here?" she laughed.

"Well, okay," he joked. "Do you have somewhere in mind?"

"How about *La Maison Rouge*?"

"Wow! You like going all the way," he laughed. "*La Maison Rouge* on Tuesday at noon," he said as he wrote in his appointment book. He then took a step toward her, kissed her on the cheek and Francine watched him walk away.

For the remainder of the day and all day Monday, Francine could think about nothing else but her lunch meeting with Richard. She felt a little guilty thinking about it so much, but she couldn't help it. When 11:15 a.m. Tuesday finally arrived and she was sitting in the back of the limousine en route to the restaurant, she was pleased that it would be just a matter of minutes before she saw her friend again.

Roger dropped her off and she asked him to pick her up again at 3:00 p.m. Upon entering the restaurant she was told that Richard had not yet arrived, but the maître d' had their reservation, and he greeted her and showed her to their table. She had called on Monday just to make sure that it had been made and was advised that Richard had indeed made it. After being seated she took her compact from her purse and checked to make sure her nose wasn't shiny. It was, so she dabbed it with the powder puff. As she finished, a waiter appeared and asked if she would like to order something while she waited. She said she would wait for her friend and then instantly changed her mind and ordered a dry white wine. She finished the glass and looked at her watch. It was 12:20 p.m.

Francine ordered a second glass of wine, wondering were Richard could be. It was half finished before Richard finally showed up. The moment she saw him, her concern dissipated.

"I'm terribly sorry to have stood you up like this," he apologized as he suddenly appeared from behind her. "The cab I was in hit another one and the two of them are still arguing. I walked the last half dozen blocks here," he finished as he sat down and wiped his brow with the handkerchief from his breast pocket.

"I was a little mad at first, but now I'm not," Francine smiled. "You've got a good excuse. Every time you were late in Roberval, you had a good excuse, too."

Richard laughed and raised his hand for the waiter. He ordered a gin and tonic and rejoined the conversation. "So tell me all about yourself. I know you married into one of the richest families in Toronto. Do you have any children? How did a poor Catholic girl from Roberval manage all of that?"

"Please, one question at a time," Francine interrupted him. "I'll answer one of your questions and then you answer one of mine."

"Deal," Richard replied as the waiter delivered his drink. He picked it up and motioned for Francine to pick hers up as well. "To old friends," Richard toasted as the two glasses clinked.

"To old new friends," Francine responded as she brought her glass to her lips.

Francine and Richard had a very enjoyable lunch. They chatted and laughed. Richard had never married, he had no plans to get married, and didn't even have a girlfriend. His work took up most of his time and for the present that gave him all the pleasure he needed. He admitted that this was his first non-working lunch in months.

At the mention of working so much, Francine admitted to him that her husband worked a lot and was rarely at home.

His next question caught her by surprise. "Are you happy, Francine?"

Francine paused for a moment. "Would you order me another glass of wine?" she asked.

Richard held up his hand and a few seconds later, Francine's glass was refilled. "That's a very difficult question, Richard. I have every-thing that a woman could want, but one thing."

"What's that?"

Francine paused again to sip her wine. She looked at her friend. "I can't tell you all my secrets, now can I?" she teased. The wine was start-ing to make her a little giggly.

"No, I suppose not," Richard answered. "Besides, if you tell me everything today, we won't have an excuse to get together again."

Francine suddenly remembered that she had asked Roger to pick her up. She glanced at her watch; it was 3:12. "*Merde!* I told my chauf-feur to meet me outside at three. I must go," she said as she gathered her belongings. As she made a motion to get up, Richard stood up as well. "I really would like us to do this again sometime," Francine said as she readied to leave. The maître d' appeared as Francine stood up. She instructed him to put the meal on her account and to add twenty percent for himself and the waiter. Richard tried to protest, but Francine insisted that she pay, considering that she had invited him to lunch. Next time, he could pay. Richard agreed and Francine passed him a card with her telephone number printed on it.

Richard escorted her to the limousine where Roger stood talking to another chauffeur. He reacted as soon as he spotted Francine and held the door for her. Richard took her arm and led her to the vehicle. They paused for a second, he kissed her cheek and Francine then stepped back into her world.

Francine slept fitfully that night. Every time she closed her eyes she saw Richard's smiling face. For the next few days, every time she heard the telephone ring she hoped it was him, calling to invite her to lunch again. She suffered through a week, and as the memory of their lunch was fading, she was summoned by Joseph to a telephone call. The fol-lowing day at 2:00 p.m. she met Richard again.

The second lunch was more enjoyable than the first. The two of them seemed much more comfortable together. After they had eaten, they went to see the previous year's academy award winning movie, *All The King's Men*. Richard held her hand in the darkened theatre and her heart raced. She felt like a teenager again, as if with a magic wand the last few years had been erased. She wanted to watch the movie, but found it very hard to concentrate. She removed her hand from his and wiped her nose with a tissue. She then folded her hands in her lap.

They chatted briefly after the movie, and Richard said he would love to meet her husband and son. Francine informed him that Denis was very busy and she doubted very much if she could convince him to have lunch with them. She would love, however, to have him meet Michel. He agreed and the following Sunday they went to the city park for a picnic. Michel took to Richard immediately, and Francine watched guiltily as Richard and Michel ran around on the grass, kicking a ball.

Francine and Richard met regularly for lunch over the next couple of weeks. She loved being with him. She felt alive again when they were together. At the same time, she couldn't help feeling grateful that, in Richard, Michel could have a positive influence, something that was missing in his life. At the end of the second week, she confided in him about the state of her marriage, and Richard seemed genuinely concerned, offering suggestions to help her make things better. But Francine was convinced that nothing could be done to improve relations between herself and Denis unless Denis himself was willing to change. And as each day passed, she grew closer to Richard.

Despite all of her best attempts to smooth things over with Denis, nothing seemed to help. Every time she spoke to him, he either chose to ignore her or gave her a surly response. They were living separate lives. They attended many social functions as husband and wife, but they went in different cars and rarely spoke to each other once they met there. Francine also attended numerous events alone, making the excuse that Denis was too busy to join her. She suspected that people were gossiping, but nothing was ever said to her directly.

Meanwhile, Francine and Richard's friendship blossomed. During the first week of November, over lunch, Richard asked her if she would go to an evening event with him. His firm was throwing a party to celebrate the president's thirty-fifth wedding anniversary and there was nobody else he wanted to go with.

Francine wanted to go, but she felt uneasy accepting the invitation. Her instinct was to refuse. What if she saw people she knew there? What if the press covered the party? At this point she was so tired of not feeling anything, of hiding her true feelings, that she didn't want to lie anymore. She threw caution to the wind and told Richard she would be honoured to join him.

Roger had committed to driving Linda to another event that same evening, so Francine went by taxi. She was glad enough not to have to lie to Linda. She wore one of her favourite dresses, a black haute couture and Richard was waiting for her at the entrance to the Grand Hotel where the event was being held. He heart leapt as she caught sight of him in his tuxedo.

The wine was wonderful, the music and food were fantastic and Francine couldn't remember the last time she had such a wonderful time. Richard was a terrible dancer and she still wasn't much better, but they overcame that. They danced only the waltzes, and the more wine Francine drank, the closer she got to Richard.

Francine realized what was happening. She had fallen out of love with her husband and was now falling in love with Richard. She knew what she was doing was wrong, but she was tired of being unloved. She wanted and needed to be held and to be made love to. As Richard held her and they danced, the desire grew. The dance floor was very dimly lit and Francine looked around to see if she could recognize anybody. She didn't. Richard's arm was around her and she moved her head from his shoulder until she was looking straight at him. Slowly she moved toward his lips. They met and kissed.

When Francine woke up it was nearly 2:00 a.m., and Richard's arm was across her bare chest. She smiled and looked at him. It had been one of the best nights of her life, and not because it had been such a long time since she made love, but because Richard had been truly concerned about her pleasure too. She tried to remember how she had let this happen, but quickly decided she didn't care. Slowly she got out of bed, dressed and called a taxi. She had to get home.

Twelve ∼

ESTHER GAGNON WAS well known among the elite of Toronto. She and Francine saw each other at least once a week at one charity function or another. They had met the previous day at a fund-raiser for hungry children, and she had suggested to Francine that they should have lunch together the next day. At 1:00 p.m. they met in the dining room of The Leblanc.

The two ladies gossiped over lunch and when dessert arrived, Esther revealed the purpose of her lunch invitation. "Francine, honey, I know this is none of my business, but we are friends and I would like to help you through this if I could."

Francine looked at Esther with a blank stare. She laid her dessert fork down and spoke. "Esther, whatever in the world are you talking about?"

"The problem you are having with Denis."

The revelation caught Francine off guard. She decided not to try to hide anything. "How did you know that Denis and I are having problems?"

"Pierre told me. You know he tells me everything."

"How would Pierre know?" Francine asked.

"Because Pierre is Denis's lawyer. You know that."

"Of course I know that, but what does Pierre have to do with our problems?"

Now Esther appeared confused, surprised that Francine had not guessed her intentions. She looked at Francine for a moment before speaking again. "Francine dear, you need a lawyer if you're going to get a divorce."

"I don't intend to get a divorce," Francine snapped.

d say too much.

"Yes, we should," Francine said, reaching across the table and grasping Esther's wrist. "Did Denis see Pierre about getting a divorce?"

Esther looked down at her plate.

"Esther?" Francine demanded in a louder than normal voice, attracting the attention of some of the other diners.

Esther lifted her head and took a quick glance around their table before looking back at Francine. Francine has no idea of the watchful eyes of the people around them, nor the ramifications of a public scene, she thought to herself. "Yes, Pierre told me that Denis had spoken to him about a divorce. He told me a little while ago, but he didn't say when it was that he had spoken to Denis."

Francine stared straight ahead. She couldn't believe what she was hearing. She couldn't speak.

"I'm sorry, Francine, but I thought you knew about it. The reason I wanted to have lunch with you today was to try and help you through this. I had no idea that you didn't know, I swear."

Francine still couldn't speak. The waiter came to take away the half-eaten dessert and when he asked if she were finished, Esther answered for her. She continued to stare straight ahead.

"Francine, dear," Esther said, "it isn't the end of the world, you know. It's not like you will be left penniless. Romeo took care of you and Michel, so you certainly won't need for anything. And besides, if he wants the divorce, give it to him and then take half of every bloody thing he owns."

"He's going to take my son from me," Francine suddenly blurted out, and tears began running down her cheeks.

Esther looked around nervously to see if anyone was watching them. No one was.

"Now don't be silly. He's not going to take Michel away from you. You're a wonderful mother and everybody who knows you knows that."

Francine picked up the napkin from the table and dabbed her eyes. "You're my friend, Esther, right?"

"Yes, of course I am," Esther answered, somewhat surprised at Francine's question.

"Good. Then I would like you to do something for me."

"Sure, if I can."

"I want you to find out from Pierre everything he knows about this. Please!"

"Well," Esther said, "you certainly don't mince words when you want something, do you?"

"Esther, I know what it is I'm asking for and I know what you've got to do to get it. But I have to know what Denis is up to. I don't care about the divorce or the money or anything else. I did something very silly a little while ago, and if Denis finds out about it, there's a good possibility that he will twist it around so that he gets custody of Michel. I have to know, Esther. I just have to," Francine pleaded as she looked at her friend.

"I don't know, Francine. You're asking me to betray my husband's trust. If he ever found out that I told you what I've told you so far, he'll be furious. My God, the Ontario Law Society would probably disbar him or something. You're asking an awful lot, Francine."

"I know, but what you tell me, I'll never tell another living soul. You know that. But if I lose my son I might as well be dead."

"What was it that you did, that you're so afraid of Denis finding out?" Esther asked.

Francine took a deep breath. "I trust you Esther, so I'm going to tell you." She paused for a few seconds before revealing her secret. "I slept with another man."

"My God, who was it?" Esther asked. She never dreamed that her innocent little friend had such a secret.

"That's not important. What is important is that I did it, and if Denis finds out, you know what he can do with it. I know he's been sleeping with other women. I actually went to his suite here once to see him. He wasn't there and I talked them into letting me in. His closet is filled with women's clothes. But it's expected that married men should have mistresses isn't it? But married women aren't allowed the same privileges. So if this comes out, you know what

I'll be branded as.

Esther didn't respond. She was torn between the trust she owed her husband and her friendship with Francine.

"Listen, Esther, when Denis and I were first married I thought he was the most wonderful person in the world. I thought it was a dream come true, that I had found the most perfect man in the whole world. Then I got pregnant and we had Michel. Our marriage was great at first, but then something happened to him. He beat me and the last time we had sex he raped me in the library. Remember you asked me about the bruising on my face and I told you it was because I fell downstairs?"

Esther nodded her head.

"Well, it wasn't from a fall. Denis beat me. Linda heard it, but she didn't do anything. If it's brought up in court, I'm sure she won't testify for me. Denis is her stepson, for God's sake. I need your help."

Esther lifted her head and looked at Francine. This was one of the most difficult decisions she had ever faced. If Pierre ever found out, it could mean the end of their marriage. But Francine was her friend.

"Okay, I'll do it for you. I'll ask him everything he knows about the case. He's not handling it, you know. Pierre is not a divorce lawyer. I'll have to be careful not to make him suspicious. He knows you and I are good friends." Esther suddenly smiled. "We're having people over for dinner this evening, and Pierre will probably have one too many cognac, and then he won't remember telling me anything. Let's meet here again tomorrow for lunch. No," she quickly corrected herself, "let's meet somewhere different, where we're not known. How about if you get your chauffeur to drop you off downtown around noon, at city hall, and we'll walk around until we find some place?"

"Okay Esther. I don't know how I'll ever repay you, but I will. I promise you I will."

The two women finished lunch and said goodbye, promising to meet again the following day. Francine was overwhelmed by Esther's news, but grateful for help,and decided to do a little window shopping before she went home. She needed some time to think. She couldn't decide whether she was mad at Denis for trying to get a divorce, or happy that she would soon be free of him. She would have to get a lawyer. Francine didn't know very much about divorce, but she couldn't think of anything that would give Denis grounds to divorce her. There could be no way that he found out about Richard, could there?

Francine wandered around the stores for another little while and then hailed a cab and went home. She played outside with Michel for an hour before they went swimming. After putting him to bed at 8:00 p.m., she had dinner with Linda. Francine's mind was preoccupied as they talked about the days activities and Linda knew it, but she never gave any indication of what the problem was. When Linda asked, Francine just shrugged off the question and said that she was tired.

Francine didn't sleep well that night and woke up several times. After waking up for the third time, she turned on her light and read a little in the hopes that she would fall asleep again. She didn't and at 7:10 a.m. she got up. When Linda got up an hour later she asked her if she wanted to go downtown, but Francine said she was having lunch with a friend. The minutes dragged by like hours until it was finally time to leave. Linda would need Roger all day, so Francine had booked a cab for 11:00. It arrived as Francine was sitting outside on the veranda telling Michel to be a good boy while she was away.

Francine spent a few minutes standing in front of city hall before Esther finally arrived, apologizing profusely for having been delayed by a telephone call just as she was leaving home. Francine told her it didn't matter, and a few minutes later they were sitting in a small inconspicuous restaurant around the corner from city hall. Just after their wine was delivered, Francine blurted out, "I can't wait any longer, tell me what you found out from Pierre."

Esther looked around the restaurant and then looked at Francine. "I don't have good news," she said reluctantly.

"What is it?" Francine asked, the concern in her voice evident.

"I was able to find out from Pierre, and for God's sake don't ever let anybody know where you heard this from, that they have pictures of you with other men," Esther said almost apologetically.

"What other men?" Francine asked, knowing of only one.

"They have pictures of you getting flowers from a man and being kissed on the cheek at several locations throughout the city. On one of them, Michel is with you."

"Oh, my God!" Francine said, and all colour drained from her face. She suddenly realized who the man was who had been giving her flowers. He was somebody obviously arranged by Denis.

"They also have pictures of you with a man in the park and Michel is with you."

Francine covered her mouth to muffle a gasp.

"That's not the worst," Esther said, interrupting Francine's thoughts. Francine looked at her without speaking.

"They have pictures of you in bed with another man," Esther continued, unable to look at her friend.

A feeling of despair swept over Francine. Denis had won before she even knew that the fight had started. She couldn't believe that he would sink as low as he had, but she should have known better. She had nobody to blame but herself. The flowers and the man kissing her in the street could easily be explained, but there was no excuse for what she had done with Richard.

"That son of a bitch!" she suddenly said out loud. "He was in on it from the beginning."

"Who?" Esther asked.

"The man I slept with," Francine replied. "He was obviously paid by Denis, and I fell for it." Francine stared into her wine. "I actually thought that he felt the same way about me as I felt about him. I can't believe he would do this. I trusted him."

Esther felt for her friend, but there was little she could do to console her. "It may not be as bad as you think," she said. "You're going to have to get yourself a lawyer and fight this."

Francine considered the comment for a few seconds before answering. "The funny thing about it is, I don't want to fight it. Nothing would make me happier than to be divorced from Denis, but he may have the ammunition he needs to get custody of Michel. He'll try and paint a picture of me as a tramp who jumps into bed with every man I come into contact with. And he'll have the pictures to prove it." Francine stopped talking. She picked up her wine glass and drained its contents in one gulp. "I'm sorry, Esther," she said as she laid her glass down and picked up her purse. "I'm just not in the mood for lunch. I just want to be alone for a while and think this through." She stood up and turned to leave. Esther didn't try to stop her.

For the next couple of hours Francine wandered aimlessly through the downtown streets of Toronto. She stood in front of store windows that normally dazzled her, but she never saw through them, nor saw her reflection in them. She could not remember ever feeling more alone, and the more she thought about it, the more she came to the realization that it would get a lot worse before it got better. She had nobody to turn to. She couldn't talk with Linda. As soon as she found out about the pictures she would side with Denis. Francine stopped at a pedestrian crosswalk and waited for the light to change. As she crossed the street, she noticed a sign in front of her. Simpson and Harris - Barristers. She walked into the building and a few minutes later was shown into the office of Norman Simpson.

Mr. Simpson was talking on the telephone as she was shown into his office by a poorly dressed, overweight woman who spoke with a foreign accent. He spoke a few seconds longer and then hung up, obviously happy that he had a client, because, judging by the meagre furnishings in his office, he didn't appear to be overly successful. Francine had a sudden urge to turn and run. If first impressions could be trusted, she could certainly afford much better than Norman Simpson. But before she could get up, he was reaching out his hand in greeting.

"This is Mrs. Leblanc," the fat woman said, and then turned and left.

"Please have a seat, Mrs. Leblanc," he said after he had held her hand briefly. "I'm Norm Simpson. Is there something I can do for you?"

Although the urge to leave was still there, Francine was able to muster enough courage to speak. "Yes, Mr. Simpson, I think I need a lawyer to handle my divorce."

Despite his outward appearance, Mr. Simpson was a kind, gentle man. He assured Francine that he would do everything in his power to assist her. Once he found out who she was and who her husband was, his enthusiasm grew exponentially. He appeared as if he hadn't had much to smile about in a long time, but with the appearance of Francine Leblanc, his practice could get the boost it so desperately needed. He asked a few questions, had her sign an agreement for his firm to represent her and advised her that until the divorce was filed by her husband, there was little he could do. He advised her to go home and wait. As soon as she was contacted by her husband's lawyer, she should advise him immediately. Then he could prepare a strategy. Francine left his office feeling a little better.

Francine didn't have long to wait. The following morning the divorce papers were delivered to her by official courier. She had no idea what all of the legal terminology meant, but a quick telephone call was made and an hour later she was sitting in Mr. Simpson's office. He looked at the papers and shook his head. "It doesn't look good," he said. That was not what Francine wanted to hear.

"I'm not worried about the divorce, and I don't care about a financial settlement, Mr. Simpson. All I care about is getting this over with and taking my son and leaving here. I don't need his money, nor anything else from him."

"Good," Simpson managed.

"But I want my son and I don't care what it takes. I will not give up custody of my son."

"That may not be as easy to arrange," Simpson said. "He is suing for divorce on the grounds of infidelity and he is suing for custody of your son on the grounds that you are an unfit mother. Is there any truth to this?"

Tears welled up in Francine's eyes as the reality of the situation began to set in. Mr. Simpson passed her his handkerchief. She took it and dabbed her eyes.

"I'm sorry to have to ask these questions, Mrs. Leblanc, but it's better that I find out from you here than in court."

"Yes, I understand," Francine said. She looked up at her lawyer's face. "I slept with another man a few days ago and apparently my husband arranged it. I know you'll find that hard to believe, and so did I when I found out, but he set me up. He also had a man give me flowers and kiss me at different locations around the city. My son was with me on one occasion in the park and I was with a man I thought was my friend. But, I know that my husband put him up to it, to get pictures to use against me."

Simpson furiously made notes. "Does he have pictures of you sleeping with this other man?"

"Yes," Francine replied.

The lawyer continued to make notes. Finally, he laid down his pen. "Your husband is a very powerful man and his lawyers are from one of the best firms in the city. I have to be honest with you, Mrs. Leblanc. This could go either way, but if I were a betting man, I wouldn't bet on our chances of winning. He could end up getting custody of your son."

His last statement was like a knife through Francine's heart. The lawyer continued to speak, but Francine didn't hear anything. All she could think of was the possibility that she could lose her son. The thought was unbearable. She closed her eyes. There was no way Denis would get her son.

"I'm sorry, but I have to leave right now," she said as she stood up.

Simpson tried to protest but to no avail. He hurried out from behind his desk and helped with her coat, all the while trying to convince her to stay. His chance at success was rapidly slipping away, and there was nothing he could do about it. But all Francine wanted was to get out of there. The words he could end up getting custody of your son repeated over and over in her head. She promised Mr. Simpson that she would come back after she got a breath of fresh air, but she knew she would never meet with Norman Simpson again. Francine left the office aware of what she had to do: Lawyers couldn't help her. The police couldn't help her. She would have to help herself if she had any hope of retaining custody of Michel.

Thirteen ∽

FRANCINE WAS AT her wits end. She was about to lose her son to a man who had beaten and raped her. A man she once loved and who had given her a son. A man who would now take him away from her, and she was powerless to do anything about it. She wondered what else he could have concocted to take Michel away. She knew about the pictures of the man who gave her flowers, her time in the park with Richard and their one night together. How much more did she not know? She shuddered when she thought about it. Francine left the lawyer's office and walked in no particular direction. She heard a clock striking somewhere. It was 5:00 p.m. She had to get home to Michel. And then she considered the worst.

Francine turned and walked into the incoming traffic. Tires squealed and horns honked in protest. Fortunately for her, she wasn't hit. She found a vacant cab stopped in the maze of traffic. Pulling open the door, she stepped in.

"What the hell is wrong with you, lady?" the cabby snapped at her. "Get the hell out of my cab. I'm on a call," he said as he reached behind him to lift up on the door handle and open her door.

Francine reached into her purse and came out with fifty dollars. "Just drive," she said, and the cabby pulled the door closed with the same hand. For fifty dollars, he could forget how crazy this lady was.

Forty minutes later the cab stopped outside the gate to the mansion. Francine instructed the cabby that she would walk the rest of the way. She got out, walked to the telephone and waited for someone to let her in. The cabby waited for a few seconds, and when he saw Francine pick up the telephone, he put the car in gear and drove away. He had a week's wages for a tip. Seconds later,

Joseph pushed the release button on the gate and Francine walked through.

Francine weighed her options as she walked through the tree-shrouded arcade leading up to the mansion. She remembered the first time she had come up this driveway. Would this be her last? Her lawyer had said it all: "It doesn't look good." She was a good mother and had been a good wife, but that didn't seem to matter. She was about to become proof that there were two kinds of law in Canada: one for the rich and powerful, and one for people like her. Law and justice were about to become distant cousins. It just didn't seem right. Francine tried to be optimistic, but as she walked up the driveway to the mansion, there was only one thing on her mind—Michel. If Denis came and took him it would all be over. Suddenly, she was overcome by the thought that at this very moment he could be doing just that. Panicking, she started to run and then had to stop and remove her high heeled shoes. When she got within sight of the mansion, her heart began to beat faster. Denis's car was parked out front.

It was still several hundred yards in front of her. Just as she spotted it, the door to the mansion opened and Denis came out carrying Michel. Francine's worst fears had become a reality. All strength left her legs and she fell to the grassy lawn that she had tried to run across as a short cut. She tried to call out, but her voice wouldn't come. All she could do was watch as Denis walked down the steps to his car and opened the driver's door. Francine buried her hands in her face and cried. Maybe if she got up and stood in the driveway and prevented the car from leaving, she could still stop Denis from taking Michel. She got up and, as she did, she could hear the car engine starting. She watched as it pulled away from the house and she ran toward the driveway. Looking back at the house, she saw that her fears had been unfounded.

Michel stood on the steps of the mansion. She could see him smiling and waving goodbye to his father. "Thank you, Holy Mother," Francine said aloud as she tried to act as if everything was okay. She brushed the grass off her skirt and wiped her eyes with the backs of her hands. As Denis's car took the sharp bend in the circular drive-way and approached her, she continued to look straight ahead to the house. The car came around to her left and disappeared behind the trees a few seconds later.

Francine ran the last few hundred feet and as soon as Michel spotted her, he began running toward her as well. When they met, Francine swept him off his feet, holding him tightly to her chest. As she swung him around, the little boy laughed.

"More, Mommy, more Mommy," he begged after Francine had stopped. Francine held his two hands and swung him around, but quickly grew woozy and had to stop. Michel pleaded for her to continue.

"Mommy is tired, sweetheart," Francine said as the little boy held her hands and tried to jump off the ground. "Can we just go for a little walk?" Michel instantly agreed and let go of one of Francine's hands. Holding onto the other, he moved to her side and dragged her in the direction of the trees.

As they walked along, Michel asked many questions. "Why is the grass so soft, Mommy? Why are the trees so high? Will I ever be able to fly like the birds?" Francine patiently answered all of his questions and every ten or fifteen minutes she would stop, kneel down and squeeze him. "I love you, Michel," she would say each time.

"I love you too, Mommy," Michel would answer.

The two of them walked for nearly an hour. During that time, despite all of Michel's interruptions Francine came to a decision about what she had to do. There was nobody in Toronto she could turn to. Especially once the pictures of her and Richard were made public. If there was anything she was sure of, it was that Denis would use the pictures to turn everybody against her. No explanation could counter pictures of her in bed with another man. And she couldn't imagine what else he might have. My God, she thought, it could be anything. Francine had only one option. An option that meant she would have to give up everything. And Michel would have to give up everything, too. That was the hardest part of all.

Michel would never want for anything if he stayed with his father. He would someday assume control of Leblanc Industries, just like his father had from Romeo. But would he turn out to be a cruel man like his father? Would he become a ruthless profiteer whose only desire was to make money? Francine was not willing to take that chance. She wanted her son to grow up to be a man who cared about people and who was not preoccupied with making money. His father would teach him the latter. He would mould him in his own image. Francine would not have enough influence to be able to change him. She had to remove him from his father's influence.

Francine put Michel to bed a little later than usual. She was so happy that he was still there when she returned home, she spent more time playing with him than she normally did. The scare that afternoon made her realize how empty her life would be without him. Michel was falling asleep in the bathtub as she tried to wash the day's dirt off him and as she sat him up and pulled on his pyjama top, he fell forward, asleep. Francine covered her son and kissed him good night. "Tomorrow, we will start our new life together, just you and me," she whispered.

Francine knew what she had to do and spent the rest of the evening preparing for it. She reflected on what she had been planning to do with her life before she had come to work for Romeo Leblanc. The only good thing to result from her coming to Toronto was Michel. She remembered what she was going to do with her life before she had come to work for Romeo Leblanc. Now the time had come to leave the bad behind, to take what was good with her, and to make a better life.

She didn't want anyone to know what she was doing so she only packed enough clothes to fit into a little bag. It was the same bag she took with her every time she took him into the city. She was able to stuff the bag with two complete changes of clothing for both herself and Michel. She dared not take another bag because somebody would be sure to ask questions if they saw her leaving the house with a suitcase. She looked at the mass of dresses and expensive clothing in her closet and knew that she would have to leave them all behind. Where she was going, she didn't need designer dresses. There were certain things though, that she had to take. She went to her closet and took out the cup that Linda had given Michel and the company shares given to them both by Romeo.

It was 7:30 a.m. when the alarm went off beside her bed. In spite of everything that was on her mind, she had slept surprisingly well. Francine showered and dressed in a loose, comfortable dress. Michel's clothes were already laid out on the end of his bed, and after she had finished dressing, she went to his room. He was still asleep and Francine gently shook him awake. Michel was not a morning person, but after a few tickles and kisses, he awoke and they chatted as Francine dressed him.

They had a good breakfast and as they were finishing, Francine rang Roger and asked if he could come around and drive them into the city. He said he would, and while they were waiting, Francine dressed Michel in his warmest coat and his warmest boots. She finished dressing herself and just as she was pulling on her coat, Linda came down the stairs.

"Where are you guys off to this early in the morning?" Linda asked.

"We're going to town to do some shopping. Michel is growing out of his clothes as fast as I can buy them," Francine replied.

"Why don't you wait until I get dressed and have breakfast and I'll go with you?" Linda asked.

Francine was not expecting that. She paused for a second before answering. "I'm meeting an old friend from Roberval and we thought we would take Michel shopping and catch up on all the news from home at the same time. She doesn't speak very good English and—"

Linda didn't let her finish. "That's okay. I just thought you might like a little company to handle the monster here," she said as she took a few steps toward him and pinched his cheek. The three of them laughed.

"Thanks," Francine said, and then kissed her mother-in-law on the cheek.

"What was that for?" Linda asked, surprised at this show of affection.

"Because you're such a nice person, and I'm going to miss you more than anybody," Francine answered before realizing what she had said.

"I promise that I'll be home when you get back," Linda replied looking at Francine strangely. "I'll miss you, Mommy," Francine quickly said in a childish voice, trying to make light of her comment. She flushed a little, wondering how she could have been so stupid. Linda was fooled, and pushed her playfully toward the door. That was a close one, Francine thought to herself.

Francine finished picking up their things and walked toward the door. Joseph was in the foyer and he held the door for them. Francine wanted to kiss Joseph goodbye, but she resisted. "Thank you, Joseph, and we'll see you this evening. We plan to make a day of it, so don't expect us until after six," she lied. Joseph smiled his usual smile and nodded his usual nod.

Francine and Michel climbed into the back seat of the limousine as Roger held the door open. Once they were seated, he slammed the door and got into the driver's seat. "Where to, Ma'am?" he asked into the little microphone.

Francine pushed a button on the armrest. "To the train station, please. I need to purchase a ticket," she lied for the third time today. Before this was over, she knew she would lie a lot more.

"Going away for a few days, are you?" Roger spoke again.

"Yes, to see my parents," Francine said, wishing the conversation would end.

Francine needed Roger if her plan was going to work. When she didn't show up at the mansion later, he would be asked where she had been driven and if she gave him any indication of where she would be going. The lie that she was going to Roberval might give her a little time. She had to cover her tracks or Denis would quickly locate her. With Roger's unwitting support, she might just escape.

As they sped toward the station, Francine suddenly remembered that she didn't have any luggage with her, and Roger would discover that before they got there. "I'm just buying a ticket today," she informed Roger as soon as she realized it. "We're going the day after tomorrow."

Roger looked in the rearview mirror and nodded his understanding. Then he spoke again. "Would you like me to wait for you and drop you off somewhere else?" he then thought to ask.

Francine wasn't expecting that question. She reached to adjust Michel's coat collar while she thought of a response. "No, that's fine. I promised Michel that he could look at the trains for a little while. We'll take a cab later."

As soon as she spoke his name and the word trains, Michel responded.

"Trains, Mommy?" he asked as he looked at her.

"Yes, sweetheart, just like Mommy said, we can go see the trains."

Michel rocked back and forth on the seat in anticipation.

Her lies must have been believable enough because she didn't get any further questions from Roger. Neither of them spoke to each other for the remainder of the trip, except to say their goodbyes once he dropped them off.

It was surprisingly warm for a mid-November morning, and Francine wished that they had dressed in lighter clothes. But they would probably need the warmer clothes later, so they would just have to be uncomfortable for a little while. Francine went into the train station and walked up to the ticket counter. "A ticket for two on the next train to Roberval, please," she requested to the uniformed man behind the glass wicket. The agent thumbed through a thick book, found what he wanted and retrieved a blank ticket from another pile. He began writing.

"Name?" he asked, coldly.

"Francine Leblanc and Michel Leblanc," Francine answered.

"Age of child?"

"Three in March."

The agent continued to write. As he finished, he spoke again. "That will be seventeen dollars and it will be leaving at eleven-twenty from Ramp Two."

Francine found twenty dollars in her purse and slid it under the glass to the man. He slid out the ticket. "Keep the change," she said as the man took three dollars out of his cash register.

The agent looked at her and suddenly became very pleasant. "Thank you, Ma'am, and may you have a very pleasant trip."

"Thank you, too, and would you mind if I asked a question?" Francine replied.

"No, of course not." She had given him nearly a day's wages. She could have asked him for practically anything.

"My son would like to wear your hat for just a moment. Would you mind?"

The agent couldn't come out from behind the glass quickly enough, and plopped his hat on Michel's unsuspecting head. Francine toyed with the man just long enough to leave a lasting impression. It was important that he remember that they had purchased a ticket to Roberval. She thanked him graciously and then, with Michel by the hand, she walked toward Ramp Two. When she was out of sight of the agent, she found a garbage can, threw the ticket in it, and left the train station.

Francine looked at her watch. It was 9:20 a.m. The bank didn't open until 10:00. She needed a cab to get there, but decided that she should walk away from the train station before she hailed one. When Denis and his cronies discovered that she hadn't gone to Roberval, they would question everyone who could possibly have seen her at the station. The only person she wanted to remember her was the ticket agent. She didn't want to have anybody remember her leaving the station so she tried to be as inconspicuous as possible. She waited until she was several blocks from the station and then hailed a cab.

The cab took her within a block of the bank and dropped her off at a little cafe. She provided only a minimal tip. She didn't want him to remember her. She ordered a coffee and Michel had a glass of orange juice. He wanted ice cream, but Francine knew that a waitress would remember serving a mother and her son ice cream at 10:00 in the morning. They finished their drinks and then walked to the bank. The last time she had been at the bank was with Linda, and with the assistance of the manager, she had opened up accounts for herself and Michel. Every month, approximately twenty-five hundred dollars was deposited into their accounts in accordance with Romeo's will.

Francine nervously walked up the steps to the bank. The steps had high risers so she picked up Michel and carried him to the top. With Michel by her side, she walked into the bank and up to the teller. She laid her purse on the counter and took out a cheque. She had cheques that she could use to draw funds out of an account she shared with Denis to purchase items for herself and Michel. An alert supervisor recognized her instantly and replaced the teller.

"Good morning, Mrs. Leblanc," she smiled at Francine. "How may we help you today?"

"Good morning," Francine smiled back as she lifted a fidgeting Michel up and sat him on the counter beside her. "I'd like to make a withdrawal. It will be Denis's birthday in a couple of days and I want to get him something special. I would like to have two thousand dollars," she finished as she passed the cheque to her.

"That will not be a problem," the supervisor said as she took the cheque, stamped the back of it and then proceeded to count out twenty, one-hundred-dollar bills. Francine watched her and after she had finished, she recounted them and asked for an envelope. Once she had it, she carefully folded the bills, put them in the envelope and put everything into her purse.

"Will there be anything else today, Mrs. Leblanc?" the woman asked.

Francine looked up at the woman's name tag for the first time. "Thank you, Miss Summers, yes there is. Do you think I could speak with the manager for a few minutes?"

Miss Summers face grew dark with concern. The Leblanc accounts were the largest accounts in the bank. "Have we done anything to upset you?" she asked curtly, her defensiveness obvious.

"No, of course not. I would just like to talk with him for a few minutes."

Miss Summers waved her hand for the teller to take her place back at her wicket. "Yes, by all means. Please follow me and I'll bring you to Mr. Corbett's office."

Francine gathered up her belongings, picked up Michel and followed Miss Summers to the manager's office.

Mr. Corbett must have seen them coming because he was waiting at his door for them.

"Good morning, Mrs. Leblanc," he beamed at her. "Marjorie," he spoke to Miss Summers, "take Master Leblanc and entertain him until Mrs. Leblanc has completed her business." Marjorie took Michel's hand and he willingly followed her. When they had gone, Mr. Corbett extended his arm to invite Francine into his office. Once inside, he closed the door and held the chair for her as she sat down.

"Well, Mrs. Leblanc, how may I help you?" he asked.

"Mr. Corbett, I would like to purchase a gift for my husband. It is a very expensive item and I don't have enough money in my account to pay for it. I took a little from our joint account, but I don't want to use our money to pay for it," she explained, emphasizing the "our." "I would like to use my own. Am I making sense?" Francine asked, trying to appear naive.

"Yes, I understand perfectly, Mrs. Leblanc."

"Good," Francine said. "I believe I have slightly more than fifteen thousand dollars in my account, but I would like to have twenty thousand dollars, please." It was only a few months earlier that she had invested a large part of her account balance on a long-term investment. If only she had known, she thought.

The bank manager never gave it a second thought. "That is very easy to arrange, Mrs. Leblanc. We will simply debit your account as the payments from your trust arrive. Are you sure twenty thousand is enough?"

"Yes, it is. I took two thousand out of our joint account to cover a few incidental expenses and I think that it should be enough."

"You're sure now, Mrs. Leblanc?" the manager asked, knowing that this would be the most secure line of credit he would ever extend.

Francine never dreamed it would be this easy. "Well, there may be a few more things I could get for him at the same time. There was a slightly more expensive one that I thought he would like, but, as I told you, I don't have the funds in my account at the present time. Maybe if we increased it to twenty-five thousand, then I would have more than enough," Francine added.

"Not a problem," the bank manager replied as he filled out a withdrawal slip. "I don't think that anything more than this is necessary," he said passing the withdrawal slip to Francine for her signature. "A bank draft will be fine?" he asked as he stood up.

Francine had not anticipated this. "No, no," she stammered for a few seconds trying to come up with a reason why the draft was not acceptable. "I have to purchase several products at different locations, and I'm sure that neither one of them will be able to cash such a large bank draft," she lied. She clasped her hands and squeezed them as punishment for not having foreseen this possibility.

"Yes, I understand, but we can easily make out drafts to each company or we can give you the cash," he quickly volunteered.

"I would prefer the cash. The gift is a special-order gift. The man I am purchasing it from will insist on cash," Francine explained. Mr. Corbett hesitated a few seconds and Francine wondered to herself if he would refuse to give her such a large sum in cash. She anticipated the worst. She decided to play her trump card. "I appreciate your concern and I am going to inform my husband how very happy I am with your service and how helpful you, personally, have been." Francine knew that it was just what Mr. Corbett wanted to hear. He smiled broadly.

"Don't give it a second thought, Mrs. Leblanc. I will have your cash before you know it. I just want you to be careful with such a large amount of money."

"But you are not to breathe a word of this to my husband," Francine warned, batting her eyelashes. "This is a surprise."

"Mum's the word," the manager said as he stood up and walked to the door. "Marjorie," he called. She appeared almost instantly. "Please get these funds for Mrs. Leblanc and put them in an envelope for her." Marjorie left immediately to fill the order.

So, I don't suppose you want to let me in on what it is you're buying for your husband?" Mr Corbett asked, smiling.

"I'm afraid not, Mr. Corbett. My husband is a very influential man and he has people everywhere. It's not that I don't trust you, but I want this to be a secret. He found out last year what his present was before I could give it to him, and I am making doubly sure that this year that doesn't happen. However, I will be giving it to him at a party tomorrow night, and you're welcome to come to the mansion."

The manager couldn't believe his ears. "Oh, that would be wonderful, Mrs. Leblanc," Mr. Corbett said, barely able to contain his joy.

"And bring Mrs. Corbett as well," Francine added. "There is a Mrs. Corbett, I assume?"

"Yes, yes, and she won't be able to sleep tonight after I tell her. No doubt she'll buy a dress that will cost me a month's salary, too," he laughed. This would be something his wife would talk about for months. She might even get her picture in the society pages.

Francine smiled. "It will be starting around eight o'clock. I'll have Joseph contact you if there are any changes." As she finished, Marjorie appeared at the door.

"Here is what you requested, Mr. Corbett," Marjorie said as she handed him a large, heavy, sealed envelope. Mr. Corbett took it and passed it to Francine.

"I assume it's all here," she said.

Both bankers suddenly realized what they had done and tried to apologize for being so presumptuous. Francine dismissed their apologies. "I trust you both, and Mr. Corbett, we'll see you and Mrs. Corbett tomorrow evening." She turned to Marjorie. "And if I could have my son, we'll get on with spending a little of this money."

Marjorie reacted instantly. As Mr. Corbett and Francine chatted about the party, Marjorie returned with Michel. Together, they were escorted to the door and Francine left with twenty-seven thousand dollars more in her purse than when she had come in.

Francine felt uncomfortable carrying so much money and as she was leaving she turned to Mr. Corbett who was still standing at the door. "Would you mind if I used your powder room before I left?" she asked. Once again, Michel was led away and Francine was taken to the executive bathroom. A few minutes later, she left the bank with the money distributed throughout her body. A little was kept in her purse for the immediate purchases she had to make.

Francine was pleased with herself. It had been a lot easier than she had expected. She knew however, that the rest of her plan wouldn't be so easy. By this time tomorrow, Denis would be looking for them. He would mobilize an army of police officers and private detectives who would search every nook and cranny in Toronto for a woman and a young boy. She would have to do something about that, and as she left the bank, she went in search of a men's store.

Francine made her purchases and then made her way to The Leblanc. The desk manager recognized her immediately, and gave her their best room. Surprisingly, he didn't ask any questions and in order to be sure that he didn't discuss it further, Francine asked that he not tell her husband that she was in the hotel. She wanted it to be a surprise. By the time that Denis finally discovered that she had been there, she would be long gone. He smiled his understanding. The bellhop helped her with her parcels and escorted them to their suite.

An hour later, Francine Leblanc was Walter George. She was dressed like a man and she looked like a man. Fortunately it was winter, and the large clothes she was wearing covered her feminine physique. She had to be careful not to let anybody hear Michel referring to her as Mommy, though. She had purchased a large bag which would serve as a suitcase, and in it she put her own clothes and the bag containing their other clothing. As long as she didn't encounter anybody who knew her, especially when they were leaving, everything would be okay. She didn't expect that anybody would recognize her once she had changed, however.

It was well after noon by the time the transformation had been made and Michel was impatient for lunch. Francine took him from the hotel through the back door and, carrying the large bag, she hailed a cab. She gave him instructions to take them to the bus station, where they arrived twenty-five minutes later. At the bus station she bought them both lunch and then a ticket to Montreal. The next bus left at 2:20 p.m. Fifteen minutes before the bus was due to leave, Francine found a telephone and called Joseph. She told him that they had a lot more to do before they would be finished shopping and so would take a room at The Leblanc for the night. She further informed him that they would be home tomorrow afternoon and would call for Roger when they were ready. Five minutes later they boarded the bus and Francine knew that she would never talk with Roger again. She would have to call her parents, too, but that could wait until tomorrow.

Fourteen ~

FRANCINE AND MICHEL spent their first night away from home in Montreal. After they got off the bus Francine had hailed a cab and asked to be taken to the train station. Twenty minutes later the driver delivered them to their destination, helped her with their few belongings and then drove off. Francine and Michel sat on a bench for ten minutes and then, acting as if they had just arrived by train, Francine hailed another taxi and asked to be driven to the nearest reasonably priced hotel. She tried to act as normal a traveller as she could so as not to draw attention to herself. She knew that by this time Denis would have started tracking them down, and she couldn't be too careful. She gave the driver a modest tip and then checked into the hotel.

She and Michel had a wonderful for dinner from room-service and after they had eaten they went for a long walk. It was nearly eight o'clock when they got back to the hotel, and, after a bath, Michel went to bed. Francine tried to answer Michel's questions about where they were going by saying they were on a wonderful adventure together and over the next few days they would be seeing all kinds of exciting things. He seemed content with her answers. Like every other young boy, he was only interested in toy and nice things to eat and as long as the trip had those things, he would be happy. He hadn't asked about his father so far, but he rarely did when they were home either. Francine had decided that she would say Denis was at work if Michel asked. That was always the answer she gave him on those other rare occasions when he inquired about his father.

Francine knew that she was bringing her son to a place that was very different from what he was used to. She was taking him away from his inheritance, away from his father, away from a life of luxury into one of the most isolated regions in Canada, but it was as much for his benefit as it was for hers. She had gone over the decision in her mind a hundred times before. Right now, however, before she did anything else, she had to call her parents.

She called from her room and asked that the charges be put on her bill. She wondered if there was a way that Denis could trace her from the call she was making but she didn't know enough about the system to make a decision. Even if he could, she would be long gone from the hotel before he found out. It was a chance she had to take. She couldn't just disappear for a couple of years without telling her mother. In retrospect, she realized that she should have called earlier, but it was too late now to second guess herself.

Her parents still didn't have a telephone, so she called Jean Gauthier who ran the local store near her parents' home, and she asked him if he would contact her mother and tell her that she would be calling back in an hour. She had made a similar request before.

It was nearly 9:30 p.m. when Francine called again, and after a brief hello from Jean, her mother was on the line.

"How are you. Is everything okay with Michel?" her mother asked.

"Good, everything is good," Francine replied. "I just wanted to talk with you and see how things are."

"That's good," her mother responded, still with obvious concern in her voice.

"Mama, Denis and I are having a few problems."

She could hear her mother's stifled gasp at the other end of the line.

"Michel and I have to go away for a while. I don't want you and Papa to worry about us."

"Francine, what's happening? What's this all about?" her mother asked, the fear rising in her voice.

Francine tried to remain calm. "Denis has filed for divorce and he's going to try and take Michel away from me. I just have to get out of Toronto for a while. I won't be able to talk to you for a few months and I know that Denis will call you and try to find out where I am, so I can't tell you where I'm going."

Francine could hear her mother crying.

"Don't cry, Mama, please," Francine begged.

"Come home to us," her mother sobbed. "Your father won't let anybody take Michel away from you."

"Denis is a very powerful man and he can do things that we can't. Please understand, Mama. I have to do this."

Her mother didn't understand.

"We won't tell anybody you're here. Please, Francine, come home," her mother pleaded.

"I can't Mama," Francine said, and by this time she was crying, too. "Denis will call you and I don't want you to tell him anything. I want you to tell him that you thought that I was in Toronto. You must do this for me, Mama. You have to help me or he'll take Michel, and you and Papa will never see him again," she said, trying to make her mother understand. "We have lots of money and as soon as we get settled, I'll call and let you know where we are. Please, Mama," she finished.

There was a pause and after a few seconds her mother spoke. "Okay, Francine, but you have got to promise to let us know where you are as soon as you get settled."

"Don't worry Mama, I will, and please kiss Papa for me and tell him not to worry. I have to go now."

"Adieu, ma fille," were the last words Francine heard as she hung up the telephone. She began to cry again. She hoped she was doing the right thing.

The next morning, still dressed in men's clothes, Francine checked out of the hotel. After she paid her bill and was bid "goodbye, sir," by the desk clerk, she picked up a lobby telephone and summoned a taxi. It arrived a few minutes later and Francine asked to be taken to the bus station. At the bus station, she took another taxi to the train station. There, she purchased a one way ticket from Montreal to Roberval in the name of Walter George.

Francine took her ticket and, with Michel in hand, left the train station and walked directly to a hotel they had passed on the way there in the taxi. It was only a five-minute walk and Francine walked through the lobby and sat on a couch outside the ladies' restroom. Michel played with a couple of magazines while his mother watched and waited until she was sure the restroom was empty. After carefully checking to be sure no one was watching them, she took Michel's hand and quickly entered. Once inside, she found a stall, stood Michel on the toilet sea, and emerged a few minutes later dressed as Francine Forest. She stuffed Walter George's clothes in a garbage container outside the hotel.

Back at the train station, Francine stood in line as far away from the agent who had sold her the ticket to Roberval as she could, for fear he might recognize her. She left Michel sitting on a seat by himself, within sight, for a few minutes so that when she purchased her ticket the agent would not remember seeing a woman with a child. A few minutes later, she had a return trip ticket from Montreal to Halifax. She scheduled the return trip for a week later, but knew that she wouldn't be on it. So even if Denis was able to trace her telephone call, and reviewed all of the train ticket sales to Halifax, he would find nothing out of the ordinary. She purchased the ticket in the name of Valerie Long and because she had purchased a private cabin all she had to do was to identify the number of people. She told the agent there were three and paid for three. She hoped that anyone looking for her would not think to look for a group of three.

They boarded the train at 11:03 a.m. and it left twenty-seven minutes later. It was her plan to stay in Halifax for a couple of days and then embark on the next leg of her journey.

It was nearly 2:00 a.m. before Francine settled into her hotel in Halifax. Before leaving the train station, she had purchased a ticket for the day after tomorrow to North Sydney. She chose the name Sandra Day for those tickets, and used the same name when she checked into the hotel.

Michel had fallen asleep on the way to the hotel in the taxi, and even though they had eaten on the train she was still hungry, so she ordered a sandwich from room service and some things for Michel in case he woke early.

Francine would spend the next day in Halifax shopping. She needed at least a day to purchase those items necessary to make her story believable. Before going to bed, she made a list of everything she needed. She took all of her money, some of which had been in her bag, and some more which had been in the pockets of her jacket, and put it in one large pile and counted it. She had twenty-six thousand, nine hundred and twelve dollars, plus a few dollars in change. Francine took it all, folded it into bundles of five thousand dollars each, put all of them in separate envelopes and put the envelopes in her purse. There were four bundles of five thousand dollars each, a fifth with three thousand dollars and the remainder she would keep for herself. She finished her list of things that she had to buy the following day and then with her money safely tucked underneath her pillow, she got into bed beside Michel.

Francine awoke a little after 8:30 a.m. the next morning. Michel slept on. She couldn't remember the last time she had slept so late. It was Friday, and, after getting out of bed, she looked out the window and saw that it had snowed during the night. Her first view of Nova Scotia in the sunlight was beautiful. The sun was very bright and the snow had already started to melt. She could see the ocean from her window the steam rising from it like a boiling kettle. As she stood admiring the scene in front of her, she heard Michel waking. He saw her standing at the window, jumped out of bed and ran over to her.

Francine helped him up to the window sill so he could admire the view along with her, "That's the ocean, sweetheart," she said. It was the first time either of them had seen the ocean, and they both stood staring at it for several minutes until Michel had seen enough and informed his mother that he was hungry. Francine quickly got the cereal and milk she had ordered from room service the night before and go dressed while he was eating.

Michel got more cereal over the table than he got in his mouth, but by the time Francine had finished dressing, he was full. She cleaned him up, put on warm clothes and they left their room. Francine carried only her purse and money. Outside, two taxi cabs were parked in front of the hotel and she walked up to one and asked if he was occupied. He wasn't and quickly got out and opened the cab door for them. Once inside, the driver spoke.

"Where to Ma'am?" he asked.

"Could you please take us to the nearest bank?" she requested.

The driver paused for a second. There was a branch of the Bank of Montreal a block from the hotel. "Yes, Ma'am," he responded, and left for a branch of the Royal Bank, two miles away.

It was Francine's intention to deposit her money in increments of five thousand dollars at several banks. Word of a single deposit of the full amount she had might be the clue Denis needed to find her, so she it would be best to set up accounts at different banks. She wanted to draw as little attention to herself as possible.

Inside the bank, Francine walked to a counter under a sign for customers opening new accounts. The young lady behind the counter was very pleasant and helped her fill out the necessary forms. Francine informed her that she didn't have a street address as of yet, but that any correspondence should be sent to: General Delivery, Dark Harbour, Fortune Bay, Newfoundland.

Francine wanted the money invested for three years. She knew that by then she would be able to leave Dark Harbour and come out of hiding. Surely after three years Denis would give up searching for them. Then she could withdraw the money and it would be available for her and Michel to make a fresh start, to be free. Francine provided the teller with a specimen signature to be used for notifying the bank when and if she required the funds. She made it very clear however, that if the bank did not hear from her, they were to reinvest the money at one-year intervals each year thereafter, and this was to continue until she contacted them and told them otherwise.

It was a very unusual request, and the young lady asked to be excused so she could seek her supervisor's approval. A few minutes later she returned with her supervisor, who introduced himself as Mr. Davis. Mr. Davis explained to Francine that she could invest funds with the bank for as long as fifty years. However, if she was choosing a term of only three years, then each year thereafter she would have to either visit the bank or write them and tell them what she wanted done with her money. Accounts that had no activity after a period of nine years were considered dormant and, by law, had to be forwarded to the federal government in Ottawa where a decision on the fund's status would be made. He emphasized the fact that she could not simply deposit the money and then forget about it. He tried to make that very clear to her.

Francine had not been aware of this, but it was unimportant. She elected to sign the bank documents as Francine Matte, using her mother's maiden name. She thanked him for his explanation, but assured him that she would communicate with the bank on a regular basis. It may take her a little longer than normal because of where she would be living, but otherwise she couldn't foresee any problems. To be on the safe side, before she signed the papers, she asked that an annotation be made to her file that five years after the last deposit was made the account was to be closed, a draft prepared and made payable to her son, Michel Matte, in care of Francine Matte, and sent to his attention in Dark Harbour. Mr. Davis wrote her instructions as she issued them and informed her that this would not be a problem. Francine knew that she would have closed the accounts long before then, but, just in case something did happen, she wanted to be sure that the money would go to Michel.

A few minutes later, when everything had been signed and stamped, she was given her bank book and a paper showing that her investment would mature in November, 1954. Francine suddenly thought of the stock certificates. It would be best, she thought, if she left them in the bank. The manager happily provided her with a safety deposit box, and she instructed him to deduct the annual fee from her account as required. She asked to make a further annotation to her file that when the account was closed and the balance sent to Dark Harbour, the contents of the safety deposit box were to be sent as well. They agreed, and thanked her for her business. Francine thanked them and asked if they could call her a taxi. A few minutes later, she was en route to a second bank.

The next cab took her back to the Bank of Montreal. She walked up to the counter and went through the same procedure as before. She was given the same information about the nine-year rule when she asked to have her one year deposit extended a further year. She chose a one-year deposit because, even though she had nearly four thousand dollars in cash, some emergency might arise where she would need more money. It would be more accessible if it wasn't locked in. She explained that if they didn't hear from her by 1960, they were to close the account and forward the money to the Royal Bank and upon producing her bankbook from the Royal Bank, the manager copied the account number.

Nothing was going to happen, she knew, but by arranging things the way she had, money from the other banks would be transferred to the Royal Bank and the new activity in her Royal Bank account would mean that her account with them would remain open until 1969. She did the same thing at the other three banks, staggering the dates when the balances were to be transferred so she would be sure of continued activity in her Royal Bank account for decades. If anything did happen to her, Michel would get it all shortly after his twenty-first birthday. It was a terribly complicated way of doing things, but at least it would keep her money out of the government's hands. And if she found that Denis was still looking for her after the initial three years, she could extend her stay in Dark Harbour an additional year without worrying about her money. In the meantime, if she needed money, she could simply write any of the banks and have them send some to her.

It was lunchtime by the time Francine had completed all of her banking. They found a little restaurant beside the last bank and Michel ate his french fries as if they were the last ones he would ever see. He had a hearty appetite, and usually ate whatever was put in front of him. After they had finished, she asked the waitress if she would call a taxi for them and left a twenty-five cent tip.

Francine told the taxi driver that they were just visiting and she wished to be taken to a store where she could purchase a typewriter. If it were possible, she would like a place where she could also purchase clothes for both herself and her son. The driver drove them about a mile, to the Barrington Street area of Halifax. He informed her that she could purchase whatever she needed on this street. There were numerous stores. As soon as they stepped out of the taxi, Michel raced for the closest one, a toy store. Nearly half an hour later, Francine had to practically drag him outside so they could finish the remainder of their shopping.

During the next several hours, Francine tried to purchase everything she thought they would need for the next couple of years. In one store she bought a typewriter and a large supply of typing paper, informing the clerk that she would return later and pick it up. It was her intention to tell the people of Dark Harbour that she was a writer so she could write her book based on first-hand experiences she had decided to live there for a few years to learn what life was like. She also planned to tell them that her husband had died in a plane crash a few years earlier.

After Francine had bought her typewriter and supplies, she concentrated on finding clothes for herself and Michel based on what she thought his size would be in a few years. At each store she visited she bought the same clothes, only a size larger than those·purchased from the previous store. Finally at 3:45 p.m. she had everything she needed, including two large steamer trunks to hold everything. At the final store, a taxi was called for her and each of her earlier purchases were picked up before the driver drove them back to the hotel.

She gave the driver a two-dollar tip and asked if he would bring her things to their room. He agreed, and Francine left the cab and quickly walked through the lobby to ensure nobody would see her. The driver had to make several trips, but eventually it was all in her room. While Michel jumped up and down on the packages strewn across the floor, Francine tried to unwrap them and pack them in the steamer trunks.

By 5:15 p.m. Francine had finished unwrapping and packing all of their belongings. Michel had tired himself out and fallen asleep a half hour earlier. Francine sat on the edge of the bed beside him and decided to see how much money she had left. She took all of her money out of her purse and counted it. At the last bank, she had opened an account for three thousand dollars. That meant that she had a total of twenty-three thousand dollars in various banks and three thousand, three hundred and seventy-two dollars in cash. She had spent over five hundred dollars today, she quickly figured out as she folded the remainder of her money. She put fifteen hundred dollars in each trunk and locked them. The balance she put in her purse. Satisfied now that she was ready to move on, she ordered supper.

Francine fell asleep that night wondering if Denis had been able to find out where she had gone. She had taken every precaution, and prayed that she had not overlooked anything. She decided not to worry about it anymore. She was with her son, and he was with her. She looked at his sleeping form and leaned over and kissed him on the forehead. Someday, she hoped to explain everything to him.

Fifteen

NOVEMBER 10TH, 1951, was a very cold morning. Light snow had fallen again the previous evening and the streets were icy. At 6:10 a.m., Francine and Michel boarded the train to North Sydney. It was scheduled to depart at 6:35 and the cab driver had delivered them with plenty of time to spare. Their steamer trunks were too large to fit in the trunk of the taxi and their ends stuck out as the driver navigated the icy streets. He had taken great pains to secure them, but Francine kept looking behind to ensure that neither of them fell out. At any minute, she expected one or both of them to fall and their contents to be strewn over the streets of Halifax. To his credit, however, the driver had secured them properly and when they arrived at the train station and the baggage handler had at last placed them in the baggage car, Francine breathed a sigh of relief. After they were safely stowed, she checked to make sure she still had the keys in her purse.

It was a twelve-hour trip to North Sydney and like before, Francine had requested and paid for a private compartment. She didn't want to take any chance on a passenger recognizing her this far from Toronto. She had not seen a newspaper since they left, and she expected that Denis would have her picture pasted on every major newspaper in Canada by now. She dared not risk reading a newspaper and inadvertently drawing attention to herself. In her compartment, she would be isolated from the other passengers and thus reduce the chance of being recognized.

She felt ill this morning. She had vomited twice shortly after she got up and she had terrible cramps. She suddenly remembered that she had missed her period last month and it would soon be that time again. Shortly after the train got underway, however, the pain dissipated and she dismissed her previous discomfort as the change of weather and food, coupled with the tremendous stress she was under. Michel was fine, and that was what was most important.

The train took them through some of the most beautiful parts of Nova Scotia. Michel kneeled on the seat opposite Francine and together they watched the Nova Scotian countryside pass by. The scenery reminded her a little of Roberval, but Roberval wasn't quite as idyllic as the scenes that flew by the train window as the two of them strained to see everything they could. The train made a lot of stops at little stations where there didn't appear to be any buildings other than the train station, but people still got on and off. There were trees everywhere and it seemed as if the communities had been cut out of the forests. Every whitewashed, clapboarded house was the same. Each had a little picket fence, and hanging onto them were children who seemed to know exactly when the train would pass. They seemed to be waiting for it, and they all waved as the train passed by. Some of them did little dances, as if they had practised them for the passengers. Michel pointed and said "Look mommy" whenever he spotted them.

The further east they travelled, the more snow they saw. There wasn't enough to for the children to make snowmen, but some had tried anyway by filling small buckets and emptying each bucketful on top of the other, to make their snowmen. Each time Michel saw one he would turn and point it out to Francine, but by the time that he had turned back, the scene was far behind them.

At noon Michel said he was hungry and Francine called the porter and asked if he would bring them something to eat, telling him that Michel was not feeling very well and she didn't want to bring him to the dining car in case he got sick. She gave the porter two dollars and asked him to bring her a few sandwiches and some milk. He returned a few minutes later with sandwiches, two apples, two pieces of apple pie and a pitcher of cold milk. He had change, but Francine told him to keep it. There was so much food that she had enough for an afternoon snack.

Michel fell asleep a little after 2:00 p.m. and shortly after, Francine fell asleep as well. The clacking of the train as it passed over the joints in the rails was very soothing. This, combined with the little dips and hollows in the track caused by many years of the frost entering and leaving the ground, turned the train car into one large cradle. It was 3:55 when Francine awakened to find Michel kneeling on his seat, again staring out the window. When she stirred, he turned.

"Sleepy Mommy?" he smiled.

"No, Mommy's not sleepy any more. She had a nice nap," Francine said as she reached for him, pulled him to her and gave him a big hug. Minutes later when they had returned to looking out the window, they heard a little knock on their door, followed by its opening a few seconds later. The porter who had brought their lunch was standing in the doorway.

"We'll be arriving in North Sydney in about two hours," he said.

"Thank you very much," Francine said, and the porter smiled and slid the door closed.

"We'll be getting to the boat in a little while," Francine said to Michel after the porter had left.

"Boat, Mommy?" Michel said.

"Yes sir," Francine said, "we're going on a big boat."

Michel stretched his hands apart as far as they would go. "This big?"

"Much bigger than that," Francine laughed.

Francine picked up their belongings and put them in the bag and sat and waited for the train to arrive in North Sydney. The tops of the hills, she noticed, were snow-covered and the air through the open window grew noticeably colder as they neared the ocean. At six o'clock, they ate what had been left from their lunch as they slowly approached the town of North Sydney.

Francine had not seen anything like it before. Everywhere there were huge smoke-stacks and reddish smoke poured out of them. The snow on the ground had the same red tint as the smoke. The train slowed as it approached the smoke-stacks, and eventually passed them. For the first time since they had left Halifax, the train seemed to be going down a slight grade and the scene changed. They travelled through several places where the rocks had been blasted to let the train pass through. The train whistle blew every few minutes and Michel tried to imitate it. As they neared their destination, the train was travelling at only a fraction of the speed that it had for most of their journey. They passed several crossings, and when they did, cars waited and its occupants waved to nobody in particular. Francine and Michel returned the waves.

The ride suddenly became bumpy as they crossed the many track intersections en route to the station. Michel remained in his seat while Francine tried to gather their belongings and she had difficulty maintaining her balance. Michel laughed as he watched his mother being thrown from side to side by the movement of the train. Finally, however, she had all their belongings packed and placed by the door. Then she put on her coat and dressed a reluctant Michel, who wanted to keep looking out the window. Over his protests, they could hear the squealing of iron on iron as the train rolled to a stop.

Francine made a quick check that nothing was left behind, and, holding onto Michel's hand, left the cabin and walked up the narrow hallway to the exit. Most of the other passengers were already near the exit and Francine queued behind them as they waited for the doors to open. The porter was waiting on the ramp outside the train and as Francine appeared, he reached up, took Michel and lifted him down. He then reached up and held Francine's hand to help her step off the train.

"We are supposed to take a ferry to Port aux Basques," Francine said as she produced her ticket. The porter looked at it.

"Yes, Ma'am, the ferry will be leaving in a few hours. There is a waiting room just up there a little ways," he stated as he turned and pointed. "We will put your baggage on after all of the passengers have disembarked, and, if you'll just proceed to the waiting room, someone there will tell you everything you need to know.

Francine thanked him, and, hand in hand, she and Michel walked toward the waiting room. For the first time they noticed that they weren't in a train station. There was a smell that she had not smelled before, and as they came out into the open air, she could see why. The ocean was just a few hundred yards in front of them and a cold Atlantic winter breeze blew straight in their faces. It carried the smells of tar and twine and diesel fuel, but was still surprisingly fresh. Francine turned up the collars on their coats and, picking Michel up in her arms, she carried him the remainder of the way.

The waiting room was actually a little shack and inside it was a big pot-bellied stove. Francine stood in the entrance for a second and the hot air struck them. A half dozen people were sitting there and the smell of stale tobacco smoke and burning coal filled the air. There were several chairs around the room and Francine pushed the door closed behind her and walked toward one and sat down. She helped Michel up to his chair and unbuttoned his coat, while he sat there with his legs stretched out trying to see everything at once. Francine spotted a wicket with the sign Information written on it. She instructed Michel not to move and walked over to it.

The man behind the wicket slid open a glass partition as she approached and spoke. "Good day, Ma'am, can I help you?"

"Yes," Francine said, "We're booked on the ferry to Port aux Basques, and I was wondering if it's on schedule."

"Yes it is, Ma'am, but it won't be leaving for another five hours. Did you just arrive on the train?"

"Yes we did. We left Halifax this morning," she said, and was immediately sorry she had volunteered that information. There was no need to tell him where they had come from.

"Are you travelling alone, Ma'am?"

"No, I'm with my young son," she said, pointing to Michel who was still sitting on the chair.

"You must be very tired then. Let me see what I can do for you. *The Cabot Strait* is being loaded right now and it will be at least four hours before we'll start loading passengers. But let me speak with the purser and see what can be done for you."

Francine returned to her chair and Michel. He was hypnotized by the flickering flames he could see through the holes in the door of the stove. As Francine sat down, he decided that he wanted to get a closer look and started to get down from his chair. Francine tried to get him to sit down again, and as she did a man in a uniform approached them.

"Are you the lady who just arrived from Halifax?" he asked.

"Yes," Francine answered.

"Hello, I'm John Chalk, the purser on *The Cabot Strait*. I told one of our stewards to get a cabin ready for you so we can board you right away. This place is going to be filled to capacity soon and it won't be a very nice wait. If you'll come with me, I'll show you to your cabin. The ship is not ready to accept passengers yet, so I hope you'll excuse the mess."

"Yes, yes, thank you very much," Francine said, excitedly. "We are not worried about a little mess." Francine welcomed the opportunity to board the ferry, but she knew that the purser would remember her. She didn't want to bring attention to herself, but when she saw another man and woman and a child follow them, she relaxed a little. Maybe this was something he did every day and would forget her and Michel as soon as they were settled.

The purser picked up her bag and Francine picked up Michel. Together they headed toward the ferry. It was moored about a hundred feet or so from the waiting room and as they walked, it felt to Francine that in the short time they had been inside, the temperature had dropped several degrees. Francine pressed Michel's face into her chest and tried to shield her own face from the biting wind. The purser walked a few steps in front of them and his open coat signified that the wind didn't bother him in the least.

Francine had never seen a ship this large before. As a matter of fact, she realized, she had never seen any ship before, except in pictures. Ropes, thicker than her legs were stretched taut and looped over steel poles that protruded up through the jetty. Had it been warmer, she would have liked to stop and look around. She knew that Michel would certainly like to do that, but he, too, realized how cold it was, and kept his face buried in his mother's chest. The ship stood motionless despite the wind, and they walked quickly toward the big, open, black hole.

Two large metal covers that would seal the stern of the ship once they were underway were open. The top was like a canopy that covered the ramp leading up to the hold. The bottom cover rested on the ramp. Train tracks led up the ramp and into the ship, and Francine could see long rows of lights on the ceiling as they got closer. The smell of diesel fuel got stronger and the wind dissipated as they stepped further inside. It grew surprisingly warmer and Michel lifted his head and pointed at the men dressed in dirty coveralls, who seemed to be everywhere. They were busy unloading and loading huge pallets, and none of them paid them the slightest bit of attention.

The purser led them through the first door to their left upon entering the ship. Francine had to step over a high metal step to get out of the hold and into an area with metal stairs that winded up into the upper decks. Holding Michel tightly, she started to walk up the winding stairs and just when she thought she couldn't take another step, they were brought into an area of the boat that was a complete contrast from where they had just come.

The floors were waxed shiny and there were handrails affixed to the walls on both sides of the hallways. It was very warm and Francine welcomed the opportunity to put Michel down. The purser kept walking without speaking, and then stopped outside an office with a big glass wicket with the word "Purser" printed on the glass. He took a ring of keys from his pocket and opened the door.

"I have to get the keys to your cabins," he said as he disappeared inside the office. He reappeared almost before he had finished speaking. "Please wait here," he said to the other couple as he locked the door again and he motioned to Francine to follow him down a set of stairs. He stopped at the bottom.

The cabin number was seven and the door was already open. The purser dropped the bag inside and turned the key in the lock. "Here we are," he said, smiling. "Please stay in your cabin until you hear the other passengers coming aboard. The heads-the bathroom," he quickly corrected himself, "is just up there," he pointed.

"Thank you, Mr. Chalk," Francine said as he turned and went back up the stairs.

The cabin was utilitarian. Directly in front of them, as they stood in the doorway, were two beds, one on top of the other. They were like two rectangular wooden boxes, neatly made, with a big U shape scooped out of the outside to let the sleepers in. A ladder led up to the top bunk and Michel immediately ran to it and started climbing. Francine held him as he climbed up and then jumped into the bed. To their left was a sink and Francine reached and turned on the tap. It hissed for a few seconds as the air left the lines and then a yellow liquid sputtered into the sink. There was a mirror above the sink and as Francine looked into it she read the sign: "Water is for washing only." As she waited for it to run clear, she knew why. She splashed a little on her face and then dried it with a very small, and surprisingly rough, towel.

Directly opposite the sink on the right side of the cabin, was a little table and chair, and with the beds, they made up the total furnishings of the cabin. Above the table and chair was a circular window with a rusted latch which Francine recognized to be a porthole. She pushed the door closed behind her as she took off her coat and hung it on the hanger screwed to the back of the door. Michel lay on the top bed and peered at her over the edge. He seemed very pleased with the new sleeping arrangements and called a playful "peek-a-boo" to his mother as she finished hanging up her coat. He then buried his head in the blanket.

Michel soon tired of his fascination with the beds and asked to get down. Francine lifted him down from the bed and stood him on the table in front of the porthole. She strained to lift up the rusted handle and then swung the window into the cabin and against the wall. Through the porthole they could look at the dock and watch the ship being loaded. This was a scene that could keep Michel busy for quite some time, so Francine found her book and lay down on her bed to read. The open window cooled the cabin quickly, but Michel would not let her close it. She put on his cap and coat and then pulled the blanket over herself to keep warm.

By 9:00 p.m. Michel's interest with his surroundings had worn off, so Francine decided to try to get him to bed. After several trips up and down the ladder to the top bunk, he reluctantly agreed to lie down and go to sleep. He had insisted that the top bunk was his, but Francine would hear nothing of it. She tried to explain to him that if he fell off he would have to go to the hospital, and then they would have to return home. When he was dressed in his pyjamas, she filled the sink with water, washed his face and hands and then put him into the bottom bunk. She lay on the bed beside him to read a little before she, too, went to bed.

Francine didn't realize that she had fallen asleep, but when she woke up the cabin was freezing. She hadn't secured the porthole window and it was now wide open. She got out of the bunk and stepped onto the tiled floor. As she did, the ship rolled and she was thrown against the cabin door. Her arm hurt as she slammed against the door again and she lifted it and looked at her watch. It was 1:15 a.m. They were underway and she had been sleeping. She staggered to the porthole and swung it closed and locked it. She shivered in the cold morning air and realized that she needed to go to the bathroom. It, like the potable water, was up the hallway. She didn't want to leave Michel alone in the room, but she simply had to go.

Francine found her boots and then with the key in her hand, she left the cabin. She locked the door behind her and walked up the hall to the bathroom. There were several people in the hallway and they held the hand-rails as they walked to and from their cabins. There were a couple of people in the bathroom, but Francine found a vacant stall. She looked at the huge toilet and the water swishing from side to side with the swaying of the ship. She managed to sit down and relieve herself and as she did, she felt sick like she had earlier yesterday morning. After confirming that her period had not started she concluded she was a little seasick.

The other women were talking as she came out of the stall. They spoke to her and Francine nodded, smiled, and left. Francine had to be very careful to keep from falling as she groped and staggered her way back to her cabin. She prayed that she would make it before she vomited, did, but just as she entered the cabin and closed the door behind her, everything that was in her stomach came up in the sink.

Francine passed the worst night of her entire life: either throwing up in the sink, or walking back and forth to the bathroom. Fortunately, Michel slept through it because Francine would not have been able to handle him as well as herself. She was sicker than she thought a person could possibly be. Her face was hot but as soon as she splashed water on it she became very cold. She tried lying down, but the movement of the ship seemed to worsen the nausea, so she had to get up and sit on the chair. She vomited again and again, and when finally there was nothing left to come up, her stomach just heaved, the muscles contracted and causing her an almost unbearable pain.

The long night wore on. Just as Francine would begin to think her sickness was starting to subside, she would have to rush to the sink again. By the time daylight finally appeared through the porthole window, she was ready to die, and wished it would come quickly. As the heaving of the ship began to subside, however, she started to feel a little better.

At 5:00 a.m. there was a sudden knock on the cabin door, followed by the words, "The ship will be docking in one hour. Breakfast is being served in the galley." The first sentence was the best news Francine had ever heard in her entire life, but the second sentence caused her to rush to the sink again. Nothing came up. The knock on the door and her gagging at the sink awakened Michel, who sat up smiling. Francine looked at him and smiled too. A very weak smile.

They dressed and followed the other passengers to the galley. It was on the same deck as their cabin and they could walk without having to hold onto the railing. Michel had slept well and he was now hungry. He pulled on his mother's hand to try to encourage her to walk faster. The air smelled fresh and each time they passed an open door, Francine breathed deeply. Finally, the smells told them they were close to the galley.

There were nearly a hundred people sitting at tables. Each table had a low wooden railing around it. Other people queued in front of a steam table, holding trays and eating utensils, while men in white uniforms heaped eggs, bacon and fried potatoes onto their plates. There were a few children holding on to their mothers' skirts, trying to see what was happening. The smell was almost overpowering, and at any other time would have been wonderful, but, for Francine, it was the worst smell she thought she would ever have to endure. She picked up a tray, filled a cup with coffee, a glass with milk, and asked for a small helping of scrambled eggs. They found a vacant table where Francine sipped her coffee, while Michel heartily ate his eggs and drank his milk. By the time she had finished her coffee, she started to feel alive again.

After breakfast they returned to their cabin where they picked up the remainder of their belongings and went out to the observation deck to watch the docking. They pushed open the heavy metal door and walked out onto the deck. The boat had already entered the bay leading to Port aux Basques, and they got their first glimpse of the island of Newfoundland.

The wind was cold, but it felt good. Still, Francine was glad she had taken mitts and hats from their steamer trunks before they left Halifax. Their first vision of Newfoundland was directly in front of them and rapidly enveloping them as they moved closer to the port. It was barren; more barren than she had ever dreamed it would be. There were no trees; only snow-covered rocks, and everything seemed to have a blue tint to it. Other people were on the observation deck and they pointed to landmarks and chatted. Michel was fascinated, but for the first time since she had left Toronto, Francine began to seriously doubt whether she had made the right decision. There were no people or animals to be seen on the land. Nothing but snow, rocks and water.

It was too cold to stay out on deck for very long so Francine and Michel went back inside and, through the windows, watched the docking. As they neared the port they finally saw signs of real life. At the entrance to the harbour, they spotted a lighthouse and were then passed by a fishing boat, its occupants waving. Then, the harbour opened and before them lay the town of Port aux Basques.

A dozen or more men in coveralls were standing on the jetty prepared to do the job they had done a thousand times before. Few of them even looked at the ship; they just huddled together to break the biting wind. Smoke from their cigarettes appeared briefly over their heads and was quickly blown away. Behind them were several buildings, steep cliffs and houses that looked like they had been glued to the sides of the hills. They were all white, but most could have used painting. There were two jetties separated by a distance of about one hundred feet and the insides of both were ringed with old car tires suspended by ropes. At the end of the jetty closest to the shore was a ramp.

The ship slowed until it was barely moving at all, and then water began to churn rapidly at the stern. The entire ship vibrated and windows and doors rattled as the captain tried to manoeuvre the ship between the two jetties. After a few minutes, the ship had turned completely around and was being backed up to the ramp. By this time the men had stopped chatting and were catching thin lines with round weights on the ends, which were being tossed from the ship by the crewmen. The lines were attached to heavy hawsers, and two men pulled on each line until the hawsers were brought onto the jetty and thrown over the large vertical posts sticking out of the jetty. Once the lines were made secure, heavy winches on the ship took up the slack and the ship began to slow. When all four hawsers were secure, the ship was slowly winched to a stop.

Loudspeakers then sounded on the boat and everyone was instructed to proceed to their vehicles, and foot passengers were given instructions on where to disembark. Francine and Michel followed the others and walked out of the belly of the ferry and stepped onto the snow-covered jetty.

Francine had read about Newfoundland, but she had never dreamed it would be this bleak. When she thought of becoming a nurse and coming here, she had become very familiar with most aspects of life on this coast, but she wasn't prepared for this. The wind was biting cold and even though she had dressed in her warmest clothes, she could still feel the wind through them. It did not seem to bother the locals though; some of them weren't even wearing gloves.

"Are you cold, sweetheart?" Francine suddenly remembered to ask Michel.

"No, Mommy," he answered as he walked beside her and kicked at the snow.

Passengers travelling beyond Port aux Basques had been instructed to meet at the baggage collection point where they could board the train to take them inland, or to catch another boat to one of the coastal communities. By the time Francine and Michel reached the baggage point, several other passengers had gathered there. It was just a shack and Francine squeezed inside with everybody else. The hot air was a welcome relief as she pulled open the door and stepped inside.

A shabbily dressed man in a blue uniform was seated beside a glass wicket and he answered questions and pointed out where the passengers should go to continue their journeys. Francine queued beside several other people and after a ten minute wait, she spoke to the agent.

"My name is Francine Matte," she began. "I have a ticket to travel on the coastal steamer *Bar Haven* to Dark Harbour. Could you please tell me where I have to go to meet this boat?"

"Yes, Ma'am," he answered. "She'll be leaving here at noon, and she's taking on supplies right now. If you'd like, you can go over to the main waiting room and they'll tell you when she's ready."

Francine stared at him for a few seconds trying to comprehend what she had heard. She had read that the dialect would be difficult to understand. "I'm sorry, sir, but would you repeat that?"

"Over there." He pointed toward where she had just disembarked the ferry. Francine turned and followed another couple who were heading in that direction. She realized that not only would she have to learn a new lifestyle, but she would have to learn a new language as well.

Francine was finally informed that their coastal steamer would be leaving from this jetty and would be boarding at noon. They had a three hour wait. Despite the cold, Michel insisted on exploring the jetty area for a while, and while Francine held tightly to his hand, he threw lumps of ice and whatever else he could find, over the sides into the water. Francine could stand the bitter cold no longer, and after a few minutes, she had to drag Michel back to the waiting room. Noon finally came, and not a moment too soon for Francine.

Francine could see the name SS *Bar Haven* painted in huge white letters on the hull of the coastal steamer as they boarded. The ship was smaller than the SS *Cabot Strait*, and after ensuring that their luggage had been transferred from the other ferry, Francine and Michel walked up the gangplank.

The SS *Bar Haven* was one of several coastal steamers which provided the only contact many coastal Newfoundland communities had with the rest of the world. There were twenty-five cabins on the boat and one large lounge where some of the travellers with only a short distance to travel had set up housekeeping. Francine held Michel's hand firmly as they stood on the deck of the ship and looked around. She wondered for the second time that day if she had made the right decision. The SS *Cabot Strait* had been very utilitarian but the SS *Bar Haven* resembled pictures she had seen of the ships that had plied the slave trade.

The deck of the boat was covered with everything imaginable. The boat brought mail, food, clothes, machinery and everything else needed to sustain life in the remote coastal communities. Whenever a resident needed something that wasn't available locally, it was ordered, and subsequently transported to that person by coastal ferry. Items as necessary as books, fishing gear, lamps, stoves, trousers, winter coats, dresses, and other essential items, could be ordered and delivered by boat. But the biggest bulk of the cargo was, by far, groceries. Dark Harbour, like all the coastal communities, had a general store and the only way to replenish the stock was via the coastal steamer.

Once aboard, the purser showed Francine and Michel to their cabin. When Francine stepped inside, she prayed she wouldn't be seasick again. There wasn't even a sink in this cabin, and she looked desperately for a bucket, just in case. She found one that was obviously meant as a trash can. Satisfied, she settled in for the two-hundred-mile trip that would take nearly two days to complete. By the time they arrived in Dark Harbour, they would have stopped at ten communities. As they settled in, Francine felt confident that Denis would not find them now.

Sixteen ～

THE WINTERS ON the south coast of Newfoundland were humbling experiences. From December through March, the wind blew constantly. If it wasn't snowing, it was just about to start. Huge waves pounded the shores and even the snow had a salty taste to it as the ocean spray mixed with the snowflakes as they were driven to the ground. It was a very unforgiving land, but the people accepted what they could not change. And there was very little they would have wanted to change even if they could have. They had grown accustomed to the harshness. They knew no other kind of life and so they accepted what they had and thanked God for what He had given them.

For the entire month of February, the harbour had been filled with ice and nothing could get in or out. Medical emergencies could be airlifted out by helicopter, but mail and other non-essentials would have to wait for the boat. As with the ocean, the ice was both a blessing and a curse. Even though the ice cut the community off from the rest of the province, it brought with it another food source and a chance for the fishermen to earn extra money—seals.

Seals were everywhere and Michel went out on the ice every day. Sealing was a two man operation, and a small flat-bottomed boat had been built just for that purpose. Pushing the boat beside them and hopping from pan to pan, two men could fill a boat with forty or fifty seals in a few hours. Because the weather was so unpredictable, they could never venture very far from shore. A sudden change in the wind and the entire ice pack could be blown out to sea, the men and their boats with it. The boats were not designed for anything other than dragging across the ice, and for traversing a few hundred feet of open water. Joe had given up sealing a few years earlier, but from his house he could watch the others in the harbour. He helped with the skinning and he appreciated a good meal of seal as much as he ever did, but jumping from ice pan to ice pan was work for the younger men.

In addition to the seals, there were also several species of birds. Turrs, ducks and puffins were in almost limitless supply, and in a good day of 'turring', two men could shoot five hundred birds. The rich dark meat of the turrs that averaged a pound when cleaned took the place of chickens and turkeys. There was always something to keep people occupied. But for the Fudge family, the letter was always on their minds.

It was the middle of March before the pack ice cleared and they got mail. It was a large envelope from The Royal Bank and addressed as Lori had requested in her letter. It had been sent registered mail, and although it was addressed to Michel, the post mistress allowed Lori to sign for it. Michel had never received a registered letter before and the post mistress joked with Lori about it.

"Your man is some important person now that he got to sign fer he's mail," the elderly woman chided her jokingly, in a heavy Newfoundland accent.

Lori just smiled, and in a way, liked the attention. I suppose we are important now, she thought. They certainly had a lot of money, even though she couldn't tell anybody about it just yet.

Michel was at home when she returned from the post office, and she passed him his mail.

"It's from the bank," Lori said proudly as Michel took the envelope, looked at it briefly and laid it on the table.

"We'll wait until after supper before you open it," he said as he stood up and put on his coat. "I'm taking Dad out 'turrin' with me now, and it'll be supper time before we're finished cleaning the birds. I'll bring Dad back with me for supper."

Lori left the letter on the table, propped between the molasses can and the bowl of sugar. She looked at it many times that afternoon, and more than once she was tempted to open it. Of course, she didn't.

Over supper, Michel described his day's hunting with his father. Lori listened, but she heard little. She was anxious to open the letter and to find out what was in it. Finally, after what seemed to be a hundred stories, Michel asked Lori to open the letter. Lori carefully tore open the envelope and found two more inside. She opened the smaller envelope first and read the letter silently. The men patiently waited until she was ready.

"It says that they received your letter, Michel, and the money has been placed in a savings account until they hear further from you. They believe that you're you." Lori smiled at Michel.

"Well, at least somebody does," he laughed.

Lori next turned her attention to the second envelope. It was much larger than the first and it tore open very easily. There was nothing written on it and although it had the same Royal Bank crest on it, it had practically faded. She reached inside, pulled out several sheets of paper, laid them on the table in front of her and picked up one. She studied it for a few seconds, but it was obvious from the puzzled look on her face that she had no idea what it was.

"I'm sorry, but I don't know what this is," she admitted.

Michel then picked up one of the sheets and examined it, while Joe sat back and puffed on his pipe.

"It looks like a certificate of some kind or another and there's a lot of legal type stuff written on it," Lori said. She continued to examine it. "The bearer of this certificate is entitled to one thousand shares of Atlantic Processing Inc." she read. She lifted her head and looked at the two men for comment. They had none. "I've never seen anything like these before. I have no idea what they are." She paused while she looked at the other papers. They were all the same and she counted them as she thumbed through them. "There's ten thousand of these shares, whatever that means," she said, obviously frustrated.

Michel and Joe, in turn, examined the papers and they too had to conclude they had no idea what they were. "They must be worth something," Michel finally said. "Otherwise, why would she have left them in the bank so long and then wanted them sent to me?"

"I'd bet Linda would know what they are," Lori said, excitedly.

"I'd bet she knows what they are too," Michel quickly replied. "But we're not going to show them to her. Now let's put these things away somewhere safe. If they're worth anything, they'll still be worth something tomorrow and tomorrow after that. Besides, we have over one hundred thousand dollars in Halifax. If these things are worth money, we certainly won't need it for a while."

Lori stuffed the certificates back in the envelope and then made them a cup of tea. While she did, she silently wondered if she could write to somebody to ask what the pieces of paper were. But who? There was nobody in Dark Harbour she could ask, she was certain of that, except maybe the teacher. But she would have to talk to Michel about it first. Maybe the easiest thing to do would be to write to the bank. Maybe she could send one of them registered, like Michel's letter, and that way it wouldn't get lost. She would have to give the whole thing more thought before she talked to Michel though, so she decided to forget about it until the next morning. Michel and his father obviously had, because they laughed often as they talked about the day they had spent 'turring', and the work that had to be done to get ready to start fishing again in a couple of months. They had a lot to do and now that he had some money, Michel was already planning to buy some new equipment for the boat.

"You're going to have to find another crew member," Joe said, as they drank their tea.

"Why is that?" Michel asked.

"I think I'm going to pack it in. My arthritis is worse now than it ever has been," Joe answered, rubbing his shoulder.

Michel had known that this day would eventually come. But he never thought that it would come so soon. "It's cold now, Dad. When it warms up a little, you'll feel a lot better," he said, trying to convince his father that it was just the weather, and it was the cold that was causing his pain.

"No, son, I've had enough. It's up to you now. I've been fishing for nearly fifty years. Al had to give it up last year and he's two years younger than I am."

Lori had listened to the same conversation between her father and brother a few years earlier. It was a conversation that most fathers and sons in Dark Harbour eventually had. Joe hadn't had it with his father though. The sea had snatched that conversation away from him. Michel would accept his father's decision and he would find another crew member. Al's son had replaced his father. And now Michel would find one to replace his own father. Fishing was a never ending cycle of joy and pain. His father's decision was a pain he would have to overcome.

Linda came home for a week in the middle of May. The ice had returned to the harbour, but with the aid of a gaff to push the pans aside, and a couple of hours longer than usual, they were able to navigate the route. She could only stay for a week because she had her first job. She had found a job for the summer working for the law firm of Hawkins and Murphy. She had six more years of study before she would be able to write the bar exam and she didn't know any more about the law now than when she had started at university, but she welcomed the chance to see how the law worked. Hawkins and Murphy hired one first-year student from Memorial each year and promised him or her a summer job until graduation. Linda had not even started her law studies yet, but her new employer had a unique way of recruiting staff. They wanted to observe a potential lawyer from the time he or she entered university through to graduation. Then, based not only on performance at school, but at the law firm as well, they could more realistically judge a young lawyer's potential. They were the most successful law firm in St. John's and employed only the brightest lawyers. Linda had been selected from some fifty applicants. Her interview had been the most nerve-racking experience of her life, but when asked why she wanted to become a lawyer, her answer got her the job.

"Because little people have to be protected from big people. Poor people from rich people. Government must be challenged. People's rights have to be protected and new rights obtained. Everything we do is based on the rules of law. I want to learn those rules."

Michel had picked up Linda in Fortune and taken her back to Dark Harbour. Her father didn't come with him, but he was waiting on the wharf when they arrived. He looked a lot older to Linda. There had always been a little twinkle in the corner of each eye; now it was gone. She knew why. Her mother and her father had loved each other intensely. She had never heard either of them speak a harsh or unkind word to the other. He was missing his wife and her passing was taking its toll. When she stepped onto the wharf he hugged her, and when he finally let her go, she noticed that his eyes were wet. He looked at her a long time before he spoke. Even though she didn't resemble her mother, it was obvious to Linda that he was seeing Millie in her.

Linda's visit was like a tonic for her father. The smile returned to his eyes and he laughed often. She spent every minute she could with him and she wished she could stay at home longer, but she had to get back to St. John's. When Michel told her that Joe had decided to give up fishing this year, she was more determined to get back to St. John's and earn the money to pay for her second year of university. Michel assured her that money was not a problem. He wanted to tell her what he knew about their real mother, but he saw how she looked at Joe. He, too, had seen the change that had come over their father since the death of their mother and he believed that his father needed Linda's love now more than ever. The doubt he might see if she knew that Joe wasn't her real father might just be too much for him. That uncertainty would be completely unfounded because Michel knew that Linda loved Joe as much as he did. It just wouldn't serve any purpose to tell her at this time. Instead, he told her that their mother had saved a lot of money for his education and now it was all hers. If she would have the university send the bills to him, he would see that they were paid. Linda was a little suspicious, but when Joe informed her that it was indeed true, she seemed satisfied.

Linda enjoyed working for Hawkins and Murphy that first year although the closest she came to any legal work though was copying it on the Xerox machine. Her job was to make coffee, clean up the conference room, do the filing, run errands and a dozen other such menial tasks. She wouldn't get to do anything 'legal' until she started her law studies. That was three years distant, that is, if the firm saw fit to bring her back next year. If all of the students had been found suitable, there would have been six students there beside herself. There were only two, one who would write the bar exam next year and another who had just received his Bachelor of Arts degree this year.

Linda particularly liked working for this firm because one of their major clients was Ocean Products International Limited. Their head office was in Toronto, but because of their many dealings in Newfoundland, they had retained Newfoundland counsel. Linda was from a fishing family and she knew what it was like to live on a fisherman's income. She understood first hand the problems of the inshore fisherman and had formed the opinion that they were being taken advantage of by large companies such as Ocean Products International Limited. It seemed a contradiction that her reason for wanting to practise law was to protect people such as her father, but that she was working for a firm that represented the big fishing companies. Before she began her studies, she had made up her mind that she wanted to practise corporate law, because in order to be able to properly defend the 'little' people, she had to understand the rules the 'big' people used. She wanted to be able to volunteer her services to the fishery unions in the way that doctors volunteered their medical services to the poor. She realized that there could be a conflict if she was offered a position with Hawkins and Murphy, but she would cross that bridge when she came to it.

Hawkins and Murphy offered Linda employment again after completing her second year of studies. They had been impressed with her attitude toward her work and had told her that if she did as well at school as she had the previous year, she could expect to work for them again. She didn't disappoint them, and got an 'A' in every subject. She had won enough in bursaries and scholarships to pay for her third year.

She was able to spend two weeks in Dark Harbour during the summer and it was a very pleasant two weeks. Her father was slowly getting over the death of Millie, and went out on the boat occasionally during the fishing season. Michel wouldn't let him do any work, but he kept himself occupied anyway. Linda even went along a couple of times. Joe hated to see her return to St. John's, and she suggested that he come and visit her. He could use some of the money that Millie had saved, but he laughed at the suggestion.

When they said goodbye in Fortune, Linda promised to try and spend a little more time at home for Christmas. Even though she had enjoyed her short vacation, she was anxious to get back to St. John's and her job. But there was also another reason, Bob Humby. During the past two years, they had become very close and the two weeks she spent away from him had seemed like an eternity. This would be Bob's final year at Memorial, and then he would hopefully find a teaching position in St. John's. In her prayers each night, Linda asked God to find Bob a job in St. John's.

The summer of 1970 passed quickly and Linda returned to her studies filled with enthusiasm. She received permission to take an extra credit and, despite the increased workload, she maintained her firm A average during the Christmas exams. Her big disappointment of the year was having to spend Christmas Day in Fortune with Bob and his family. A terrible snowstorm that had started on December 22nd lasted until Boxing Day, making the trip to Dark Harbour impossible. She had never spent Christmas Day away from home, but the Humbys were very nice and they tried to make her feel at home. Her father was devastated and Michel was equally distraught. They refused to open their gifts until Linda arrived. When she finally did, they celebrated Christmas one day late. Nevertheless, they had a wonderful New Year's celebration together. On January 3rd, Linda returned to St. John's.

In February, Bob was assigned to a school, but it wasn't in St. John's. He waited until Friday, when he was meeting with Linda to go to a movie, to break the news. Together they took the bus to the Bond Theatre and as they sat in their seats waiting for the movie to start, Bob blurted it out.

"I got assigned a school," he whispered, from a mouth stuffed with popcorn. He lifted the Coke to his mouth and waited for her reaction.

"Oh, God, you didn't!" Linda shouted as she turned to look at him, as did everybody else within earshot. She turned bright red as a couple in front of them chuckled and she realized how loud she had spoken. She turned her gaze from Bob to the others and smiled weakly. They returned their attention to their snacks. "When did you find out? Is it St. John's?"

"Whoa, whoa," Bob whispered. "One question at a time."

"Okay, okay, but where is it?" she asked, with an impatient ring in her voice.

"It's not St. John's," Bob answered, trying to sound disappointed.

"Damn!" Linda said, forgetting to whisper. The couple in front of them turned again. "Oh, why don't you two mind your own business!" Linda snapped. They turned like soldiers on parade after having been given the order to "About face." Bob didn't speak. He continued eating his popcorn and drinking his pop. "You're taking the news well,"

Linda said sarcastically as she turned her attention back to him. Just as she finished speaking, the lights dimmed.

"Shhh!" Bob said. "The movie is about to start."

Linda couldn't believe what was happening. Her mouth dropped open and all kinds of thoughts flashed through her mind. Bob sensed her discomfort and turned to her. "Well, aren't you going to ask me where I got the position?" he asked, with a smirk on his face that Linda couldn't see in the darkened theatre.

"I don't suppose it makes much difference now," Linda answered, the entire evening obviously ruined. She paused for a few seconds. "Okay, where is it?" she finally asked.

Bob laughed. "Did you see that?" he asked, pointing at the screen.

Linda had had enough. She jumped up from her seat and her box of popcorn went flying. She pushed past Bob who was sitting in the aisle seat and rushed toward the exit.

"It's Mount Pearl," Bob shouted after her. "I got offered a position in Mount Pearl."

Linda stopped dead in her tracks as Bob's words sunk in. "Mount Pearl, that's practically St. John's," she whispered. Then she realized what that meant. "Thank you, God," she shouted in her loudest voice as she looked up with folded hands at the dark theatre ceiling. As before, every eye in the theatre was on her as she ran toward Bob who was now standing beside his seat. She left the floor four feet in front of him and jumped into his arms. "I hate you, I hate you, I hate you," she shouted, between rapid kisses. All attention had switched from the screen to the crazy couple in the aisle. Suddenly, flashlights appeared and the ushers escorted Bob from the theatre with Linda still in his arms, amid the applause of the remaining audience.

Outside her dormitory later that evening, Bob proposed, and Linda accepted without hesitation. They would be married in July.

Seventeen ∾

LINDA AND BOB were married in Dark Harbour; nearly every person in the community attended the reception. Including the guests from Fortune, there were nearly four hundred people. Tearfully, Joe gave Linda away in the church where she was baptised. Equally tearfully, he said goodbye a week later when she left once again to begin her summer work for Hawkins and Murphy.

They had found an apartment in Mount Pearl and Bob had found a summer job pumping gas at a downtown St. John's service station. Their finances had been a little tight and they were concerned about paying their bills and making ends meet until Bob received his first teacher's pay check. But all those doubts vanished when they opened Michel and Lori's wedding gift. It was a cheque for five thousand dollars. At first they vehemently refused to accept it, but Michel was able to convince them that he had had an excellent couple of years fishing and he wanted to do something for his only sister. She thought it funny that the cheque was written on a Halifax bank account, but decided against grilling her brother any further. Then she opened her father's gift, and it too contained a cheque. It was for four thousand dollars. He explained that it was really a one thousand dollar gift. The other three thousand was to pay for her expenses at school. Linda was pleased with her new found wealth, but felt very uneasy about accepting such large sums of money. She knew her mother had somehow saved money for her education, but she wondered where Michel was getting it all. Obviously fishing was paying a lot better now than it had just a few years earlier.

That had been two years earlier. Linda was now in her first of three years of law studies. Unfortunately, Memorial didn't offer a law program and so she had to attend the law school at Dalhousie University in Halifax. She had found accommodation at the university residence, but it meant she was away from Bob for three or four months at a time. There was the increased expense, but she had won enough in scholarships to pay for everything.

Bob had considered a summer position working on the Provincial Marking Board correcting exams, but chose instead to return to university. Just before Christmas, they had purchased their first home and they could use a little extra money, but Bob wanted to get his Master's Degree. Linda fully supported his decision and they knew that they would have to make a few sacrifices until Linda began working. They had refused any financial assistance from Joe the previous year, saying that now that they were married, they could not have him paying for Linda's education. He was visibly hurt, but accepted their refusal. Michel wanted to help as well and he was also thanked and his offer politely refused. They were committed to making it on their own.

In the summer of 1974, with her first year of law studies completed and having finished third in her class of seventeen, Linda once again went to work for Hawkins and Murphy. She was now the senior student at the firm, which meant that the other students reported to her and she directed their daily activities. Also, the typing staff and cleaning staff were her responsibility. It was the firm's way of teaching her to manage. It was very efficacious. Linda learned to appreciate the problems of the so-called working class; not only did she supervise them but on occasion she was invited to their homes and socialized with them. When a typist called in sick or a cleaning person failed to show up for work, she either had to redistribute the work or do it herself. Many times that summer she could be seen typing law reports or vacuuming offices. It gave her a new appreciation of low status, low paying work and the people who did it. Hawkins and Murphy believed in treating all its employees with dignity and respect regardless of the service they provided to the firm. They not only preached that philosophy, they practised it. All of their lawyers for the past fifteen years had travelled the same route as Linda.

Linda returned to the firm the following year. She had again done well, finished fifth in a class of sixteen. This was the year she would get her first opportunity to actually practise what she had been learning. She became law clerk to Jeremy Hawkins, the son of one of the founders; he challenged her to her limit. Jeremy was in his mid-thirties and one of the brightest legal minds in the province. He had been educated at Oxford, as had his father who had died of cancer two years earlier. Jeremy was in the office every work day at 7:00 a.m. and rarely left before 8:00 p.m. Linda kept similar hours except she often had to work weekends to keep up with the work Jeremy assigned her throughout the week. She and Bob saw each other only at breakfast and at night in bed.

Jeremy was the lawyer for Ocean Products International Limited(OPI). It was the firm's largest client and it occupied nearly half of his time. One of the junior lawyers had also been assigned to the company account and all of his time had been dedicated to servicing the legal needs of OPI. Unfortunately, he had died in an automobile accident a few weeks earlier and now Jeremy had to devote all of his time to the company. Soon after Linda joined the firm for the summer Jeremy called her to his office.She had never been in his office before and as his secretary showed her in, she could only dream that some day she would be so successful that she could have an office half as sumptuous as Jeremy Hawkins'.

"I see that you've done well at school again this year," he said, as he motioned for her to have a seat.

"Yes, I have, thank you. There's a few in my class, though, who are very bright, and I'm afraid that I'm not going to finish at the top of the class."

Jeremy laughed. "Permit me to let you in on a secret. I finished thirty-fifth out of class of forty. I'm still more successful than any of the others, so don't let that bother you. School is one thing. Doing the actual work is another."

Linda didn't speak.

"Okay, now that you know my secret, let's get down to the purpose of our meeting."

Since Linda had entered the office he had not looked up. Instead he had busied himself signing papers. Finally, he signed the last and looked at her. He smiled, replaced the top of his fountain pen and placed it on the table beside the signed documents.

"You may know that OPI is our main client. I trust you know what OPI is?" he asked as an aside.

"Oh yes," Linda replied promptly.

"Good. You also know that Brent Sears was recently killed. You may not have known that he was the only other lawyer in this firm who was involved with the OPI account. Currently, we are very busy and I can't spare another lawyer to assign to this account. That means I'm having to work a lot more than I would like. We've begun to look for someone to replace Brent, but it's going to take a while. So I need some help and that's where you come in. There's a lot of routine stuff that you can be doing for me. But before you can do anything you have to become completely familiar with everything that's in our files. We have represented OPI since they started business in the province, so our files are quite comprehensive. I don't expect you to read everything. What I want is for you to skim through everything and get a feel for what the company is all about. If you have any questions, don't hesitate to ask. I caution you that there's a lot of sensitive material in those files and I don't want you discussing any of it with anybody but me. Understand?"

"Yes, sir."

"Fine. I'll give you a week and after that I expect you to be able to lay your hands on anything I require. So don't move anything. Just make yourself some kind of note or whatever you need, to be able to find things as I require them. What makes it all the more difficult for us is the fact that Sarah, who was the file clerk responsible for these files, just had a baby. She may not be returning to us. She has a system and if you can't figure it out, call her at home. Any questions?"

"No sir, none."

"Good. Let's get right at it then. All the files are in the office beside Brent's. Ask Marie to give you a key and a key to his office. Maybe you should just keep that office until you join us next year. Then after you've returned to school and if your workload permits, perhaps you can continue to maintain the files when you get home for breaks. Every long weekend, book yourself a flight and have the bill sent to us. Then you can keep everything up to date. That way you'll get to spend a little time with your husband and do us a favour as well."

"Yes, I'd like that," Linda answered.

"Great. Now get outta here and let me earn a little money to pay the high salary that you're going to demand from us now that you're proving yourself to be invaluable," he laughed.

Linda just laughed, turned and left.

Marie provided her with a key to Brent's office and asked that she gather up the few personal items belonging to him and put them in the storeroom until they received disposal instructions. A few hours later she was deeply engrossed in OPI files.

OPI's head office was in Toronto and had operations in New Brunswick, Nova Scotia, Prince Edward Island and Newfoundland. Its largest operations by far were in Newfoundland, where it owned and operated twenty-seven fish processing plants employing nearly seventeen thousand people, directly or indirectly. It was the single largest employer in the province. On its board of directors were several former cabinet ministers and the elite of the Newfoundland business community.

Linda spent the first day reading about the current status of the company. She read that it traded both on the Toronto and Montreal Stock exchanges at a current price of eighteen dollars and twelve cents. She also read about the shares outstanding and the principal shareholders. Fortunately, she had take a stock market course a couple of years earlier at the recommendation of the firm, and she was now reaping the benefits. She examined financial statements and stock issues and, with the assistance of the firm's accountant who helped her interpret the statements, she had a good grasp of the current status of the company. It was very healthy, financially.

Next, Linda turned to the history of the company and read through the files with increasing interest. She devoured the information. The company had started from very humble beginnings in 1948. It purchased its first two processing plants in Nova Scotia that year and the next year moved to Newfoundland where it grew rapidly, purchasing its first Newfoundland plant in Bonavista and the next in Bay de Verde later that year. There was a file on each acquisition; Linda thumbed through the aged sheets absorbing the information. The first few purchases appeared to have been reasonably simple transactions. A letter was sent to the owner with an offer to purchase. From there, negotiations began and eventually they settled upon a price. But after the company had acquired a half dozen or so plants, the province began to get involved. There were letters signed by the premier, and the minutes of several meeting held with the premier were also in the files. Essentially, the purpose of the meetings with the premier was to seek tax relief. At first, she read that the province was reluctant but with each acquisition, the province became increasingly generous.

Linda began to see the same names over and over again. A cabinet minister who had approved a purchase or had given crown land to the company was appointed to the board of directors. She remembered the stunning defeat a few years earlier of the member of the House of Assembly from her riding. He had also been the Minister of Fisheries. She noted that he was now on OPI's Board. She remembered seeing his name on a document she had read a few days earlier. Quickly, she found the file and the letter. She reread it. It had to do with the building of a new plant in Carbonear. It was a very thick file and Linda had only skimmed through it when she first read it, but now she read it with more interest.

Lake, the owner of the fish plant in Carbonear, refused OPI's offer to purchase. When it did, OPI sought approval to build a second plant. Walter Lake had written several letters of opposition to the Minister stating that the community could not sustain two fish plants. Linda found it strange that Mr. Lake's letters were on file at OPI. Then she discovered something even more intriguing. In addition to the grant of land to build the new plant that the minister had approved, the government provided a half million dollar grant under the auspices of creating jobs. Additionally, the company was given preferential tax treatment for five years.

Linda wasn't quite sure what she was reading. But from all indications, it appeared that the government was deliberately giving OPI an advantage over Mr. Lake's operation. When Lake refused to sell his plant, the government gave OPI the means to drive him out of business. And the former minister's reward was a plum job with OPI. He was now one of the company's directors, getting paid forty thousand dollars annually.

Linda found all of this very disturbing. She was only a second year law student but she knew enough to know that this wasn't right. It appeared that OPI, with the assistance of government, had conspired to put Mr. Lake out of business. And the person who had approved the process was now on OPI's payroll. The last eight acquisitions had similar involvement with government. Even when OPI succeeded in purchasing an existing plant, the government rewarded it with tax incentives. Linda spent sixteen hours a day reading the files. She couldn't believe what she was reading. It occupied her every waking moment and interfered with her sleep. There was something she had to know and there was only one way to find out. On Friday, she arranged to meet with Jeremy at the end of the day.

"Hello Linda," Jeremy said as he welcomed her to his office. Jeremy was a very distinguished looking person and in his intimidating office, it was hard to be at ease. "How's your education on OPI coming along?" he asked as he pointed to a plush leather chair in front of his desk.

"Good, great," Linda answered.

"Well, what is it I can do for you? You must have a million questions."

"Yes, but they can wait. I've made myself a lot of notes and they are just general questions of law and I can ask one of the junior lawyers, if you don't mind. It's nothing to do with OPI specifically."

"Okay, but remember what I told you. There's some very sensitive information in those files and you know about lawyer-client privilege," he finished, winking at her.

Linda just smiled. "I'd like," she continued, "to visit one of the plants so I can get an appreciation of how they operate. There's a lot of expressions and references to equipment that I'd just like to be able to see. I think it would help me to understand everything a little better. Do you think that I could go visit one for a couple of days? I'm considering the one in Carbonear. It won't cost anything. I went to university with a girl from there and she's been after me to come out and visit her for a weekend. I could stay with her."

Jeremy looked at her for a few seconds and then broke into raucous laughter. Linda felt embarrassed. She got up to leave.

"No, no, sit down," Jeremy said, still laughing. "I apologize for my behaviour. It's just that when I first started with the OPI account, I asked my father if I could visit one of the plants."

Linda felt relieved.

"He refused, giving me a hundred reasons why not. But I went anyway. So, the answer to your question is yes. And I won't have any employee of this firm going through the back door anywhere. You ask Marie to book you the best hotel room in Carbonear. OPI will pay for it one way or another," he laughed. "I'm going to Montreal for the weekend so you can have my car and driver until Sunday. I'll need him to take me to the airport this evening and to pick me up on Sunday at 4:00 p.m. Ask Marie to call the plant manager and tell him you're coming. And whatever expenses you have, make sure that accounting reimburses you. Take a few people out to dinner. Let them know who you are and who you represent. It's all good PR and as I said, OPI will end up paying for it."

Linda certainly hadn't expected any of this.

"Now go and have a good weekend. Take that husband of yours with you, too. Let Marie know where my driver can pick you up and have her book him a room as well."

Linda managed a thank-you before she made her way back to her office.

Bob was as excited about the trip as she was. The trip meant an entire weekend together. They hadn't had that luxury since they were married. Linda was not only excited about spending the weekend with her husband, however. She would also get a chance to speak with Walter Lake. Ever since she had read the file on the attempted purchase of his plant, she had been intrigued. She had contacted her friend Cynthia earlier and she confirmed that Walter was now retired and living in Carbonear. He had indicated that he would be happy to meet with her.

Linda spent most of Saturday morning and a portion of the afternoon at the plant. It was located on the south side of Carbonear, directly across the harbour from Lake's former plant. Lake's plant had gone out of business two years after the OPI plant opened. That wasn't in the files. George Earle, the OPI plant manager, was very accommodating and she learned a lot. She had grown up around fish plants, so the visit was just a refresher. The equipment had changed, but the process was basically the same.

Although the visit to the plant was ostensibly the main reason for her visit to Carbonear, her visit with Walter Lake was of equal importance. She had to hear from him and get his side of the story. If she was going to work for Hawkins and Murphy she had to believe in what they did. She remembered how her father had been taken advantage of by the fish buyers, so she had no great desire to protect them. But she had to know if she was going to work for a firm that cared only about the law and not justice.

She walked to her meeting with Walter Lake. She didn't want Jeremy questioning his chauffeur and finding out that he had dropped her off at Walter Lake's house. Walter's home was very impressive and was located one street above Water Street. She paused for a moment to admire the ornate carving on the face of the house, then walked up the concrete steps to the main door. She lifted the heavy door knocker; as she did she heard chimes sounding inside the home. She lowered the knocker until it rested against the door. Seconds later the door opened.

"Good evening Miss Fudge," a very distinguished-looking gentleman greeted her. "I've been expecting you." She had arranged the meeting using her maiden name.

He was dressed in a smoking jacket and wore a tartan ascot around his neck. His face was cheery but weather-beaten, and his gray hair was thick and full. His eyes were blue like the water he had depended on for his living. Walter was a big man and he stretched out a hand that swallowed Linda's, but his handshake was gentle. "Good evening Mr. Lake," she responded as he gently drew her inside the home. She guessed his age at sixty.

She stepped into a windowed porch filled with plants and then followed him into a beautifully decorated foyer. The walls were covered with a bright wallpaper and imprinted pictures of spouting whales. A large winding staircase was directly in front of them and pictures, which she assumed were family, hung evenly on the wall leading upstairs. A huge chandelier hung suspended from the high ceiling on a chain that looked large enough to not only hold the light but to moor a large boat. The floor was hardwood and a circular rug with a picture of a sailing ship in its centre covered most of it. She followed behind Walter Lake and then almost ran into him as he paused and held open a door at the left of the foyer. She smiled and walked through it.

It was small room with a desk up against the wall at the back. It was a study, library, office, and trophy room all in one. She would have liked to spend some time in the room just admiring it and its contents. Two chairs separated by a low table were placed in front a fireplace. Walter asked for her coat, hung it on a rack and then held a chair for her as he took the other.

"Well, Miss Fudge," he began as he went to a large coffee urn on the table beside him and poured her a cup of coffee. "I haven't had such a pretty visitor in a long, long time. How may I help you?"

Linda blushed a little. Walter Lake was a very charming man. He passed her a tray containing cream and sugar and she held up her hand, indicating that she required neither.

"Mr. Lake," she began, "I'm not sure how to start, but I suppose the best way is to get right to the point. Unfortunately, I can't tell you everything about me at this time, and I can only hope that you will answer my questions believing that my reasons for talking with you are strictly personal."

Walter sipped his coffee. "We'll see after you've asked your questions," he smiled.

"Fair enough." Linda placed her cup and saucer on the table and pulled a notebook out of her purse. "In 1963, OPI offered to buy your fish processing plant. You refused and then when you found out that OPI was planning to build a plant directly across the harbour from yours, you wrote several letter to the Fisheries Minister, voicing your concern." Lake continued to sip his coffee, showing no reaction to Linda's questions. She watched for a reaction as he placed his coffee on the table, got up, selected a pipe from the rack over the fireplace and returned to his chair to fill it.

"I trust that my pipe won't bother you?" he asked.

"No," Linda replied. "Mr. Lake," she continued, "I have reason to believe that there may have been improprieties surrounding these events. Could you provide me with your feelings and thoughts about what happened back then?"

Walter finished filling his pipe and then pressed the tobacco lightly into the bowl with his index finger. He reached into his jacket pocket and brought out a box of Eddy matches. He struck one to the side and then drew the flame into the bowl. He blew the smoke from the side of his mouth, until satisfied that it was lit, then removed the match and blew it out. He paused another few seconds before he spoke. Then his eyebrows wrinkled and his expression suddenly turned very cold.

"Miss Fudge," he said, "are you sure that you want to drag up the past? You may find out that the system doesn't work like it's supposed to. No, let me correct myself. You may find out that the system doesn't work like it was designed to. You faith in our democracy might be shaken a little."

This was a much more sombre Walter Lake. Clearly there was a bitterness in his voice.

"Yes, I'm sure."

"Okay, let me see, where will I begin," he said, leaning back in his chair and looking up at the ceiling. "My father and his father before him were fishermen. My great-grandfather fished in a twenty-five foot boat out of Carbonear. Every morning during the fishing season, he and the men who worked with him, rowed the boat out to the island," he said, pointing at the wall in the direction of Carbonear Island about a mile off shore. "It was hard living but it was an honest living. They salted all their fish and sold it to the merchants." He took a break for a puff on his pipe.

"But you have to understand what it meant to sell to the merchants. The fisherman never got anything for the sale of his fish but credit in the merchant's stores. Everything the fishermen needed was available in the merchant's stores: fishing gear, clothes, food, everything. And always at the end of the season, there was money owing to the merchant. So even if he wanted to sell his fish somewhere else, he couldn't. Fishermen were held hostage."

"Then of course, the demand for fresh fish developed and my father and a few friends built the fish plant to process it. It was a way, they felt, to break the control of the merchants. I want to point out that there were many merchants who also got into the fresh fish processing business and continued to screw the fishermen. But my father had been a fisherman and he treated the other fishermen fairly. He and a couple of other fishermen had been able to accumulate a little money to build the plant because they sold to the Cubans and the Portuguese and whoever else was willing to buy from them. He later bought his partners out. It was just a small operation when he got started, but by the time I took over, it had the most modern equipment we could buy. We employed as many as five hundred men and women at our peak. More than anybody outside of St. John's," he added proudly. "And we were fair. We paid a decent wage to our workers and we paid a decent wage to the fishermen.

Linda continued to make notes.

"When the plant was started, it was with the understanding that father would make a profit but that profit would not be made at the expense of the fishermen. When markets in the states and in the Carribean improved, father increased the prices paid to the fishermen. There's not a fishermen in this bay who ever sold fish to us and can say that we did him wrong. If you can find one, I'll call him a god damn liar to his face."

He paused again to draw on his pipe. It made a whistling sound as he drew air through the unlit tobacco. With a practised stroke he drew the match against the side of the box and held it to the bowl of the pipe. The sweet smell of tobacco soon wafted through the room.

"We made a good living from the fish plant," he began again. "None of the Lakes will want for money. But despite all that's happened, there's one thing we didn't do."

"What's that?" Linda asked as she looked up from her notebook.

"We didn't get in bed with the goddamn politicians. Joey Smallwood is a good man. When he was premier of this province and he brought it into Confederation, times were good. His wife comes from Carbonear. Did you know that?"

Linda shook her head.

"Well, she was. Anyway, Joey was in office and a lot of rogues got elected on his coattails. Other than Joey, not one of them gave a damn about this province. All they cared about was themselves. The whole lot of them. But I'm getting off track. Where was I? Oh yes. I got this letter from OPI saying that they wanted to buy me out. It was a fair offer, but my father would have turned over in his grave if I had sold it. You see, OPI is greedy. They don't care about the fishermen. All they care about is making a profit for their shareholders. What they're doing is buying up plants in this province so they can control the entire market. Then they can pay fishermen whatever they want.

There'll be no competition. I knew what they were up to and so I told them 'no'."

He poured himself a second cup of coffee. "Well, the fun began. I started getting visits from government people from St. John's. The 'safety experts' they called themselves," he said sarcastically. "All of a sudden I didn't have enough lights in the plants. The floors had to be covered with an anti-slip product. The freezers had to have special locks on them. Just one piece of bullshit after another. Even the workers themselves couldn't believe it. So, I did what they wanted despite the expense. But they still came. I was supposed to have a foreman for every ten men and I had to have a man full time on the fish elevator. I did that too. They couldn't break me."

"Are you saying," Linda asked, "that the government of this province tried to force you to sell to OPI by forcing you to adhere to safety regulations designed for that purpose?"

"Yes, Miss, I'm as sure of that as I'm sure that you're sitting in that chair. OPI had those sons of bitches in their pockets and were getting them to harass me."

It was all coming into perspective for Linda. It was incredible. "But what happened? Why did you have to shut down?"

"You've heard the expression that you can't fight city hall," he replied.

Linda nodded.

"Well, I can fight city hall and I can win. But I can't win against the entire goddamn government. You see, when they couldn't buy me out and they couldn't force me out with the safety bullshit, they authorized the construction of another plant right across the harbour from me. I wrote the sons of bitches in St. John's and I told them that there wasn't enough fish here for two plants, but they wouldn't listen. I was buying all the fish the fishermen could bring me. Harbour Grace, up the road, was buying all they could and so was Bay de Verde, further down the shore. None of us were working to full capacity and we could all use extra fish. OPI owned the plants in Bay de Verde and in Harbour Grace. I was in the middle. Anyway, they built the plant and the first thing they did was to pay their employees twenty five cents an hour more than mine. Then they paid the fishermen more per pound for their fish. There was no way they could make a profit. They were willing to lose money until they drove me out of business. And it worked. The fishermen sold to OPI. I couldn't blame them. I couldn't afford to pay the fishermen what they were paying and I certainly couldn't pay the wages that they were paying. I had to shut down. Then the next year, the wages dropped lower than they ever were and the same thing happened to the price of fish. It didn't take a genius to figure out their plan."

"Why didn't you open up again?"

The old man looked at her for a few seconds before he spoke. "Okay," he began, "let's say I spend my money to bring the plant out of mothballs. Then I convince my customers that I can supply fish to them. I won't be in business for a month before they drive me out again. My pockets aren't deep enough."

"I can't believe what you're telling me, Mr. Lake."

"Well, you believe it Missy, because it's true. Every stinking word of it is true. But I can't prove a thing. I suppose the safety issues were real. But I was the only plant singled out to make the changes. I know in my gut that the politicians were involved with this in some way or another. Hell, half the board of OPI is filled with ex-politicians."

"I didn't mean to say that I don't believe you, Mr. Lake. It's just that I can't believe that this happened."

Walter picked up his pipe and knocked it several times on the ashtray and then began the process of refilling it. "I've told you my story, Miss Fudge. Don't you think that you should tell me your story?"

Linda looked into his eyes. She was convinced that every word he had told her was the absolute truth. She had the proof in the OPI files. "Mr. Lake, first let me tell you that I believe every thing that you've told me. I'm afraid though that I can't tell you why I believe you, but let me just say that now you've confirmed the information I already have. I realize that this is terribly unfair, but I can't tell you any more than that. I can tell you, though, that this issue is not over. I don't think that you were the first person victimized like this and I can't stand idly by and watch it continue."

"It's not me who was the victim. Sure, I lost my business. But look at the fishermen. Right now OPI is selling fresh frozen fish to the States for almost fifty cents a pound. You know how much they're paying fishermen?"

Linda shrugged her shoulders.

"Four cents. Four goddamn cents. I was paying four cents a pound when I was selling it for twenty three cents. So don't call me the victim, Missy."

Linda looked at the man in front of her. She saw him in a completely different light after his last outburst. He truly was an honest man and he was a victim whether he wanted to admit it or not. Maybe by not acknowledging it, he could convince himself that he had not been beaten. She knew that she could learn to like this man. He was very much like her father; honest and direct.

"Yes, you're right," Linda responded.

"Just tell me that you're not working for the government."

"Yes, Mr. Lake, I can tell you that I am not working for the government."

"Good," he mumbled.

Linda knew now that she had what she had come for. She got up from her chair and as she did, he also rose. On top of everything else, he was a gentleman. "I can't thank you enough for everything you've told me," Linda said. "Let me assure you that this issue is not over. I don't know how and I don't know when, but I do know that some day all of what you told me will be revealed."

"It has been a very enjoyable conversation, Miss Fudge. And let me apologize for my language. Since my wife passed on I've been alone and it's not very often that I get charming young ladies such as yourself dropping by. Usually my only visitor is my son and he lives in New York and doesn't visit very often. So, my language gets a little coarse."

"No, Mr. Lake, you don't have to apologize. I've heard a lot worse from my father," she laughed. "Would you mind calling a taxi for me so I can return to my hotel?"

"No, not at all. Go and sit by the fire while I call."

Linda return to her chair beside the fireplace and a few minutes later Walter returned. "They said he'll be here shortly. They have a cab just around the corner." He had barely finished talking when they heard the front door chimes. "There you go," he smiled.

Linda got up from her chair and followed Walter to the door. He held it for her, then rushed to get the second door for her. "Goodbye

Mr. Lake, and thank you for a very enjoyable and informative evening. I would like to come again and chat, if you don't mind?"

"Yes, please call again anytime," he said.

Linda could clearly see that he had enjoyed their time together. She made a motion to leave and then turned and kissed him on the cheek. "Good night," she whispered.

He stood on the step until she was in the taxi and then waved goodbye. He truly was a gentleman.

As she showered away the day she remembered the wonderful smell of tobacco as she kissed his cheek. She liked Walter Lake and she didn't like what had been done to him. She considered talking to Bob about it, but quickly changed her mind. If what she thought was true and that certain government ministers and OPI had conspired to create jobs for the former and a monopoly for the latter, then it would be better if she waited until she had more proof before discussing it with her husband.

Bob returned to the hotel from his walk just as Linda was getting out of the shower. They had a wonderful late dinner and made love for the first time that week. They fell asleep in each others arms and awoke refreshed, but Linda was troubled with what she had discovered after talking with Walter Lake.

She had made up her mind that she had to do something for him. She couldn't just ignore what had happened. Upon returning to St. John's, she worked late every evening and stayed long after Jeremy had gone home for the day. She had made a decision that she knew might haunt her for the rest of her life, but she had to do it. She photocopied everything in the files that had to do with Walter Lake because she knew that if she ever decided to bring this to the police, she would need something to back up her story. But she felt like a traitor. Hawkins and Murphy had given her employment ever since she had finished her first year of university, and would undoubtedly offer her employment when she graduated. But the law they were practising was not the law she wanted to practise. She needed somebody to talk to; someone who was a lawyer and could advise her and assess what she had uncovered. For the first time in her life, Linda had serious doubts about her future.

Eighteen ∿

LINDA RETURNED TO school for her final year disillusioned with the legal profession. She had spent the entire summer working with Jeremy on the OPI account, and the more she learned about the company the more disenchanted she became. Her career, up to this point, had been very structured and directed. But now the structure and direction were disintegrating.

She had tried talking with her law professors, but because she couldn't be specific, they were as vague with their answers as she was with her questions. There was no doubt in her mind that in nearly every dealing, OPI had broken the law, or at the least stretched it very thin. But Linda's problems and confusion didn't arise because of the actions of the politicians. It was that her belief in the law and lawyers was being shaken. Jeremy Hawkins, her idol, and one of the most influential and respected members of the Newfoundland legal profession, was apparently condoning all of this. By Christmas, Bob could tell that something was bothering his wife.

He tried to find out what the problem was, but Linda insisted that it was just the pressure of her last year and that she'd be okay as soon as she graduated. But when next spring came and she graduated, Bob could sense that whatever had been bothering her had caused a change in her. She always seemed preoccupied and sad. Her tenure with the firm was secure because Hawkins and Murphy offered her a job, as was expected, and her starting salary was nearly twice as much as Bob was earning. Though Bob was very happy for them, Linda didn't seem happy for herself. In November, three months after joining the firm, she wrote the Bar Exam and passed with flying colours. It was Friday and Bob took her out for a special celebration dinner, hoping that with the passing of the Bar her disposition would improve. It didn't. On Monday, however, he found out what was bothering her.

Jeremy had arranged a celebration party for Linda at the Newfoundland Hotel for Monday after work. He called Bob on Sunday at home and asked him to be there, but not to tell Linda. Jeremy explained that it was traditional to have a party for lawyers when they passed the Bar and that the half dozen or so lawyers who had written the exam and passed would be toasted that late afternoon and evening. All of the firms in town had staff attending and the press would be covering the event. Bob confirmed his attendance and his promise that he wouldn't tell Linda.

Bob arrived at 4:30 p.m. and Jeremy spotted him as soon as he entered the ballroom. They had met at a Christmas party a few years earlier and had sat together the entire evening. Jeremy explained to him what was going to happen and that Linda could be expected around 5:00 p.m. She and the others who had passed the Bar were presently in Justice Robert's chambers being sworn into the Newfoundland Bar Association. Bob was on his second glass of wine when the main doors were opened and the seven new lawyers were marched into the large ballroom.

In turn, each of the young men, and Linda, the only woman, were brought up onto a stage and their merits were lauded by the new employers. It was very obvious that everybody was enjoying themselves. Everybody that is, except Linda. Linda's speech was saved for last and Jeremy was introduced to the stage by the Master of Ceremonies.

"Fellow members of the Bar, family members, ladies and gentlemen, members of the press, it is with great pleasure that I present to you a man who needs no introduction. So I won't introduce him." With that he left the stage.

Everybody laughed and clapped as Jeremy walked to the stage. As he stepped to the microphone the MC rushed back to the stage again. "Jeremy Hawkins, ladies and gentlemen", he shouted, smiling.

Jeremy, with drink in hand, stood in front of the microphone. "Thank you, Judge Seabright," Jeremy said as he looked across the stage at him. The judge acknowledged him by raising his glass. Jeremy turned to the crowd.

"Ladies and gentlemen, I have the distinct pleasure of intro-ducing you on behalf of Hawkins and Murphy to one of the newest members of the Newfoundland Bar Association. Not only is this person one of the youngest ever to write and pass the exam, she is also one of the brightest."

"She topped her class at Dalhousie this year and despite lower rankings in previous years, I knew that when it came time to graduate, she would show her true mettle. I am, of course, referring to Linda Humby and I am very pleased and honoured to introduce her to you and announce that she will be joining our firm. In fact, she has been working at our firm since her first summer break from university. Ladies and gentlemen, please welcome Linda Humby."

Loud applause erupted and Linda, who had been holding a glass of wine and standing with a couple of other lawyers from Hawkins and Murphy, placed her wine on a table and walked to the stage. Bob followed her with his eyes and felt more proud of her than he had ever felt before. She stepped up to the stage as Jeremy twisted the ring on the microphone stand and let it drop to her height. Linda smiled her thanks.

"Judge Seabright, fellow members of the legal profession, ladies and gentlemen, and especially my wonderful husband, Bob," she said. "I was born and raised in a Newfoundland community that until a few years ago didn't even have electricity. My father was a fisherman. His father and his father before him were fishermen. My brother is a fisherman and there is a good chance that his children will become fishermen."

She paused to clear her throat.

"It's a terrible thing to have to admit, but my father can't read or write. My mother couldn't read or write. My brother can barely read and write. But they can catch fish. Boy, can they catch fish."

Everyone laughed.

"As a little girl growing up in Dark Harbour, I witnessed how people who could read and write took advantage of people like my father and my brother. They created feudal systems not unlike those amongst farmers in Europe in the middle ages. And they cheated them."

The trails of laughter suddenly died.

"I remember returning from fishing with my father and watching as the fish buyer deliberately miscounted his catch to give him credit for less than what he actually had caught. My father was just one of thousands who were cheated. So as a very young girl I decided that I would try and do something about it and the best way I thought I could help was to become a lawyer. Today I am a lawyer. I don't know what it means to be a lawyer yet, because I certainly don't feel any smarter today than I did yesterday."

Once again the crowd laughed.

"I have been very fortunate. As Mr. Hawkins pointed out, I began working for his firm after I finished my first year of University. I was young and naive, but I can't tell you how much I learned from them and how deeply indebted I am to them, especially Mr. Hawkins, for everything they have taught me. I don't know how much you others are getting paid," she said, pointing at the other new lawyers, "but I think it's a crime how much I'm getting."

"Everybody broke into a much louder bout of laughing.

Linda cleared her throat and looked across the stage at Jeremy before she began again,

"But," she began again, "I cannot accept the offer of employment from Hawkins and Murphy,"

Suddenly the room went deathly quiet. Nobody, not even Bob, had expected this turn of events. Everybody looked shocked, but Jeremy was flabbergasted. He stood staring at her, mouth open and in a apparent case of shock.

Linda didn't wait for him to recover. "Thank you and I wish all of my fellow inductees to the Bar every success."

Then, carefully, as if practised a hundred times before, Linda walked across the room, took Bob by the arm and walked out of the room while everybody stared in complete disbelief.

They didn't speak until they reached the car. Bob unlocked the door and held it open for her. He then walked around and got in on the driver's side. He pushed the key in the ignition and turned to Linda.

"What the hell was all that about?" he asked.

Linda turned to look at him. "It's something that I should have done months ago," she said smiling. "But before I tell you what it's all about, I would like you to take me somewhere to get something to eat and then I want to go dancing. I want to stay out late and then go home and make love until the sun comes up," she laughed impishly.

Bob just stared at his wife. He had never seen here like this before, but it was obvious that whatever was troubling her, had suddenly disappeared. "Okay," was all that he could manage as he leaned over and kissed her. She returned his kiss and he could tell that the old Linda had returned.

They had a great meal and Linda felt relaxed as they danced after dinner until well after midnight. Neither of them were in any condition to drive and a Bugden's taxi dropped them off at their house at 1:35 a.m. It wasn't until the next morning in bed, that Bob raised the subject of her decision not to return to work at Hawkins and Murphy.

"Are you ready to talk about what happened yesterday?"

"Yes, but get me a drink of juice first. I feel like I swallowed an old dust mop."

Minutes later Linda was drinking her juice and began to relate her story.

She began by telling him what she had discovered in the OPI files at her office. She went on to explain where she had really gone in Carbonear when she had lied to him that she had a meeting with the plant manager.

Bob hung on every word. With each revelation he got a clearer understanding of what she must have been going through.

"I had to quit when I did. I just couldn't start working as a lawyer for a company who took and is still taking advantage of our families. I can't let this drop without doing something. And I can't do what I feel must be done if I continue to work for them. I realize that I'm throwing away a lot, sweetheart, but I can't sell my principles. You understand don't you?"

Bob moved closer to her and took her in his arms. He kissed her. "Of course I understand and do you know something else?"

"What?"

"You smell like a brewery in spite of the juice."

Linda pushed him away playfully and turned away from him. She was glad that he could make light of the entire issue. She got out of bed, feigning pain, and then returned to give him a quick peck on the cheek.

They had breakfast after they showered and then decided they would spend the day shopping. Bob joked that it could only be window shopping now that he was the sole breadwinner in the family. They were putting on their coats and getting ready to leave then the telephone rang. Bob picked it up.

"Hello."

"Hello, may I speak with Linda Humby please?"

"Yes, sure," Bob said as he passed the telephone to her.

"Hello, this is Linda Humby."

"Mrs. Humby, this is Bill Saunders. I was at the Newfoundland Hotel yesterday when you told Jeremy Hawkins what to do with his job. I'd like to offer you a job now that you're unemployed. We can't give you as much as he was offering but it's honest work and I think you'll like working for us."

Linda couldn't believe what she was hearing. Bill Saunders was a prosecutor working out of the Crown Prosecutor's Office. "This is quite a shock, Mr. Saunders. I wasn't expecting to get a call from anybody after what I did yesterday."

"I understand, Mrs. Humby. I don't expect you to make a decision right now, Think about it for the rest of the weekend and come in to our offices on Monday morning. Say around 10:00 a.m.. We can discuss it further and I can answer any questions you may have."

"Fine, yes. I'll see you then," Linda said, barely able to contain her exitement. She hung up the receiver carefully and turned to Bob who had been listening to the conversation.

"Who was that?" he asked.

"Oh, nobody," Linda said. "Just Bill Saunders from the Crown Prosecutor's Office and they want me to come to work for them," she finished, shouting with increased volume as she spoke each word.

"Great," Bob said as he took a step toward her, picked her up and swung her around. After a couple of twirls he let her drop back to the floor.

"Let's go shopping, Mr. Humby," Linda said, after she had straightened her clothes. "And it doesn't have to be window shopping. "I'm no longer your dependant."

Linda reported to Saunders' office at 9:50 a.m. on Monday morning. The receptionist showed her to the conference room, where she served Linda coffee and informed her that Mr. Saunders would be with her in a few minutes. At precisely 10:00 a.m. two very well dressed men and an older, plainly dressed woman, came into the conference room. Linda was seated and as they entered she stood up to greet them.

"Good morning, Ms. Humby, I'm Paula Rogers, this is Clarence Simms and I believe you have already spoken with Bill." Each of them walked to Linda and shook her hand. They exchanged pleasantries; Linda stood drinking her coffee as the others got coffee and then motioned for her to join them at the table.

"Please sit down," Clarence asked as he held out a chair for her at the head of the large rectangular table. She took her seat as the others sat along the sides.

"Well, Linda," Bill began, "that was quite a performance you gave Friday afternoon. Want to let us in on what it was all about?"

"Not particularly," Linda replied very coolly. "It's just that the way Hawkins and Murphy practise law is a little different that what I had expected."

Her answer got quite a response from the others, who laughed and looked at each other. "Good answer, Linda," Paula responded. "Now, let's get down to the real reason for our meeting. We've watched you working with Jeremy Hawkins and we like the way you do things."

"You've watched me?" Linda asked, surprised to discover that somebody had been observing her work other than Jeremy.

"Yes," Clarence said. "On the last couple of occasions that Jeremy appeared in court, he was much better prepared than he has been in the past. We wondered why, until we were told that he had a very bright student working for him who was doing the majority of his research. So, we put two and two together, as only we lawyers can do, and concluded that the bright student was you."

Linda blushed a little.

"For the past several months we've been looking for another lawyer to join us, and to be perfectly honest, we were looking for somebody with a little more experience than you have. It seems that prosecution does not have the glamour that defence has. When we saw you turn down Jeremy Hawkins' offer, we all agreed that we should try and get you. Jeremy only selects the brightest and the best. This could be a great learning experience for you. I don't think for a moment that you'll spend your entire career with us, but you'll get hands-on court experience with us quicker than with any law firm in this city. That will serve you well when you finally get an offer that you can accept."

"Thank you," Linda said.

"I believe," Paula said, making her pitch, "you know the type of work we do. It is varied and even if you don't choose to stick with it, it will give you some great experience. We believe that you could find work with us very rewarding and challenging. What do you think?" she asked.

Linda looked at the three of them for a few seconds before she responded. "I have to be perfectly honest too. I never once considered going to work for the Crown Prosecutor's Office. I'm honoured to be offered a position. Without sounding sanctimonious, the thought has crossed my mind that because Hawkins and Murphy do meet with you as adversaries in court..."

"Whoa, whoa," Pauls interrupted her. "I believe I know what you're about to say. We're not offering you to join us because of what you may or may not know about Hawkins and Murphy. I want to make that perfectly clear. We want you because you're a bright young lawyer."

"I had to get that clarified," Linda said, sounding relieved.

"We understand," Bill said. "Now what do you say, or do you want more time to think about it?"

Linda drank the last of her coffee before answering. "I need a job," she laughed. "And you're offering me one. What are you offering to go with the job?"

"Low pay, hard work and slave-driving bosses," Bill laughed.

"Then I accept."

"Great," Paula said. "When can you start?"

"How about this morning?"

"I like your attitude," Clarence laughed.

"But," Linda said very sternly, "I'll consider myself on the payroll as of 8:00 a.m."

"I suppose you'll want a raise next week," Paula laughed.

Linda was assigned an office considerably smaller than her previous one and the furniture was clearly 'early modern leftover.' The staff was friendly, and even though the wages were less than one half of what Jeremy was offering, there were good medical benefits and she enjoyed working with Bill. She did the bulk of his research and got the privilege of sitting as his assistant whenever they had to make a court appearance. Finally, at Christmas, six months after becoming an assistant prosecutor, she was assigned her first case.

It was a drunk-driving charge against a repeat offender and Bill was in court to observe her. She sat at the table by herself and in Bill's opinion, obviously shared by the judge, she handled herself well; the defendant was fined fifty dollars and lost his license for three months. Linda confessed later than she had never been more nervous. She was afraid that the judge would hear her knees knocking. That afternoon at the office they celebrated her win. She then took over all prosecutions for drinking and driving charges. Linda welcomed the extra work and the challenge.

For Christmas 1977, her father, Michel, Lori and their two children Millie and Fred, came to Mount Pearl to celebrate Christmas with her and Bob. It was the first visit to Mount Pearl and St. John's for all of them, and the shopping malls and the traffic were quite a thrill.

But the visit wasn't all fun. Michel explained to his sister that it seemed each year fish prices were getting lower and lower. The previous year the price for fish was the same as it had been seven years earlier. When Michel saw the one pound packages of fish Linda brought home from the supermarket, he simply refused to believe the price. Even with Michel's meagre arithmetic skills, he realized that somebody was getting very rich from his and the other fishermen's labour. Linda's suggestion was for him to sell his fish to somebody other than his current buyer.

"Who?" Michel asked. "It's the same price at all the plants. OPI owns every one of them so there's nobody else to sell to."

Lori remembered her conversation with Walter Lake. He had been one of OPI's victims. Now her own family was becoming their victim.

It was a very enjoyable two weeks that ended too quickly. Before they left, Linda and Bob promised to come and visit for at least one week the following summer. It had been too long since they had been home.

Linda returned to work after the holidays to a very busy schedule. Dozens of drivers had been picked up for alcohol-related offences and Linda was kept busy well into March. But her conversation with her brother was always on her mind; she thought oftenabout what was happening to fishermen all over the province. She knew that she had to do something and had to confide in someone. She chose Paula.

It was late Friday afternoon. She noticed Paula's office door was open, knocked on the door front and walked in. Paula, sitting behind her desk, looked up from a mountain of papers.

"Hello, what are doing here this late on a Friday?"

"I'm either ambitious or stupid. I can't figure it out," Linda answered.

Paula laughed too, "Is there something I can do for you?"

"I'm not sure, but I've got to talk to somebody abut it."

"Well, you've got my attention."

"You remember when I first came to work here?"

Paula nodded.

"I said then that I didn't want to talk about why I left Hawkins and Murphy. But now I do."

"Okay, I'm all ears."

"When Brent Sears was killed, Jeremy asked me to become familiar with the OPI account. You know, of course, that they handle all of OPI's business.

Paula nodded again.

"My job was to take charge of all the files, become completely familiar with everything in them and to assist Jeremy with the account. I was still only a student, and it mostly involved filing and retrieving information and things like that. Anyway, as I read the files, I started to see a pattern. The government was helping OPI to take over fish processing plants in this province. And it seemed that government ministers, after leaving politics, were being appointed to OPI's Board. In one particular case, the Lake Plant in Carbonear, I actually went out and visited the owner, Walter Lake. There were even letters in the files that he had written to the Minister of Fisheries. I didn't tell him who I was, of course. He nevertheless agreed to talk to me and what he told me confirmed all of my suspicions. The government and OPI are in bed together."

Paula couldn't believe what she was hearing. "I always suspected that things weren't right with that company," she blurted out. "Everything always seemed to fall right into place for them. But I never dreamt it was anything like this! Are you sure of this?"

"Yes, I'm positive. You may end up firing me for what I'm about to tell you, but I'm going to anyway. I made copies of some of the documents in those files. I don't know why I did it, but I suppose I thought that if I ever told somebody about this, they would never believe me unless I had some proof."

"You did what?"

Linda just nodded her head.

"I can't believe this, You're telling me that you have information that would connect OPI and the government of this province in some sort of scheme to drive private fish plant owners out of business."

"Yes, I do."

Paula got up from behind her desk. "And you acquired this information illegally."

"Yes, I suppose."

"I've just got to say that you never fail to surprise me, Linda Humby. So what are you planning to do with all of this?"

"I don't know. You see, my brother came to visit with us over Christmas and he told me that he's getting paid the same price for his fish now as he was getting seven years ago. Where he lives, there is nobody to sell his fish to other than OPI. I believe that OPI is deliberately keeping the price of fish low. I want to do something, but I don't know what.

"Jesus Christ," Paula whispered. "If what you're telling me is true, you're talking about a scandal that will rock the very foundation of this province. My God, Linda, what you're saying is unbelievable. Would you mind showing me some of the papers you have?"

"No, come to my office."

Paula spent several minutes skimming through the files. "It looks like what you're saying has some basis in fact. These papers, even though they were obtained illegally, seem to confirm your claim that if this ever got to trial some fairly senior people would be doing jail time. I still find all of this hard to believe. I understand now though why you didn't want to return to work for Jeremy Hawkins. You realize, of course, that if you had gone back to your office after you had been sworn in, you wouldn't have been able to reveal any of this without a real fear of being disbarred?"

"You know I never realized that until now. I just didn't want to work in a firm where I knew this type of stuff was going on. But that still leaves me with the question of what am I to do with all of this."

"That's the sixty four thousand dollar question. We know one thing. It wouldn't be advisable to take the government to court. Those papers would not be allowed to be entered as evidence. And you haven't been victimised, so there is no way you can bring a civil suit. You could go to *The Evening Telegram* but they won't print anything derogatory because of the legal implications. I really don't know what to tell you. But I agree with you that you simply can't ignore this. There are corrupt people both in government and in OPI and they have harmed and are continuing to harm the fishermen of this province."

"That's my point," Linda said.

"Give me the weekend to think about this and first thing Monday morning let's get together again and talk about it, okay?

"Okay."

"Good, and don't discuss this with anyone else, because the implications are incredible."

"I know," Linda admitted. I've been living with this for over a year and I'm just glad to be able to talk to somebody about it, especially another lawyer. I'll look forward to talking again on Monday."

They parted company and Linda spent a very relaxed weekend with Bob. OPI didn't ever cross her mind again until Sunday evening. She went to bed, hoping that Paula would have something constructive to offer on Monday morning.

Paula was already in her office when Linda arrived. "I think I know how to get this to court," she said as Linda entered her office.

"Good morning," Linda laughed.

"Sorry. Good morning," Paula apologized. "I've been thinking about this OPI thing all weekend."

"Welcome to the club," Linda said, frowning.

"The solution," Paula continued, " is to find somebody who's willing to bring suit against OPI. Somebody who feels so aggrieved that they want to sue them. Can you think of anybody?"

"Yes, of course. My brother."

"Think again. On what grounds? To prove price-fixing will be extremely difficult if not impossible. You will have to find something else, and show that the price-fixing was the benefit to OPI."

Linda thought for a few moments.

"You need somebody who has been directly affected by the actions of OPI, and you need to show that the actions were illegal and caused financial or other distress."

"Walter Lake. Walter Lake lost his fish plant because he couldn't compete with the deep pockets of OPI who were given government support to compete against him."

"Yes, Walter Lake. If you want to get this matter out in the open, you have to talk with h im and convince him to hire you to sue OPI. Then, if you're successful, not only will you win damages for him, you will be able to bring out the corruption in government. But before you even consider this, let me caution you about the downside. You're taking on one of the biggest corporations in this part of the country. They'll have the best lawyers and unlimited resources to support them, and as soon as you start talking about government corruption you'll be tackling a whole new problem. I'd give you a snowball's chance in Hell of winning your case. You won't be able to enter into evidence any of the files that you have and if that's not enough, you're a public prosecutor working for government. You'd have to quit your job and, if you lose, you'll have one hell of a time finding employment in this city again. Even if you win, you'll have a hell of a time finding employment."

Linda stared at her boss. She was right. She'd have to be crazy to pursue this any further. "I suppose you're right," Linda admitted.

Paula looked at her long charge. "Yes, I am right."

"But what they're doing is wrong," Linda said, frustrated.

"Of course it's wrong. It's corrupt and the fishermen of this province have been the victims of corruption ever since the first one of them pitched a basket over the side of the *Matthew*. And the corruption will continue."

Linda looked directly into Paula's eyes. She saw something there that she had not seen before. "What would you do?" she asked.

"That's unimportant, what I would do." I'm fifty-two years old. In three years I'm going to get a pension and I've already bought my retirement home in Florida. But you've got your entire career in front of you. I can't decide for you. I can only say that thirty years ago when I was in university, I met a young boy who practically begged me to marry him. Even though I loved him, I thought that getting married would interfere with my career. I've always wondered how it would have been if I had married him."

"What are you telling me?" Linda asked.

"There's an old adage that I can't remember where it came from or who wrote it, but it goes something like this: It's better to have loved and lost than to have never loved at all. Just ask yourself why you became a lawyer. Was it because you wanted a nice safe eight-to-four job, was it because of the money and the prestige that goes with the job, or was it something else?"

Linda never responded.

"I think that you've answered your own question. You became a lawyer to fight for the rights of those who have nobody to fight for them."

"My God, Paula, what am I letting myself in for?"

"Probably the biggest and dirtiest fight of your life. And it will be a fight to the end. You'll be playing with the big boys and they play dirty."

"I don't care. I just have to do this."

"I knew you would," Paula smiled. "But there are a few things you have to do first. You've got to convince Walter Lake to go along with your plan and you've got to find out everything you possibly can about OPI. Legally, that is. You have the papers, but like I said, you won't get them entered as evidence. But you know they exist and you've got to find a way to get your hands on them legally. I suggest, however, that before you quit your job, you give this one hell of a lot more thought. From what I've seen they're all as guilty as hell. The trouble is, they're some of the most influential people in this province."

"You're not helping," Linda said, smiling.

"You asked for my opinion and now you have it. You've no experience and you're going up against the best legal minds in this province and no doubt the rest of Canada, if OPI deems it necessary. I know you want to fix this but I suggest you give this a lot of thought before you decide what to do. Think about what you're giving up. And talk to your husband. He'll have a big stake in this as well."

Linda leaned back in her chair and stared up at the ceiling. After a few moments she spoke. "You're right. I'll talk with Walter Lake and tell him who I really am. If he doesn't want to go through with this, then that will be the end of it. If he does, then now that I know what I have to do, I'll have to make a decision. You've been a big help, Paula. And let me assure you, I'll give this job my full attention for as long as I'm working out of this office. The moment I make up my mind either way I'll let you know."

"I couldn't ask for anything more. Now get outta here and go see Bill. He tells me that you're ready to take on something a little more challenging."

Nineteen ∽

LINDA WAS VERY busy during the spring of 1978; the little free time she had, she spent with Bob. They had promised each other early in their marriage that they would make time for themselves just as they made time for their jobs. They always attended Sunday morning church service and reserved one evening a week to go out for a meal, to see a movie, or some other form of entertainment.

Linda thought about OPI a lot, but she never seemed to have the time to do much after meeting with Walter Lake. She told him everything. He was impressed with her honesty and her personal motives for wanting to get OPI in court. He was aware of what he might be letting himself in for, but at the end of their meeting, admitted that he wanted her to proceed in whatever manner she deemed appropriate. Linda explained that it might be a couple of years before she was ready to bring the matter to court. He realized what was required and gave her his support. She left Carbonear promising to keep in touch with him as often as she deemed it necessary. That had been a few months earlier.

She spoke with Michel at least once a month. He was becoming disillusioned with the fishery. It seemed that the cost of fishing kept going up, but the price he was getting for his catch remained the same. Their talks renewed her desire to quit her job and dedicate all her efforts to pursuing OPI. But it simply wasn't in her best interests to proceed at this time. She had talked it over with Bob and he told her to do what she felt she must. She just wasn't ready to take the big step. Instead, she spent a good part of her spare time trying to find out what she could about OPI.

Through a contact at the Fishermen's Union she got the number for the major buyer of Newfoundland cod, in Boston. She was shocked to find that the price was set daily, but it had nearly tripled in the past five years. Yet the price paid to fishermen, according to Michel, remained the same.

She kept in regular contact with Walter. She tried to sound positive, but she knew there was lot of work to be done before she could hope to get into a courtroom. Getting OPI in court was relatively easy. But once she got them there, nothing would be easy. She knew that the company traded on the Toronto Stock Exchange and she had to find out as much background information as she could. That's why she arranged a meeting with Ian Rose.

She had met Ian at a Government House New Year's Day Levee. He was a young stockbroker who accidentally spilled his drink on her dress. Despite the reason for the meeting, they became good friends. He had been accompanied by his wife Sally, and since their accidental meeting they had gone out as couples several times. Ian had convinced them to open an account with his firm and true to his word, he had increased the value of their investment nearly eight percent in four months. He had been a broker for only a couple of years, but possessed the instructs of a seasoned veteran. Linda knew that if there was someone she could consult with to get information on OPI, it was Ian. She had called him a few days earlier and they agreed to meeting for lunch at The Admiral. He was there when she arrived.

"You're late, Counsellor," Ian said as the maître d' escorted her to his table. He always referred to her as counsellor.

"It was your choice to eat at a restaurant with parking half a mile away," she exaggerated. "I did see however, that your car is parked just outside and the meter has expired. As an officer of the court, I consider it my responsibility to call and have it ticketed."

Ian laughed. "And I would probably buy you five thousand shares in a company that is building deep freezers to sell to the Inuit." He reached to kiss her cheek as the maître d' held her chair and took her order for a glass of white wine.

"It's been a couple of weeks since I've seen you and Bob. How is the old school marm?"

"Fine. I guess it's our turn to have you and Sally over for dinner if that's what you're hinting about. How about this Friday evening?"

"Sounds fine. I'll check with her and I'll call your office later this afternoon."

"I won't be there, I've taken a couple of weeks of vacation. Have Sally call me at home this evening. Now, what have you got for me on OPI?"

Ian drained the remainder of his Chivas and held it up for a refill. "It's a big company," he said as he reached down to the floor and picked up his briefcase. He flipped open the locks and retrieved a large folder. He passed it to her and closed the case and returned it to the floor.

"Wow," Linda said as she took the folder and placed it on the table beside her drink. "Can you give me a overview of what's inside?" she asked.

The waiter arrived with Ian's refill. ""Do you mind if I order for us?" Ian asked as he picked up his drink.

"No, not at all, as long as it's a bowl of the wonderful seafood chowder and a small Caesar salad."

The waiter looked at her and smiled. He scribbled her order without looking at the pad.

"I'll have the same," Ian said.

The waiter left smiling from ear to ear. Linda was laughing. They both enjoyed these games.

"Okay then," he managed after she had composed herself, "Do you want me to brief you on what's in that file or not?"

"Yes, please" Linda answered trying to sound apologetic but not sounding convincing.

"Right then. OPI is part of a much larger company. But before I get to that, let me tell you a little about OPI. It owns and operates 53 fish processing plants in New Brunswick, Nova Scotia, Prince Edward Island and Newfoundland. It has a fleet of 16 trawlers, 7 freezer ships, and 3 meal processing plants where it turns offal into pet food. Additionally, it has interests in numerous other companies which produce many of the products used in offshore fishing operations. You can have a look at the latest financial statements that are in the folder and you'll see why I encouraged Bob to buy 100 shares in the company for your account a few months ago. We paid fourteen and an eighth for them and today they are trading for seventeen and three quarters," he said proudly. He continued with the background of the company, its management and pro-jected growth.

While he talked Linda found the financial statements and exam-ined them as she sipped her wine. When he took a break to drink his Scotch, she whistled softly as she looked at the balance sheet. "They are pretty healthy, aren't they?" she admitted.

"That's an understatement," Ian said laughing. "The company began in 1948 and its history has one success story after another. The Board of Directors of the company is filled with a who's who of Newfoundland politics, as well as former politicians of other provinces, and that's probably a good reason for its success. They don't need to spend money on lobby groups. Their own board is a lobby group in itself."

Linda continued to look through the folder as Ian spoke.

"We have a student working with us this summer and I asked him, after you called me, to trace the stock history of the company. He finished it this morning just before I left for lunch. It's at the back," he added, pointing at the folder. "The stocks have split numer-ous times and the names have changed as often."

"What do you mean, split?" Linda asked.

"When the price of a stock reaches a price that the company decides might be out of the reach of the average buyer, the stock is split. For example, let's say the stock trades at $20. Normally the minimum purchase, a board lot, is 100 shares. They would cost $2000. So, they split the stock which puts its price at $10 and every person who holds shares now has twice as many. That way an investor can purchase a board lot for $1000."

"And the name changes?"

"Companies change names, acquire partners, that sort of thing. So they change the name."

Linda continued to flip through the pages.

"The big news however, is who the parent company of OPI is," Ian said proudly.

"With a company this size, one wouldn't think that there would be a parent company," Linda commented.

"That's what I thought," Ian quickly added. "But they are owned by somebody else and that somebody else has a sixty percent share in all outstanding securities. Any idea who is it?" Ian teased.

Linda looked up and shook her head.

"Leblanc Industries."

"The hotel people?" Linda asked.

"The hotel people, the garment people, the transportation people, the 'you name it they're involved in it' people," Ian answered.

"That's incredible. What's his name, the fellow who runs Leblanc Industries, isn't he a recluse or something? I've heard him referred to as the Canadian version of Howard Hughes."

"His name is Denis Leblanc and he is a very private guy. He's apparently alive and kicking though, and lives in Toronto. Apparently, he's one of the richest people in Canada."

The waiter delivered their chowder at that moment and the two of them ravenously attacked what was unquestionably the best seafood chowder in the province. They concentrated on their food and the subject changed to family and vacations and politics. As they progressed through their lunch however, the subject switched back to OPI. Ian continued to brief her and by the time the bill arrived, she knew as much as he did about the company.

The maitre d' arrived as they were finishing their coffee and after being assured that the meal was excellent, he placed the bill in front of Linda.

Ian laughed. "Touché," he said.

Linda laughed too. "You really are a good sport," Linda said. "When I went to powder my nose a few minutes ago, I asked the maitre d' to give me the bill. But now that the point is made, you can have it. I'm sure that with those huge fees you charge our account whenever you make a transaction, there's lots available for your expense account."

Ian took it without speaking, added fifteen percent and scribbled his signature on the bottom. The maitre d' held her chair and Ian held the door as they left. They briefly hugged outside the restaurant and Ian stepped to his car as Linda made her way up the street. When she has travelled a short distance, Ian called out to her.

"Hey Linda," he called out.

Linda turned and could see him waving over the heads of the many shopper on the sidewalk.

"I signed your name and put your address on the bill," he called out, laughing as he stepped in is car and sped away.

Linda returned home and spent the remainder of the day poring over the information that Ian had given her. School had finished a few weeks earlier and Bob had decided to take a few classes at the university. They both lay in bed with piles of papers in front of them. It was nearly midnight when the telephone rang on the bed table beside Linda. "Hello," she answered.

"Who is it?" Bob asked, before Linda even knew who it was herself. She held up her hand for him to be quiet.

"Lori," she said, placing her hand over the mouthpiece. Bob turned back to his papers. He didn't notice the smile on Linda's face suddenly disappear and the tears begin to run down her face. He only noticed when he heard the telephone drop to the floor. He looked over and her face was buried in her hands.

"My God, what is it?" he asked as he dropped the papers and reached for her. "What is it sweetheart? What's the matter?"

Linda cried out. "Nooooooo? Oh God, nooooo."

Bob didn't know what to do. He suddenly remembered the telephone, jumped out of bed and picked it up from the floor. "Who is this?" he yelled into it.

"It's Lori, Bob. I'm afraid that Linda's father has had a stroke. He didn't suffer."

Bob sat on the end of the bed with the telephone to his ear. Lori continued to give the details but he wasn't listening. He just looked at his wife. The death of her mother had been traumatic and she still cried sometimes when she thought about her. But she had been even closer to her father; the next few weeks would be a living hell for her. He wanted to console her but couldn't think of anything to say.

Linda wanted to leave for Dark Harbour right away, but Bob convinced her to wait until morning. Sleep would be out of the question, so they got up and he made coffee. He spiked it with a little alcohol and she knew it. She insisted that he return to bed because he would have to do the driving in the morning. She would be okay. He knew she wouldn't be. Her eyes were already red and swollen. But he did have to get some sleep.

He was up again at 6:00 a.m. Linda had packed a couple of suitcases and she was dressed, sitting in front of the blank television screen, still sobbing. They didn't have breakfast. Later in the afternoon, they arrived in Fortune where Michel was waiting for them at the wharf. Bob had called from Boat Harbour and told Michel when they would be arriving.

Joe was buried two days later. Everybody from Dark Harbour attended the funeral; the tiny church was overflowing with mourners. Many stood outside and watched the service from the open doors. Linda had barely slept since the late night telephone call, and the nurse prescribed a sedative, which she took after the funeral. She slept until noon the following day. When she awoke the redness had gone from her eyes, but the sadness and the sense of loss could still be seen.

Michel did not show his sadness as openly as Linda, although his voice cracked when he talked about his father. Lori confessed to Bob shortly after they arrived that Michel had cried like a baby when he was told of his father's death. But he remained strong afterwards. Several times he approached Linda as if he had something to say, and then withdrew.

A week later, the worst had passed and Michel and Linda sat at the kitchen table drinking coffee. It was a cool summer evening. Linda, with the help of the others, had come to realize that her father was old and that a stroke at his age was not totally unexpected. He had not suffered and that was a blessing. Michel told her that Joe had not been ill and had actually been out in the boat with him a few times. They tried to remember all the good things.

They were smiling as they talked about growing up and the fun they had as children and young adults. The door opened and Bob and Lori entered. They had gone out to give Michel and Linda some time together. As they saw their smiling faces, they knew that the time together had been good for them.

"It's a beautiful night, isn't it?" Lori commented as they came in.

"Yes, it's lovely," Linda answered as she got two cups from the cupboard, filled them with coffee and placed them on the table. Bob sat beside her.

"How are you managing, deary?" Lori asked.

"Oh, I'm gradually coping," she said, smiling weakly.

"Good," she said. "And you too, Michel?" she asked.

He nodded. Then he turned to his sister.

"Linda," he began, "I've got something to tell you and I know I should have told you this before and I know you're going to be mad at me, but I can't put it off any longer."

Linda looked at Bob, then Lori and back to Michel.

"Sis," he spoke again. He hadn't called her Sis since they were children. He looked down into his cup as he spoke again. "Dad wasn't our real father."

Linda drew a quick breath of air and put her hand over her mouth. "What are you saying? What kind of nonsense is this you're saying, Michel? Of course Dad is our real father!"

Michel looked to Lori for support.

"I'm afraid that he's telling the truth, Linda. Your father, Joe, that is," she said, correcting herself, "told us that after your mother, I mean Millie, died. We wanted to tell you, but your father, I mean Joe, wouldn't let us."

Linda looked at Bob again. She opened her eyes and raised her eyebrows in disbelief. "You say that Dad isn't my real father and that Mom isn't my real mother? This can't be a joke. It must be a dream. Please God, make this a dream," she pleaded as she looked skyward.

Tears appeared in Michel's eyes. "No, this isn't a joke. I just wish it was. We have all the proof. We have a whole lot of papers and stuff that proves our real mother was a woman called Francine Matte and she came to Dark Harbour when I was really small. That's her name on the boat. I really don't know who I am. She died when you were born and so Mom and Dad became our parents. I couldn't believe it either when I first heard it. You have to believe me. My name isn't even Michel Judge. It's Michael Lablank or something like that. She told Mom, I mean Millie...I don't know what I mean," he said throwing up his arms in frustration.

Lori took up where he left off. "When Francine was dying she confessed to Millie that her name was 'Forest.' But we found a birth certificate that says Michel's last name is Lablank," she said, mispronouncing it. "He even got mail and it was addressed to Michel Matte. So we don't know what his name is."

"It's Michel Judge as far as I'm concerned," Michel shouted.

"What's this proof you have?" Linda managed.

Lori got up, went into another room and returned with a large envelope. She placed it on the table in front of Linda. Linda looked at Bob, reached for it, and pulled out its contents.

Slowly she examined each piece of paper and then passed it to Bob. She examined the birth certificate. "It looks authentic," she said. Suddenly she drew a deep breath. "Do you have all this money?" she asked as she looked at the letter from the bank.

"No, it's still there. At least the bulk of it is still there. Michel took a little to do repairs on his boat."

Then Linda got to the stock certificates. "Oh my God," she gasped, when she read the writing on them. "How long have you had these?"

"They came with the second letter from the bank. We didn't know what they were so we just put them in with the rest of the papers. What are they?"

"They're stock certificates. There's ten thousand shares. That means, the holder of these owns a little of the company named on the certificate. I've never heard of it," she added. "I have no idea what they're worth now, or if the company even exists today."

Linda continued to look through the papers until she finished with them. "Is this all there is?" she asked.

"No, there's more," Michel said. "Dad kept a trunk full of her things over at his house. There's an awful lot of papers and things in it. He showed it to us once, but we never looked in it very long. There are a lot of papers that Lori was going to read, but Dad put the trunk away before she had a chance to read them."

"Do you know where it is now?" Linda asked.

"Yes, of course. It's in the attic?"

"Good, let's go and look in it."

"Now?" Michel asked.

"Yes, right now," Linda said as she stood up from the table and walked to the door. Michel and Bob followed her. Lori remained with the children.

Michel found the old steamer trunk and with Bob's help, carried it downstairs. They placed it in the centre of the kitchen; before it was on the floor, Linda was already lifting up the cover. It creaked as it opened.

For the next hour, while Michel and Bob watched, Linda emptied the contents of the trunk. There were some old dresses and jewellery. An old typewriter and at least a hundred pages of typing. It appeared to be a diary. There were also two purses, but they were empty. Linda didn't speak as she examined each item. Occasionally, she would make a grunt or a gasp, but otherwise she didn't give the others any suggestion as to what she was discovering. Finally, she got up from the floor and sat at the table holding a picture.

"The name on the back indicates that this person is Linda. Any idea who this person is?" she asked.

They shook their heads.

"I suppose I should have told you sooner," Michel said trying to apologize again.

"Yes, you should have," she said very sternly. "But I suppose I might have done the same if I had been in your place," she added in a much softer tone.

"What did you find out from all of this?" he asked, pointing at the trunk.

"Well, it looks like you're right. I'll need more time to look at it, but there's no doubt that Mom and Dad weren't our natural parents. It appears as if this Francine woman is our mother and she kept some kind of diary. I'll have to read it. Did Dad tell you anything about her that you haven't told me?"

"No, I don't think so. He just said that she came here and told them that she was a writer. She also said that her husband had been killed a couple of years earlier. But then Mom found out that she was pregnant with you, and on her death bed after giving birth to you, she admitted that she was running away from her husband. She also told Mom that she didn't want us to go back with him and that Mom should take us and rear us. That's what Mom and Dad did. I didn't know anything about this until I got the letter from the bank in Halifax. We opened it over at Dad's house and that's when he told us."

"This is all simply incredible," Linda managed. "All these years I didn't suspect a thing. All these years they let us believe that they were our natural parents."

"Just a minute," Michel interrupted her. "I don't care who our natural mother and father were. All I know is that Mom and Dad will always be our parents."

Tears suddenly began to run down Linda's cheeks. "You're right," she sobbed. "I'm sorry, but this is all such a shock. Dad's death followed by this is more than I can take."

Bob had spoken very little the entire evening. "Come on sweetheart, let's go to bed. All of this will still be here in the morning. We'll stay an extra day so you can look at it. Once you've had a chance to read everything, then maybe it'll make sense."

"You're right," she said as she got up and kissed him. Michel got up at the same time.

"Yes, Bob's right. We'll talk about this some more in the morning. Good night," he said as he walked to the door to make his way home.

Bob insisted that Linda take a sleeping pill. She slept soundly until 9:00 a.m. the next morning. As soon as she was up she began re-reading the papers and her mother's diary.

By late afternoon Linda had finished reading and she walked to the graveyard. Lori had told her where to find Francine's grave. She paused to stop at her mother's and father's graves. The ground had been covered with sods and someone had watered it earlier. She looked around to find Francine's grave and was surprised to see that it was just a few feet from her mother's. She tried to remember if she had seen it before but she had no such recollection.

She stood silent for a few moments, reading the inscription. "So, you're my mother, Francine Matte?" she whispered. "You may have been my biological mother, but the woman beside you will always be my real mother."

Linda stood for a long time staring at the two graves. Occasionally she would turn her gaze to her father's grave. "You should have told me Dad," she repeated several times.

Linda spent nearly an hour at the graveyard and during that time she tried to absorb what had happened in the past week. The death of her father had been a terrible blow, but the news that he wasn't her natural father was equally hard to accept. But the evidence was buried in front of her. She had hoped that her mother's papers would tell her who she was and who her father was. Unfortunately, all of the typed papers were stories about Francine's childhood and her experiences in Dark Harbour. Many of the pages were written about what she wanted to do after she left Dark Harbour. But there was no real substance to the stories. The only thing she had was Michel's birth certificate. It that was real, it was a starting point. All she knew for sure was that her mother's real name was Francine Forest. Matte had been her maiden name. Surely that was the truth, for that was what she had said on her death bed.

There was one other thing that might help Linda find out more. In several of her mother's stories, she had talked about a town in Quebec called Roberval. That was where she would have to start. Nothing else mattered now. OPI would have to be put on hold until she found out who she really was. Her entire life had been shattered. She had always been Linda Fudge, the daughter of Millie and Joe Fudge of Dark Harbour. That had been a lie. But Millie and Joe would always be her parents. The woman buried deep in the ground beside the moss-covered headstone may have given her life, but Millie was her mom. Joe was her dad. But she had to find out who Francine was and she had to find out who her father was. Maybe he was still alive. Why did Francine leave him? There were many questions for which she had to have answers.

Twenty

LINDA DID A lot of thinking on her way back to Mount Pearl. She said a tearful good bye to Michel in Fortune as they had so many times in the past. The new road to Dark Harbour would be finished the next time they returned and as they stepped off the boat onto the wharf in Fortune, it was, she realized, the end of an era. Linda stopped for a quick visit to Bob's parents, but despite the appeals of Bob's mother, they wouldn't stay for lunch. Both of them were anxious to get home. Bob had left Dark Harbour a day before so he could visit with his parents.

Normally Linda chatted a lot in the car on the trip between Fortune and Mount Pearl. Wildlife was plentiful and there were always berry pickers or something else to talk about. But not today. Linda remained surprisingly quiet. Bob knew that she was thinking and it was best to leave her alone, Even though they had been married a short time, they knew each other very well, When the time came for him to be consulted, he knew that she would talk with him. The time just hadn't arrived yet.

It was late Thursday by the time that they arrived home. They had left in a hurry and in the week and a half that they had been gone, the house plants were nearly dead. Linda had a pitcher of water and was watering them before she had even removed her coat. Bob unloaded the car and unpacked the suitcase while Linda cleaned the dishes that had been soaking in the sink. She finished before he did and then thumbed through the telephone book to find the name of her friend. She was talking on the telephone when Bob came into the living room.

"Ian," he heard her say as he walked to the TV and turned it on.

"Yes, thank you. It was quite a shock to both of us."

"Thank her for us. Neither of you ever had a chance to meet him. I'm sure that if you had, you would have liked him."

Bob listened to the one-sided conversation and it became obvious that she was talking to Ian Rose.

"Ian, I wonder if you could do me a favour."

There was a pause as she waited for a response.

"Thank you. I have some old stock certificates. I wonder if you could meet with me tomorrow morning and tell me what they're worth?"

Pause

"Great."

Pause.

"Yes, sure I could. Wait a minute until I get them." She placed the receiver on table, rummaged through her purse and found a small envelope. She opened it, took out several papers and picked up the receiver. "It reads, East Coast Sea Products, and there's ten of them with 1,000 on each of them," she said, while reading from the papers and speaking into the receiver.

There was a pause until she spoke again. "Okay, fine. See you at eleven."

"What was that all about?" Bob asked.

"That was Ian. I wanted him to check out these old stocks and tell me how much they're worth. He wanted to know the name on them so he could do some checking before we meet tomorrow morning."

"I see," Bob said.

"Michel wants me to keep them, but we don't need the money, do we?" she asked.

"Are they worth anything?"

"I really don't know, but if they are, I wouldn't say they're worth very much. If the price of fish doesn't improve, Michel and Lori and going to need the money from these things and what they have in Halifax."

"Then find out what they're worth and send it to them," Bob said.

The two of them relaxed for the remainder of the evening. It was good to be home. Linda made them some tea and they went to bed after the ten o'clock news. The past week and a half had been an exhausting experience for the two of them and it wasn't until 9:00 a.m. the next morning that they awoke.

Linda decided to stop off at her office before meeting with Ian. Bob dropped her off and she said she would take the bus home. Bob asked that she call before she left just in case he was at home. He was going to the university to see if there was any way he could salvage the course he had abruptly left without informing the professor.

Paula was happy to see Linda and to find out that she had safely made it back home. Linda informed her that she would be returning to work on Monday. She had a meeting dealing with her father's death at 11:00 and she didn't know how long she would be. They had coffee and chatted about the events of the past couple of weeks. Paula expressed a real interest in Linda's grief and it was sincere. They had become close friends, but not close enough for Linda to confide in her that Joe hadn't been her biological father. At 10:40 she left for her appointment with Ian.

She arrived a few minutes early, and to a very enthusiastic Ian Rose. He was pacing the foyer to the entrance to the corporate offices, as she got off the elevator.

"Linda," he called out to her as he looked up in response to the footsteps on the tiled floor. He ran to greet her and then wrapped his arms around her and kissed her on the cheek. "Once again, let me offer our deepest sympathy over the death of your father," he said as he drew back from their embrace.

"Thank you Ian," she managed, smiling weakly.

"Now," he spoke again, moving from her front to her side and then leading her up the hall to his office, "where in the name of God, did you get those stock certificates?" Before she had a chance to offer, she was greeted with several "Good mornings" from the members of the staff as they neared Ian's office.

"They're my brother's. How much are they worth?" she asked as he held her chair to sit in front of his desk.

"Not so fast," Ian smiled. "How much do you know about the stock market?"

"A little," she answered.

"You remember when we had lunch and I explained to you about stock splits?"

Linda nodded.

"Well, that was a part of the problem we faced when we tried to track down those certificates. You see, your brother had shares valued at twenty thousand dollars."

"Wow!" Linda said, "they're worth that much?"

"Don't get ahead of yourself," Ian laughed. "They used to be worth that much when they were first issued in March, 1948 to raise capital for a new company called East Coast Sea Products. The company began operations in Nova Scotia and a few years later, after Newfoundland entered Confederation, it began operating here as well. A few years after than, it opened up an office in Boston and was renamed Ocean Products International."

"Are you telling me that these are shares in OPI?" Linda asked with obvious disgust in her voice.

"Yes, I'm afraid so," Ian admitted.

"Well, if that's the case, you can dispose of them right now," Linda snapped.

"It would be a pleasure ma'am," Ian answered, obviously very pleased with Linda's decision. "And what should I do with the proceeds of the sale?"

Linda stopped for a few seconds. "As I mentioned, the shares belong to my brother. You can deposit the proceeds to my account, if they're worth anything now, and I'll make arrangements to send him a cheque."

Linda got up to leave. Ian remained seated, still smiling like he had won the sweepstakes. As she reached the door he spoke.

"Linda, you have no idea how much they're worth do you?" he asked.

"No, and I don't particularly care either," she answered as she opened the door.

"Not even the tiniest bit interested?" he asked.

Linda turned and closed the door. "Okay, how much?" she asked, with more of an irritated tone than an interested one.

"Remember stock splits?"

"Yes, yes, yes. I'm sick of hearing about stock splits."

"East Coast Sea Products, now Ocean Products International, has split a total of five times since the shares were first issued. So, instead of ten thousand shares, your brother now owns a total of three hundred and twenty thousand shares. This morning when the Exchange opened in Toronto, shares of Ocean Products International were trading at eighteen dollars and twenty five cents. That means that these old pieces of paper here are worth..." he paused for effect, "are you ready for this?"

"Yes," Linda said, "get on with it."

"You have shares worth a total of five million eight hundred and forty thousand dollars."

Linda suddenly felt weak. She looked for a place to sit down. Ian got her a glass of water.

"Here drink some of this," he directed.

Linda drank a little. She then placed the glass on the table.

"You can't be serious?" she finally managed.

"I couldn't be more serious. That's the value of those shares if you sold them today."

"In my wildest dreams I thought they might be worth a few thousand dollars, but five million? That's incredible!"

"That's incredible all right and I think you consider now about keeping them."

"No," Linda snapped. "I still want to sell them, but even the little I know about the market tells me that I think it would be wise if we sold them a little at a time."

Ian smiled his agreement. "Yes, you're right, but leave that to me. I'll take care of everything. Now, you know that there will be a fee to dispose of them," he quickly added.

"I know," Linda answered. "And your share of the fee will probably pay off the mortgage on your house."

Ian continued to smile. "And it couldn't happen to a nicer guy."

"But there is one thing I want to be sure of," Linda said.

"What's that?"

"I don't want anybody knowing who's selling the shares. Can that be done?"

"Sure, just leave it all to me."

Linda didn't even remember the taxi ride home. She didn't call to see if Bob was there. Normally, she took the bus, but now that she was a millionaire, she could afford to take a taxi. Michel had told her that the shares were hers. But that was out of the question. When the shares were sold there would be enough money to make both of them very rich. She would call him.

He was out fishing when Linda called. She wanted to tell him herself, but instead broke the news to Lori. There was a long silence after Linda mentioned the amount. Finally she spoke and her words were in short excited little bursts while she danced around the kitchen trying to hold the receiver to her ear. Linda hung up leaving instructions for her to have Michel call her when he arrived home.

Ian called shortly after she finished speaking with Lori. A large pension fund in Montreal had purchased all of their shares. He had even managed to get eighteen and five eighths for them. He had recommended that they be sold in small lots as to not cause a drop in price, but with a block purchase such as this, a price fluctuation was of no consequence even if it did occur. After commission, her account had been credited with five million, seven hundred and twenty thousand dollars. She asked that fifty thousand dollars be transferred to her account at the Bank of Nova Scotia immediately. Ian promised to call the bank personally and inform them that the cheque would be hand delivered before the bank closed. Ian asked her to give him 15 minutes. Exactly 15 minutes later, Linda called him back.

Bob arrived home shortly after 2:00 p.m. and was surprised to find that she was home. She greeted him at the door and then, saying that she wanted him to accompany her, they left in the car with her driving.

It was a short drive to the bank. It was just a few blocks from their house. The manager was waiting for them at the door. They were escorted to his office while Bob kept nudging his wife to find out what was going on. Linda just smiled and told him to be patient.

"Please have a seat, Mr. and Mrs. Humby," the elderly bank manager said as he pointed to a couple of chairs in front of his desk. He walked around his desk, sat down carefully and opened a folder. "As of today, the balance outstanding on your mortgage with us is thirty-four thousand eight hundred eleven dollars and twelve cents. That is of course if it were fully paid off today. There is a no-penalty clause in our agreement."

Linda opened her purse and without speaking, began to write a cheque. Bob looked at her and the bank manager. Still he said nothing. Linda tore off the cheque and recorded the amount on her record of cheques. "I trust this will make us no longer indebted to your bank," she said, smiling, as she passed the cheque to him.

"Is this a joke?" Bob asked, before the manager could speak.

"I'm not sure I understand what you're asking Mr. Humby," the manager said with an blank look on his face.

Bob quickly concluded that this man had never joked about anything in his life.

"Yes, Mrs. Humby, this will do very well," the manager said, managing a weak smile.

"Good," Linda responded, and then carefully removed another paper from her purse. She placed their mortgage documents in a large ashtray on the manager's desk and then using a heavy ornate lighter, lit one corner. As it caught fire, she stood up. "Thank you for everything, Mr. Rideout, and I trust that the remainder of our financial dealings will be equally as pleasurable."

"Yes, thank you Mrs. Humby, and I look forward to it," he answered as he quickly stood up. He reached across the desk and they shook hands being careful to stay away from the burning papers.

Bob remained in his chair with his mouth open. He had no idea what was happening. He just stared at the burning papers that the two other people in the office had completely ignored.

"Are you coming?" Linda asked him as she reached the door.

Bob looked first at the manager and then Linda. Without speaking he got up and followed her outside the bank. As they exited the bank and walked down the stairs, Bob finally couldn't take it any more. He held her arm and stopped her progress.

"Linda, what in the Hell was all that about? Have you gone completely mad?"

Linda turned and looked at him. "Remember those shares Michel gave me when we were in Dark Harbour?

"Yes," Bob said. "You were seeing Ian about them today."

"Do you have any idea how much they are worth?"

"You guessed maybe a few thousand."

"Well, I guessed wrong by a few thousand," she said as she continued walking.

"How wrong?" Bob called after her.

"A little more than five million dollars wrong," she answered as she continued toward their car.

It took a few seconds for her response to sink in. "*How* wrong?" he shouted as he ran and grabbed her two arms and spun her to face him.

"Ian called me this afternoon after our meeting and informed me that he had deposited five million seven hundred and twenty thousand dollars to our account."

Bob felt his knees suddenly become weak. He let go of Linda and leaned against the car. His eyes rolled up in his head.

"Are you going to make it?" Linda asked.

"How could the shares be worth that much?" he managed.

"It's complicated, but let me assure you that that's what they were worth and we have the money for them in our account."

He waited for a moment. "We're rich!" he shouted and picked Linda up and swung her around. "We're rich! We're rich!" he continued to shout as he dropped her to the ground and ran around the car.

Linda had not seen such exitement from Bob before. She just stood and looked at him as he gave his best impression of a drunken fairy. After several minutes she finally convinced him to get in the car after several people had stopped to ask her if they could help.

The went to The Fishing Admiral for dinner. They drank the most expensive champagne on the menu and admitted they didn't particularly like it. After dinner they went to The Garage and danced and drank some more. The taxi dropped them off at home at 2:30 a.m. and they fell asleep a few minutes later after a feeble attempt at love making.

Michel's telephone call at 5:30 a.m. awoke them and Linda went through the same experience with him as she had with Lori the previous day. Like her, he couldn't believe his new found fortune. He couldn't appreciate the full extent of their new wealth, but it did not take a great deal of convincing to accept half the money. She also convinced him to allow her to deposit his half of the money in an account with Ian. Later in the week Ian would contact him to determine how the money should be invested. A family trip to St. John's to meet with Ian would be necessary.

On Monday, Linda went to work. Paula was already there, seated at her desk and drinking one of the many cups of coffee she consumed daily. "Good morning," Linda greeted her as she walked into her office.

"Welcome back, stranger," Paula said, referring to the long time she had been away from work.

Linda passed her an envelope.

"What's this?" Paula asked as she took it and removed the single sheet of paper. She read it quickly. "You're quitting?" she blurted out as she finished reading.

"Resigning. There's a big difference," Linda responded. "This is my two weeks notice."

"But why?"

"You know why," Linda answered her. "I can't pursue this OPI issue while I'm still working as a crown attorney. And I must pursue it."

"I understand, I suppose," Paula admitted. "Have you decided where you're going to set up your office?"

"No, I haven't given that much thought, but I'll find a place. Paula," she continued, "I know that what I'm about to say is going to upset you, but I can't work out my two weeks notice. Something besides the OPI thing has come up. It's personal, and there's something I have to do and I have to do it right away. I'm owed vacation and overtime of more than two weeks. Please understand. I don't even want to get paid but I have to get away right now."

Paula had not been expecting this. A terrible backlog had built up in Linda's absence. She waited a few seconds before responding. "You know you're leaving us in a terrible state, don't you?" Paula asked.

"Yes, I know that, and if there is ever a way that I can make it up to you, I will"

"Okay, but you know the Crown Attorney is going to have a fit and he will make it difficult for you if you ever need our services because of this notice that isn't notice."

"Thanks. I'll come back later and clear out my office."

"Keep in touch," Paula said as she came out from behind her desk and hugged Linda.

Linda hated herself for what she had done. Paula was a good friend and had given her a job when she most needed one. She had also been a confidante and she was going to miss confiding in her and seeking her advice. But she could not allow those things to get in her way. Her feelings about OPI had not changed. OPI had unknowingly given her the financial freedom she desperately needed to stop the company from taking advantage of Newfoundland fishermen. It seemed ironic that thanks to OPI, she had the financial wherewithal to start her own firm and to take on Walter Lake as her first client, with OPI as the defendant.

After her father's death, when she learned who her real mother was, it had been her plan to go to Roberval and to trace her roots. She had taken her mother's writings with her and Roberval played an obviously important role in her life. She would have to go there and she what she could uncover. But there would be time for that. First, she wanted to set up her new law practice and to do that she needed lawyers and office space.

Linda placed an ad in *The Evening Telegram* that same afternoon, She was very specific about the type of lawyers she wanted in her firm. Her ad took up half a page and indicated that she was starting a new firm, and was looking for experienced criminal and civil lawyers interested in becoming partners without needing money up front. She knew only too well that the biggest hurdle facing a lawyer was finding the resources to set up his or her practice. Many good lawyers had spent their entire careers without getting their own firms or getting a partnership in an established firm. She also advertised for an office manager.

The following morning she went looking for office space. She called Marian Wareham who had sold them their home. Marian spent the next couple of days with her, and by Friday she had signed a five year lease for the top floor of the Chaulker Building. The rent was four thousand dollars a month and would have been six thousand if she hadn't signed for five years. Utilities would cost an additional one thousand dollars a month and she shuddered to think how much it would cost to furnish the offices. And she still didn't have a paying client, nor did she have any staff.

On Monday she hired a decorating firm to decorate and provide the furnishings. She gave them two weeks to finish the project and a budget of one hundred and twenty-five thousand dollars. She received the first response to her ad that same day, and on Tuesday, received two more. By Friday she had a total of twelve resumes and held interviews for her office manager position. Marilyn Cole had taken time off six years earlier to have a baby and now that the baby was in school, she wanted to return to the workforce. Marilyn became her office manager.

Over the weekend, Linda contacted each of the applicants. She decided to interview five of the twelve. She needed three. It took all day Monday to conduct interviews and select her staff. They had to agree to come to work for her with only two weeks notice to their current employers. All agreed.

Marilyn immediately took charge of the offices and worked with the decorators and the delivery people. She ordered all the suppliers, arranged for a janitorial service, prepared the ads for secretarial staff and set up the interviews with the lawyers the day they arrived. She had been a legal secretary for four years and she knew what was needed.

During the weekend, Linda and Bob visited Carbonear again. This time they stayed with Walter Lake at his home. He was very pleased to have the company and even more pleased to find out that Linda had started her own firm and that he would be the firm's first client. Linda used the time to get to know Walter and to explain to him that she simply did not have the experience to prosecute OPI in court. But her staff certainly did. They didn't discuss the fee but Linda made it clear that her firm would take it from the settlement which she was confident they would win.

On Monday, Linda met with her new staff and welcomed them to her firm. She repeated what she had told them when offering them jobs and explained to them who she was and her experience. She was brutally honest and informed them that she had come into a very significant amount of money and that by forming her own firm she had put all of her eggs into the proverbial basket. She wanted to punish OPI for what it had done and what it continued to do. She had committed one half million dollars to prosecuting OPI and her only hope of recovering it would be in a successful prosecution. The firm would concentrate exclusively on its case against OPI, and would not accept any other cases. If, at the end of the litigation they failed, she would commit an additional one million dollars to find new clients and to make the firm a success. However, if that should fail, then they would all be out of work. Marilyn had made copies of all the files on

OPI and gave each of them a copy. She asked that each of them review the files and the following day recommend a course of action.

The following morning, Linda and the other lawyers met and they agreed, to a person, that what OPI had done was indeed worthy of pursuing. Bill Parsons, the most senior, believed that the route to go was to sue both OPI and the Government. Roger Brake thought that the best way to proceed was with what he called a "shotgun approach": sue everybody even remotely involved. Marty Simmons had not made up his mind who should be named in the suit. They needed to get together and to hash it out. They all agreed.

Linda listened and learned. When she had heard enough she asked Bill to act as lead counsel. The others recognized this as a wise decision. They would examine the files more thoroughly and, using their group experience, they would decide upon a course of action. She wouldn't insult them by asking them to work hard and to help her to help Walter Lake. They knew much better than she did what was involved. But she wanted to give them more than just a salary and a desire to see that justice was served. Following a successful prosecution, she promised them, she would offer partnerships.

Linda now would not have to stay and mind the store. They now were working for themselves. That following morning, Linda left for Roberval, confident that her team of lawyers would begin the process of bringing OPI to justice.

Twenty-One ~

BOB DROVE LINDA to the airport for her 1:15 p.m. flight to Montreal. He wanted to accompany her, but she told him that this was something she wanted to do herself. She had considered going to Toronto and attempting to find an address at the hospital for the names on Michel's birth certificate, but Roberval just seemed the right place to start. Her mother had seemed happy when she was writing about Roberval; when she had written about Toronto, she appeared sad. Linda had a picture and she had a dying mother's confession that her name was Forest. That was what she had to check out first. She would go to Toronto after.

The whole idea of going to Quebec and searching for her roots was frightening; she prayed for the strength she would need. Her biggest fear was the language. She had studied French in school and she could read and write it a little, but her teachers had been taught the same way she had and the spoken word was as foreign to them as it was to her.

The trip to Montreal took four hours. It seemed as if nothing ever left St. John's and went direct to anywhere. She remembered her trips back and forth from Dalhousie. The trips from Halifax stopped at Stephenville, Deer Lake and Gander. Today she had only two stops, Gander and Halifax, where she had to deplane and catch a second aircraft to Montreal. In Montreal, she had a two hour wait for a small commuter flight to Chicoutimi, a half hour north. She had never flown in a small aircraft before and when she landed, she was tempted to bend over and kiss the ground.

She picked up her rental car a little after 8:00 p.m. and got directions to the nearest hotel. She had room service for supper and was pleased to find that the food was excellent and the waiter spoke surprisingly good English. She took advantage of his English skills, asking and receiving excellent directions to Roberval. The rental company had provided her with a road map and André, the waiter, traced her route and marked with 'x's' the places he thought she should stop and visit. She didn't tell him she wasn't on a sight-seeing trip.

Linda took breakfast the next morning in the dining room; this time she wasn't as lucky. The waitress spoke as much English as Linda did French. The menu was in French, but thanks to her schooling, Linda managed to pick the 'oeuf, jambon et cafe.' Still, the young girl was very pleasant and the English-speaking manager came over after she had ordered and asked if everything was okay. They laughed and the young man explained that he often let English speaking customers try and order before offering help. It was part of the "Quebec experience" as he put it. They chatted for a few minutes and he even joined her for a cup of coffee. Like the rental car agent, he suggested a few places to visit.

Linda didn't know how long she would be staying in Roberval but wanted to ensure that a room would be available for her when she returned. The manager assured her that the hotel was rarely full this time of year and she need not worry about a room. She guessed she would be in Roberval two or three days; the manager provided her with his card and asked her to call him when she would be returning. He would ensure that a room was available.

The drive up to Roberval was as pleasant as the staff of the hotel had said. A portion of the trip took her through the Laurentide Park and the route was very well maintained. Where she had grown up there hadn't been any trees, just low bushes. One of her most memorable experiences as a child was seeing her first tree. It had been a tiny spruce that her father had cut for Christmas and brought home by boat. She thought it the most beautiful thing in the world. The trees here were tall and straight and made even the tallest trees in Newfoundland look small by comparison.

Halfway to Roberval she stopped at a little *casse-croûte* and had a wonderful meat pie lunch. It was located on a small lot that seemed as if it had been cut out of the forest. She sat at a little table outside and the smell of the forest was almost overpowering. As before, there was somebody on the staff who spoke English and she left an hour after arriving, not only with a wonderful lunch but a greater appreciation for the people and the province.

She was anxious to get to her destination; nevertheless, the many places to stop and visit enroute were compelling and it was after 6:00 p.m. before she arrived. A sign at the entrance to the town indicated that there was a Holiday Inn ahead and she found it without any difficulty.

Later that evening before she went to bed, she checked the telephone directory for the name Forest. It was a very common name and calling each of them to ask if they knew a Linda Forest was out of the question. But that had never been her intention unless there were only a few names listed.

She got instructions to the town hall from her waitress at breakfast and drove into the parking lot at exactly 10:00 a.m. It was an old brick building and the heavy steel door took a great deal of effort to push open. Inside, the floor was done in black and white tiles, yellowing from years of waxing. Ornate mouldings bisected the wall at waist height and above that hung pictures of what she guessed were former and present town officials. A huge chandelier hung from the cathedral ceiling though it failed to light the area appropriately. In one corner of the large foyer she spotted a tiny window with a round opening. She walked toward it.

"Good morning," she greeted the woman behind the glass.

She glanced up and went back to her work. Her desk was covered with papers and she was busy entering figures into a calculator. Linda waited a moment and spoke again.

"Good morning, I wonder if you could help me please."

This time the woman didn't even look up.

Linda spoke again, only this time in a louder voice. "I wonder if you could help me please."

The young woman looked up, but this time had a scowl on her face. "*Je ne parle pas anglais,*" she mumbled, and again returned to her work.

Linda looked at the woman in disbelief. She understood that she had said she didn't speak English but she couldn't understand her tone. For the first time she was experiencing the rudeness of a society that hated English-speaking Canadians. Linda looked around for help, but knew that she wouldn't get any there.

She left the town hall discouraged, realizing that it may have been a mistake to try and do what she was attempting. As she walked to her car, not knowing how to proceed, her spirits lifted. Across the street she saw two nuns walking in her direction. She crossed over and waited for them to reach her. She smiled as they approached.

"Good morning," she greeted them

They smiled. "*Bonjour,*" they said in unison.

"Do you speak English?" Linda asked, pronouncing each word as carefully and as slowly as she could.

The both shook their heads and smiled again.

Linda smiled her thank you to them anyway and headed back to her car. As she did, the younger of the two spoke.

"Come," she said and pointed in the direction they were heading before Linda had stopped them.

Linda smiled and looked where they were pointing. There must be someone there who could help her, she thought. The older of the two took her arm and together they walked up the street.

As they walked, they would occasionally look at her and smile. Finally, ten minutes after they had linked arms, Linda could see a large stone structure that she quickly concluded was a convent. Obviously, there was somebody there would could speak English.

The two nuns lead her through a huge gate with a large cross at its top. The building was surrounded by a beautifully manicured lawn and there were flowers everywhere. She could see several nuns gardening as she walked the cobble stone path to the entrance to the convent. Some of them looked up and smiled as she walked by, and then returned to their work like bees gathering pollen.

The interior of the convent smelled musty, but there was a warmth there that she could feel as soon as she stepped inside. Everything was spotless; as the two sisters ushered her up the long hall, Linda tried to take in as much of the scene around her as she could. Once she tripped on the edge of a beautiful rug and she would have fallen if the older sister had not caught her. They laughed and continued on their way.

It was a large building and the trip took them up several flights of stairs and through several large rooms. Finally, they arrived at a tiny room that Linda guessed was perhaps in the centre of the convent. Inside the room were several shelves of books. On a ladder retrieving one of them was a nun, her back turned to the door.

The older sister said something in French that Linda did not understand and without looking to see who had spoken, the sister climbed down the ladder, straightened her habit and turned to greet them.

"May I help you, Miss?" she asked in perfect English, and then lifting her hand, she shooed away Linda's two companions. She was a very imposing figure and despite her apparent young age, gave the impression that she was very sure of herself.

"Yes, thank you very much," Linda said, relieved. "My name is Linda Humby. I'm a lawyer from St. John's, Newfoundland."

"I've always wanted to visit Newfoundland," the sister said mispronouncing the name. She walked to a desk and pointed to a chair for Linda. "Maybe I will someday," she said longingly. "I'm Sister Marie Claire," she added as she sat down.

Linda sat down facing her. "I came to this town," Linda began, "in the hope that I might find my mother. Actually," she quickly added, "I have found my mother, but I don't know anything about her. I don't even know for sure if this is where she is from. I just have a lot of questions and I need some answers. Unfortunately, I don't speak your language and maybe you could help me by telling me where I could find a translator. I would be very willing to pay him or her."

Sister Marie Claire paused before speaking. "I tell you what," she said, smiling, "classes are out now for another couple of weeks and I really do not have that much to do. But don't tell that to the Mother Superior," she said laughing. "For a donation to our little convent, maybe I could help you find what you are looking for."

"Oh yes, I would be willing to donate whatever you feel is fair," Linda said, pleased with her good fortune.

"Good, now tell me what or who you are looking for."

For the next half an hour, over tea, Linda told the Sister everything she knew about her mother. It was like talking to a doctor or a psychiatrist and very quickly Linda began to confide everything, knowing that what she said would not be repeated.

Sister Marie Claire commented that if Francine Forest was born in Roberval she could locate her records. It might take a while but they would find her birth certificate.

From what she had learned from her father, Linda had been able to guess that if her mother were alive today, she would be between sixty and sixty-five years old. That meant she was born sometime between 1910 and 1915. It was only a rough guess and could be out by several years. But at least it gave them a starting point.

It had been Linda's intention to search through the birth records at the town hall starting at 1910, to see if she could locate her mother's birth certificate. Sister Marie Claire agreed, but stated very proudly that the convent's records were much more thorough, and having listened to Linda's story about her experience at the town hall, commented that she was much more pleasant.

They decided to have lunch before they began their search and at precisely noon, she sat with Linda and approximately fifty other nuns in a large dining room. After Grace was said, several novices delivered steaming bowls of soup accompanied by delicious warm bread rolls that Linda dipped into her soup like the other sisters. Huge pitchers of cold milk complemented the meal and what she had expected to be a solemn affair was just the opposite. They laughed and giggled like school children and Linda could tell that they enjoyed each other's company. She was introduced to everybody and after a chorus of '*bienvenue*' she responded with a '*merci*'. There was no dessert served and Linda was glad.

The records room was small. After opening the ornately carved door, Sister Marie Claire walked directly to a shelf of large leather-bound books. Besides the shelf and the books, the only other furniture was a small desk and a chair. Each book measured nearly two feet long by eighteen inches wide and six inches thick. The Sister strained to remove it and bring it to the desk, delivering it with a resounding thump that caused the legs of the tiny desk to wobble under the strain.

"This volume contains the birth records of the town from 1905 through to 1933," she said proudly. "As you can see, the people of Roberval follow the directions of the Bible well," she said laughing.

Linda laughed with her. For the short time she had known Sister Marie Claire, she had grown to like her sense of humour.

"This is going to take a lot of work." the Sister said as she sat at the desk, opened the large book and thumbed through the pages until she came to the year 1910. "Now, in the left column is the month, the next, the date, then the child's name and sex, and finally the name and address of the parents. What I suggest you do," she continued, reaching for a pencil and note pad, "is to search through the years that you believe she may have been born, record all the particulars, and then, once you're finished, I'll help you search through the telephone book and find out if any relatives are still living or if they are still in Roberval. "How's that?" she finished.

"That would be great. I don't know how this is going to turn out, but however it does, I'm already in your debt."

"Just remember the donation you promised," the Sister said, smiling. "Now, I am going back to my office. When you are finished, put the book back where it was and come to my office. If I'm not there just have a seat; I won't be long."

"Thank you," Linda said as she took the Sister's place behind the desk and began the examination of the book.

The pages of the book were heavy and the years had yellowed them. All of the entries were written in the same hand with an obvious skill for the task. Over the years the ink had been absorbed into the paper; even though the paper was quite thick, it had seeped through to the other pages. The entries were small and in the poor light of the room, Linda began the tedious process of searching through the book. At 3:00 p.m. a novice appeared and without speaking, placed a pot of tea and plate of cookies on the desk beside her. Linda knew whose idea it was.

By 4:30 p.m. Linda had gone through the book and had fourteen names and addresses on her piece of paper. The earliest record of a child with the name of Francine was 1912 and the latest was 1930. She returned the book to its position on the shelf, tucked the piece of paper in her purse, picked up her tray, closed the door, and went back to Sister Marie Claire's office to find her sitting at her desk working. She looked up when she heard Linda enter.

"Well, did you have any luck?"

"Yes, I did," Linda answered, removing the piece of paper from her purse and showing it to her.

The Sister examined it for a few seconds. "Now the work begins. We will have to see if we can find the names of the parents in the telephone directory and then call and ask where their daughter Francine is. But that is going to have to wait until tomorrow. Right now it is time for supper and prayers."

"Okay then. I'll return to my hotel and meet you here again tomorrow morning, if that's okay?" Linda asked.

"Yes, and you are welcome to join us for dinner."

"I certainly appreciate your offer, but I can't wait to crawl into a hot bath and I would like to call my husband," Linda said apologetically.

"I understand," the Sister smiled. "I will show you out."

Sister Marie Claire accompanied her to the gate, and they said goodbye until the following morning. Linda walked quickly back to her car and then drove to the hotel. She called Bob first to tell him how pleased she was with her progress. Then, after her bath, she went to dinner in the hotel dining room; the staff were as pleasant as they had been in Chicoutimi. She finished dinner at 9:15 p.m. and then went for a little walk around the town. By 10:30 p.m. she was asleep, content in the thought that she was making real progress in finding her roots.

Linda drove to the convent the next morning and parked just outside the gate, She walked directly to Sister Marie Claire's office and found her working at her desk. They greeted each other, then, sitting side by side, they began to compare Linda's list with the telephone directory.

Nine of the fourteen names were in the directory. The Sister moved the directory to the centre of the desk and began the process. She called the first three names on the list. The first Francine was married and living in Toronto. She actually talked to the second Francine. The third had died from Polio in 1950. Sister Marie Claire called the fourth number and then laughed as soon as someone answered. She held her hand over the telephone and spoke. "The number is for the nursing home. I've been there often enough I should have recognized the number. Sister Rolande tells me that they have a resident named Esther Forest. She is gone to get her."

They waited a few more seconds and the conversation began again. A few minute later, Sister Marie Claire hung up the telephone.

"It looks like we may have found what we are looking for. That was Madame Forest. She is quite old and desperately wants to meet you. I told her you were looking for a Francine Forest and that you thought that you may be her daughter. She became very excited when I said that and then said that she would not tell me anything else unless I brought you to meet her. Are you willing to meet her?"

"Yes, of course I am," Linda said quickly. "When can we go?"

"Let me see," Sister Marie Claire said while thumbing through her calendar. She paused for Linda's reaction. "Right now, of course," she laughed.

"Great," Linda said, standing up and pulling the Sister up from her chair.

"Okay," she said as she ran behind Linda who practically began running from the building.

Sister Marie Claire provided directions as Linda drove anxiously to the nursing home. Each red light seemed to stay red for an inordinatly long time, but finally, the large apartment-style building came into view. Linda parked and walked very quickly toward the entrance.

She pulled open the large door and stepped inside. There was a large area filled with tables and around each table people sat participating in various activities. They were in varying states of health as was obvious by the number of wheelchairs parked around the tables. Some were playing board games, some were watching television in a little adjoining room and others were putting together puzzles. A nurse spotted them as they entered and approached.

"*Bonjour, puis-je vous aider?*" she spoke.

Sister Marie Claire responded and then informed Linda that Madame Forest was in her room waiting. They followed the nurse to the room.

The took an elevator to the second floor and down a hall until they came to a room with a closed door and a sign with the name 'Esther Forest'. The nurse knocked gently, then they stepped inside. The nurse spoke in French as she entered.

The room had a warmness to it and was very tastefully decor-ated. Outside the door was an institution, but inside the room was a home. Linda looked quickly around the room until her eyes came to rest on a woman she guessed to be at least eighty years old. She somehow looked familiar. She was sitting in a chesterfield chair and was dressed in a pretty flowered dress. Her gray hair was tied in a bun at the back of her head and her eyes were glued to Linda.

The three women spoke in French and after a short conversation, the nurse left and Sister Marie Claire sat on the couch and patted for Linda to join her.

"Madame Forest does not speak any English and she had a stroke two years ago. She now has a little difficulty speaking. I will tell her your story and then I will translate for her." The Sister then turned to Madame Forest. The old woman continued to stare at Linda.

Linda understood a little of what the Sister was saying because she spoke very slowly and pronounced each word very carefully. The old woman's expression never changed and her only reaction was to turn her gaze from Linda to the Sister. She talked for at least ten minutes. Finally, the old woman spoke.

"I have a daughter and her name is Rollande Esther Francine Forest. We call her Francine. You have my daughter's eyes. Would you smile for me?"

Linda looked at the Sister and then the old woman. She smiled weakly.

Tears suddenly appeared at the corners of the old woman's eyes. She continued to speak, but her voice was lower and there was pain in it.

"When she was very young she went away to Toronto to work for a very important man. I didn't want her to go." She reached into the arm of her dress, found a tissue and dabbed the corners of her eyes with it. "It was not very long after she went there that she got married. We went to the wedding. Romeo paid for everything. He brought all of our family to Toronto. It was the first time we had ever been to Ontario." She smiled as she remembered. "It was the most beautiful wedding that I have ever seen and Francine was the most beautiful bride." She shifted a little in her chair. It was obvious that the stroke had affected her right side as her arm remained in her lap as she tried to get comfortable.

She suddenly became very quiet. Sister Marie Claire spoke to her but there was no response. Then she began to speak again.

"She had a beautiful son. She brought him to visit us once."

"What was his name?" Linda suddenly interrupted her. "You must tell me his name."

Her sudden outburst caught both women by surprise. Sister Marie Claire looked at Linda.

"Translate," Linda ordered.

The old woman smiled as the question was asked and then put the crumpled tissue to her nose. Her eyes seemed to brighten. "His name is Michel," she said in a half cry. "His name is Michel Romeo Claude."

Linda suddenly felt very warm. Her face flushed and she reached to undo her sweater, but it was already undone. She looked at Sister Marie Claire and then the old woman. She got up and walked across the room to a tiny sink. She found a glass, filled it with water and drained it. Her throat still felt dry.

"He was a beautiful baby," she heard from across the room.

Linda couldn't hold it in any longer. She ran across the room to the old woman. "Grandmother," she cried. "Oh, Grandmother," she repeated as she picked up the old woman's hands and drew them to her face. Sister Marie Claire translated and then watched as the old woman's good hand attempted to raise Linda's face. Tears streamed down both their faces.

"Where is my Francine?" she cried. "Where is my baby? She left us so long ago."

"She went to Newfoundland," Linda said, and Sister Marie Claire translated. "I am her daughter. I'm Linda." She suddenly remembered something and ran to her purse. She emptied it on the floor and then found what she was looking for. She raced back to the old woman.

"Michel," she said, holding the picture up for her to see. "This is my brother Michel."

The old woman reached for the picture and then gasped when she recognized the features of the boy who had become a man.

"I think we should go now and let your grandmother rest for awhile," Sister Marie Claire said to Linda.

Linda looked at her, surprised at the suggestion. It had taken her so long to find any traces of her mother, but reluctantly, she had to agree. The Sister pushed a button on the wall and summoned the nurse, who appeared almost instantly.

The old woman protested when she was told that they were leaving. They promised they would return in a couple of hours after she had rested a little. She held up her hand and motioned for Linda to come to her. Linda bent down and the old woman kissed her and pressed her frail hand into the back of her neck.

They had lunch at a tiny restaurant near the nursing home. Linda ordered a sandwich but only picked at it. She felt like a good stiff drink, and had she not been having lunch with a nun, she might have had one.

They talked about finding the old woman and Linda commented on how ironic it seemed that now that she had finally found her grandmother, she needed a translator to talk to her. The time passed slowly as they waited to give the old woman an opportunity to rest. Two hours after their first meeting, Linda met with her grandmother for the second time.

This time she knocked and then ran to her grandmother's arms. No translation was necessary. They just hugged and looked into each others eyes.

Linda sat at her grandmother's feet, filled with questions. When she was told that Francine had died giving birth to her, the old woman drew a breath and moaned. Linda could feel her pain and wished there was something she could do. But she quickly added that Michel was alive and married with two children of his own. She seemed to temporarily forget the grief of knowing that her daughter had been dead such a long time. She asked many questions about Michel and the children.

An hour passed, the nurse appeared and insisted that they end their meeting until tomorrow. Madame Forest would not be dissuaded. Her voice turned very hard and she held onto Linda and she wouldn't let go. "I will not go to bed tonight until I know everything my little girl has to tell me. It has been too long not knowing." She looked at the nurse with resolve that was determined.

By the end of the next hour Linda had learned more than she could ever have hoped. She found out that she had more aunts, uncles and cousins than she would ever have the time to meet. She also found out that her father was Denis Leblanc and he was from Toronto. Her grandmother didn't know where he lived in Toronto, but *his* father's name was Romeo. The last time she had heard from Francine, she related, was in a telephone call very late one night. Francine told her that she was going away for awhile and that there was no need to worry. She never saw nor heard from her again. A few days later a man came to their house looking for her. He was very rude and he wouldn't believe that Francine and Michel weren't living with her. Francine's brother Paul went to Toronto and tried to see her husband, refused to see him. The police were called but they couldn't find her either. Her husband said that she had run away from him and taken a lot of money.

By late afternoon the old woman showed signs of the day's excitement. Linda suggested that her grandmother rest, saying tomorrow she would come and visit again. She agreed. Before Linda left, Mme. Forest asked Sister Marie Claire to go to her bed table and bring back an envelope. She refused assistance as she fumbled with it and then pulled out a single item. She passed it to Linda.

"This is your mother, child," the old woman said, and for the first time Linda saw a picture of her real mother. She cried as she fell to her knees. "Oh, Mother," she moaned as her tears dropped onto the old photograph.

During the next few days, Linda met many of her new relatives. Unlike her grandmother, they could all speak a little English and what they didn't know, Sister Marie Claire translated. Her mother's brother Paul told her about his trip to Toronto and how Denis, her husband, had refused to see him. A "big nigger" as Paul referred to him, had called on him a few days after his mother had received the call from Francine, and accused him of hiding his sister. It was a very difficult time for all of them, and despite their best efforts they were unable to find her. All that they were able to find out was that Francine had called from a hotel in Halifax where she stayed for two nights. But after she checked out, it was as if she had disappeared.

By Wednesday, Linda thought it was time to leave Roberval. Her new aunts and uncles and cousins gave her many pictures of her mother, and she promised to keep in touch with each and every one of them. She had a tearful goodbye with her grandmother, promising that she would come and visit often.

Saying goodbye to Sister Marie Claire was as difficult as saying goodbye to her newfound family. It had been less than a week, but it was long enough for a friendship to develop between the two women. It had been because of the nun that she had found out who she really was. She owed her a debt that she would never be able to repay.

Through her relatives, she found out that her mother had been a student at the convent and that was how she ended up in Toronto. She was brought there by Mr. Leblanc to teach French to his children. When Sister Marie Claire went through the records she confirmed that Francine had been a student. Before Linda left Roberval she wrote a cheque to Sister Marie Claire for twenty thousand dollars. The money would be used for a scholarship named in honour of her mother. Francine promised to returned to Roberval every year thereafter and present it. She left Roberval happy to have found her mother's family, but sad to have to leave them. She didn't expect the same reception in Toronto.

Linda knew that a trip to Toronto was inevitable. Her father was there. She knew who Denis Leblanc was. He was one of the most influential and powerful men in Canada. It had to be him because that was how her mother had shares in the company. Denis Leblanc was the head of Leblanc Industries and Ocean Products International, a man she despised even though she had never met him. A man who had done something to drive his wife and his son from a life of luxury to a remote community on the South coast of Newfoundland.

On the plane trip home Linda looked at the pictures of her mother often. She examined the few wedding pictures her uncle had given her and examined her father's face. There could be no doubt that Michel was his son. The resemblance was phenomenal. She felt that her father had killed her mother as surely as if he had driven a knife through her heart. If she had been living anywhere other than Dark Harbour, she would still be alive today. Linda knew what she had to do. But she would do it in the courts. She would destroy the man who had caused so much pain to so many people. Then she would meet him. Then she would introduce herself. Then he would know what it was like to feel pain. The pain of an old woman in Roberval. The pain of a dead wife. The pain of a son and daughter.

Twenty-Two

BOB NOTICED THAT Linda had changed in the week she had been away from home. She seemed distant and preoccupied. But he also detected something else. He noticed it in her eyes the moment he greeted her at the airport. It was a look that would result in many sleepless nights for her as she tossed and turned in bed, plotting and preparing for the trial. He knew that there was something festering inside of her. She had given him most of the details of her visit over the telephone and he wished he could have been there when she found her grandmother. He cursed himself for not going with her.

Linda decided that she needed a few more days off before going back to work. Bob helped her make that decision. School would soon be starting and she knew that once that happened, they would have even less time for each other. Neither of them had eight-to-four jobs. Bob would have to spend most evenings preparing lesson plans for the next day and Linda wouldn't get home until 8:00 p.m.

Linda thought a lot about what she was planning. She fully expected that it would be a year to a year and a half before this was all over. She would have to foot the bill for everything until then in the hope that they won their case. If they lost, then it would all have been for nothing. She could never hope to get a cent of government business, regardless of the outcome. Businesses trying to remain on good terms with government would also shy away from her firm. If they won the suit, the fees would more than pay all her expenses. There was so much uncertainty.

Bob and Linda spent a leisurely weekend together, but Linda was preoccupied with things other than the weekend. Her family in Roberval filled her every thought as she tried to figure out why her mother would leave Toronto for the isolation of Newfoundland. She asked Bob's opinion often, but he could offer nothing. She also asked his opinion of whether or not she should tell her associates, especially Walter Lake, that Denis Leblanc was her father. He thought that she shouldn't. She agreed, but she was committed to finding out why her mother left her father. To that end she decided one of her first tasks would be to hire a private investigator.

The office had run as smooth as clockwork in Linda's absence. Marilyn had taken charge of administrative duties and Bill and the team were making good progress. Linda got a quick briefing from Marilyn, then set up a meeting with the lawyers for 10:00 a.m.

"Welcome back, stranger," Bill said as he poked his head into her office on his way to his own.

"Thanks. It's good to be back. Keeping banking hours?" she said laughing as she looked at her watch.

"Don't I wish," he laughed. "We've been burning the midnight oil ever since you assigned me this job. I was at the Justice Department this morning to pull in a few favours. I'll brief you later. Marilyn just said you want to meet at ten. I was hoping you'd be gone a few more days so we could have firmed up a few things, but I think you'll be pleased with what we have."

"I'm looking forward to it," Linda said.

A half hour later when Linda went to the conference room, her three associates were already there. Marilyn followed and closed the door. Two other staff members had been hired to provide secretarial service to the associates and one of them had already moved to Marilyn's desk to man the telephone.

"Welcome back," both Roger and Marty said in unison, as Linda walked into the room. "Good trip?" Marty asked.

"Yes, thank you very much. It was very good indeed," she said, taking her place at the end of the table. Marilyn placed a carafe of coffee in the centre and they all chatted as they filled their cups. When they had their coffee, Linda began the meeting.

"Okay, it's been over a week since we last met. What do you have to tell me?" She looked in Bill's direction.

"As I told you a little while ago, we've been keeping very late hours and they have been very productive. We've decided to take a three-prong approach to this case with each of the three of us being assigned very definitive areas of responsibility. We also need your assistance and I'll come to that in a little while. We've met several times in your absence and developed our strategy. At this point we'd like to brief you on what we've decided and we obtain your input."

"Fine," Linda agreed, "but like I said when I hired you all, I'm a newcomer to this game. You're the experts in all of this. Sure, I'm the boss, but I depend on you guys to get this on the right track."

They all smiled their agreement.

Bill began again. "We haven't even decided yet, who, if anybody, we're going to sue. The information you gave us was very damning to any number of people, but you know as well as I do, that no judge in the world is going to let us admit it into evidence. In fact, if became known that we even have it, the entire firm could be prevented from representing Walter Lake. But the files do have value. A tremendous amount of value. It tells us what actually happened and because we know that this correspondence exists, we can request the information. We can't specifically refer to the pieces of correspondence, but perhaps we can get it by asking, for example, for correspondence between OPI and the government regarding the location of the plant in Carbonear. And don't get your hopes up that we'll ever get it but there is a side benefit. Because we know what actually transpired, we can then ask questions based on that information. Do you follow?"

Linda nodded.

"Now, hopefully, before this meeting is concluded, we are going to decide whom we're going to sue. As I said when we began, each of us has been assigned definitive responsibilities. Marty was assigned the responsibility of rounding up witnesses. For the past week, he has been doing just that. Tell us what you have, Marty."

Marty put his coffee cup on the table and pulled a file closer. "Well, the first person I went to talk to was our client. I spent two days with him in Carbonear and I believe he's going to be one hell of a witness. He's got a grandfather image that could convince a jury he's as honest as Santa Claus. I also talked to a number of his former employees, including the former plant manager. I got some great information from him regarding the situation at the time that OPI built the plant. Among other things, he can confirm that there just wasn't enough fish around to support two plants. He's a packrat and kept a lot of information. He's rough but very credible."

"I also was fortunate enough to speak with the plant bookkeeper. She worked there for twenty-two years. She knew what they were getting for the fish in Boston and she also knew what OPI was getting. She'll be a great witness when we get into the price war that developed after the OPI plant was opened. I spoke with a half dozen or so fishermen as well, and I've been trying to find people who can support our claim that fish for a second plant simply did not exist. I have found one former senior government employee who questioned government's approval of the second plant. I still have a lot to do," he finished.

"Good work, Marty," Bill said. "Okay Roger, what do you have to offer?" He turned to Linda. "I've had Roger trying to find out where some of the players in this little charade are hiding these days. I also had him checking out OPI and its parent, Leblanc Industries," Bill added.

Roger smiled as he opened a folder in front of him. "I hope you've got a treasure chest somewhere, Boss," he laughed, "because I've blown this year's telephone budget."

"Let's hope it was worth it then," Linda commented.

"We're playing with the big kids now," he began as he passed out several sheets of paper. The first was the balance sheet for OPI. Marty whistled as he looked at the numbers. Then Roger handed out the balance sheet for Leblanc Industries. Marty whistled again. Linda had seen the financial figures when she worked for Jeremy Hawkins.

"As you can see, Leblanc Industries is quite a diversified company. And the people I spoke to tell me that it's Denis Leblanc who calls all the shots. He's chairman of the board for every one of these companies, except one. His stepmother, Linda, is the chairperson of Leblanc Travel."

Linda gasped. "His stepmother?" she asked.

"Yes, his stepmother," Roger responded, apparently surprised by Linda's reaction.

"She's still alive?" she asked.

"Yes, as far as I know. Why, is there something about her that I should know?

No, nothing other than the fact that she's my stepgrandmother, Linda thought, *and I wasn't aware that she was alive*. Instead, she said, "Oh, nothing, just curious."

Roger continued to brief them on OPI and the parent company. His main goal had been to examine the board composition of the various companies, and in particular, OPI. He had found that two former provincial fisheries ministers were on OPI's board, He had meetings set up with them for later in the week. He had been able to set up the meetings in the guise that he was an historian working at Memorial University. He doubted they would check it out. It was fine, though, if they did. He had used his brother's name. His brother just happened to be the historian and although he wasn't particularly pleased with the idea, he did accept a dinner as compensation.

Bill made notes as both men spoke, and when Roger had finished, he spoke again. "I've also been very busy," he said. "I've prepared all of the documents to begin the process. I've just got two things to finish. The first is the Statement of Claim and the second is whom we are actually going to sue. Roger, I asked you to get me financial statements of Lake's company for the five years before OPI built their plant, and the final year of operation."

Roger thumbed through his papers and finding what was needed, handed them to Bill.

He examined them for a few moments while the others chatted.

"I'll run these by our accountant and come up with a figure. I don't suppose we have an accounting firm lined up, do we?"

Linda shook her head.

"I'll find us one," Marilyn interjected.

"Good," Bill said. "Now, whom do we sue?"

"Well," Marty spoke, "we have to name OPI."

They all nodded.

"And Leblanc Industries is the parent company, so they have to share responsibility."

They all nodded again.

"And how about one of those crooked politicians," Linda added. "Joe Crocker was the Fisheries Minister when the approval was given to OPI, and then two years later he's sitting on the board where he remains to this day. By suing him we'll get their attention real quick."

They discussed Linda's suggestion at length. Finally Bill spoke. "We have to be careful about how we approach all of this. We know that government is as guilty as OPI, but if we name too many in the suit each person named could ask for a separate trial and even if they're all heard at the same time, which I doubt, each would have his own lawyer and we'll all be old men and old women before this thing actually gets to be decided by a jury."

"Now I know why you're the lead lawyer on this one," Marty said. "I agree, we don't want to turn this into a three ring circus. Why don't we just name OPI and let the press take care of the rest of them? OPI has more than enough money to pay all our bills and to make Walter Lake independently wealthy."

"Yes," Linda said. "If we concentrate on OPI and try and prove that there was collusion between OPI and the government, the Opposition will call for an investigation and that will serve our purposes."

They all nodded their heads in agreement.

"Great," Bill said. I'll finish filling out these forms and see if I can get them filed this afternoon. Then get set. This is going to be the big news and every TV person and newspaper reporter will be wanting interviews. Linda, that's where you could help. How about if you handle the press?"

Linda was surprised by this sudden request. "I'm not sure I can handle it," she said.

"I think you can. You're capable of answering their questions. Just don't give them any specifics. I'll brief you daily. Once the trial starts, I'll give you enough to keep them interested. How about it?"

"Okay," Linda said.

"Good. Let's get in contact with Walter Lake and tell him to refer all calls to you." He turned to the others. "So, if there's nothing else, I'll get on it."

They all nodded their agreement that nothing else was needed. "Okay, we'll meet again the same time on Friday," Bill said.

As the other two men left, Bill turned to Marilyn. "Marilyn, when the press starts to call, what I want you to do is to say that Mrs. Humby is busy right now and she'll return their call. Try and find out what they want and that will give Linda some time to think through a response before she speaks with them. We'll work on a press release in the next little while and then we'll deal with each issue as it comes up. Is that okay with you, Linda?"

"Sure."

Bill gathered up his papers and left a few minutes later. Marilyn and Linda remained to discuss several administrative issues.

Bill filed the papers later than afternoon, naming OPI as defendant and Walter Lake as the plaintiff. OPI was given thirty days to respond to the suit. If they failed to respond, which was extremely unlikely if not impossible, the court would rule in favour of Walter. Once OPI responded, a date would be set for the trial, which Bill anticipated would take eight months to a year. They would need every day until then to prepare.

For lunch, Linda went downstairs in her building and picked up a sandwich. Marilyn had asked if she would like to have lunch with the new girls and use the opportunity to get to know them. Linda suggested they do it tomorrow because she had a few things to do over lunch. As she sat eating her sandwich, she telephoned the Ontario Bar Association and asked if they could recommend a good Toronto-based private investigation agency to do some work for her firm. They gave the names of several companies and from them she chose one. She telephoned Davis Investigations, the first on her list, and asked if they could send someone to St. John's on the next flight. They telephoned while she was in her meeting with Roger later that afternoon and said that Harry Thistle would be arriving on the 4:25 p.m. flight the next afternoon.

She hadn't been given any information to identify Harry Thistle, so she stood at the arrival gate wondering how she could identify him. After everybody had deplaned she paged him and a man approached her a few minutes later.

He was a lot older than she thought a detective should look and he wasn't dressed as she thought he should be. She blamed her expectations on television's portrayals of private investigators. He was dressed very casually and she guessed him to be close to sixty. His hair was thinning, but despite his apparent age, Linda could tell that the man was in good physical condition.

"You must be Mrs. Humby," he said as he approached her, carrying a small overnight bag and briefcase.

Linda was standing beside the counter where she had made the page. She held out her hand. "Yes, but please call me Linda," she said smiling. "Is this your first trip to Newfoundland?"

"Yes, it is. I've heard a lot about the place. I'm really looking forward to seeing a little of the province."

Linda pointed toward the exit and held his arm. "I'm afraid you won't get to see much of the place this trip," Linda said. "What I would like you to do for me has to be done in Toronto. It won't take me very long to explain to you what I want you to do, but you'll have this evening and tomorrow morning to see a little of St. John's. There's a 2:05 p.m. flight back to Toronto tomorrow. I've booked a room for you for tonight at the Newfoundland Hotel. That's where we'll go now and I'll tell you what I want."

"You certainly don't waste time or words," Harry said as they left the terminal and headed for Linda's car.

During the twenty minute drive to the hotel, Linda detailed what it was she wanted. She explained that her company was preparing a law suit against OPI. She interspersed her request with descriptions of prominent landmarks and by the time they had reached the hotel, she had only briefly talked about the lawsuit. She ended by saying that the details of the lawsuit were not important to the job she wanted him to do.

The doorman took Harry's overnight bag to the room and returned the key to him in the bar a few minutes later. Harry had a local beer and Linda had a glass of Chablis.

"What I need from you, Harry, is everything you can find out for me about Denis Leblanc. I don't mean the stuff I can find out in the *Financial Post* or sources like that. I want to know everything about him from the time he was born, to today. I want to know if he's married or if he's ever been married. I want to know his likes and dislikes, that kind of thing. I've heard for example, that his first wife left him, but the details are sketchy at best. I want you to find out everything about him."

Harry had taken a tiny pad of paper from his windbreaker pocket and was quickly scribbling notes. He finally took a break and drained his beer glass. He look at Linda after he had finished.

Linda continued with her request. "I want to know more about

Denis Leblanc than he knows about himself. And I need this information before Christmas. You can wait until you've finished and then I'd like you to come back and brief me. If I like what I hear, with respect to detail, in addition to your fee, I'll pay for a week here for you and your wife so you can really see the province. You do have a wife, don't you?" she asked.

"Yes, I have a wife and I think she'd like that a lot. There is one thing that bothers me though. You could have told me all of that over the telephone."

"Yes, I could have," Linda answered. "But over the telephone, I would just have been another faceless client. I wanted to meet you and to impress upon you the importance I am placing on the information you are about to get me. I want to know everything. No detail is to be left out. I don't care how you get it. And other than your boss, no one is to know for whom you're getting this information. Is that clear?"

"Perfectly," Harry said as he held up his hand indicating that he wanted another beer. He pointed to Linda's glass. She shook her head.

Linda finished her wine and then made a motion to leave. "Okay Harry," she said as she stood up. "You know what I want and how soon I want it. I hate to leave you alone on your first night here, but you're only a few minutes from downtown and any taxi driver will take you on a sightseeing tour. Signal Hill is just behind the hotel and for a man in your excellent physical condition, it's easy walking distance. Here's my card," she said, taking one from her purse and handing it to him. "I'll be at home all evening if there's anything you need. So, until we meet again," she finished, holding out her hand.

Harry got up and shook her hand. "Thank you," was all he said as she turned and left the bar.

Linda checked into her office before going home. Marilyn had left her a few telephone messages, but a quick check revealed that they could wait until the morning. Everybody had gone home earlier and Linda decided that, for a change, she would go home before 8:00 p.m. Maybe she would even cook supper for Bob. Tomorrow she would answer her first questions about the suit against OPI. One of the telephone messages had been from a reporter at *The Evening Telegram*.

Twenty-Three

THE PROCESS SERVER was shown into Jeremy Hawkins' office a little before lunch. Marie looked a little intimidated; before she got to introduce the little man beside her, he spoke.

"Are you Mr. Jeremy Hawkins, legal counsel for Ocean Products International Limited?" he asked.

"Yes, I am. Who the hell are you?"

He didn't answer. Instead, he just passed an envelope to him, turned and left the office.

"What was that all about?" Jeremy asked his secretary.

"He said he was from the court and had papers he had to serve you."

"From now on, don't let anybody in here unless I know them. Especially not process servers."

"Yes, sir," Marie answered and she turned to leave.

Jeremy looked at the envelope for a second and then, using his letter opener, he ripped it open.

"Holy Jesus," he called out after he had read the first page. "Marie, get in here." Marie heard his scream through his open office door and came running.

"What is it, Mr. Hawkins?" she asked.

"That ungrateful bitch. After everything I've done for her. Now she wants to take us to court."

"I'm afraid I don't understand," Marie said apologetically.

"Just get Henry and George. I don't care what they're doing. Tell them I want to see them right this minute."

Jeremy turned back to the papers. He tried to read them, but he was so filled with rage that the words were only a blur on the pages.

He had been able to determine, though, that Humby and Associates, representing Walter Lake, were suing Ocean Products International Limited, for six million three hundred thousand dollars.

Jeremy had only been indirectly involved with the majority of the details of that case, but he knew exactly what had happened. His father, before he died, had tried to tell Denis Leblanc that what they were doing was illegal, but his counsel had fallen on deaf ears. Joe Crocker, the Fisheries Minister, had been bought and paid for. Jeremy had only met Crocker once, but after that one meeting he had formed the opinion that if one looked in the dictionary under the word 'crooked', one would find a picture of Crocker.

Fortunately, the other two partners were in their offices. Jeremy was still holding the court documents when they came in. "What is it?" George said as he walked in. Jeremy just passed him the papers. Standing in front of Jeremy's desk, George took them and started to read, Henry looking over his partner's shoulder.

George Saunders had been with the firm for over thirty years. He had been made a partner by Jeremy's father. He was a very distinguished looking man with a full head of hair despite his sixty-some years. He wasn't wearing a jacket and his trousers were held up with a very colourful pair of suspenders. He was about thirty pounds overweight and puffed on a pipe as he looked at the documents.

Henry Flight was about the same age as George, and had founded the company with Jeremy's father. He was a tall, thin man; standing beside George, the two of them looked like Mutt and Jeff. He wore very thick glasses and strained to see what was on the papers.

"Jesus Christ, Jeremy. Is there anything to this?" George asked, as he finished skimming the papers and then passed them to Henry.

"Sit down, George. You too, Henry." Jeremy got up from his desk, walked over to his office door and closed it. He returned to his desk, pulled the chair out from behind it and sat beside his two partners.

"Henry, you know it was Dad who got the OPI account. He and old Mr. Leblanc were friends, and when Dad found out that Leblanc Industries was coming to Newfoundland, he talked to him and got the account. Dad looked after the account and I never got involved with it until five years ago when he got sick. I tried to talk to him about it on a number of occasions."

"Yes, I know all that," Henry interjected. "When we first got the account I worked on it a little with your father, but as we got other accounts, he kept it and I moved on to others. Why? Is there something about the account that we should know?"

Jeremy paused for a few seconds before speaking. "It's not good," he admitted, bowing his head.

"What does that mean?" George asked.

Jeremy lifted his head. "From what I can see in the files, Denis Leblanc bought a few politicians."

"Sweet Jesus," Henry whispered. He looked at George and then back at Jeremy. "Who knows about this?"

"Obviously, Walter Lake knows something about it," George said. "And his lawyers. Who are these people, Humby and Associates?"

"It's a new firm. The owner is Linda Humby."

Henry hesitated for a second and then looked at Jeremy. "You don't mean the Linda Humby that used to work for us?" he asked.

Jeremy nodded his head.

"What in the hell was she working on when she was here?" George asked, and from the tone of his voice, it seemed as if he already knew the answer.

Once again Jeremy hesitated before answering.

"Tell me it wasn't the OPI account," Henry said, before Jeremy had the opportunity to answer George's question.

"I wish I could," Jeremy admitted.

The two older men looked at each other. "Did she have access to the account files?" George asked.

"Yes, she looked after them for me when Brent died. I didn't have anybody else. She had been with us ever since she started school. I trusted her. I even authorized her to go to Carbonear and see our operation there. That's when she must have met with Lake and they cooked this whole thing up. The last thing I expected was for her not to continue working for us after she got admitted to the Bar."

"I suppose that everything is in those files," Henry thought out loud.

Once again, Jeremy nodded.

"God damn it, Jeremy, you should have told us about this when she wouldn't come to work for us. You should have known that there had to be a reason. Did you ever call her and try and find out?"

"Yes, I called her several times and left messages to call me each time. She wouldn't return my calls. After a while I just gave up calling."

"Well, now you know why she quit, don't you?" George asked.

"Yes, unfortunately I do," Jeremy said.

"Okay then," Henry said, trying to change the subject. "Let's get a look at those files and see what's in them. You can bet that she's going to try and subpoena them. So to protect our collective asses we better see what we can do to clean them up."

"I don't know what good that's going to do," George said.

"What do you mean?" Jeremy asked.

"She was just a goddamn law student when she worked here. Whoever is running the show for her, because clearly she doesn't have the experience or knowledge for this, has to simply put her on the stand and she can testify as to what's in the files."

"That will never happen," Jeremy shouted. "No judge would allow that to happen. Even though she was a law student, she was still in a position of trust and if she is called to the stand or if even one piece of information is produced that we know was copied from our files, we'll have them all disbarred."

"This still doesn't look good," Henry said to Jeremy. We're going to have to see what's in the files before we do anything. Then, while we're doing that, you had better give our client a call and tell him what's going on. If we get served today, you can bet it won't be too much longer before he's served too. And I strongly suggest you talk to him before then. Claude is assisting you with the account now, isn't he?"

"Yes, he is," Jeremy answered.

"Good, we'll get the files and you speak with Leblanc. We'll talk again after we've looked at them. In the meantime, we better have somebody see who's working with Linda Humby on this."

"Right," George said. "We'll get Claude to find that out for us. We're going to have to bring him up to speed on this, too." The two men then left Jeremy's office.

Jeremy moved back behind his desk and reached for the intercom to his secretary. Marie answered immediately.

"Get me Denis Leblanc on the telephone, Marie please. Tell whoever answers that it's an emergency and I have to talk with him right away."

"Yes, sir, right away," Marie answered.

While Jeremy waited, he tried to assess the situation. He looked at the court documents again and wondered why she had chosen to sue only OPI. If she had seen everything that was in the files, she could have filed suit against any number of people, including Hawkins and Murphy. As Jeremy continued to wait, the telephone buzzed.He picked it up.

"Yes, Marie."

"I have Mr. Leblanc for you," Marie answered.

"Good," Jeremy said, without meaning it.

"Hello Mr. Leblanc, how are you today?" Jeremy asked, trying to sound cheerful.

"You didn't call me to ask me how I am," Denis Leblanc answered. "I was told that it was an emergency."

"Yes, sorry Mr. Leblanc. It is an emergency." Jeremy cleared his throat. "Walter Lake from Carbonear is suing OPI for six million dollars."

"Who in the name of Christ is Walter Lake?"

"It started in 1963 when OPI wanted to buy his fish plant in Carbonear."

"Yes, so what?

"He's stating in his affidavit that OPI bribed government officials and that, as a result, he was driven into bankruptcy."

Jeremy waited for a response, but all there was was the crackling of the telephone lines. "Mr. Leblanc, are you still there?" Jeremy asked.

"Yes, I'm still here," Denis shouted. "What do they have?"

"It's not good sir. Not good at all."

"What the fuck do you mean, not good? What do they have.?"

This was what Jeremy was fearing. "We had a young student working in our office. She had access to the files. She now has her own firm and is representing Lake."

"Goddamn it. Goddamn you. You knew the sensitivity of some of our dealings and you let a goddamn student have access to our files?"

"It's not like it seems, sir," Jeremy tried to apologize.

"It better goddamn well not be," Denis shouted. "You get your ass to Toronto right now and I'll expect full disclosure on this. And if you're not in my office by tomorrow morning at 8:00 a.m. you better be dead or in hospital. Is that clear?"

"Yes sir," Jeremy answered to the sound of the heavy slamming of the telephone receiver.

He immediately buzzed Marie.

"Book me on the next flight to Toronto. I have to be there by eight tomorrow morning. If the flights are booked, tell the agent to find somebody who's willing to sell their ticket. I'll give them what they paid for it and five hundred dollars besides." He didn't wait for an answer before hanging up.

Henry, George and Claude were in Claude's office poring over the OPI files when Jeremy walked in.

"Did you speak with Leblanc?" Henry asked.

"I wouldn't say I spoke with him. I said a few words and he blew up. I have to be in his office tomorrow morning. What am I going to tell him?"

"That's the big money question," George said. "We haven't seen what's in these files yet, so we can't assess the damage. You know what's in them. Depending on when your flight is, we may have a chance to look at them together before you leave. We haven't even met with Humby yet."

The buzzing of the telephone interrupted them. Claude picked it up and passed it to Jeremy. He listened for a moment and then hung up.

"That was Marie. I have to return to my office."

Marie met him at the door. "There's a flight leaving at 2:05 for Halifax. You can make a connect there for Toronto," she said.

Jeremy looked at his watch. It was 11:20 a.m. "I'm gone to pack a few things," he said as he ran to his office. Marie followed behind him.

"Your ticket will be waiting for you at the reservation desk," she said as she stepped into his office.

Jeremy reached his closet and took out his raincoat. He pulled it on quickly and half-ran to his desk, where he threw a pile of papers into his briefcase. "Tell George and Henry that I'll call them from the hotel. Make me a reservation at The Leblanc. When am I due to arrive in Toronto?"

Marie looked at her note pad. "Eight twenty," she answered.

"Okay, tell them I'll call as soon as I land," he called out as he left.

The flight arrived ten minutes early, but it was still 8:40 p.m. before Jeremy got access to a telephone. "I'm here," Jeremy said as soon as George accepted the collect call. "What do you have to tell me?"

"It doesn't look good, Jeremy. But we've got the advantage. If she took copies of those files, there's no way she is ever going to get them entered into evidence. I think they'd have a hell of a time proving this without the cooperation of Joe Crocker."

"I feel the same way, Jeremy," Henry said on the extension. "She's got Bill Parsons working for her. I had heard he was getting bored with Wells and Wells. He's done this kind of work before but never at this level."

"You're not telling me anything new. I know what's in the files and I've heard of Bill Parsons. I want to know what to tell Denis Leblanc tomorrow morning."

There was silence for a few seconds. "Tell him there's nothing to worry about," George said breaking the silence.

"I agree," Henry said. "Give him the facts and tell him that we have everything in hand. Remember, we only did what we were told. They were the ones who met with Crocker. We take responsibility for giving a student access to the files. Explain to him that we have always hired our new lawyers by first hiring them as students. Tell him about Brent's death. Tell him that Humby was the first and only student to quit on us."

"Good," Jeremy said. "I feel better now. I'll let you know how it goes. Goodnight," he finished as he hung up the telephone.

The chauffeur from The Leblanc had met Jeremy as he got off the plane. He waited beside the telephone booth as Jeremy made his call, and then lead him to the limousine. Thirty minutes later he was checked into his room and waiting for room service to deliver his Scotch and water.

Jeremy was too agitated to sleep, but finally drifted off just before dawn. The call from the front desk startled him. He looked at the clock on the night table: 6:45. He picked up the receiver and then put it back in its cradle without speaking. Then he picked it up again and dialed 8. When a voice answered he spoke: "A pot of coffee to room 1507 as soon as possible please," he said, and didn't wait for a response. It was on the table when he finished his shower.

The hotel limousine took him to Denis's office. As he was getting into it, he thought he saw Denis getting into a limousine in front of his. He laughed at his paranoia as the chauffeur took him to his destination. He arrived outside the office of the president of Leblanc Industries at exactly 7:45 a.m.

A very young woman, too young to be a company president's secretary, was seated at a desk outside Denis's office. Jeremy had only been there once before with his father, but he couldn't remember how it looked. The young woman looked up from her desk. She could have been a model.

"Good morning, Mr. Hawkins, Mr. Leblanc is expecting you. Please have a seat and I'll let him know you're here," she said.

Jeremy took a seat and watched as she got up, walked to the big oak door behind her, knocked softly and walked in without waiting. A few seconds later she reappeared and held the door open.

"Mr. Leblanc will see you now," she smiled as she stood inside the office and held the door.

Jeremy suddenly remembered the luxury of the office as he stepped inside, but had little time to reflect as he was met with the powerful voice of Denis Leblanc.

"Come in. Sit down. Tracy, get Mr. Hawkins a coffee."

"How would you like it Mr. Hawkins?" she asked.

"Black," Jeremy answered, as Denis pointed to a leather chair on the other side of the office. He walked to the chair, sat down, and placed his briefcase on the floor beside him, and watched as Denis signed a couple of documents. It had been nearly ten years since he had seen him but he didn't look as if he had aged a day. Jeremy guessed that Denis would be fifty or fifty-five years old, but he could have easily passed for thirty-five. His face was very heavily tanned and there was a long scratch on his right cheek. Jeremy wondered if he tinted his hair. After a couple of minutes, Denis got up and joined him. By this time, Tracy was putting their coffee on the table.

"I got served with papers just after you called yesterday. I've given them to our senior legal counsel and asked him to join us here at 8:15. Now, before he gets here tell me what this is all about."

"Well sir, my staff hasn't had much of an opportunity to assess this, but our preliminary assessment is positive."

"What does that mean? I only want to know two things. How do we beat this, and how much is it going to cost me?"

"There is a little complication with this case, sir," Jeremy admitted reluctantly.

"Yes," Denis responded. "I suppose this has something to do with this student."

"I was assisted on your account by a young lawyer who was killed in an accident a few years ago. I needed help and there was a young law student in our office who had been with us six or seven years. I had her maintain the OPI account files. Well, she quit unexpectedly and now she has her own firm. She's representing Walter Lake."

"What's in those files?" Denis snapped.

"Everything, sir."

"Goddamn you, Hawkins. You mean to tell me that you let a student have access to the files of our account?"

Jeremy nodded.

"I can't believe that you could be so fucking stupid! Don't we pay you enough to put a real lawyer on the account? Who else has access to the files?"

"Just one of our lawyers and my two partners."

Denis got up from his chair and walked to the door. "Tracy, get Winston in here. Never mind," he said as he saw his lawyer step out of the elevator. "Come in, Winston," he said holding the door open. "I believe you know Jeremy Hawkins."

"Yes, good morning Jeremy," Winston said as he walked toward Jeremy with his outstretched hand.

"Good morning, Winston," Jeremy responded as they shook hands.

Tracy appeared and placed a coffee cup on the table in front of Winston.

"Hawkins here has just given me some very disturbing news, Winston," Denis said as he sat down. "One of his law students had access to our files in Newfoundland and now she's representing one Walter Lake who claims we put him out of business."

Winston lifted his eyebrows. "Really?" he managed.

"Yes, really," Jeremy said. "We had a law student working with us. She had been with us every since she started university. Then the day she got admitted to the bar, she quit and went to work for the Crown Attorney's office. Now she's got her own firm and she's representing the plaintiff."

"A law student one day and the owner of her own firm the next day. Is she independently wealthy?"

"I never thought of that," Jeremy commented.

"I'll need those files," Winston added. "What's in them?"

"Everything," Jeremy admitted. "Letters, contracts, everything that has ever been generated affecting OPI interests in Newfoundland.

"What's in there that she can use against us?" Winston asked.

"There's copies of a letter from Lake to the Premier when we tried to buy him out. There's letters from the fisheries minister, Crocker, giving us tax breaks."

"Isn't he on the board?" Winston asked.

"Yes, he is," Jeremy answered.

Winston turned to Denis. "I thought I advised you to get rid of that drunk," he said.

"I never got around to it," Denis replied. He then turned to Jeremy. "Goddamn it, Hawkins. You knew the sensitivity of those things. What the fuck was on your mind?"

Jeremy had been looking down and suddenly he jumped to his feet. Both men drew back. "Listen, you son of a bitch," he screamed at Denis. "I'm tired of being held out as the whipping boy for this and you better change your God damn approach or I'm on the next flight back home. I made a mistake by giving a student access to our files and I've admitted it. But it was you who bought Crocker. My father tried to tell you not to do it, but you ignored him. I'm your goddamn lawyer and I'll do everything in my power to represent you as fairly and as impartially as I can. But I won't sit here and take any more abuse from you. You can fire me if you want, but I won't be treated like this."

"Maybe I should have done that. Maybe if I had...."

"All right, Jeremy," Winston said, interrupting and reaching across and putting his hand on Jeremy's shoulder. "Let's keep our cool.

This may not be as bad as it seems. She may have seen everything, and if worse comes to worst, she even may have copied some of the documents. If she did, she must know that she can be prosecuted and no judge will allow illegally obtained documents to be admitted. They've still got to prove that we bribed government officials. We'll have to admit that there may have been some improprieties, but they could easily be explained as bad judgement calls on Crocker's part. How important is Crocker to you?" he said, turning his attention to Denis.

"He's a goddamn leech."

"That may be, but what we have to be careful of is having him turn against us. He may have to be the scapegoat for this and if he is, it may have to be with his co-operation. Understand what I am saying?"

"I think so," Denis said. "We'll just have to get him to say that he made a few mistakes. The son of a bitch is nearly seventy-five years old anyway. I can throw a couple of hundred thousand dollars at him. He can go to Florida somewhere and by the time they decide to charge him and get through extraditing him, he'll be dead. Then whatever happens in the future, we can say that we thought it was okay because Crocker told us it was okay. That might be a weak argument but it might work." Denis smiled for the first time since he had been advised of the suit.

"Let's not get too far ahead of ourselves," Winston added. "I'm assuming that there are documents in those files, that if they were presented in court, could be a big help to their case."

"If those files contain what I think they do, then the answer is yes," Jeremy admitted.

"Could the information be so damning that they could win the suit?" Winston asked.

Denis and Jeremy looked at each other and then to Winston. Jeremy nodded.

"I want to go back to St. John's with Jeremy then," Winston said, "and have a look at them. I also want to talk with the Humby girl."

"Good," Denis said, standing up. "Keep me advised of everything. Winston, you take charge of this. Hawkins, if this ends up any way other than the way I expect it, we'll be looking for another law firm. Understand?"

"Yes, fully," Jeremy said as he got up.

"Okay now, let's get this looked after."

Jeremy gathered up his papers and his briefcase and followed Winston out of the office. Winston paused in front of Denis's secretary's desk. A much older woman was seated behind it.

"I hear you were not feeling very well," Winston commented.

"Yes, but I'm much better now. I had to go to the hospital for a test first thing this morning and they'll know the results of the tests this afternoon."

"Well, let's hope it's good news. Now, could you make reservations to St. John's on the next flight for Mr. Hawkins and me, please. Let Cynthia know the details."

"Yes, sir," the secretary replied.

"I supposed the only thing for you to do is to come back to my office with me and wait until we find out when we're leaving," Winston said as they walked toward the elevator.

"Yes, I suppose," Jeremy said, not sounding very confident.

"Don't worry about it," Winston said, patting Jeremy on the back. "Denis's latest whore must have given him a hard time last night," he laughed.

Jeremy looked at Winston for more details.

Winston just smiled.

Twenty-Four ~

By November, Linda had given more interviews than she could remember. She had talked with reporters from every major newspaper in Canada, done telephone interviews with numerous radio stations and appeared on both local televison stations. The OPI story had been front page news for a week. The "letters to the editor" columns of both local newspapers were filled daily with letters from readers supporting Walter Lake. The overwhelming majority of them were from fisher-men or the wives of fishermen and the gist of all of their letters was that it was time that somebody did something about the stranglehold OPI had on the Newfoundland fishery.

Walter Lake had been coached very carefully and in the numerous interviews he had given, he had concentrated on what Linda had advised him to say. He focused on the fact that a lot of good men lost their jobs and now they had nothing, and trying to get the message across that he was just one of many who had lost their jobs because of OPI.

Lake came across as a grandfather whose grandchildren had been brutalized. And the wonderful thing about it all was that he was believable. Whenever he was asked a question on a subject that he had been advised to stay away from, he just smiled and said that that question would be best answered by his lawyers. It worked well.

In the second week of December, Linda got a call from Harry Thistle. He advised her that he was ready to come to St. John's and brief her. Linda remembered the promise she had made regarding a week's holiday in Newfoundland and suggested he bring his wife. Regrettably, his wife's sister was ill and she had gone to spend time with her in Winnipeg. He would be joining her there after he had fin-ished in Newfoundland.

Linda met him at the airport and they chatted about the weather and other trivial things on their way to the hotel. Once in the hotel, though, the subject changed to the purpose of his visit.

"I believe that during the past couple of months, I've gotten to know Denis Leblanc better than he knows himself," he laughed as they sipped drinks that room service had delivered.

"Good," Linda said. "I expect that you've put everything you're going to tell me into a report."

Harry moved from the table to the bed and opened his briefcase. He returned with a large binder and placed it carefully on the table in front of her. Linda opened it and inside was a rather large, typewritten report.

"That's your report," he said.

Linda riffled through the pages. "I'm impressed," she said.

"I hope you feel that way when you get our bill," he laughed.

Linda laughed with him. "Okay, tell me what's in this," she said, turning serious.

Harry drained his glass and leaned back in his chair, "Okay," he began, "Denis Leblanc, this is your life."

"Denis Leblanc was born in Toronto on June 6th, 1920 to Romeo and Josephine Leblanc. His mother, Josephine, died of pneumonia in 1932 when he was twelve. I found one of his old school friends and he told me he remembered that Denis took his mother's death very hard. I also found one of his school teachers and she told me that before his mother's death Denis was a very pleasant child and every person in his class, especially the girls, really liked him. But after her death, he got into fights with girls and, oftentimes, for no reason, punched them. That may explain his later treatment of women."

"What do you mean?" Linda asked.

"I'll get to it in a little while," Harry said. "Okay, where was I? Yes, okay. His father married Linda Peterson in 1935. She was from a good family in Toronto and although much younger than Romeo, from all indications they loved each other. Denis appeared indifferent to the marriage, but he was civil to her and as he matured, he grew to accept her. She was given several awards by the City of Toronto and the Province of Ontario for her charity work but despite her volunteer work, she found time to have two children, Alain and

Marie, who loved and admired their older stepbrother. Alain was killed in a skiing accident in 1963 and Marie lives in Toronto, married to a very successful plastic surgeon. They have two children.

"Was Alain married?"

"No. He had trained as a lawyer and was working for Leblanc Industries when he got killed. He was an avid skier and was glacier skiing in Austria. It was very foggy and he was skiing off piste. Apparently, he went right off the side of the mountain. It was several days before they found his body."

"That's terrible," Linda said.

Harry just nodded. "In 1941", he began again, "Denis joined the Royal Air Force despite the fact that his father was vehemently opposed to it. His father, sixty-four at the time, had become a very successful and wealthy businessman and he wanted Denis to join him in the business. According to the people I talked to, he wanted nothing to do with the business. Denis trained as a pilot, reaching the rank of Flight Lieutenant, and flew a total of twenty-seven combat missions. He was shot down over Germany, but the underground helped him to get out of the country safely. In 1945, when the war ended, he transferred to the Royal Canadian Air Force and was posted to Camp Borden, Ontario. He came home to visit occasionally to visit with his family and that's when he met his wife."

"In the summer of 1946, Francine Forest, from Roberval, Quebec, was brought to the Leblanc mansion to teach French to Denis's stepbrother and stepsister. Denis's father, Romeo, had been born in Roberval and he found Francine as a student in a convent there. She was nineteen at the time and she willingly accepted the job. I talked to some of the staff who used to work in the mansion and they told me that the children loved her like a mother. In fact, Linda Leblanc depended on servants to raise her children and Francine became more of a mother to the children than Linda."

"Do you have any pictures of her or anything like that?" Linda asked.

"There was quite a write-up in the newspapers about the wedding. I've placed copies in the report."

Linda thumbed through it, "Where?" she asked.

Harry took the report and within seconds he had found them.

Linda stared a the pictures. "Was this her?" she asked, pointing to the newspaper copy. Francine has seen pictures of her mother in Roberval and recognized her. But she wanted to be sure.

"Yes," Harry said, leaning toward her to confirm it.

Linda examined the pictures. Her mother had been very pretty. Suddenly, she gasped. "My God, is this Denis?" she asked.

Harry leaned toward her again. "Yes," he said, obviously surprised at her surprise.

It was like looking at a picture of Michel. Denis's hair was styled a little differently, but it was like looking at twins. It was an incredible likeness.

Harry continued. "Denis was quite the charmer and in the spring of 1947, after courting Francine for several months, he proposed. They were scheduled to be married in July, but Denis, a short while after their engagement, had a flying accident that nearly resulted in his death. His legs were broken and his right arm was severely mangled. As a result, he was medically discharged from the Air Force. For Romeo, the discharge was great news because his son would now have no choice but to join the family business. However, Denis became very bitter and became a recluse. Anyway, it seems that Francine had more of an influence over him than anybody could have imagined. He suddenly changed. It was like she had given him a reason for living. I was able to find one of his physiotherapists and he told me Denis changed overnight. He made a rapid recovery and Denis and Francine were married on August 13th, 1947."

"Francine and Denis set up house in the Leblanc mansion and Denis went to work for his father. His father put him to work doing the most menial of tasks in every facet of Leblanc Industries, which by this time had become a multi-million dollar operation. People I talked to who worked with him at that stage of his life, were very impressed. He was a kind, caring and responsible person, who very quickly learned the way his father's businesses were run. He was a quick study and things were going very well for him. On March 16th, 1948, their only child, Michel, was born."

"Are there pictures of him in here too?" she asked.

"Yes, just flip a few pages. His birth announcement, accompanied by a picture, was in the papers.

Linda flipped to the picture.

"Things seemed to deteriorate in his marriage after his son was born. I found a young girl who worked upstairs in the mansion and she told me she heard them fighting a lot. Also, Denis started sleeping at The Leblanc and he began using the services of prostitutes. I talked to a couple of the bellhops who used to work there and they told me it wasn't common knowledge, but he spent practically every night there. And usually with a different woman each night."

"Did you find out why?" Linda asked.

"Yes, I think so. Just bear with me for a few minutes."

"Okay," Linda said.

"On June 12th, 1950, Romeo died and Denis took over control of Leblanc Industries. It came as a shock to everybody, but it seemed that Denis was the strength in the family and he took charge of everything. I have included a copy of Romeo's will with the package and there were no surprises. Denis took control of the company and, despite his personal failings he led the company from one successful acquisition to another. He became fanatic and spent nearly every waking hour at work. He rarely went to the mansion to see his wife and son; on the few occasions he did, he usually fought with her. I talked to some of his wife's friends and they told me that many times they saw her with bruises on her face as if somebody had beaten her. I couldn't find anybody who had actually seen him striking her, though."

"Did he mistreat Michel?"

"I found no indication of that," Harry answered.

"Now, to your other question. It appears that the only way Denis Leblanc could enjoy sex was to beat up his sexual partners. I spoke with several retired cops and they talked about numerous prostitutes who had been hospitalized for broken bones and bruises. Not one of them would press charges against anybody. What the cops found disturbing was that it seemed that after these hookers left the hospital they disappeared off the streets. It seems they suddenly had enough money so that they didn't have to hook any longer. I found an old prostitute who had been on the streets of Toronto during that period and she told me it was Denis Leblanc who had been beating them up. She had gone to his room once and when he got violent she managed to get out of there. But she had a few friends who had not been so lucky."

"That's incredible," Linda said.

"But that's not all," Harry continued. "Now for the shocking news. On November 15th, 1950, Francine and Michel disappeared and were never seen again. I talked with the cop at the Toronto Metropolitan Police who was in charge of the investigation to find her, and what he had to tell me came as quite a shock. He told me that Denis hired a private firm to find her. Nobody from the firm would talk to me. I found that rather surprising. But then I discovered that the guy who owns the detective agency was an old Air Force buddy of Denis's. Anyway, the cop told me that Denis placed ads in every newspaper in the country offering rewards to anybody who could find her. They're also in the file," he added. "Because of his influence, he was able to put a lot of political pressure on the police departments to put extra men on the case, but despite everything, they never found a trace of her or the boy. But that's not what shocked me. The cop said that his investigation showed that Denis Leblanc was probably a sadomasochist. Like I just said, he gets his jollies beating up women. He, the cop, figures that Denis had his wife done away with and used the elaborate search scheme just to throw suspicion away from him. He told me he wouldn't admit it publicly, but that was the only conclusion they could come to. For a woman and a boy to disappear and to not be found considering the resources available to Denis Leblanc, the woman had to be extremely smart or Denis Leblanc had something to do with the disappearance. The woman did not give the impression that she was extremely smart. Anyway, the cop concluded that if it had been somebody other than Denis Leblanc, they might have been able to pursue it. He was questioned at length, with the assumption that he may have been responsible for his wife's disappearance, but any potential investigation with that goal in mind was squashed by the brass before it even got started. The cop was convinced that Leblanc had done away with his wife and son and he insinuated that to Leblanc during his interrogation. He almost got fired as a result. Leblanc called the mayor and the whole thing was suddenly stopped."

"I understand now the political influence you mentioned he had," Linda said.

"In the end," Harry continued, "they didn't find them and their whereabouts are still a mystery."

"Not any more," Linda blurted.

"What do you mean?" Harry asked.

"Oh, nothing," Linda apologized and turned a couple of pages quickly. "I was just thinking about something else."

"Leblanc gave up looking after about a year or so, never remarried and became more of a fanatic with respect to his business dealings than ever. He turned Leblanc Industries from a multi-million dollar industry into a multi-billion dollar industry. I've devoted several pages to his personal net worth and the worth of the company in the package you have.

"His stepmother," Harry continued, "is still alive. She lives in the mansion on the outskirts of Toronto. She never remarried after Romeo's death. Denis lives at The Leblanc and still spends sixteen hours a day at the office. His sexual perversions haven't changed except he's now a lot more discreet. He took a trip to Cuba a few years ago and beat up a prostitute so bad that it cost him over fifty thousand dollars to keep it out of the news. I would guess that if I were to check further, I could probably find several other situations such as the one in Cuba.

"He's a highly respected businessman and has contacts at the very highest levels of government. He's on a first name basis with the prime minister; when he married Margaret, Romeo was a consideration for best man. He's got contacts all over the world and surrounds himself with only the best people. Nobody who works for him now would talk to me about any aspect of his life.

"That's about it. There's a lot more detail in the package and if you have any questions or would like anything investigated further after you've read it, just call."

"Well, Harry, at the risk of repeating myself, I'm impressed. I didn't imagine that you would provide me the detail you have. I plan to inform the owner of your firm how pleased I am with what you've given me," Linda said.

"Thank you," Harry said, "but right now another scotch would be thanks enough."

Linda got up and walked over to the telephone. "Hello," she said when room service answered. "Please send a bottle of your best Scotch up to Mr. Thistle's room right away please. Have the bill sent to Humby and Associates. This is Linda Humby. I'll sign the receipt when I come down to the lobby on my way out," she finished. She hung up and smiled at Harry. "You don't mind if I join you for one too, do you?"

"No, ma'am," Harry said.

A few minutes later the Scotch was delivered. Linda drank with him and then they said their goodbyes. She expressed her appreciation for what he had done and reminded him to call her when he wanted to take advantage of her vacation offer. He promised that he would call in the not-too-distant future.

Linda's mind was working overtime as she drove back to the office. Harry Thistle had given her a lot of information. She wasn't quite sure how she could use any of this information in their suit against OPI, or if she should even give it to Bill. Maybe what she should have done was to have Harry dig a little into what happened in Carbonear. She considered discussing that with Bill.

Linda returned to her office and found her staff discussing Bill's first visit to see the government letters promised to him in court. None of the information he had hoped to find was in any of the files. "It's like having a murder weapon, and having a picture of the murderer committing the crime, and not being permitted to admit them into evidence. Damn the bloody law," Bill said.

The others laughed, as did Bill, when he realized how silly he must have sounded.

"Is there no other way to get what I have into evidence?" Linda asked.

"There is, but I'm not sure how much good it will do," Bill answered.

"What is it?" she asked.

"I could put you on the stand and ask you if you had ever seen anything in the files that would indicate that OPI and the government were in bed together. But I'm not sure how much credibility you'd have considering that you own the firm representing Walter Lake."

They all agreed that it would be a last ditch effort.

"How about if we can get Crocker on the stand and try and get something out of him?" Mary asked.

"It wouldn't hurt I suppose. But that old bastard could claim that his memory is failing or any other of a hundred excuses. You have him on your list don't you, Roger?"

"Yes, I have, but I'm having a hell of a time trying to find out where he is. I'm still on it though."

"Good," Bill said, "How about people who may have been working in the Minister's office at the time and might remember something about this?"

"I've contacted a few of them," Roger said, "but the details are scanty. Many of them are a loyal to Crocker and are not willing to say anything negative against him. I'll tell you who I do have though. Just this morning I spoke with Crocker's ex-wife. She hates his guts and called us saying that she may have some information that may help our case. I'm meeting with her tomorrow. Let's hope she has something useful."

"Great," Bill said, "but I have to say that by not getting access to those letters, our case is not very strong. Also, I was advised today that our court date is February 15th."

"Jesus Christ," Henry said.

"My sentiments exactly," Bill responded. "I tried to get more time but Judge Somers, who'll be hearing this case, says that OPI complained that any delay would cause them more harm than the suit has already. Their shares are down two dollars and they want to get this over with as quickly as they can. I'd guess the Justice Minister may have influenced this decision. Denis Leblanc has a very long reach."

Linda remembered her briefing from Harry Thistle. He had said that Denis was a very influential person. Now she was starting to feel a little of that influence first hand. With the court date so close, schedules would have to be readjusted. The Christmas holiday would be short.

Linda was starting to realize, for the first time in her very short legal career, that the law sometimes could help the guilty at the expense of the innocent. She began second-guessing herself. Maybe she should just cut her losses and get on with her life. But then she remembered Walter Lake and everybody else who had been beaten down by Denis Leblanc. She had to see it through to the end.

Twenty-Five ✌

THE TRIAL BEGAN as scheduled on February 15th. Jury selection took a full week. Bill had successfully argued earlier for a jury trial. Judge Somers, who had been scheduled to preside over the trial was suffering with the flu. He stayed at home on Wednesday and Thursday. Bill wanted fishermen on the jury and Jeremy, of course, wanted nothing to do with fishermen. Bill believed that fishermen might be sympathetic to their case and Jeremy, realizing this as well, could use his right to dismiss them. The case was being heard in St. John's and only a very small percentage of the population were fishermen. The two who were called for jury duty were rejected by Jeremy.

Bill and his team were ready despite the shortened time they had to prepare. In spite of the fact that they had been unable to legally obtain any of the correspondence that Linda had copied, they felt that they had a strong case. Joe Crocker had been located and subpoenaed. He would be identified to the court as a hostile witness, but Bill still felt he might be able to get Crocker to admit to one or more transgressions. He had refused a meeting with them before the trial and insisted on having a suite in the Newfoundland Hotel. If he had to testify, he would milk Humby and Associates for everything he could.

Jury selection ended just before lunch on Friday and the judge adjourned proceedings until Monday morning at 10:00 a.m.

The trial began in the largest courtroom available and still, hundreds of people milled around unable to get inside. It could seat nearly one hundred spectators and by 8:00 a.m. nearly half the seats were filled by members of the media. Few of the faces had changed since they began to select the jury, and each was busy with a note or a sketch pad. Linda watched with interest as the young people who had been paid to give up seats for press people exited the courtroom to be replaced by reporters. She sat with Roger and Marty in special seats behind Walter and Bill.

Bill was very eloquent in his opening statement. It lasted nearly two hours, as he outlined the injustice that had been done to his client and how it was the responsibility of the jury to hear the evidence. He told them they would see very clearly how OPI had deliberately set out to drive Walter Lake out of business.

Jeremy was equally eloquent in his address, taking the stand that Walter Lake, faced with legitimate competition, went bankrupt because of his lack of ability to run a successful business. Linda judged the opening statements a draw.

Bill began their case by putting Walter Lake on the stand. They felt it best to begin with Walter, to set the stage for everything that was going to happen thereafter. Bill estimated that it would take at least two full days to get Walter's testimony. They had spent a lot to time preparing him, and Bill felt very confident that he would prove to be a very effective and credible witness for his own case. Roger had played the role of defence lawyer during the preparation and spent many days cross examining him. When Walter was called to the stand they knew he was ready.

"Do you swear to tell the truth, the whole truth and nothing but the truth, so help you God?" the court clerk asked as Walter stood in the witness box with his right hand held up and his left hand holding the Bible.

"I certainly do," he responded in a loud clear voice.

Bill stood up from behind his desk and began to speak. "Would you please tell the court your name, address and what you do for a living."

"Walter George Lake from Carbonear, and I haven't done anything for a living since OPI drove me out of business."

Jeremy jumped to his feet. "Objection! My lord," he shouted.

The judge looked toward the jury. "You will ignore the witness' last statement and you, Mr. Lake," he said, turning to look at Walter, "will refrain from making such inflammatory statements.

"I swore I would tell the truth, judge," Walter said, "and that's the truth."

There was snickering in the gallery.

"That's not for you to determine Mr. Lake," the judge countered.

"You asked me to swear to tell the truth, Judge, and now you're telling me that someone else is going to determine what is or not the truth. I'm a Christian, Judge. I swore on that Bible to tell the truth. The truth is, that OPI crowd drove me out of business."

Jeremy jumped to his feet. So did Bill. It took the judge several minutes to straighten out Walter but he finally succeeded.

This had been planned. They had to establish from the beginning that Walter felt he had been beaten up by OPI. Bill knew that Jeremy would object to the statement.

"Okay, then, Mr. Lake, would you tell us please what type of work you did before you stopped working?" Bill asked.

"I owned a fish plant in Carbonear. My grandfather built it. My father took over from him and I took over from my father."

For the next half hour, Walter testified about the history of the plant, the people who had depended on his plant for a living and some of the awards he had received from the municipal and provincial governments.

"How many years did you operate the plant, Mr. Lake?" Bill asked, continuing the questioning.

"I ran it for thirty-two years," he answered triumphantly.

"And would you tell us how many people you had working in your plant?"

"During the summer, that's from June until the end of September, we worked twenty-four hours a day, seven days a week. There were three crews with nearly one hundred and fifty people on a crew. Now, they didn't work every day, of course. Sometimes there just wasn't any fish. But it was a very rare occasion when one of the people on shift didn't get fifty or sixty hours a week. Then of course, there were the refrigeration people, the office people and mechanics. I'd say that we provided work for about four hundred people."

"So you provided direct employment for nearly four hundred men and women?" Bill asked to emphasize the numbers.

"Yes, sir," Walter answered.

"How about indirect employment?"

"Well, we had a lot people who didn't work for us, but they got work from us driving trucks and stuff like that. Then of course there were all the people who handled the fish after we had it frozen and ready to ship."

"Would you say that you were the largest employer in the region?" Bill asked while looking at the jury.

"Yes, by far," Walter answered, looking at the jury.

"My lord," Jeremy spoke while rising to his feet. "We concede the fact that Mr. Lake's operation provided employment in the area. We wonder where Mr. Parsons is going with this."

"My lord, we are simply showing the jury the contribution Mr. Lake and his company made to the community. Before we can examine the effect of the closure of Mr. Lake's plant, we have to establish what conditions were before the plant was closed," Bill explained. "Surely my learned colleague does not want his client to erase the memory of Mr. Lake's contributions to this region as well as the plant."

Jeremy jumped back to his feet, but before he could protest Judge Somers raised his hand.

"That comment is out of order, Mr. Parsons and you know better. Make such an error in my courtroom again and I will find you in contempt. Now continue with the questioning of your witness."

Bill turned to look at his notes, having received the message very clearly, but also having achieved his goal. "Now then, you told the court that you operated this business for thirty-two years and your father and your grandfather operated it before you. You must have made a profit then," Bill said.

"Yes, we made a good profit, but I'm not a millionaire if that's what you mean," he laughed, as did several of the spectators.

The judge banged his gavel. "Order," he spoke.

Walter continued. "We were fair to the fishermen. We made a good dollar, but we paid the fishermen top dollar for their fish and we gave our fish plant workers an honest wage."

"How many people do you have in your employ today, Mr. Lake?"

"Not counting you lawyer fellers, not a single soul."

A few spectators laughed. "Order," the judge said as he banged his gavel for the second time.

"So what happened?" Bill asked.

"OPI happened," Walter answered bitterly.

"Please explain."

"I'd be happy to. It was in 1963 that I got a letter delivered to me. It was signed by a Denis Leblanc and in that letter he said he was interested in making me an offer for my plant."

Bill picked up a letter from his desk. "My lord, we would like to enter plaintiff Exhibit one, which is a copy of the letter Mr. Lake is referring to. Denis Leblanc, for the jury's information, is the chairman of the board of directors of Ocean Products International." Bill walked toward the clerk and passed the letter to him. He then provided Jeremy with a copy. The clerk marked the paper and passed it to the judge who examined it briefly.

"So ordered," the judge said.

"What was your response to this letter?" Bill asked.

"Well, I suppose I was a little shocked. I had heard that OPI had bought up plants in other places in Newfoundland, but I didn't think they were interested in mine. Anyway, I didn't waste any time. I sent a letter back to him the following day telling him that I wasn't interested."

Copies of the reply were produced by Bill and distributed in the same way as the first.

"Was that the last you heard from them?" Bill continued.

"No, I guess it was a couple of weeks after I had told them I wasn't interested that I got a visit from a couple of fellers. I was in my office and I wasn't expecting them, but I agreed to see them anyway."

"What was the reason they wanted to see you?"

"They told me that they were from OPI and would like to discuss my refusal to sell the plant. They said they were here to ask me to reconsider and that they were offering top dollar."

"What was your reaction?"

"I listened to them and then told them that I wasn't interested in their money. My plant wasn't for sale for any amount. I then informed them that I was busy and didn't have the time nor the interest to talk about it any longer. I then asked them to leave."

"Did they?'

"No, they didn't, They told me that unless I sold the plant, times could be very tough for me."

"What do you think they meant by that?"

"Objection, My lord," Jeremy said as he stood up. "The question asked the witness to state what he thinks these people were thinking."

"Sustained," the judge said solemnly.

Bill rephrased the question. "When these two men told you that times would get tough, what was your reaction?"

"I considered it a threat of some kind. They looked like goons and quite frankly, I thought they were more suited to heaving around fish pans than acting as messengers from OPI. But I had dealt with lots of people like those two before, so I told them to leave or I'd have them thrown out."

"Did they leave?"

"Yes, they did, but they told me I was making a big mistake by not selling. OPI always got what it wanted."

"Objection," Jeremy shouted.

There was a pause.

"On what grounds?" Bill asked.

"I was about to ask that question myself, Mr. Parsons," the judge said.

Jeremy appeared flustered. "Hearsay, My lord."

Bill laughed. "Your honour, the two men were from OPI, they identified themselves as employees of OPI and Mr. Lake is simply stating the facts."

"Objection overruled."

"Was this the last time you heard from OPI?" Bill continued.

"I wish it was, but no. I suppose that perhaps six months had passed when we found out that OPI was building a plant of its own in Carbonear."

"What was your reaction to this?"

"I couldn't believe it at first."

"Why was that?"

"First of all, I wondered where they were going to get the people to work in their plant. In 1964 there weren't very many people out our way who didn't have a job. We had to go over to Trinity Bay to find enough people to work for us, and we had a hard time finding them. Then I wondered where they were going to get the processing licence because there was only one licence for Carbonear, and that was mine. Finally, I wondered where they were going to get the fish. We were buying everything we could buy. I would have bought more, but there wasn't any. I even took the overflow from the plant in the next community, Harbour Grace. No town in this province had two processing plants and I couldn't believe that government would issue two permits in Carbonear, especially when there was a plant in Harbour Grace."

"So there was another plant in Harbour Grace?"

"Yes."

"How far is Harbour Grace from Carbonear?"

"I'd suppose it's about two or three miles."

"So, what you're telling us is that you didn't think that another plant in Carbonear would be a viable operation."

"Objection, My lord," Jeremy said. "Mr. Parsons is asking his client whether or not he thought OPI could make a profit in Carbonear."

"Yes, My lord. That is exactly what I am asking Mr. Lake to do. Mr. Lake operated a fish plant in Carbonear for thirty-two years. He has also testified that he bought all the fish that was available and he even bought the overflow from another plant close to his. Therefore, Mr. Lake can be considered an expert and can offer an opinion as to whether or not another fish plant could be viable in the area," Bill argued.

"My lord, OPI conducted a very extensive market survey and as a result of its survey, it came to the conclusion that another plant could be profitable. Whether or not Mr. Lake thinks it was a viable operation is irrelevant. The fact remains that OPI decided to build the plant."

"Approach the bench," the judge ordered the two lawyers.

"My lord," Bill said as he reached the bench, "there is only one plant in Carbonear and that's the OPI plant. We are attempting to prove that OPI knew, before they built the plant, that the area could only sustain one plant. Their intentions, therefore, were to drive Mr. Lake out of business. I will call the former manager of the plant in Harbour Grace and he will testify that, in his opinion, a third plant could not survive while the other two were operating. Therefore, in order for it to make money, it had to draw away the present customers of the plants in Carbonear and Harbour Grace."

Jeremy was about to speak, but the judge held up his hand. "Step back," he ordered.

"I'm going to allow this line of questioning, Mr. Parsons, but I caution you to be very careful not to try my patience."

"Thank you, My lord," Bill said.

"Now, then Mr. Lake," Bill continued, "in your expert opinion, do you think that another fish plant in Carbonear was a viable operation in the 1960s?"

"Definitely not," Walter said. "As I said earlier, there simply was not enough fish, and workers if they could be found, would have to come from outside the area."

"So then, why do you think that a company with the experience and expertise that OPI obviously has in the fish processing business, would decide to built a plant in Carbonear?"

"Objection," Jeremy said.

"Overruled," the judge responded. "Answer the question."

"They must have determined that they could lure away employees from my plant and the plant in Harbour Grace, and they could convince the fishermen who were selling to us to sell to them."

"Did you lose any of your employees to the new plant once it was built?"

"Yes, I did."

"And why do you think that these employees left your employ?"

"Objection."

"Sustained."

"Let me rephrase the question. When these people left your employ, did they give you a reason why they were leaving?"

"They did," Walter answered resolutely.

"And what was that reason?"

"OPI was paying fifty cents an hour more than I was."

"And how much were you paying an hour?"

"Well, the majority of the people that I lost were filleters. We were paying them two dollars and thirty cents an hour. Those were the workers we had the most difficulty finding."

"How much was the plant in Harbour Grace paying?"

"Two dollars and thirty five cents."

"Why were they paying more than you were?"

"They had a union."

Laughter broke out again. Even the judge smiled.

"Okay," Bill said, after the laughing had subsided, "so you've told us that employees who left you said that the reason they were leaving was because OPI was paying fifty cents an hour more than you were paying. How did you feel about that?"

"I told the boys to go for it. I was paying them a fair wage. If I had to pay my filleters fifty cents more an hour, I wouldn't have lasted a year."

"How many people did you lose?" Bill asked.

Walter rubbed his chin while he thought. Then he answered. "They finished building the plant in March, 1965. By June I had people working twelve hour shifts. The overtime was killing me. But by the end of July, it didn't make much difference anyway."

"What happened in July?"

"Over three quarters of the people who had been selling me fish, starting selling to OPI. I only got what our own boats brought in and the loyal fishermen who stayed with me. I only needed one shift to clean up my fish."

"How much were you paying the fishermen for their fish?"

"I was paying them five cents a pound. I met them increase for increase, but I couldn't go any higher than five cents. I was losing money."

"How much was OPI paying them?"

"Ten cents a pound. Three times what I was paying them when this all started. Add that to the wage increases that I tried to match, and you see the result."

Bill waited for the jury to digest what Walter had just said. "How much was the Harbour Grace plant paying the fishermen for fish?"

"Three cents a pound."

"Why didn't they sell to OPI?"

"Because the law states that you have to sell to the plant that services the fishing region. Carbonear gets this region, and Harbour Grace gets that region."

"How much was the Bay de Verde plant, fifty miles from you, paying for cod?"

"Three cents a pound."

"How much was every other plant in Trinity-Conception paying for cod?'

"Three cents a pound."

"Then why do you think that OPI decided to pay ten cents a pound?"

"Objection," Jeremy shouted.

"Overruled," the judge countered, "I'm willing to let Mr. Lake answer this question because of his knowledge of the fishing industry and the prices at the time. Go ahead and answer the question, Mr. Lake."

"Because they needed fish and the only way to get fish was to pay a higher price. The same as they did with the wages," Walter answered.

"Yes, Mr. Lake, but that's business."

"No sir, that's not business. The market could not bear a purchase price of ten cents a pound."

"Where were you selling your processed fish?"

"We transported it to Boston and sold it to a fish wholesaler."

"How much were you paid?"

"Twenty-three cents a pound on average.'

"But you paid the fishermen three cents a pound and you got paid twenty three cents a pound. That's still quite a profit."

"I suppose it is when you look at it that way. But when you consider all of our costs, which included maintaining freezer ships to send it to Boston, it wasn't that much. It cost us twelve cents to deliver a pound of cod to Boston. That's the cost to buy it and to transport it considering all of the costs attributable to the ships. It cost us six cents a pound for wages and plant operating costs. That left us with five cents a pound profit. If we were able to net two cents a pound I was happy. When the price in Boston went up, we paid the fishermen more. When it went down, we paid them less."

"Perhaps," Bill suggested to him, "OPI could do it a lot cheaper. They were bigger, they owned other plants in Atlantic Canada. They could control the market."

"Yes, they were bigger and they might have been able to do it a little cheaper than us, but their wages costs were twenty percent higher, and the price they were paying for fish was three times what we were paying. There's no way they could make a profit."

"Objection, My lord," Jeremy interrupted. "Mr. Lake has no way of knowing whether or not the OPI operation in Carbonear was profitable or not."

"Sustained," the judge said.

"So then, Mr. Lake, what happened next?"

"We tried to stay open, but without fish and without men to work in our plant, we had to close. In March of 1966, we closed."

"That left only OPI to process fish in Carbonear, is that right?"

"Yes, that's right."

"So, at the start of the 1966 fishing season, OPI was the only place in Carbonear for fishermen to sell their fish."

"Not only in Carbonear, but in Harbour Grace as well."

"What do you mean?"

"I mean that in 1966, they bought the Harbour Grace plant."

Bill looked over at the jury. "So the only place for the inshore fishermen to sell their catch was an OPI plant."

"Objection, relevance," Jeremy shouted.

"I'll make that very obvious with my next couple of questions, My lord," Bill answered.

"All right, I'll permit it, but get to the point, Mr. Parsons," the judge ruled.

"After you closed down, how much did OPI pay the fishermen?"

"Two and a half cents a pound."

A few of the jury members gasped.

"They paid ten cents a pounds when you were still operating and as soon as you closed the price suddenly became two and one half cents a pound?"

Jeremy was on his feet again, but his objection did not sit well with the judge.

Bill continued. "How much did they pay their filleters?"

"Two dollars and forty cents."

"A drop of forty cents an hour."

"Yes," Walter answered.

"Do you have any explanation as to why there was a decrease in the price of fish and a decrease in wages?"

"Yes, I heard that it was because the price that OPI was getting for fish in Boston had dropped significantly."

"Objection, that is hearsay," Jeremy stated.

"Sustained," the judge ruled.

"When the price of fish increased in Boston, you testified earlier that you increased the price you paid to the fishermen. Is that correct, Mr. Lake?"

"Yes, that's correct. We wouldn't increase our price if the price in Boston increased minimally, but if there was an increase of a few cents we normally made a small price increase to the fishermen."

Bill returned to his desk and retrieved a piece of paper.

"My lord, I have here an invoice for fish purchased from OPI on July 5th, 1966." He showed a copy to the judge and then provided a copy to Jeremy. It was stamped as a certified true copy. He passed it to Walter.

"Mr. Lake, would you tell us, please, what the price OPI was paid for the fish supplied to it on this invoice?"

Walter looked at it. "Thirty-four cents a pound."

"Thirty-four cents a pound," Bill repeated. I believe that you testified that a year earlier you were getting paid twenty-three cents a pound."

"Yes, that's right," Walter answered.

"And how much was OPI paying the fishermen?"

"Objection, My lord," Jeremy said.

Bill returned to his desk and retrieved another couple of pieces of paper. He distributed them as before. "This is a receipt provided to a George Butt of Carbonear. It is dated June 16th, 1965, and it shows that he was paid ten cents a pound for his fish."

The judge looked at the paper. "The witness may answer the question."

"They were paying ten cents a pound."

"And one year later, when OPI is being paid an additional eleven cents a pound for their fish in Boston, they reduced the price that they are paying fishermen to two and one half cents a pound. Do you have an explanation for this?"

"Yes, they wanted to recoup their losses from increasing wages and the price they paid fishermen so they could drive me out of business and buy the Harbour Grace plant."

Jeremy erupted. He was almost frothing at the mouth. Bill said and did nothing. He knew what Jeremy's response would be.

The judge said, "The jury will ignore Mr. Lake's last response. And as it is nearly lunch time, we will adjourn until 2:00 p.m." He banged his gavel on the bench, the jury was marched out and everybody stood. After the judge had left, Bill walked up to the witness box.

"Great job, Walter. The judge might have cautioned the jury to ignore what you said, but they will remember it all over lunch and for the duration of this trial. I think we're winning points with them. This afternoon, we'll get into what happened after your plant closed. For now, let's go have lunch."

Linda, who had been sitting as a spectator with Roger and Marty, joined them. The five of them then left the courtroom for lunch.

When the court reconvened, Walter's testimony continued. "Mr. Lake," Bill began, "Let's go back to the time when you first heard the OPI plant was going to be built. Did you do anything to try and question the construction?"

"Yes, I certainly did. I wrote several letters to Joe Crocker, the Fisheries Minister, telling him what the consequences would be."

"We would like to enter these three letters as plaintiff's Exhibits numbered four, five and six, My lord," Bill stated as he presented them to the clerk. They were copies of letters that Linda had copied from Hawkins and Murphy, but it could be easily argued that they were from Lake's own files.

"So ordered," the judge ruled, after he had examined them for a few seconds.

"So what did you tell the Minister in those letters?"

"I told him that another plant in this area would drive me out of business."

Several minutes of heated argument ensued between the two lawyers. Jeremy objected to the insinuations and Bill argued that all he was trying to do was to have his client testify as to the content of the letters. Bill was permitted to continue.

For the next hour Walter testified how, even with the support of the town council and a petition with over four thousand names on it, their pleas went unanswered. The minister never gave Walter the benefit of a reply, and the plant went ahead as scheduled. After Bill was satisfied that the jury understood everything that Walter had done to try and stop the construction was not only for his benefit, but for an overall community benefit, he spent the remainder of the day in the labourious process of bringing Walter through all of the things that caused him to have to close his business. It was very detailed testimony, and in order to ensure that the jury fully understood what had happened, Bill took particular care to make sure that everything was explained in as simple a manner as possible. Bill's quick checks of the jury's faces whenever they dealt with a particularly complicated issue, appeared to confirm that they were understanding what was being said.

On Tuesday, Bill began the routine of determining the effect of the closure of Lake's plant on the people and the area's economy. Those people who had remained loyal to Lake had not been able to secure jobs with the OPI plant when Lake closed; the majority of the work force in the OPI plants were from outside Carbonear and made an insignificant contribution to the town's economy. By lunch on the second day, Walter's testimony had finished and Jeremy now had the opportunity for cross examination. At 2:00 p.m. his examination began.

Jeremy, despite his age, was a very experienced and skilled lawyer. He was used to defending OPI policies and practices. His cross-examination was very professional and deliberate.

"Mr. Lake," he began, "you testified that you operated your plant in Carbonear for thirty-two years."

"Yes, that's correct." Walter said proudly.

"You also testified that during that period, you treated the fishermen who sold you fish and your employees fairly."

"Yes," Walter said again proudly.

"Do you remember an accident in 1960 when one George King was crushed to death in your plant?"

"Objection," Bill interrupted. "Most companies have accidents. What is the relevance to this line of questioning?"

"My lord, Mr. Lake has testified that he was a fair employer. We are attempting to show that he wasn't as fair as he would like this court to believe."

"Overruled," Judge Somers ruled.

"I repeat, Mr. Lake, do you remember such an accident in 1960?"

"Yes, I do."

"Could you explain to the court what happened?"

"The fish elevator had a malfunction and it didn't stop at the top, crushing George."

"What did you do for the family of that man?"

"I promised his family that they would have a job in my plant for as long as they wanted one. They would have had one too, if it hadn't been for you and that crowd from OPI."

Judge Somers banged his gavel. "You will refrain from making such comments. The jury will ignore Mr. Lake's last comment."

"So, Mr. Lake, one of your employees was killed in your plant because a piece of your equipment failed and all you did was offer his survivors a job. Did you help pay for the funeral expenses? Did you offer any financial help to the widow and her eleven children?

Once again Bill objected and was overruled.

For the remainder of the afternoon, Jeremy continued with the line of questioning he had started when he began his examination. He had been very thorough in his investigation, and despite the fact that Walter had done everything he was required to do under the law whenever there was an accident, Jeremy was painting a picture of a man who appeared uncaring over the death of an employee.

Jeremy next turned to several employee firings. At the end of the afternoon, Walter was feeling the effect of a very tough cross-exami-nation. Jeremy's plan was working and it was obvious on the faces of the jury.

The following morning Jeremy began again. This time he took the approach of undermining Walter's qualifications to actually manage a fish processing plant. Very expertly, he showed the jury that Walter's lack of formal management training, and the fact that he didn't even have a high school education, were the real reason the plant failed. Everything was being done to show the jury that Walter simply was incapable of handling the competition from OPI.

Jeremy continued with his cross-examination for the second day and for half of the third day, By the time he had finished, any gains that Bill had made with the jury were gone.

That evening, Bill and his team assessed the damage that Jeremy had done. At this stage, they had to conclude that Jeremy had been able to counter much of the sympathy Walter had been able to win from the jury. Jeremy might have continued with his examination, but it was evident that Walter was tiring and his continued grilling could bring back some of the sympathy that has been lost.

On Thursday morning, Bill began the process of trying to show

how government gave an unfair advantage to OPI and this, coupled with their immense financial resources, enabled OPI to increase employee wages and the price they paid fishermen for their fish. A copy of the company's financial statements for the first two years of operation were obtained and there were, indeed, tremendous losses. In year three, however, the profits skyrocketed. Several witnesses were called to support this and won points with the jury.

For the remainder of the week, and half the following week, Bill called witness after witness in an attempt to try and determine what benefits the company had been given by government. In all attempts he was only mildly successful. The only thing he had been able to show the court was that OPI had been given access to crown land to build their plant. Bill knew that they had been given tax breaks and incentives, but he was having difficulty finding someone to confirm it. The entire crux of their case was their belief that Joe Crocker has been bribed to give the company what it needed. As each day passed, it was becoming increasingly difficult. Government secrecy was working. On Friday of the third week, Bill called Joe Crocker.

Bill identified him to the court as a hostile witness and got the judge's permission to treat him as such.

"Mr. Crocker," he began, "you were the Fisheries Minister of this province from 1962 to 1965. Is that correct?"

Crocker was a very distinguished looking man with an infectious smile. He was nearly seventy years old, but he had a full head of white hair and gleaming white teeth. His skin was very heavily tanned and surprisingly, his face contained very few wrinkles. His nose was large and red from half a century of excessive alcohol consumption. He was dressed in a very expensive suit and looked at ease in the witness box.

"Yes, that's correct," he answered, smiling.

"Mr. Crocker, while you were Fisheries Minister, were you approached by Ocean Products International regarding the construction of a fish processing plant in Carbonear?"

Crocker looked at the jury and then at Bill. "No, I was not."

Bill looked at Crocker in complete shock, He hadn't been expecting this at all, He paused for a few seconds before speaking.

"I find that difficult to believe, Mr. Crocker. You were the

Fisheries minister when the plant was built in Carbonear. In that capacity you approved the location and construction of all new plants. How can you tell this court that you weren't approached by OPI when they contemplated building a plant in Carbonear?"

Jeremy rose to argue that Crocker had answered the question. The judge nevertheless directed Crocker to answer the question.

"Yes, My lord," Crocker answered with the same infectious and innocent smile. "You see, I was having personal problems when I was minister. I had a lot of people working for me at the time. Some of my closest staff members knew of these problems and they handled things for me."

Bill couldn't believe what was happening. It was crucial to their case that they get Crocker to admit that he was involved with the location of the plant in Carbonear. Clearly, he had been paid to make himself look like a fool. It could do him no damage now.

"I understand, Mr. Crocker, that since you left government, you've been a member of the board of directors of OPI. Is that correct?"

"Yes, I have been a member of the board of OPI."

"Why do you think that you were appointed to their board?"

"I've wondered that myself," he said.

Raucous laughter broke out and Judge Somers attempted to get order.

Bill tried to establish that he was getting paid handsomely to sit on the board and that he was appointed because of what he had given OPI when he was Minister, but it was like dealing with a complete idiot. Bill had no choice but to end the farce. Judge Somers, to Bill's relief, adjourned until Monday at 10:00 a.m.

Linda met with her staff back at the office shortly thereafter.

"I don't like the way this is going," Bill admitted. "Obviously, OPI bought Crocker off and he is willing to act the fool. We have nothing."

Linda sat silent, watching and listening. She didn't like what she was hearing. She had sat through every minute of the trial so far and she, too, had to admit that if the trial ended today, they would win nothing. They had the weekend to develop a new strategy. But Linda knew there was little they could do. From the outset, everything had been stacked against them. OPI was just too big a company to take on and they were just too small and inexperienced.

She excused herself from the meeting, knowing that she had to do something. Ever since Harry had briefed her on what he had found out in Toronto, she had thought that it might have to come down to what it looked like she was about to do.

She returned to her office and thumbed through her personal telephone directory. She found Jeremy Hawkins' personal number and telephoned him. He picked it up on the second ring.

"Jeremy, this is Linda Humby. Arrange a meeting for me with Denis Leblanc. I don't care what you have to do or say, just get me that meeting. I'll be in my office waiting."

"Why should I do that, you ungrateful bitch?" Jeremy shouted.

"Because if you don't, I'll give the press copies of the letters I copied from your files. I don't care about the consequences. Just arrange the meeting Jeremy. Winston Cummings is there with you, I'm sure. Have him arrange it. I'm in my office. I'll expect your call," she finished as she hung up.

A half an hour later the telephone rang. Marilyn had gone home earlier. "Hello," she answered.

"9:00 a.m. Monday morning, in his office," she heard Jeremy say before she heard the click.

She immediately telephoned the airport and made a reservation for Sunday. Then she returned to the conference room where her staff were still considering strategy. "I'm going to Toronto on Sunday," she said. "I'll be back late Monday or Tuesday. I'll call before I come back."

"Does this have something to do with our case?" Bill asked.

"It's an urgent personal thing. I'm sorry to leave like this."

"It's fine. Don't worry about it," Bill said as she left.

She had a lot to do before leaving for Toronto.

Twenty-Six

LINDA HEADED FOR home. It had been a busy week, filled with disappointment. She shuddered, more from anticipation than from the cold, as she started her car to go home. The drive took about twenty minutes and then she would have an even longer drive.

Bob was home when she arrived. He had fixed supper and the dining room table was set, accompanied by a bottle of Linda's favourite wine. She hated what she had to do.

"Hello, sweetheart," Bob greeted her as she entered the kitchen.

She laughed as she looked at him. He was wearing an apron and he looked like a young grandmother. "Hello," she answered as she walked to him and they kissed. "What smells so good?"

"I made lasagna," he said proudly.

"Mmmmm," Linda managed. "But I hate to say this honey, I can't stay and have some."

"What?" Bob asked.

"I have to drive to Dark Harbour right now. I don't want to discuss why and I'd love it if you didn't ask me. Just trust me on this one please."

"Is there something wrong with Michel?"

"No, it's nothing like that."

"My goodness, Linda, you can't leave and drive to Dark Harbour at this time of night. You've been working all day. You're tired. You're asking for an accident."

"I don't want to fight about this, Bob. I have to do this. You can't talk me out of it. I simply must go," she said as she left the kitchen and headed for the bedroom. Bob followed her.

"What could be so urgent that you have to go to Dark Harbour right this minute? Is there something wrong with somebody there?"

"No, everybody is fine." She reached up to the shelf in her closet and removed a small overnight bag. She threw it on the bed. "Bob," she said, turning to him, "we have never kept any secrets from each other and I don't want to start now. But this is something I have to do and I can't tell you about it. I have to go to Dark Harbour. There is something there that I have to get. Don't ask me any more than that. I have to go now, because I've leaving for Toronto on Sunday afternoon. If I wait until tomorrow to go, it will be too late and I won't get back in time for my flight. When I get back from Toronto I will tell you everything."

"Okay," Bob said reluctantly, "but at least let me go with you and do some of the driving."

"No, Bob. I need the time alone to think out what I'm about to do. I'll be okay," she said as she finished her packing. "If I feel that I'm too tired to drive, I'll stop at a motel for a nap. I'm not tired. I'll be back late tomorrow. Tell me you understand."

"No, I don't understand, Linda, but I suppose you have to do this. At least stop for the occasional cup of coffee and call me when you do, so I won't worry."

Linda finished packing and pulled the zipper closed. "I promise," she said, smiling. "Now, wrap up that lasagna, put the wine in the fridge, and when I get back home tomorrow night, we'll have a wonderful meal. I'll bring the dessert," she said smiling as she moved her hips suggestively.

"You're a witch," Bob said as he hugged her. "Just promise me that you'll be careful," he ordered as he pushed her away and looked sternly at her.

"I promise," she answered.

Driving conditions were excellent. The roads were bare and there was a full moon. *We finished the drive in '65 thanks to Mr. Pearson* signs were everywhere. She stopped every couple of hours for coffee and called Bob to let him know she was okay.

The trip was a perfect opportunity for her to work out the details of her plan. She had placed a pad of paper and a pen on the seat beside her and every few minutes she would make a note. Occasionally she would frown, followed by a smile and then the writing of something on the pad.

It was shortly after 2:00 a.m. when she arrived in Dark Harbour. Six months earlier, the first road to the community had been finished. It was gravel and filled with holes and bumps caused by the frost but it eliminated the need for a boat. Most of the lights were out in the tiny community as Linda arrived, but she could see the numerous cars parked beside the homes. There had not been a car in Dark Harbour until a few months earlier and now it seemed as if every home had one. There was even a stop sign, and the horse path that had been the main road through the community had been widened and covered with crushed stone.

On her second knock on Michel's door, a light appeared, and then the door opened. Michel's big frame filled the entrance. He rubbed the sleep from his eyes as he peered out into the night.

"I could have frozen to death waiting for you," Linda said as she pushed him aside and walked into the warm kitchen.

"My God, Linda, what are you doing here?" Michel asked, as soon as he recognized his sister. "What's the matter? Where's Bob? Why didn't you call?"

His loud voice roused Lori and she suddenly appeared at the door to their bedroom followed by the children.

"Linda," Lori said, as soon as she saw her. "What are you doing here?"

"Can't I come home for a visit?" she laughed.

"I'm sorry," Lori said, "I didn't mean it like that."

"I know," Linda answered, "I came here to get something. Don't worry, everything is fine. Bob is fine. I'm fine, I just have to get something before I leave to go to Toronto, Sunday afternoon. I didn't want you worrying about me as I drove here, so I didn't call. It was a last minute decision. Now, I'm exhausted. I want to go to bed and when I get up, I'll tell you why I'm here. Where do I sleep?"

Linda got what she had gone to fetch, and arrived back home shortly after 6:00 p.m. Saturday. During the return trip she didn't need to make notes. She had found everything she needed and more. She had telephoned Bob and told him when to expect her. He had the lasagna hot and the wine chilled.

The next day, *en route* to the airport, she stopped at her office to pick up some papers. She had called Marty from Dark Harbour and asked him to draft something for her. When she explained to him what she wanted and that she wanted it ready before her flight on Sunday afternoon, he told her she was crazy. She confessed that that might be true, but she wanted it done anyway. It was on her desk. She took a quick look at it and scribbled a note to Bill. She knew he would find it before he went to court Monday morning.

During the plane trip she made more notes and ensured that everything was in order. At the airport in Toronto, she took the limousine to The Leblanc and had dinner in her room. After dinner, she went over everything that she had to do and when she was satisfied that nothing could go wrong, she went to bed.

Breakfast the next morning was taken in her room, and then she arranged for a taxi to the head office of Leblanc Industries. Her stomach churned with anticipation as she took the elevator up to her father's office.

A mature woman greeted her as she stepped from the elevator. "Good morning, you must be Mrs. Humby. Mr. Leblanc is expecting you. Please have a seat and I'll let him know you're here."

"Thank you," Linda said as she sat down.

Linda watched and listened as the secretary buzzed her boss. She smiled as she spoke and then turned to Linda after she had finished. "Mr. Leblanc will see you now. Please go right in."

Linda stood up, straightened her clothes and walked toward the big oak door. The secretary beat her to it, held it open and indicated that Linda should step inside.

Linda stepped on the plush carpet as the door closed behind her. Directly in front of her was a large desk, but nobody was behind it. The room was the most impressive office she had ever seen.

"Mrs. Humby, I presume?" a very handsome man asked as he stepped out of the bathroom.

Linda was standing just inside the office door and the moment she saw him and he spoke, her knees suddenly felt very weak.

"You look a little familiar," he said, before she had the chance to respond to his question. "Have we met before?" he asked as he pointed to one of the leather chairs.

Linda closed her eyes before speaking. Give me strength, God, she thought. "No, we haven't Mr. Leblanc," she answered in a firm voice. Her face remained expressionless.

"Would you like a cup of coffee?" he asked as they sat beside the table and he picked up an urn.

This was not at all what Linda was expecting. He was charming and quite nice. "Yes, I would, thank you," she said, trying to smile as she spoke.

Denis poured her coffee and passed the cup to her. She reached for it with both hands and her left hand touched his fingers. She shivered as she touched her father for the first time.

"Are you cold, Mrs. Humby?" he asked as he noticed the shiver.

Linda cursed herself for what he might judge as a sign of intimidation. "Yes, a little. I must have caught a chill."

They didn't speak as they fixed to their coffee. Linda's mind swam as she tried to decide whether or not she should make the first move. Denis beat her to it. "Well, Mrs. Humby," he said, after he had tasted his coffee, "I think I know why you've come to Toronto to see me."

Linda smiled. "And what do you think that reason is?"

"I spoke with Winston Cummings on Friday and he informed me that things aren't going very well for you and your suit against us," he answered.

"That's very presumptuous of Mr. Cummings. I'm surprised that he feels so confident about the outcome."

Denis's smile suddenly disappeared. His face turned very hard. This is what Linda had been expecting from the outset. "What can I do for you, Mrs. Humby?" he asked, very coldly.

"Now, that's the greeting I was expecting," Linda replied after she had tasted her coffee.

Denis stood up threateningly.

"Sit down, Mr. Leblanc," Linda said. "I'm not easily intimidated." Linda remained seated in front of his desk.

Linda removed a file from her briefcase. She opened it and placed it on the desk in front of Denis.

"What's this?" he asked as he looked at it.

"It's an agreement that you're going to sign before I leave this office."

Denis skimmed through it. "What does it say?"

"It says in consideration for Walter Lake dropping his suit against your company, you will agree to purchase his plant in Carbonear, in its present state, for six million dollars. Additionally, you will set up a trust fund in the amount of three million dollars and it will be used to provide employment opportunities for those persons who are now unemployed as a result of your actions regarding the construction of the OPI plant in Carbonear. And last but not least, you will fire the firm of Hawkins and Murphy and appoint another firm to represent your interests in the Province of Newfoundland."

Denis closed the file and picked up his coffee cup. He took a sip and then started to laugh. He leaned back in his chair and laughed long and hard. "Mrs. Humby," he finally spoke as he dried his eyes with a napkin, "I've heard a lot of Newfie jokes, but I must admit, this is the best. I don't know what's been going through your deranged little mind, but I think that you should leave now." He stood up.

"Sit down, Mr. Leblanc. I remind you again that I am not easily intimidated. I haven't told you why you're going to sign this agreement, because sign it you will," Linda said staring into his eyes.

Denis's gaze suddenly turned quite cold. "Who the hell do you think you're talking to?" he shouted at her. "Get the hell out of my office before I have you thrown out. No, before I personally throw you out."

"Yes," Linda said, "I hear you enjoy that kind of action," Linda responded with a smirk.

Denis sat down.

"Let me answer your first question,"Linda said. She pulled another file from her briefcase. "Who the hell I think I'm talking to, is a ruthless businessman, who, when the rules don't suit him, makes his own. A sadomasochist whose reputation for beating up women stretches from Cuba to most cities in Canada and the United States. A wife beater and a..."

"Where the hell did you get that information?" Denis shouted, again jumping to his feet. "Get out of my office this instant," Denis screamed at her, "before I forget I'm a gentleman," he added.

Linda remained seated, continuing to look at her papers and not reacting to Denis. "And a wife murderer," she said as she stood up and looked at him straight in the face with her face only inches from his.

"What are you talking about? I don't have a wife," he responded in a slightly lower voice.

"Sit down, Mr. Leblanc," Linda said in a calming voice, "or my next stop after leaving your office will be the police station."

Denis sat down.

Linda read from her file. "On August 13th, 1947, you married Francine Forest."

"So," Denis said, "that information is available to anybody who wants it."

"Don't interrupt me, Mr. Leblanc. On November 15th, 1950, after nearly three years of marriage, your wife and infant son disappeared. Prior to the disappearance, you had hired a firm to report to you on everything she did, Also, there were numerous times when you beat your wife and she appeared in public with bruises and cuts. Furthermore, on one occasion, you beat and raped your wife in the library of your home and a witness recalls you threatening to kill her."

"That's crap," Denis interrupted her.

Linda looked up and then down to her papers. "During the police investigation, you were considered a suspect in her disappearance, However, because of your influence, the investigation was terminated. But, the officer in charge of the investigation filed a report stating that, in his opinion, you murdered your wife and son and disposed of their bodies."

"That's absolutely ridiculous," Denis shouted once again jumping to his feet. I never killed my wife and son and I tried everything to find them. I loved my son more than anything in this whole world. I would have given up anything for him."

"That's very sweet of you," Linda said with obvious disgust. "But you see, I have proof that you murdered your wife. I have pictures and I have something else."

"That's impossible."

Linda reached into her briefcase and removed a gold cup with the letters Michel engraved on it, She passed it to Denis.

"Where did you get this?" He sat down to examine it. "My stepmother gave this to Michel when he was born. Where did you get this?!"

Linda reached into her briefcase and removed a second object. She passed this to him as well.

"Oh God. This is the ring I gave her when we were married," he said after he had looked at the engraving on the inside of the band.

"I asked you where you got this?" he asked, looking at her.

Linda reached into her briefcase a third time. This time she pulled out photographs and passed them to him.

He gasped as he looked at the first one. "It's Francine," he said as he exhaled.

The pictures were of Francine in her casket.

"These are pictures of your wife after her body was found," Linda said. "After you murdered her"

"That's impossible. I never killed my wife. Sure, I wanted a divorce and I beat her a few times, but I never killed her."

"You won't have to convince me, Mr. Leblanc. You'll have to convince a jury. But only after the jury is told that you beat up a prostitute in Cuba and nearly killed her, and there's a list of prostitutes in this city who are willing to testify that you nearly killed them. Add that to the fact that you hired a detective agency to tail her, there are witnesses who saw you beat her, you acknowledged wanting a divorce and it all supports the fact that you murdered her. And the witness to all of this is your son, Michel."

"Michel...he's still alive?" he said, almost in a whisper.

"Yes."

Denis paused for a moment. Then he smiled. "This is very good Mrs. Humby. Very good indeed. You went to a lot of trouble and I have to admire you for it, And I got caught up in it for a few minutes. But this has gone on long enough. I don't know where you got my wife's things, if they are my wife's things, which I doubt. They are probably copies. The woman in the casket is a nice likeness but you see, I didn't kill my wife. I think it's time we ended this game."

Linda paused for a few seconds. "I don't play games, Mr. Leblanc. Buzz your secretary. There's someone in your outer office you just might like to meet."

"This has gone on long enough. Leave now."

Linda got up and walked to the office door. She held it open. "Come in, Michel," she said.

Denis looked up as he heard Linda speak. Michel suddenly appeared.

"Jesus Christ," he said, as soon as he saw Michel. It was like looking into a twenty-five year old mirror. Linda closed the door and Michel stepped inside.

"Michel, is that you?" Denis asked as he came out from behind his desk.

"Yes, I'm Michel," he said remaining standing.

"You might be thinking," Linda said, "that the Michel here is an imposter; who has had plastic surgery to look like you. You, of course, would be wrong. Blood tests and whatever other tests the court orders, will prove that the man in front of you is your son, Michel."

Denis continued to look at Michel. "Is it really you after all these years?"

"Yes, it is," Michel said, coldly.

"Let me see your back," Denis ordered.

Michel turned around and raised the back of his shirt to reveal an apple-shaped red birthmark on his lower back.

Denis gasped.

"The court will also find that this mark is indeed a birthmark and your stepmother will confirm it as a mark she knew was on her grandson." She turned to Michel. "Please go back outside and I'll join you shortly."

Michel turned, straightened his clothes, and left.

When they were alone again, Linda spoke. "He's a very rich young man," Linda said.

"What do you mean?"

"Twenty-five thousand dollars a year for the past twenty-five years. That was what your father left to him in his will."

Denis nodded.

"Now then, Mr. Leblanc, there's some forms I would like you to sign. And after they're signed I'd like you to make a telephone call to Newfoundland and tell your lawyers that you've settled out of court. I'll call my staff and tell them I've accepted your offer. Otherwise, our next stop will be the police station.

"But I didn't kill my wife," Denis said.

"I know. You didn't kill her, but you caused her death. You'll never be brought to trial and held accountable for her death, but you killed her nevertheless. You drove her from her home to her death. I may not be able to have you convicted in court but I sure as hell can have you convicted in the court of public opinion. Every dirty secret will come out. You and your companies will be blacklisted by every decent person in Canada."

"This is extortion. This is blackmail," he shouted.

"Yes, it is," Linda said, smiling. "But it's no different from what you've been doing to the fishermen of Newfoundland since the day you opened your first plant. It's payback time and you have a decision to make." Linda pushed the documents toward him as he sat once again behind his desk.

"My lawyer tells me that you'll never win the case in Newfoundland. You'll never get the files you stole from us admitted."

"You may be right, but what I have need not have been legally obtained for Revenue Canada, the Ontario Securities Commission and the newspapers to begin an investigation. I'm asking for six million dollars for my client and three million dollars for the people you raped, just as you raped your wife."

"I need to consult with my lawyer," he said as he looked at her, defeated. "I can't sign this."

"You can and you will," Linda said. "That man outside your office is your son. He was only made aware of that fact a few days ago. He doesn't remember his mother, but when he found out you were his father, he wasn't sure he even wanted to meet you. He's a Newfoundland fisherman. His adoptive father was a Newfoundland fisherman. He hates what you represent. He doesn't know you well enough yet to hate you. But if you fail to sign these papers, you can be assured that he will hate you."

"Nine million dollars is a lot of money," Denis whispered.

"Nine million dollars is spare change to you, Mr. Leblanc. It's the principle that you're concerned with. You've never lost before. And if you fail to sign these documents, you will win the court case in Newfoundland. But you will lose a son. That is, if you ever had a son. He certainly doesn't want anything to do with you. The only reason he came with me is because I was able to convince him that perhaps by coming, he would help Walter Lake win his case.

Denis Leblanc suddenly began to look his years. He knew he shouldn't sign the papers without speaking with his lawyer. There was no doubt that the man in the outer office was his son and perhaps by giving up this case, he would have a chance at winning him back. He reached for the telephone. His secretary answered.

"Call Cummings in St. John's and tell him to advise Judge Somers that I have just settled out of court." He hung up without waiting for a response. He then pulled the papers toward him and he scribbled his signature without looking. He then pushed the papers toward Linda, who picked them up and placed them in her briefcase.

"I'd like to see my son," Denis managed just as Linda reached the door. She turned and walked to front of his desk.

"You had lots of opportunities to see your son before now. You had everything. You were a war hero, handsome, rich. You were more than a young naive girl from Roberval could ever dream of having. You swept her off her feet and you gave her a son." Denis, made an effort to stand up. "Don't stand up sir, because, although I have never before struck a person, this may be a first. You sit there and you listen to what I have to say."

"Francine Leblanc escaped from you and took her son. What you did to her to cause her to have to do what she did, I don't know. To get outside of your considerable reach, she had to go to an isolated community in Newfoundland. She died there shortly thereafter, and although nothing would make me happier than to see you sent to prison for the rest of your life for her death, unfortunately that will never happen. But there is a higher court and you will be judged there." Denis sat back down.

"Michel was raised by an illiterate fishing family and he has turned out to be one of the finest human beings I know. He is a loving father and husband who is that way because he was not influenced by you. But you took away his birthright and the life that he was born into."

"No amount of money and no apology will ever make up for the loss he now feels. No amount of money and no apology will ever bring back his mother. You do not deserve to have a son and I don't think that he will ever want to see you again. I want you to spend the remainder of your miserable life thinking about a young, naive girl from Roberval named Francine. I also want you to think about her son Michel who hates you, second only to me."

Denis came out from around the desk and as he did he spoke. "You said he didn't hate me."

"I lied," Linda said.

"I suppose then," he said, "I can understand why he hates me, but why do you hate me so much?"

Linda turned and walked again toward the door. Denis got up from his chair.

"How did you find out all of this?" he asked.

Linda stopped but she didn't turn."That's not important. What's important is the last time you saw your wife. Do you remember the last time you saw your wife?"

"I'm not sure," Denis managed.

"Then let me refresh your memory. It was in the library of your father's house. You raped her."

"How do you know that?" he asked.

"That is not the issue. The fact remains that you did."

Tears streamed down her cheeks. Denis was in an obvious state of shock and to prevent himself from falling, he held on to the side of the desk.

Linda continued. "I wish I could feel sorry for you but I only feel loathing. Goddamn you Denis Leblanc. Goddamn your soul to hell."

Linda wiped the tears from her face with the back of her hand, walked toward the door and pulled it open. Michel was sitting in the secretary's office waiting for her.

"Come on Michel," she said. "Let's go home. Let's go back to Newfoundland."

Twenty-Seven ∼

LINDA RETURNED HOME to Mount Pearl. They used the plane trip on the way home as an opportunity to talk. Michel would never again have the need to drop a fishing net in the water. In addition to the millions he had gotten from the stock shares, there were millions more owing him as a director of his father's company. In fact, someday he could make a claim on everything his father owned.

They talked about that and other things, but Michel said he wanted nothing to do with his father. It was the fisherman in him speaking. OPI had done fisherman more hurt than all the governments combined. He could not go from being a fisherman to the owner of such an entity.

Lori was in St. John's waiting for him when they arrived, and they were going to talk about moving to St. John's and buying a home. Linda knew that that would be hard sell on Lori's part.

Linda's law firm took thirty percent of the settlement for Walter Lake and ten percent of the settlement for the fishermen. The balance of that three million would be set up in trust for fishermen and fisherman's families who fell on hard times. Ian Rose would look after managing the trust; he had agreed to do it for free, considering the fact that his two largest accounts were those owned by Linda and Michel.

It didn't take long to clear up the loose ends of the OPI trial. Linda's company needed work after that but they didn't have long to wait. News of the settlement with OPI spread quickly and there was a lineup of new clients. They could pick and choose who they wanted to represent and they could diversify their activities into other areas of the law. That would mean more lawyers, more support staff and more office space.

Linda had planned to take a few weeks off for a much deserved vacation after the case was over but there was so much to do that she just couldn't leave. It was less than two weeks after she returned from Toronto that she received a most unexpected telephone call.

Linda pushed the button on her intercom. "Hello," she answered.

"Mrs. Humby, there's a Denis Leblanc on line three. He calling from Toronto and would like to speak with you," her secretary said.

Linda leaned back in her chair and just stared straight ahead. When she didn't speak her secretary spoke again. "Shall I take his number and tell him you'll call him back?" she said.

"No," Linda said. "I'll speak with him." She pushed line three.

"Good afternoon, Mr. Leblanc. How may I may help you?"

"Good afternoon, Mrs. Humby. How are you?"

"You certainly didn't call me to find out my state of health, sir," Linda responded very curtly.

"No, that's true," he chuckled. "I telephoned Michel this morning and he said he didn't want to speak with me and if I had to something to say I should call his lawyer. That would be you, I assume."

"You're right about that, and I'm sure that you're not surprised by his response," Linda commented.

There was a pause and then Denis spoke again, this time sounding a little less cocky. "Michel is my son. He's my only son and, yes, I understand why he refused to talk to me. But what led to all of this happened a long time ago."

"Whether it happened yesterday or twenty-five years ago, you were responsible for the death of his mother, sir. He's carrying a lot of baggage and it's especially heavy when we, I mean he, still doesn't know what happened to drive his mother to Newfoundland."

"That's a long story," Denis said.

"Well, sir, it's a story you're going to have to tell. Michel has asked me to hire a private investigator to find out what really happened in Toronto so long ago, so he can gain closure to all of this."

"That won't be necessary," Denis blurted. "I'm willing to talk about it."

Linda paused. "Are you willing to come to Newfoundland, to meet with me and to answer my questions? All of my questions?"

"If it will help to get Michel to talk to me…"

"I can't guarantee that. But I do know that it's a good start. When can you come?" Linda asked.

"I can be there tomorrow. If you can have your secretary book me a hotel I will have mine call her when the flight is confirmed."

"That would be fine," Linda said as she hung up the telephone without waiting for a response.

Later that day Linda was advised that Denis would be arriving in St. John's at 2:20 p.m. and could be at her office for a 3:30 meeting. She confirmed.

Linda didn't sleep much that night in anticipation of what was going to happen the next day. She didn't know how she would respond. She had left his office the last time in tears. She would have to compose herself. She desperately wanted to know about her mother and what had happened. She wanted to be a vengeful daughter, but she had to put her lawyer face on and keep it on.

Denis showed up at 3:15; and Linda thought about keeping him waiting, but realized it would be petty. He was shown into her office and they sat facing each other with only a coffee table between them.

"Welcome to Newfoundland," Linda said as they moved toward the chairs.

"Thank you," he anwered.

The resemblance to Michel was uncanny. He was a distinguished looking man and his dress showed his stature as one of the top ten business men in Canada. Linda's secretary poured them coffee.

"I trust you had a safe flight," Linda said as they drank their coffee.

"I think perhaps you would have been happier if the flight had not been a safe flight," Denis said smiling.

"Despite our last meeting, I don't wish you any harm, sir."

"Please, call me Denis, and I'd like to call you Linda, if you don't mind? There's no need for us to be adversaries. We've settled our legal battle. I was hoping we could move on."

"Okay, Denis, but we still have the moral battle that we have to overcome. You said you were going to answer my questions."

"I expected Michel to be here."

"We'll talk, and if I'm satisfied with your answers, then perhaps Michel might join us."

Denis nodded his approval.

"Okay, let's begin. Tell me about his mother, Francine."

Denis leaned back in his chair. He held his coffee cup and his saucer in his hands. He smiled before he began to speak.

"She was the most beautiful woman I have ever seen. I was in the Air F,orce stationed at Camp Borden, north of Toronto, when she came to our house in Toronto. Father found her in Roberval where she was a student in the convent. He wanted someone to come to Toronto and to teach my stepbrother, Alain, and my stepsister, Marie, the French language. My mother died of pneumonia when I was twelve and a few years after she died, he met Linda and they were married. I think father was 48 when he married Linda. She was much younger than he was. You have the same name as her." He smiled at her.

"She was there for nearly six months before I came home. I'll never forget our first meeting. Our home was, as I'm sure you can appreciate, quite large, and I rang the doorbell expecting to hear the familiar voice of Joseph, our butler, answer. Francine wouldn't let me in at first." He smiled as he thought about that day a long time ago. "But Linda was there and she rescued me."

To celebrate my visit, father had a big party and all the usual high society people were there, including the usual women. Francine was there with Alain and Marie, and halfway through the evening I asked her to dance. She refused. I couldn't believe it. I had never been refused by a girl before. I just didn't know how to deal with it."

Linda smiled seeing the picture in her mind.

"Anyway, later that evening when Alain and Marie had gone to bed, she returned to the party and this time she agreed to dance with me. I don't know whose heart was beating faster, mine or her's. We just had one dance and like the lady she was, she excused herself. Before she left however, I asked her if I could telephone her some time after I returned to the Base. She said that I could.

I not only telephoned her, I wrote her letters. Long letters and she wrote me, too. I came home as often as I could and we spent every moment together. In June, I proposed and she accepted. We were to married on July 8th, 1947."

Denis drained his coffee. "Do you have anything stronger than this?" he asked, pointing at the cup.

"Yes," Linda said, "there's a bar there. Help yourself."

Denis went over to the bar, found a bottle of Scotch, and half filled a glass. He stood there and threw back half of it. He then returned to the couch.

"As I said earlier, I was in the Air Force, and after she accepted my proposal I had to go back to base. I was a pilot, you know. You did know that, didn't you?"

"No, I didn't," Linda said.

"Yes, I was pilot. I was in the RAF during the war and then I transferred to the RCAF. Anyway, it was a routine training mission. I don't know what happened. I suspect now that my mind was occupied with Francine instead of the aircraft and I crashed. It was pretty bad, and I was injured." He held his right arm in the air and shook it. "This is useless. I couldn't use it to hold the stick and so I was discharged."

"I spent a few weeks in the hospital and I suppose the medical people would say that I went into denial. I would say in retrospect that I turned into an asshole. I didn't want to see anybody, especially Francine. I lost weight and turned into a recluse. But Francine wouldn't give in and she came to see me and told me she would love me regardless of my physical condition. But the thing that brought me back to my senses was her admission that she was pregnant with our child. We changed the date and married on August 13th, 1947."

"Sounds like a story book engagement and marriage," Linda said sarcastically.

"Yes, in fact it was. We were very much in love. Father had wanted me to join the family business ever since I was old enough, and I just wanted to be a pilot. After my accident I had no choice. We moved into the mansion and I went to work for Father. He was sixty two and he admitted to me that he wanted me to be his successor, but that I had to start at the bottom and learn the business."

"What business were you in?" Linda asked.

Denis drained the remainder of his Scotch and returned the glass to the table. "Leblanc Industries began in father's house and grew from there." Denis was very proud of his father and he it was obvious in his voice.

"Father started a clothing business and won some very lucrative contracts supplying uniforms for the military during the Second World War. In a few years the company had grown and had real estate interests, several restaurants, three automobile dealerships, and The Leblanc Hotel. Dad owned everything."

"As I said, I started at the very bottom and learned every business from the bottom up. Francine understood why I had to spend so much time away from her. Then on March 16th, 1948, Michel was born."

"Do you have any children, Linda?" he asked.

"No, I don't," Linda answered.

"Well, it's hard to explain, but that first time I saw Michel, I knew that my life was complete. I loved him with all my heart."

Linda listened to the man in front of her. This was not what she expected.

"Father even took the afternoon off work to come and see Michel, he was so proud. This was his first grandchild. In fact this was his only grandchild. We named him Michel Romeo Claude after my father. He had been talking about buying a fish processing plant in Nova Scotia and expanding into Newfoundland. He had just finished forming the new company and listing the shares on the Toronto Stock Exchange. He gave Michel five thousand shares of that new company and he gave the same amount to Francine."

"So that's where the shares came from," Linda said.

"Yes," Denis answered. "It was only after you began the court action that the sale of these shares was brought to my attention. I just didn't make the connection at the time."

"You're still not telling me why she left you," Linda said. "She did leave you, didn't she?"

Denis got up and went to the liquor cabinet again. He didn't speak as he returned with another good helping of Scotch.

"Yes, she left me. And it took me a long time to deal with that."

"I'm not going to make excuses for my behavior. I liked the power and I knew that someday I would have it all. I suppose it went to my head. I blamed Francine but it was my fault."

"This is very hard for me to tell you. I found that the only way I could enjoy sex was to be dominant. Dominant to the point whereby unless I was inflicting pain on my sexual partners I couldn't enjoy it. I want you to know that I loved Francine. I can't tell you how much I loved her. What hurt so much is that I wanted to make love to her but the only way I could was to beat the hell out of her. You don't want to know how much money I spent trying to find out what was wrong with me. It took me a long time just to admit I had a problem and then even longer to find a cure."

"I'm not sure I fully understand this," Linda commented.

"I didn't go home. I stayed at the hotel where I slept with prostitutes. Prostitutes that I beat he hell out of. When I did go home to Francine, I beat her."

He put the glass to his mouth and returned it to the table without drinking.

"I loved her and I wanted to be with her but I couldn't love her without beating her. It's a sickness and as I said it took me a long time to deal with it."

"Francine tried, but there was always that between us. Everything she did I found fault with. I even blamed Michel for it. That's how sick I was. I missed his first birthday party. I came home late that evening and I tried to rape her. She had never seen me like that. I wasn't able to overpower her, and so I went to the hotel and I beat the hell out of a prostitute and nearly killed her."

"Things got worse after that. I would go to the mansion and take Michel when she wasn't there and not bring him back until late at night. I used to frighten the hell of out her."

"I stayed away even more after the attempted rape and I gave all my attention to the business. Then it happened. Father died. Is your father alive?" Denis asked.

The question hit her with no less force than if she had been standing in the path of a speeding car. She stared straight into his eyes. "Dad is dead, yes," she answered.

"Were you close?"

"Yes, very close."

"Then you know what it's like. I was devastated. I didn't know how to deal with it. I wasn't particularly close to Linda. I wanted to put my arms around Francine and have her comfort me. I cried when Mother died, but I was twelve then. I thought I had been over that kind of pain, but it was even worse with Father. Only two weeks earlier we had been fishing in Chibougamau. Perhaps if I could have cried, it wouldn't have been so hard."

"But once again Francine came to my rescue. She hugged me and she comforted me. For the first time in a long time I wanted to be held by her and to make love to her. But I had gonorrhea. I made some excuse and I went back to the hotel."

"There were no surprises in Father's will. I replaced him as the head of Leblanc Industries. Linda was given the mansion and all of Father's personal wealth. Francine, Alain, Marie, Michel and Linda were appointed to the Board of Directors, and you know about the annual salary they were given. They were also given substantial numbers of shares in the company. Everybody got something."

"I didn't get any better. If anything I got worse. I never went to Michel's second birthday party and when I showed up at the house again that evening I believe that what I did made up her mind for her. She had to get away from me."

"What did you do?" Linda asked.

"She lectured me about never being there for either her or Michel. A week or so earlier she had taken him to Roberval to visit her parents. I told her that she could never take him out of the city again without my permission. Things really went downhill from there. I pulled her into the library and I raped and beat her. While she was still on the floor bleeding, I told her that I had given her everything she had and I could take it away from her just as easily as I had given it to her."

The hatred Linda had for this man suddenly surfaced, and he could see it in her eyes.

"You don't have to say anything. I was an animal, but if it's any consolation I was sick. I am just as repulsed at my behavior as you are."

"No, I don't think you are. Maybe it has something to do with being a woman," Linda said.

"It gets worse," Denis said.

"You know, other than my doctors I have never told anybody this before."

"I wanted Michel and I was willing to do anything to get him. I talked to people about having her killed. Yes, I was willing to go that far. Fortunately, I was talked out it."

"Yes," Linda said smiling. "Someday I'd like to shake the hand of the person or persons who talked you out of that."

Denis shrugged, not quite understanding why.

"Anyway, for me to get custody we had to be able to prove that she was an unfit mother and cavorting with other men."

"Let me get this straight," Linda said, "you were screwing and beating the hell out of half the whores in Toronto and you wanted to prove Francine unfit. Is that what you're saying?"

Denis bowed his head slightly. "Yes."

"Go on," Linda said.

"I hired a team of men to just walk up to her and kiss her on the street. Then someone else would photograph her. They would then testify in court that she was having an affair with them while her son was at home with a babysitter."

"You sick son of a bitch."

"You're right. Francine found out about our plan from the wife of my lawyer. I didn't know this until much later. But as soon as she did find out, she knew she had to leave Toronto."

"But why Newfoundland?"

"I really don't know. I suspect it was because she thought it was the last place I would look."

I became a madman when she disappeared. She took the stock certificates with her and she emptied our bank account. I had a small army looking for her and they were always one step behind her. I hired the best private investigator in the country and she still made me look like the worst hide and seek player there was. She bought train tickets in her own name all over the place and gave great tips to people so they would remember her. We thought we had her several times only to find out that she had sent us on a wild goose chase. I offered a reward that could have ransomed a prince. But there were no takers. She pulled a stunt with our bank manager to get the money in our account that was a stroke of genius. Only now can I admire what she did."

"So what happened? Did you just give up?"

"No, I didn't give up. I never gave up. I'm still looking for her. When you told me she was dead it was as if you drove a stake through my heart. In the early years, I wanted to find her so I could have revenge. In later years, when I began to address my sickness, I wanted to find her so I could apologize. In all of it I guess, I sort of forgot about Michel. My hatred of Francine and then my profound sadness for what I had done, clouded any feelings I had for him. That's why

I'm here. I want to tell him what I've told you. I want to apologize to him and to beg him to forgive me."

Linda reached and wiped the corner of her eye. "Is there anything else?"

"No, there's not. I just want you to understand all of this. I want to be able to explain to him what I have explained to you. I take full responsibility for what I've done. I am responsible for Francine's death. I am responsible for what Michel has become."

"No, that's not true," Francine interrupted him. "Michel is what he is today because of the father Joe Fudge was to him. There is not a kinder, gentler, person than Michel Fudge. The only responsibility you have for what he has become is that you put Michel and Joe Fudge together."

"You're right, of course. This is very difficult for me."

"Okay, then go back to your hotel and I'll let you know what Michel has to say about all this."

Denis stood up, they shook hands and he left the office.

Linda went back to her desk and she just sat there. She had hated Denis Leblanc more than any person alive. But his story had changed all of that. He had a sickness. His sickness wasn't an excuse, but it did provide the explanation that Linda so desperately wanted.

She left the office early and went home. Bob was busy marking papers and Linda just sat in front of the TV without even knowing what was on. Finally she got up and started making numerous telephone calls. She went to bed at 11:00 p.m. and she got up he next morning at 7:00 a.m. She told Bob she would be going away for a few days. She would call him and let him know where she was.

She got in her car and drove to the Newfoundland Hotel. She found Denis at breakfast. He was surprised to see her. They exchanged greetings.

"I'm going somewhere and I'd like you to come with me," she said.

"Is it to see Michel?" he asked.

"Not right away, but perhaps, eventually, depending on a few things."

"What few things?"

"That's not important right now," Linda said.

Twenty-Eight ∼

IT WAS THE middle of July but it wasn't warm. It was a typical Newfoundland July; enough to "free the arse of ya". They left the hotel parking lot and Francine drove north along the Conception Bay Highway. All the while she talked about what fishing meant to the area and how dependent everything was on the lowly cod fish. Denis asked lots of questions and Linda had all the answers.

They arrived in Carbonear, two and a half hours after leaving, and Walter Lake was standing in his doorway when Linda pulled up in the driveway. They hugged and kissed like parent and child. She introduced him to Denis Leblanc and then over supper and until nearly 10:30 that evening he bent Leblanc's ear like it had never been bent before.

The next morning at 4:30 a.m. Leblanc was roused from his bed and brought to the public wharf where Bill Slade was waiting. They went aboard his ship and a few minutes later they steamed out of Carbonear Harbour on his long liner.

Denis was given rubber clothes and boots and when they reached the nets he was put to work and he did so without a grumble. By 9:30 a.m they were back at the wharf and Denis was put to work cutting throats. At 11:30 a.m. they went to Bill's house for lunch. Pan fried cod, fresh bread, tea and the conversation of fishermen and their families. Again that afternoon they went out to the fishing grounds and by 9:30 that night the fish had been cleaned. Denis spent the night with Bill and his family and the next morning, which was Sunday, he went to church with them and shared their Sunday dinner. They rummaged around between the neighbours and other family members and they found clean clothes for him.

Sunday afternoon they left Carbonear after a goodbye that seemed more appropriate to lifelong friends, and headed for Dark Harbour. Mrs. Slade had even packed him a lunch for the trip. They never spoke for the first forty five minutes until finally, just before Whitbourne, he spoke.

"I'm so sorry,"he said. "I have never before met people like these." Tears rolled down his face. "I didn't realize what I was doing. All I was interested in was making money and I didn't care at whose expense. I have to fix this. I can't let this go on. How many of these plants do I own?"

"Most of them," Linda said smiling. "Most of them."

Denis didn't say much more after that. They drove and only spoke when Denis asked a question. Later that afternoon they arrived in Dark Harbour.

Michel was expecting them. The house was full of family and friends and Denis was welcomed. There was no malice against him. He tried to apologize but Linda had already told them that she wouldn't be bringing him unless he understood them. They waved off his apologies.

They had a wonderful meal and Denis met his grandchildren. And there was not a prouder grandfather in the province. He promised them everything, but all they wanted was his love.

After dinner Linda took him aside. "I want to take you somewhere," she said.

"Where?" he asked.

"Just come with me."

Together they left the house and walked the road toward the church. Before the church they came to the graveyard and Linda twisted the wooden closure and pushed the gate open. She led the way.

"Why are we here?" he asked.

Linda never spoke. She walked to a place that she could have found with her eyes closed. She stopped when she reached there. Denis caught up with her, slightly out of breath.

"Your search is over," she said as she reached for and held his hand.

He looked at the head stone. The most impressive head stone in the entire graveyard. Denis read the words:

Rest in Peace

Francine Leblanc
Born Roberval, Quebec, August 30th 1926
Died Dark Harbour, Newfoundland June 6th 1950
Survived by her son Michel and her daughter Linda

Honor Thy Mother

Linda felt her father waver but she held on to him.
"Steady, Dad. Mom is watching."

Acknowledgements

Many of us assume we are writers when in reality, without our editors we would still be looking for publishers.

I am forever grateful to the editors who worked on my book.